Whatever Next?

Whatever Next?

Lucilla Butler

ATHENA PRESS
LONDON

Whatever Next?
Copyright © Lucilla Butler 2008

ISBN 978 1 84748 041 5

First Published 2008 by
ATHENA PRESS
Queen's House, 2 Holly Road
Twickenham TW1 4EG
United Kingdom

Printed for Athena Press

One

If you slash the price of cornflakes, slash it again, and again, at some point you're not going to have much left and certainly the price will be a derisory couple of coins at most. Well, that seemed totally reasonable to Enid's mathematics. Really, given the slashings that went on, there should be a bevy of beautiful girls handing out for free all the mutilated goods slashed to extinction.

Funny, though, they never slashed black olives. Indeed, these weren't always in stock, let alone on slashing terms. But loo paper! First they slashed it, then they promoted it by building pyramids of the damned stuff; so if you were a little unsteady on your pins – and Enid was the first to admit she felt just a tad tottery some mornings – it was like being faced with the Matterhorn just after breakfast. But even the softest tissue was no competition for snow; the very thought sends a shudder.

Enid had made her list, but the biro had run out and some of the items were rather a blur. There were, of course, the items she didn't know she wanted until she saw them. Gerry would be so cross, but he never said no to crumpets with hot melted butter. Enid wished the supermarket had boards advertising a dish of the day; after all, it's so difficult dreaming up meals for just two.

Just look at the time! She must fly – not easy with a trolley – then the inevitable wait for a till with a harassed mother with two snotty-nosed children hell-bent on slowing down the works even more. Enid made faces at the children, who giggled.

'Look at the lady, Mum; ain't she funny?'

Ain't I funny? mused Enid, screwing up her face oblivious to the dour, 'not amused' queue.

'Well, bugger 'em, that's what I say.'

Soon she was driving home to her Gerry.

'Lunch!' Enid shouted, as she put the plate of scrambled egg on the table. She liked to think the plate was piled high with fluffy eggs resting on a piece of toast oozing butter, just as he liked it. Actually, the eggs were rather leathery and the toast a touch mouldy – she had forgotten to buy any more bread. She never bothered about eating lunch herself but inevitably ended up munching a couple of chocolate digestives, an apple, the lump of cheese not worth saving, a handful of raisins, some peanuts and possibly the remains of last night's apple crumble. Gerry had long since stopped explaining the fatuity of it all. Enid swore it helped keep her weight down.

'Come on,' she added, surprised that he hadn't ambled through already.

Usually he was hovering at her shoulder as she cooked, like a large shambling bear. The silence continued. She put her head round the door.

Gerry was sitting slumped in his chair. His mouth was open and he was dribbling.

It was his eyes that frightened Enid – they stared at her as if he wanted to tell her something. There was a stain on his trousers; she'd reminded him that morning but, as usual, he had done nothing about it. He wasn't wearing any socks – he never wore socks, just kept them in the drawer. In fact, he looked a right scruffy mess. But his eyes…it was his eyes. They looked particularly belligerent and furious about nothing, unless it was the indignity of not being able to say anything. Sophocles was laid out in front of the fire sleeping peacefully…so much for the guard dog!

'What on earth…' she murmured, as she bent over the inert body.

She shook his torso, tried to feel his pulse, couldn't find anything and so phoned for an ambulance. Her hand shook. The 999 bit she could remember, her name she blurted out somehow but the address was more difficult; she couldn't for the life of her remember the postcode. There was a holly tree at the entrance to their house and she kept repeating on and on about that damned holly tree. Gerry had told her it was good luck to have a holly tree; what the hell did he know about good luck? Wasn't doing him much good, the damned holly tree.

'Look, I think he might be dead, I can't tell. I mean he could just be unconscious.'

Soothing words followed. She was to do nothing and they would arrive as soon as possible. She couldn't just do nothing with Gerry slumped in that chair. Should she cover him with a blanket, give him some brandy? She only had Spanish brandy for the brandy butter at Christmas; he'd hate that and complain it wasn't the proper stuff. Enid stared at her husband. Spit still dribbled out of the corner of his mouth. She thought his face twitched, but it was those staring, empty eyes that really got her. Wasn't there something she should do with a mirror? She didn't have a small mirror, only the big elaborate gilt mirror in the dining room; she couldn't even lift it. She looked back at Gerry.

'Do stop staring at me like that,' she pleaded, adding very quietly, 'Gerry, are you really dead?' She swore he nodded.

Sophocles looked up; brain box that he was, he sensed something was wrong. He came over to Enid and whined.

At last the ambulance arrived. Enid only had television ambulances to go by. This lot wasn't as young or glamorous; they were slower too, talking quietly as they scooped Gerry up and took him away on a trolley.

Enid, with a wary Sophocles, watched. She felt she was in the way and she didn't know what to say. The oldest member of the crew put his hand on her shoulder and gave a gentle squeeze. Enid was very touched; she looked at the kindly middle-aged face and no longer felt excluded like she had when they first arrived.

'He's in good hands now, Mrs Tanner.'

'I'll follow in the car,' said Enid. 'There are one or two phone calls I want to make.'

Enid wanted most of all to ring her daughter. The others would have to wait till she knew for certain. No one would tell her if Gerry was dead or alive. She hated this kind of limbo. The nice ambulance man had told her that it was unlikely he'd survive, but that wasn't the same as being dead, was it? She was working herself into a tizz. She must ring Sal; Sal would know what she should do.

Sal was wrestling with the washing. One of her twins had put a coloured felt-tip pen in the machine and the result was green. Diminutive pants in green, socks in green, the T-shirts were mud-coloured, Douglas's shirt for visiting the bank manager was a smeared green, and her other bra was now green. And to crown it all, the bloody telephone was ringing.

'Sal, is that you? Look, I don't know if he's actually dead but Gerry's been carted off to hospital – a stroke or something.'

Poor Ma, she sounded rather hysterical, not her usual self. Anyway, Pa couldn't be dead, it wasn't possible, he was too irascible to die. Just when she must feed the twins lunch. Bloody typical!

'He can't – oh shit! Sorry, it's the twins – what a bloody nuisance; why did he have to choose now to die, especially when you've given him that lovely new dressing-gown for Christmas?' There was a scuffle at Sal's end of the telephone.

'Beatrice, for God's sake, stop feeding the dog your fish fingers; Granny is phoning to say something very sad. Grandpa might be dead... Ma, look, don't panic, ring me from the hospital and you'd better come here. Mrs Boots has chosen the spare room to have a litter so I'll fix something up for you, possibly Beatrice's room. It will be a glorified stew for supper; I haven't had time to shop but Douglas will open some decent wine. We'll prop you up, don't worry. Ring when you know definitely whether he's dead or not. Must fly, the dogs are eating the twins' lunch.'

The green wash was bundled into the tumble dryer. The twins settled down to fish fingers and peas, most of which were surreptitiously given to the dogs. Sal sat down heavily.

'I just don't believe it, not Pa.' The busy mother allowed herself just for a moment to forget the green washing and the fish fingers and remember as a small child how her father had ruffled her hair and smelled utterly safe. She mustn't cry now, not in front of the twins.

Enid felt better having rung Sal. Sal was always spot on. She didn't gush – the last thing Enid wanted was someone gushing at her. Sophocles didn't gush either. He could spend the rest of the day in the back of the car. She drove to the hospital, making mental lists of people whom she would have to inform. She practised the necessary sentences. They sounded so formal and insincere; not what she wanted to say at all. She wouldn't say 'passed away', but rather practised with an imaginary game of golf, which Gerry didn't play anyway.

'My husband has died. He won't be playing golf on Thursday.'

Playing golf my foot! Gerry loathed golf, along with conservative politics and middle-class bores. It ruled out an awful lot of people. Enid tried again.

'Mr Tanner has died. Can you let me know about his account and send me any paperwork I'll have to sign?' (And don't remind me the old boy had a stand-up row with the manager just before Christmas.) She had to smile.

She tried again.

'Scotty, guess what! The old bastard has died.' That's more like it and, unlike the golf, Scotty was for real. She was getting somewhere now, although other phrases sounded about as spontaneous as God Save the Queen.

At the hospital she parked the car in the visitors' car park. Sophocles looked resigned. She trudged what seemed like miles to the Accident and Emergency Department. She went to the desk and asked tentatively for Mr Tanner. She was handed over to a Dr Ahmed, a chubby little fellow with an engaging grin. He wore what looked like blue pyjamas and signalled her to follow him into a small office. Enid wondered if he was from India – Gerry spent a lot of time in India. Dr Ahmed let her know that he did in fact come from Leeds. He had never set foot on the Indian subcontinent and when he married he had chosen the Bahamas for his honeymoon. Enid took a deep breath; so did Dr Ahmed.

'Your husband was dead on arrival. There was nothing we could do for him. He has had a massive stroke. I won't go into the technical stuff unless you would like me to, Mrs Tanner. Perhaps you would like to see him?' Dr Ahmed made it sound like an opportunity to look at the Mona Lisa.

No, she would not. Enid was feeling mildly hysterical and light-headed. The last thing she wanted to do was see Gerry's protruding eyes – perhaps they were shut. All the same, Gerry was dead. Let's begin as we mean to go on, she told herself, in a bold but premature attempt at independence.

Dr Ahmed picked up the telephone and called the counsellor, Mrs Kenton, before scuttling away, deeply relieved that Mrs Tanner had been so easy to handle. There had been an occasion not so long before when an enraged wife had accused him of murdering her husband. As for the quiet lachrymose types, Dr Ahmed found them quite dispiriting, as if they too blamed him for their dear one's death. No one ever saw death as a natural termination of life; they seemed to think that modern medicine had overcome that nonsense. Mrs Tanner had behaved perfectly; mind you, it was early days. He looked at his watch. He'd be late for his lunch but he really couldn't blame her for that.

Mrs Kenton had handled countless grieving families. She had attended endless workshops, seminars and conferences to discuss grief, anger, loss and the whole panoply of emotions that erupted at the time of death. Just the other week she went to a one-day seminar about partners and family for gay bereavement. If everything went according to plan, a gay fellow could expect several lovers, a bevy of siblings and some bemused parents to share his death throes. It never worked out like that. Usually it was a weeping mum, a weeping lover and the hangers-on looking like prunes in the room next door.

She took one look at Enid and decided on the brisk approach. She positively ran Enid through the formalities. She made arrangements for signing the death certificate and seeing the undertaker and finally offered Enid the comfort of the hospital chapel. Actually, all Enid wanted was a stiff drink.

'Not bloody likely.' It just slipped out; Enid's voice was rising like dough. 'I mean, I'm not a Christian.'

Mrs Kenton assessed that Enid had had quite enough of hospitals and dead husbands for one day, and would really like to sit down and forget the whole wretched business. How right she was! At this rate Enid would miss *Pet Rescue*, a programme she adored. She and Gerry would watch with incredulity the fate of geckos, rabbits, three-legged dogs and injured pigeons.

'Eat the bugger!' Gerry would scream as a vet put a splint on a pheasant's leg. 'Edie, let's have pheasant for the weekend, and we'll have a bottle of that nice claret.'

Enid was well aware that she was not beginning as she meant to go on. She just wanted to sit down with Gerry, turn on the telly and watch the soothing sight of a three-legged cat looking for a happy home because Sooty deserves a second chance...

'Absolute crap! "Sooty deserves it" – my foot! You can't have rights without responsibilities, Edie. These twits haven't a bloody clue and they confuse animal rights with our responsibilities. Animals have no rights.'

'I wouldn't half like a second chance, though,' said Enid on her way back to the car park, 'after all these years. Now's the time, I suppose.'

Sophocles would watch *Pet Rescue* too, looking exceedingly smug. In theory, he was a white Highland terrier, bought from a lady in Ripon. Years of cheerful neglect had made him grubby grey. As for training, the dog knew that crapping on the lawn was a no-no and led to a boot up the backside. He sat, sometimes came when called and had a tendency to puke up the contents of the dustbins over the carpet, which led to more boots up the backside. He didn't bear grudges, adored Gerry and never demanded his so-called rights – sensible dog.

'You know, Edie, we'd never pass muster with the home search or whatever they call it. They'd see the pheasant tails in that jam jar and suspect us of letting Sophocles hunt rabbits.' At the word 'rabbits', Sophocles would go into reheat.

Enid almost ran back to the car. This time Sophocles went into reheat with excitement at seeing her, even if she wasn't a rabbit. He twirled and thrashed around, bouncing from the back seat to the front. It was on the drive home that Sophocles sensed something was seriously wrong; he leant over Enid's back resting his muzzle on her shoulder, his back legs stretched and on tippy toes to keep his balance.

The house was cold when she got home. The cat gave her a baleful stare and continued washing her paws. It was the scrambled egg that particularly revolted her; it was congealed and slightly slimy. Enid thought wryly that the Egyptians would have popped it in the sarcophagus – the cat too, probably. She left it where it was. She was quite lucid enough to know that Gerry wouldn't want it, but part of her just felt an urge to leave it there, just in case. Well, why not? She wandered into the sitting room. She couldn't face *Pet Rescue* now, in the same room as that chair. She wondered vaguely how long 'that chair' would remain 'that chair'.

'Shit, I've forgotten to call Sal.' Enid found it hard to remember the familiar numbers; they danced and leapt in any old order, slithering out of her mind, refusing to be pinned down.

'Sal, it's true, he arrived dead – a stroke. Yes, I'm home, it's horrid, particularly the chair. It's all rather spooky. I'll come over when I've fed the cat.'

The cat got dog food in Enid's confusion. The cat, any other name long forgotten, felt about as interested in dog food as Enid would feel about a camel's diet. Constipation is one thing but the pent-up need to cry that produces no tears, no relief, is quite as uncomfortable. Enid sat in the kitchen in suspended discomfort; a ball of tension weighed down her throat but it was 'the time factor' that preoccupied her most. She had played this game for nearly eight hours. That was long enough. Would someone please tell her it was over, finished? Then she could collect Gerry and they could both go home.

'Please,' she whispered. There was no answer. She stood up and found a toothbrush and some clean undies before driving over to Sal and her twins. Sophocles hitched a lift too. The cat might like an empty house, apart from the mice, but after a day in a hospital car park, Sophocles wanted a bit of action.

Enid drove over to her son-in-law's farm like a drunk pretending to be sober. She clicked her seat belt with memories of Jimmy Savile leering at her...how many years ago was that? 'Clunk-click every trip.' Those were the days when Gerry, in their courting period, would place his hand over hers as she changed gear. What about that time when they tried to have sex in the back of the car and Gerry was compromised by two riders on grey ponies with his bum half outside the back window! And when they were skint and broke down on holiday in France and had to pay the mechanic in wine they had just purchased for themselves. It's funny, she hadn't thought about those incidents for years. Bugger death, it had no right to taunt her like this.

Sal stood at the front door before gathering her mother in a great big bear hug. Her hands were floury.

'We're making jam tarts for you.'

'Not for Grandpa, he'th dead,' lisped Sophie, clinging to her mother's skirts. No sooner had they piled into the kitchen when Beatrice, the other twin, bless her little heart, who was lying on the kitchen floor, produced a drawing of dead Grandpa.

Enid found herself looking at a large, lumpy, angel-like figure, flanked by the sun, some stars and blue sky. There were some bright round things in a pile by his feet.

'What are those, Beatrice?' asked Enid, eyeing her grand-daughter dubiously.

'Apples and pears – it's a long way to heaven.'

'Who said anything about heaven?' retorted Enid.

'Beatrice believes in the Egyptian theory of the afterlife,' said Sal, as she cleared a space on the kitchen table for the tarts. They were burnt and disgusting. The girls were delighted and Enid was resigned; she'd have to eat one. This at least was taking her mind off things.

Sal was very sad about her father's death but too preoccupied to do much about it. She anticipated her mother's state of shock. Mum would put on a brave face till the wine started running, while she, Sal, would curl up next to Douglas in bed recalling all those snippets of memory that death dredges up and have a good old cry before going to sleep. Over the next few weeks, despite the twins, she would be able to mourn, but would her mum? That was the problem. Enid would behave exactly as Gerry would want her to. It was only when she stopped doing that... What's the use? Her mum had lived all her married life completely dependent on Gerry. Pathetic, really! It was that generation, though, with its God-awful attitudes about class and women's role in life. Sal shuddered.

Enid trailed round Sal as she bathed the twins and put them to bed. Sal got her mum to load the washing machine; inevitably, she forgot to put in any powder. She tried to tidy away some of the day's debris, picking up a single shoe and putting it down absent-mindedly. When Sal read a story to the girls, Enid sat on the bed, listening to some interminably boring saga about a rabbit's birthday party. Then Beatrice piped up, 'When will Grandpa stop being dead?'

'He won't, he's going to be dead for ever and ever.' It was Sal who answered; she was answering for them all, particularly her mother.

'How will he get to heaven?' Sophie was clearly perplexed.

'Beatrice drew some apples and pears. I expect that'll help,' said Enid. But that wasn't theologically sophisticated enough for Sophie.

'No, but how?'

Sal looked at Enid who seemed utterly defeated by this challenge.

'It comes from going to a Church primary.' She turned to the two little girls; they were like a pair of fledglings, their beaks wide open for knowledge.

'Grandpa has gone away. Where? We do not know. Some people think dead people go to a place called heaven; others like Granny believe that when you die the bit of you that matters simply stops. Either way, we have to get rid of the body; the body doesn't matter.'

Enid smiled bleakly at the two blonde girls, large eyes fixed on her.

'Everybody dies, that's the easy part; it's learning to live without...' Her voice cracked. She looked away.

Douglas was waiting for them in the sitting room; he hugged his mother-in-law and said simply that he would miss Gerry. He gave Enid a stiff drink. Sal's dogs, two grubby terriers, Gin and Tonic, were hurtling round the sitting room floor with Sophocles. A well-aimed kick, very un-*Pet Rescue*, caused an aggrieved yelp and the dogs took their hurtling into the hall.

Sal, whose midweek cooking was pretty bad at the best of times, excelled with some revolting splodge. No one felt very hungry. Over the wine they made a list of people who ought to be told. Enid's composure slipped.

'I can't face Phyllis, she'll only gush. I don't want to talk to the gushers.' All gushers were ticked in red; Sal would phone them. Anyone inclined to cry was also put aside. Douglas was regarded as tough enough to handle them.

'Ma, you don't have to speak to anyone.'

That did it. Enid began to cry. She also continued to drink. Douglas opened another bottle. He opened it more for Sal and himself. Let's face it, a lachrymose mother-in-law is no fun.

Enid sobbed and indulged in a trip down memory lane – including the inevitable, 'Was it Tuesday or Wednesday?' – having already established that the event was over twenty years ago.

'I remember it clearly…' fresh sobs – 'he had just come back from Zambia, I think it was.' Out came a large, soggy hanky. 'You know what those places are like.'

Everyone nodded, as only those who have never been near the place can. 'Well, I called the doctor at once, and guess what he diagnosed!'

Sal and Douglas made faces of someone guessing. Enid was being a bore.

'Housemaid's knee!'

The unfunny denouement cheered Enid up but left the other two cold. Sal scraped back her chair. Stimulated by the wine, she was feeling sad and rather frightened; a life without her pa in the background was strangely alarming. It wasn't that he did much – did anything, come to think of it – but his nuisance value alone had been endearing.

The phone calls were, on the other hand, curiously reassuring. They gave legitimacy to Gerry's death, taking it off Enid's shoulders, defining at the same time her role as the widow.

Lovely people dreamt up comforting thoughts, such as Bodger.

'You mustn't do a thing, not till you've had time to have a jolly good think.' Dear old Bodger – he had never done anything in his life, and certainly not got as far as thinking.

Then there was Maggie.

'My darling girl, go out and buy something really scrumptious; it will cheer you up.' Maggie always had been a lightweight, albeit dressed to kill.

Douglas got cracking on Gerry's immediate family. They were far too well bred to indulge in such common nonsense as tears. His two sisters stiffened their upper lips and asked about the funeral. The gushers were rather more time-consuming. Some told lengthy stories of other people's strokes. Others were tactless enough to imply that maybe Enid might be better off without the old devil.

'I mean, he was pretty unreliable, Douglas, all that gallivanting. Mark my words – the pigeons will now come home to roost.'

Too right, as Douglas was to remember at a much later date.

That observation was from Richard Thompson, himself a self-respecting philanderer, known locally as 'the Shropshire Lad', having left a pregnant wife in Shropshire for the vicar's wife, also in Shropshire. The couple had arrived in North Yorkshire a little sheepishly and taken to Bible reading classes in Ripon. Gerry had thought Richard was an ass. However, they were neighbours and exchanged gardening tools. The ass brayed insensitively – could Douglas remind Enid that Gerry had borrowed the shears recently?

All three were exhausted as they rang the various names they had written down.

'Really, some people,' began Sal, as she replaced the phone after a particularly garrulous friend launched into an anecdote best told after dinner. 'Talk about neither the time nor place!' Then she proceeded to pass the risqué story on to Enid.

'Nowt so queer as folk,' slurred Enid, adding, 'I wonder what their sex life is like, anyway. Tommy is an awful bottom-pincher.'

'Ma!' Sal was tired, quite irritable and wanted to be with her Douglas on their own. She tried changing the subject.

'What do you want to do about the funeral?'

Enid had a blotchy face and swollen red eyes; her speech was definitely slurred and, quite frankly, she looked ghastly.

'The funeral – what about the funeral? Does it really matter two hoots about the funeral?' Enid wanted to go to sleep. 'I haven't the energy to be original, whatever that means; an ordinary cremation, I suppose. I'm seeing a Mr Summerhayes tomorrow.'

That was enough. They were all tired and the strain was showing. Mrs Boots and her kittens having taken over the spare bedroom, Sal had done her best with Beatrice's room. This still left Beatrix Potter posters, one-eyed teddies, some picture books and a toy farm, which looked as if a tornado had hit it.

Enid didn't bother to undress properly. She lay crumpled and tired with enough wine sloshing around inside to give a deep sleep for a couple of hours followed by thirst, headache and tormenting thoughts. The ghastly realisation of her Gerry's death started to dawn around the cold chill hours of darkness.

There were telltale signs of Sal having wept during the night. That and a hangover made her pretty sharpish with her daughters.

'For God's sake, find your bloody shoes. Why do I always have to do everything in this bloody house?'

Beatrice burst into tears. Then Sophie started.

'Is Grandpa still dead?'

'Oh, shut up! You know he is.'

Sophie's face puckered. She began to cry and speak at the same time.

'It's going to be my news at news time. Annie's grandma died and we all said a prayer.'

Sophie continued to weep; so did Beatrice, but she was probably weeping about her shoes. Just then Sophocles, who was thoroughly enjoying this unexpected night away with Sal's two dogs, dashed into the kitchen followed by the other two and managed between them to knock over the rubbish bin and leave a trail of tea leaves, grapefruit skins, soggy cereal and mince all over the floor. At that moment Enid made her entrance. She looked frightful.

'Fucking, bloody dogs!' yelled Sal. 'Find those bloody shoes for the last time, Beatrice, or I'll send you to school in your welly boots, do you hear?'

'"Our Father, which art in heaven,"' sobbed Sophie. 'That's the prayer they'll say.'

'No they won't, that's for Lord God; they'll do a different one for Grandpa,' announced Beatrice from the depths of the play box, still looking for her shoes.

'And there was me hoping it was all a bad dream.' Enid flopped into a chair. 'I know it's not, though; it hit me sometime in the middle of the night – a horrid realisation, may I say! Any chance of a cuppa?'

'Sorry, you'll have to get your own. I must get the kids off to school. Now, have you found your bloody shoes yet?'

Beatrice stood her ground. 'Not really, look!'

Sophocles had chewed one shoe beyond recognition. Beatrice had found it, and with noisy tears showed it to Sal.

'Just look at what your fucking, bloody dog has done. You might have shut it in the car.'

Sal waved the chewed remnant in Enid's distraught face. Enid started crying again.

'Mummy's using language again,' whispered Sophie to Beatrice.

Beatrice went to school in her wellies. Sophie went mouthing her important piece of news and Enid sat in the kitchen and wished she could find some Alka-Seltzer. Instead she made some tea and sat in mournful reverie till Sal returned, feeling consumed with guilt at her intemperate outburst.

'I try never to swear in front of the kids, but this is all too much. I'm sorry, Ma; you deserve better.'

It was time to visit the undertaker. Enid felt that leaden lump of dread at the pit of her stomach. She wasn't dressed for an undertaker, wasn't ready to see him. What the hell would she say? Then paranoia arrived on the scene. Rubbing it in, that's what all this was about; they would rub it in until she got the message: she was a widow. Sophocles hopped into the car. Enid started the engine, deeply self-conscious about every action, repeating over and over, 'I'm a widow.'

Mr Summerhayes, the undertaker, was a delightful man with an office that was warm and friendly – quite an achievement for an undertaker. He had inherited his business from his father and tried to maintain friendliness with the many families he'd dealt with over the years. He had a good memory and could frequently remember the dear departed from several years before.

'We try our best to give you and your family a really personal experience. Now, wherever possible, we like to work in partnership with whoever is taking the service. I understand that in your case the curate, Gavin Weatherall, will be officiating. He's been in touch with me and I believe he'll be coming round shortly to have a word.'

Was it all just as easy as that? Enid wondered as she drove home.

Enid was bathed, changed and ready for ecclesiastical action. She watched the curate park his car and walk to her front door, thoroughly squishing one of Sophocles' turds as he did so. He'd arrived to have a word. But first he wiped his shoes on the doormat several times, looking at them with meticulous care.

'Dog shit,' diagnosed Enid.

The curate sat a little awkwardly, his buttocks pressed together. He had a very pronounced Adam's apple, which bobbed up and down, on the edge of his dog collar. It was pink and blotchy and very unattractive. Enid found herself watching it as he spoke, jerking and bobbing up and down.

'Mrs Tanner, I am so sorry about my shoes – just a little bit of whoopsie. I've cleaned them very carefully.' This was followed by a long silence. 'My condolences in your hour of need. Can you tell me a little about the late Mr Tanner? I would like to say a word or two about him in my address.'

Enid found herself thinking.

Late Mr Tanner! If he was late, he wouldn't be dead yet.

'*Sorry, chaps, can't make it today, running late.*' She could hear Gerry's voice perfectly clearly. It was by no means the first time he'd spoken since being dead. Gerry, the man of few words and which more often than not included an expletive, was becoming positively garrulous in death.

'Oh, do shut up.' She found herself saying it aloud.

'I'm awfully sorry,' she added for the curate's benefit, 'I keep hearing him speak.'

'What was he like?'

'He was like some dear, smelly, old, irascible dog – very grubby, you know.'

The curate looked at Mrs Tanner rather nervously, his buttocks clenched together more firmly than ever. There were times when God went on the blink, and without a robust sense of humour, which the Rev. Gavin Weatherall didn't have, it was difficult to know how to proceed.

'I just need something I can say to his family and friends. What was his job before he retired?'

Enid Tanner was a lady who liked clear, well-spoken English, the Queen's English. She felt quite unreasonably that people who spoke with a common accent probably wore white socks and drank sweet sherry. This one certainly had white socks. She decided she hated vicars. Poor vicar, how was he to know that the shock of Gerry's death had unleashed the two incompatible sides of Enid's nature, snobbishness on the one hand and vague left-wing ideals on the other?

How was he to know? If the truth were known, the Rev. Gavin Weatherall came from a modest house on the Uxbridge Road in London with net curtains.

Most probably, Enid would have found this knowledge quite fascinating. She was a keen observer of the lower orders. On the dinner party circuit, Enid would have championed his class but, faced with it in her hour of need, everything he stood for repelled her.

Bet he says 'passed away', Enid thought to herself and leant forward to catch the *bons mots* of the Reverend. But first her reply. She said rather primly, 'He was a spy.' There, she had said the forbidden word – never mind whether it was true or not.

'Any hobbies?' Gavin Weatherall knew that people sometimes showed off when in adversity.

Enid thought about hobbies. The word itself was pretty naff. Gerry didn't have hobbies and he'd have snorted with rage at the very thought. He mooched around with Sophocles, but not because he liked the dog much. He went to the pub. It was a chance to have a drink with his mates, or rather mate, for Gerry wasn't a great one for mates.

'Not really, he was the kind that simply sat and farted periodically.' That was the absolute truth, even if Enid was saying it for effect. Actually, the word just slipped out, like the spy business. It was vicars. They had that effect on Enid. Maybe it was Gerry's death having an effect too.

'He used to collect stamps; is that any help?'

The Rev. Gavin looked gratefully at Enid, then wrote down 'stamps' in his little booklet.

'Did he have a penny black?'

'Dozens. They're two a penny, I gather.'

'What about charities? Did he have any special ones he supported?'

'God, no! Charity began at home with Gerry.'

A silence, rather like a large chasm, fell between them. The Rev. Gavin Weatherall scrambled around for spiritual guidance. No one would deny that he merited an alpha for sincerity.

However, there are occasions when sincerity is a liability as well as a killer.

'A family man?' he suggested cautiously.

'A family man?' queried Enid. 'Not really; the responsibilities for fatherhood didn't venture much further than coitus. No, my Gerry was a worthless old curmudgeon. He had few redeeming features, so don't go making up a load of crap about him.' She began crying.

The Rev. Gavin Weatherall's eyes had been glued to Enid, who covered her face and sat sobbing in a shabby old chair. His eyes shifted to the picture on the wall behind her, one done by her daughter, Sal, at art school. It was of a naked man with a large slug-like pink penis decorated with a ring. The curate's eyes bulged as if he had dislocated eyeballs. He sought desperately for some familiar piece of furniture he could latch onto. He had buried several hundred souls; he knew the routine, or thought he did. With God's support he was able to comfort the bereaved, able to build up a picture of their loved one. But, faced with a nude man with a ring through his penis, his faith in providing any support wilted, as if it was his own penis on the block.

The picture was a wow with first-timers to the house but palled after a while.

'One thing, Vicar, please don't refer to my Gerry as a 'loved one'. He was many things but never, I repeat never, a loved one. It's such a presumptuous term.'

There are times when a man of the cloth feels he has to shake someone, confront them with God, and this was such a time. The Rev. Gavin Weatherall sank to his knees. Enid was nimble enough, despite her tears, to leap out of her seat and stand on the opposite side of the room. Her worst fears were about to be realised.

'Let us pray,' thundered, albeit in the upper register, the good Reverend, pronouncing 'pray' as 'pry', his Adam's apple jerking like a demented puppet.

'What on earth for?' inquired Enid, looking quite alarmed at his antics, her tears miraculously forgotten.

'God will give you courage.'

'But I don't want courage, I just want to bury my husband! It's you who wants to say a few words, as you put it. Frankly, I wouldn't bother.'

'Our Father...' began the Reverend, extemporising furiously. The gist was easy; here was a godless household and he would show Enid the error of her ways. Enid, however, would have none of it.

'Oh, do shut up, you'll frighten the cat! I think I'd better cancel the whole damn business. It's outrageous that one can't even bury one's husband without the bloody Church making a song and dance about it. I thought the point of having an established Church was that it was rather like an extension of the Social Services, but if you think you can come into my house and start banging on about God, you're wrong. It's crassly insensitive of you for starters, so out you go, please, Mr – I mean Reverend – Weatherall.'

But the Rev. didn't want to leave that easily.

'Mrs Tanner, let God into your life. He can support you at this difficult time.'

'Look, just get out of my house. I'll phone the undertaker and organise whatever rubbish they dole out for non-believers like Gerry. I only asked you because the service is rather pretty. I like the words.' Enid walked towards the front door, opened it and stood waiting for the Rev. to depart. The cat walked in carrying a half-dead mouse, which she delicately dropped at his feet, before giving a loud meow.

The 'Oh' that spontaneously fell from his lips was almost identical with the noise the cat had made.

'Leave it, she's always bringing them in,' said Enid.

'Look, Mrs Tanner, I feel we've got off to a bad start. I apologise. Funerals are very fraught affairs. Let's begin again and together we'll try to arrange for Mr Tanner the funeral you would like him to have.'

'Out! As far as I'm concerned, his body can be turfed out with the rubbish. He's dead. But I tell you something, I'm not having the likes of you stuffing God down my throat like some form of oral sex.'

'Believe me, Mrs Tanner, it is a time of great distress. Many of us say and do things we regret later. Perhaps we can spend some time in prayer before we decide what would be most appropriate for Mr Tanner…'

It was a strange sight: the curate, his Adam's apple all of a bobble, standing awkwardly by the cat, which was busily and with great fastidiousness decapitating a mouse; Enid, her back to the wall, in a state of fury, determined to get rid of this spiritual nightmare; while between them was the hotchpotch muddle of a sitting room that had grown organically over the years. Apart from the picture of the male model with his ringed penis, there were several prints of ancient forts in India, a mask of a Melanesian gentleman with cowrie eyes, a table full of clutter, magazines, packets of sweets, some newspapers, a beautiful bronze figure and a dog's lead. The floor was covered with kilims distributed casually and covered with dead mouse and dog hair. Some books lay at reclining angles in a bookcase – lightweight novels and biographies. It was a warm, chaotic room – a room that spoke of a happy muddle; but the happiness had left.

'Please, just leave.'

The Rev. Gavin Weatherall fled. He drove back with a hideous fantasy of God with a ring through his penis hovering over the lips of some unknown vast 'all-sucking' mouth. Mrs Tanner hadn't even offered him a cup of tea. When he got home he put the kettle on, sat down at his kitchen table and felt a profusion of emotions, from rage at the arrogance of that woman's rejection of Our Lord, to equal rage at his own naivety and ineptitude at handling the situation. He sipped his strong tea, the pain and embarrassment receding enough for him to bundle God's penis back where it belonged, close the monstrous mouth and wonder if he ought to have elocution lessons. He felt sure his accent was a drawback with some people. It was being in a rural parish. He had to deal with all classes of people. Really, some of these middle-class people were such snobs. He must learn to couch the love of God in more subtle ways. That was it: he'd pray for Mr Tanner; she'd never know, but he'd give him the whole works. She could bury him as she chose, but he would make sure Gerry's soul was saved.

Enid rang the undertakers.

'The vicar, or whatever, was a disaster. I've decided not to have a Christian burial after all. Do you have a service for non-believers?'

Yes, they did. Why didn't she come in and speak in person with Mr Summerhayes. No, he wouldn't be available in the morning but Thursday afternoon would be ideal.

Enid rang her daughter.

'Sorry, Sal. It was dreadful. That vicar, he had an accent you could cut with a knife. I kicked him out in the end. Summerhayes wants to meet me tomorrow afternoon and discuss a non-Christian "do". I just couldn't face the idea of a vicar in white socks and a frightful accent getting his paws into poor Gerry. Could you come and see the undertaker with me? Bring the twins. Sorry, love, but I can't somehow giggle. If I'm on my own, the weeps keep getting in the way.'

Mr Summerhayes was delighted to see Enid again. He quite understood the problem, even if he wasn't told about the white socks or dreadful accent. He even welcomed the twins; he kept some sweets in his office for such a contingency. He made Enid and her daughter completely welcome with quiet courtesy as he sat them down in his office. The twins, with bulging cheeks full of sweets, took some crayons and paper that prudently their mother had supplied and lay on the floor drawing Grandpa going to heaven.

'I don't want any crap,' said Enid, her voice rather unsteady.

'Is that the same as shit?' asked Sophie, looking up, her mouth still full of sweets.

'It's a grown-up word. Now draw a nice picture for Granny,' hissed her mother.

The child sighed and went back to drawing Grandpa in heaven. Mr Summerhayes's shrewd eye missed nothing; distraught women say many things they regret, and he made some suggestions.

'A little Shakespeare, Tennyson's "Crossing the Bar", the St Crispin's speech – Harry and St George – that's very popular. "To be a man, my son" – Kipling – again very popular. Perhaps there is something special you'd like, Mrs Tanner?'

'Look, I'm sorry, I just can't see it – not dignified poetry with

Vaughan Williams. Gerry wasn't like that.'

'Do be reasonable, Ma. Pa might have enjoyed bawdy verse but it's hardly appropriate to have "Eskimo Nell" for his funeral.' Sal was irritable.

'I like "Away in a Manger",' said Beatrice, kicking her heels as she lay on the floor, putting the finishing touches to yet another drawing of dead Grandpa.

'Shut up, Bea,' said her mother.

'What do you think I should do then, Sal?'

'Look, Ma, this isn't about Pa, or you for that matter. It's about all those ghouls who will turn up at the crematorium. OK, you don't want a vicar or a Christian service, but you must have something. What about getting someone to say a few words before the coffin slides into the incinerator?'

Enid winced at the word 'incinerator'.

'It makes him sound radioactive. Anyway, who would say something? And what if they come up with a load of lies, or worse, tell the truth?' Enid was silent before adding, 'I know, I'll ask the Brig; he's perfect at saying nothing convincingly.'

There followed a silence as if this 'nothing' was not going to be enough. Enid sighed first, followed by Sal's sigh of relief. So back they went to Mr Summerhayes's suggestion about dignified music and uplifting poetry.

'Got it!' declared Enid. 'What about that poem by Auden they had in that film Gerry liked? What was it called? "Four some-things…" I know, "weddings and a funeral".'

'Excellent,' beamed Mr Summerhayes. He coaxed 'All the World's a Stage' out of Enid before turning to music. Enid belonged to the tumpty, tumpty school of musical illiterates and was quite incapable of choosing anything remotely suitable. She'd heard of the Beatles and suggested 'Yellow Submarine'.

Mr Summerhayes had heard much worse; indeed, Enid was a doddle. It was overdosed addicts and suicides, whose friends were arranging the parting shot, that were really tough going. Only last week he had had to find a friendly vicar who would allow a salvo of empty beer cans to land on the coffin as it was being interred. The vicar had agreed on condition that they didn't drink the contents in church.

The day of the cremation arrived. Enid kept doing deep-breathing exercises; she felt they stopped her from weeping. Sal took her for a muddy walk with the unruly dogs. They trudged into the wind. The grass was about to burst out of its winter pallor, the hedges were bulging with buds and some rooks croaked balefully from the tall trees where they had gathered. Enid saw little and didn't hear the rooks at all. Her mind was swirling with visions of Gerry emerging from his coffin and grumbling at everyone.

'Sal, I dread it! I know it's just a social rite like a wedding, but I don't like ritual, nor did he.'

'I know, Ma, but it's a must, and Pa would be furious if you messed it up. Douglas and I will be with you and lots of your friends will be there. It's a chin-up occasion – think of it like that.'

'The worst part is people saying they understand, Sal. I don't want them to understand or know what I feel. I mean, it wasn't that I loved him or anything. It's more than love, much more after all those years. Part of me has died too, the part that was the devoted wife of Gerry; it's our marriage that is being buried. Do you realise I will never have to eat liver ever again, or dumplings? I don't know why, but I loathe dumplings. No more quarrels about the telephone bill or toothpaste; Gerry would never rinse the basin after he cleaned his teeth. I will be able to watch what I like on television. The old bugger, he restricted me. I suppose I'll now restrict myself. Old habits die hard. I must buy some nightdresses; I haven't worn a nightdress since I was a kid. I know everyone says that funerals are cathartic; frankly, I think they stink.'

'Come here, you brute; what the hell do you think you are doing?'

Sal missed the end of Enid's bellyache; the dog had caught a young rabbit and was munching it enthusiastically.

'There,' said Enid, looking at the young rabbit jerking in its death throes. 'We won't have to go to that rabbit's funeral, so why do we have to go to Gerry's?'

Sal eyed her mother. It was time to get back and change for the crematorium.

'I'm not going to even discuss it, Ma. What's more, you are not going to let your family or your friends down. You might find the whole thing absolute purgatory, but that's just tough luck.'

Enid thought of crying – very easy to do, nowadays – but she'd promised the cat she wouldn't. Sal's pomposity was out of character. Had she forgotten her eighteenth birthday?

'Don't worry, I won't let you down.'

That eighteenth birthday had been quite something. Twenty friends to stay, sleeping bags everywhere, dancing in the spare bedroom – the only room big enough with the beds removed. They hitched or arrived in cars that looked as if they had come from the scrap-heap. One young man arrived with a rucksack, having walked most of the way. All thirty-two of them turned up – some with long hair, some with short. One girl had shaved her head. There were red, pink and green heads, plaited heads, fuzzy heads, and a young man who had a tattoo on his head. Then the rings: the model with a ring through his penis insisted on showing it to Enid; then there were the ear, nose, nipple and tummy-button rings. It was rumoured that one girl had her clitoris ringed. Thank God Enid wasn't asked to see that. Their dress was universally grubby, dirty and dowdy – ripped jeans, torn shirts and long droopy skirts. Enid was naive enough to assume that deeply significant conversations would counterbalance their appearance. But no, they rolled joints and puffed away with serious, rather vacant expressions.

It was at that point that Enid and Gerry became all pompous.

'Sal, can you tell these young friends of yours that sitting around my house smoking dope is damned offensive. I'm not aware anyone had the courtesy to ask me. I'm not aware that some of your friends have had the courtesy to say as much as "hello". If I have to spend my weekend with gormless twits, I feel the least they can do is ask before they puff away at noxious weeds.'

Oooh! The fur didn't half fly. Those were the days. Enid blinked back her tears. She couldn't imagine a future, not without Gerry. She looked at her watch. It was funeral time – not his, but their funeral time; that was what it felt like, going to the funeral of their marriage.

It didn't feel like a death yet. Damn it! She hadn't even changed the sheets. His muddy shoes were still by the back door and his half-read book by the television. Only that morning the postman had delivered a pompous reply from the council, something about the refuse collection. That had been Gerry, always poking his nose into things. She wouldn't. All that was Gerry's scene, not hers. After years of listening to Gerry bang on, it would be silence now – a horrid drawn-out silence. Enid shivered. After years of 'Gerry thinks and Gerry says', it would be her doing the thinking and saying... But what would she have to say?

Douglas wore the partly green shirt; he felt that his late father-in-law would have been amused. They piled into the car and arrived without incident outside the crematorium. It was about fifteen minutes before the service. Luckily, the twins had been banned. Already there were several ladies in deepest black huddled together looking like crows. They were in fact Gerry's sisters and a cousin; a pity they hadn't asked what clothes were being worn, as their black outfits were way over the top.

Soon there were many more in a hotchpotch of safe, muted colours. A few men wore black ties; others had safe, dark ties, worn with a dark suit. There were a few anoraks, making the whole business look like an Irish funeral after a shooting. It was March. A shrill wind blew and noses grew rapidly red. Enid, looking distinctly suitable in tweed skirt done up with a safety pin and a three-quarter-length camel hair coat and no hat, shook hands mutely. Sal was looking all grey, washed out and rather dreary, very suitable and far removed from her art student days. Enid was tight-lipped in case she cried. She was adamant that the thing should be simple and dignified. 'The thing' was how she referred to the service.

'That bunch in black had no right to tart up like that. Pulling rank – that's all they are doing.'

Some people had sent flowers to the undertakers, others arrived with bunches held upside down behind their backs in case they had done the wrong thing. They had.

'What a bloody waste of flowers,' grumbled Enid. 'Anyway, Gerry wasn't interested in flowers.'

'Come on, Ma, you're all for people doing their own thing. People like sending flowers.' Sal was worried.

Enid could be quite a handful. Not that she'd burst into tears. Far from it! She was more likely to show off in some inappropriate way, picking a quarrel or loudly announcing some unnecessary information, like when she and Gerry last had sex. It was pathetic, really. Enid was bottling up her distress and trying desperately to pretend she was taking it all in her stride.

'You know, Sal, this reminds me of Disneyland. It's all unreal – the dinky little crematorium, the gravestones and the poor bloody flowers standing to attention like soldiers in the narrow borders or, even more like soldiers, dead in the service of their country, heaped on the coffin in plastic shrouds. I suppose poor old Gerry is wrapped up in a shroud. I feel we should be singing some Disney special like "Whistle while you work". But poor old Gerry wasn't Mickey Mouse. He'd have hated all this.'

'Come on, Ma, it will all be over in fifteen minutes.'

Mr Summerhayes had printed an order of service, which laid out carefully what was going to happen. As he explained to Enid and Sal, it was difficult for mourners to follow a service specifically designed for someone unless they could see exactly what was going on. The mourners shuffled into the crematorium. The soothing music had been switched off at Enid's request; not for her Gerry the strains of mutilated Mozart.

Some took their places in the front pews, like Gerry's sisters, while others nipped in at the back. The flowers had been left in the porch. Enid couldn't help noticing some daffodils and tulips bearing a card which said, 'Gerry, we'll miss you,' signed by John and Phil.

'That's those two queers who run the Blue Dragon. I bet he owes them a small fortune. Do they go to all their customers' funerals?'

'Sssh, Ma! In we go.'

The interior was silent, broken by the clip-clopping of their shoes.

'We should have organised proper music,' muttered Enid.

'Mr Summerhayes did advise more music,' murmured Sal.

'I know, but I didn't realise it would be like this. Oh shit!'

Enid walked down the aisle noticing, as far as she could from the back view, who had turned up.

'There's Sam and Jane. She's a catty old bag if ever there was one. And Mr Stoneham – whatever is he doing here?'

The small chapel was very carefully designed. Lots of well-polished wood, stained glass and brass. The coffin sat on a specially designed block. It looked rather stark, maybe because it was the cheapest Mr Summerhayes had. Enid and Sal slipped into the front pew where Douglas joined them. The silence that followed was an embarrassing one; no one knew when it would all start. Then Mike, an old friend of Gerry's and popular with the family, rose to his feet and walked to the front.

'We all knew Gerry – not an easy friend to bury, I mean cremate – not too keen on vicars and all that. Enid has put together one or two poems which Gerry liked. I'm going to kick off with some Shakespeare.'

Mike launched into 'All the World's a Stage'. He read it rather badly; he hadn't rehearsed much. He read it like a teenager having a stab at Shakespeare and failing to understand what it was all about. Enid felt let down.

'This is too embarrassing,' she whispered, quite loudly. Several mourners were thinking the same thing.

'Much better to go for the C of E option, if you ask me,' said Sam to his wife. She nodded in agreement.

'Mike's not exactly a Shakespearean scholar, is he?' Jane said, smirking. She liked to think she could remember every word of – what was it now?

This time it was Douglas, the son-in-law. He explained that Gerry had seen a film with a poem by WH Auden in it. Douglas stopped the clocks and silenced the dogs in a good style. Everyone felt more comfortable. There followed several more poems, Kiplingesque in style, before the Brig stood up and praised Gerry as a 'good sort, one of the best'.

The Brigadier went on to praise his career as a... and here, however hard you were listening, it was still difficult to say what Gerry did, or rather had done. The Brig looked immaculate: 'a distinguished elderly gentleman,' was how many of the congregation described him.

Somehow, whatever Gerry had done must have been all right, if that was his boss. Then the tape of 'Yellow Submarine' started and the congregation witnessed the sad sight of Gerry's mortal remains sliding silently into the furnace.

The next cremation was forming up as Enid and the mourners left for the private room at the Crown. Some people slipped away straight after the cremation, mumbling excuses, having shaken hands with Enid and Sal.

'Such a sad event. Unfortunately I have a meeting.'

'Our heartfelt condolences. The bitch has just whelped.'

And Enid said, 'Where do they hear these frightful phrases?'

At the Crown, the mourners sipped their wine and button-holed each other.

'Did he leave her suitably off?' asked a distant cousin, his hands firmly shoved deep in his pockets.

'Wouldn't have thought so; you know what he was like.'

'I really do think Enid was very wrong not to have a proper church service. Whatever her private opinion, this is not a time to indulge.'

'I agree, Maud, but it's typical, if I may say so. Wasn't that a Beatles tune he disappeared to?'

Enid circulated among her guests. She kissed cheeks and listened to hackneyed phrases of condolence. She preferred the tongue-tied sentiments, particularly those of William – a genial old buffer who had been a friend for years. Tears were coursing down his face as he clasped Enid, announcing at the same time, 'It's tickety-boo time, Enid.'

She agreed, adding, 'William, we're all under starter's orders.'

There was an awkward moment as one of the women in deepest black bore down on Enid.

'Enid, so sad. Why on earth did you choose such a ridiculous little service? You can't beat the church at a time like this. No one's asking you to sign on for the Mothers' Union!'

'I'm sorry, Florence, I'm not like you. You appear to like deepest black and all the trimmings; I prefer the minimalist approach, subfusc, if you like.'

'Well, I hope life treats you kindly, Enid. You've got a tough row to hoe – but then you married him.'

'Florence has always been a patronising, stupid cow,' Enid observed. She was being driven back to the twins.

She was mildly tiddly and feeling sorry for herself. Sal and

Douglas were tired. It had all been a bit of an ordeal; the DIY service, frankly, had been pretty awful. At least there were no ashes to spread. The undertaker had been asked to leave them where they were – not that Enid had any idea where that would be, but hoped an incinerator had enough ashes of its own not to notice a few more. Gerry, for better or worse, was now truly dead.

The twins dominated breakfast the next morning.

'But Granny, did you actually *see* Grandpa go to heaven?'

Sophie stood with stomach protruding and wispy hair lingering round her thoughtful face. Beatrice scooped up a spoonful of cereal and put most of it in her mouth. The remains gradually dropped off her chin onto the tablecloth.

'Because naughty people don't always go there, and you sometimes called Grandpa a wicked old sod.'

Another spoon was shovelled into her mouth; eating with your mouth shut was a lesson yet to be learnt.

'They go to hell, which is very hot.'

'Yes,' added Sophie, who was sitting down by now and eating a piece of toast by licking off the jam.

'Mummy says that Grandpa was sometimes a real son of a bitch. God doesn't like sons of bitches; anyway, that makes him a puppy dog.'

'Will you two stop talking a lot of rot! Finish your breakfast and get ready for school.'

Sal was trying to feed the cats, find the appropriate number of shoes and open the letters that had just tumbled through the door. The dogs, including Sophocles, were hell-bent on playing tag under everyone's feet.

'I think I'll sit next door, Sal. I don't feel up to six-year-old theology just now.'

Enid took her cup of coffee and went into the sitting room. Sitting rooms are never at their best first thing in the morning. The cushions were squashed and carelessly littered about the sofa and on the floor. A messy pile of magazines lay on the floor. Enid picked one up. The front picture advertised a worming drench and she turned the page and came face to face with a pair of castrators and an article on dagging sheep. There were several dirty glasses from the night before, when she, Sal and Douglas had gone through every moment of the funeral, as if it hadn't been real at the time but could only exist in retrospect. Enid looked at the tattered curtains. As long as Sal and Douglas had lived here they were about to get new curtains.

I suppose I ought to offer to make them now, Enid thought.

She didn't feel too thrilled at the idea. Making curtains was too… well, not the image Enid wanted; not that she had any idea what she wanted. After Sal had returned from the school run, Enid suggested she went home.

'Sure you're ready, Ma?'

'I've just realised that I haven't dealt with that scrambled egg yet. It will be utterly disgusting by now. I must go.'

Two

It was utterly disgusting. If you must keep a memento to your loved one, don't choose scrambled eggs. Enid almost retched as she scooped the week-old, cold, congealed egg into the rubbish bin. She had met the dreadful vicar; otherwise she had clung to Sal.

Gerry was everywhere. There were crumbs in the butter dish, butter in the marmalade and the fireplace was full of tangerine peel, old envelopes and wrapping paper from a bar of chocolate. Books reclined or lay on the windowsill. The odd auction list for a stamp sale was tucked down the side of the chair. His desk was a frenzy of unpaid bills, unanswered letters and brochures from wine merchants, even though he couldn't afford their wine. The bedroom was scattered with loose change. A filthy handkerchief lurked under his pillow and a pair of elderly bedroom slippers was by his side of the bed. His dressing room – a posh word for a tiny room next to the bathroom – was a tip.

Gerry never put clothes away. They clung to an old chair – pants, trousers, shirts, jerseys, several newspapers, a pair of scissors and a pair of gloves he had sworn he'd left in someone's house. But it was the bathroom which Enid found most painful. Not just his shit clinging to the lavatory bowl – despite being told by Enid to clean the loo every time he used it, he never did – but the whiskers clinging to the basin. God knows what orifice they came from. There was toothpaste liberally smeared round the basin, while from the bath a great deal of the water had sloshed onto the floor and remained there. On the shelf were his pills, an assortment of nail clippers, a razor and mouthwash. Finally his towel lay crumpled by the radiator.

Enid didn't don a pinny and start scrubbing. Instead walked slowly from room to room, picking a comb up here, a letter there. She sighed a great deal but, though she wanted to cry, she couldn't. There was a pile of letters to attend to: several reminders, a number of letters offering condolence. Enid could just see the different friends chewing the end of their pens and wondering what the hell to say. 'Your sad bereavement' was popular, so was the word 'condolence'. Gerry was described as a 'loving husband', 'quite a character' and 'from the old school'.

A reminder from the log merchant who still hadn't been paid since the autumn was worded slightly differently. There was also the will. Gerry didn't have enough money or possessions to warrant a complicated will.

Enid fed the cat. The cat showed no signs of sympathy but was very hungry. It hadn't been fed since the vicar fiasco. Enid wasn't in the least hungry but thought she ought to eat something. A banana was rapidly turning brown. The milk was off so she couldn't have a cup of coffee; instead she drank a can of beer, and it was disgusting. Let's face it, the whole place was disgusting. Enid wished she were an ostrich. She did the next best thing and went to bed.

'Fine,' she lied, when Sal rang later.

The call forced her out of bed. Already the evenings were getting longer; she'd go for a stroll. She chose one that she and Gerry often did together. Sophocles, after his sophisticated holiday with Sal's lot, seemed rather subdued. He trotted by Enid's side, pausing only to pee or smell some particularly fragrant odour. Enid had reached saturation point and was only too happy to watch catkins dangle in the early March sunshine. She found a clump of aconites.

She looked at them for quite a time, thinking of absolutely nothing. Bliss! – a mind full of aconites before her unquiet spirit ruined it all by remembering how Gerry would tease her about wild flowers. He would almost reduce her to tears by being disparaging.

'Edie, you're impossible. There are starving millions, tyrannies, disease and unmentionable horrors, and all you can do is wax eloquent about a bloody buttercup!'

He never gave her flowers. He never gave her anything much – a box of chocolates at Christmas, if he remembered.

So, the mind's moment of ease was broken, the aconites vanished and Enid's mind was back thinking about Gerry. It was by no means through rose-coloured spectacles, either. She remembered the hurts, the slights, the crass insensitivity. She remembered with irritation the times he didn't turn up, food left in the oven to shrivel. She remembered the light bulbs that needed changing, a desk handle that had come loose – was it fifteen years ago? And Gerry armed with a screwdriver, causing mayhem with his clumsy ineptitude.

Then some early daffs caught her attention as they bobbed and nodded in the wind. She could give more time to gardening now. But gardening was strictly for the future. Her real immediate problem was no milk, and she'd be too late for the shops. She'd have to go to the garage; they stayed open till eight. She finished her walk and had to drive a good four miles for her pint of milk.

That first evening was interminably long. Enid couldn't face cooking. There were no more digestive biscuits but there were nuts, raisins, a rather nasty apple, some crackers and peanut butter; Enid ate it in front of television. The banality of the programmes irritated her. She found her radio. It was only seven o'clock. She thought about going to bed, suddenly remembering that the sheets were the dead ones, so to speak, and she hadn't changed them. She hadn't noticed earlier when she had crept off for a kip.

No way was she going to sleep in the same sheets that Gerry had used the day he died. It would be like sharing a shroud. How had she managed in the afternoon? Mind you, she had been knackered then, now she was merely maudlin. Enid opened the airing cupboard; her toe hit the big china potty which lived there and had been used by Gerry when he had the 'dizzies' a few years back. There were also clean sheets and pillowcases smelling that lovely clean warm smell. Enid stripped the bed and remade it.

After remaking the bed, hospital corners and everything, she looked at it but didn't like what she saw; throwing Gerry out of bed was something she'd often fantasised about over the years – particularly when he decided he'd like drunken sex – but now the bed looked so empty. Did she really relish the idea of sleeping in an empty bed for the rest of her life?

The telephone rang; it was Dolly, a dear friend just down the road.

'You are coming to supper tomorrow; no excuse, just come.'

'But…' began Enid, for no particular reason.

'Have you a better offer?' snapped Dolly.

'No, but—'

'Then you're coming! The first rule of widowhood, never turn down an invitation.'

Enid turned the television back on and sat half-watching some police drama, at the same time making lists of things she must do; it seemed endless. There was probate; she'd have to get his affairs sorted out by then. His clothes could go straight to Oxfam, if they weren't too choosy about what they took; otherwise it would be the Scouts. Fishing rods and tennis racquets could stay – they added character to the house. The house – it was in her name, wasn't it? The mortgage paid in full – and everything in order? Enid had taken all these grisly matters for granted. It was bad enough with the car MOT, tax and insurance all falling due at different times.

The programme had changed to comedy with hysterical laughter coming from an unseen audience. Gerry would have been infuriated, probably thrown the newspaper at it. There was the inevitable joke about sex. Enid watched grimly. As a widow, she was just a sexless nonentity, the butt of jokes, among the first to leave the sinking ship, along with women and children. Enid had to admit that their sex life over the past few years had been a little lopsided. Gerry had grown out of relentless nightly coitus and in his later years preferred what he referred to as his nibble from time to time…'Just to keep the old chap up to snuff.'

Well, he was kept up to snuff, but did little about it. Occasionally, a merry twinkle would light his leering eye and he'd make a loving leap 'at' rather than 'on' Enid, who would scuttle under the bedclothes like a demented beetle. It was hardly sex as described in the Kinsey Report, but more a case of granny abuse. In his day, give him his due, he was a lusty, loving man with a healthy appetite for 'Come here, my girl, and let's have a spot of fun.'

Then Enid remembered his videos. How the hell would she get rid of those? They were very embarrassing, and the last thing she'd want Sal to find. She opened a small cupboard in their bedroom and scrambled around for the offending videos.

Shoelaces, a camera, a stack of stamp catalogues, a pair of worn-out espadrilles from that holiday in Brittany, a piece of rope (with no sexual connotations) and a waterproof from that time on the boat.

No videos! Where the hell were they? It was after midnight when Enid found the damned things in the downstairs cloakroom behind the wood basket. There they were and then she remembered: Gerry was going to get rid of them, or rather, find them a happy home. He knew of someone, or was it somewhere, where they were welcome.

It seemed perfectly appropriate to Enid that she should watch a couple. She made herself a hot coffee and then put on the video called *Star-studded Venus*. Venus was working in the office when she caught the eye of a strapping young man who desperately needed to get his boxers off. Foreplay was minimal before they leapt into a camera angle that enabled the photographer to do a close-up of the man's exceptionally large penis plunging in and out of her vagina. They grunted, moaned and said 'Aah' a great deal before he removed himself and had an orgasm all over her enormous breasts. She seemed very grateful and licked it.

Our Venus was some girl...just about to get down to some typing and bingo! Another young man would enter the office and plead with her to take her clothes off. She never refused. The poor girl must have been exhausted by the time she left the office. She must have had a very understanding boss, for she never got any typing done.

The next video was about a hotel manager showing guests their rooms. Every bed had to be tested, and not just by sitting and bouncing to test the springs. Dear me, no! The springs were tested in far more demanding ways. The bodies displayed their techniques for oral, anal and good old missionary-style sex. Enid watched both videos for a while. The last time she had watched them they had aroused her – not much, but she'd been aware of that heightened sensitivity at the anticipation of sex. She supposed it was too much to expect them to have the same effect so soon after Gerry's death.

It's not that I want sex, I just don't want to be sidelined from sex, she told herself. It's sex, it's love, life, vitality. I can't bear the idea of being discarded as an old lady. Gerry, did you have to die, you rotten sod? She began to cry.

It was nearly three when she went to bed. She left the lights on everywhere. A dead Gerry was one thing; the ghost of dead Gerry was quite another. She wasn't ready for that.

Enid wasn't ready for anything, really. She had spent all her married life relying on Gerry to do and be and think. She had been just a cipher, and that's not an exaggeration. Now she was nothing, or so she felt – simply lonely and bored.

Dolly was older than Enid. She was one of those fierce ladies who dye their hair. She was also more, much more. She was funny, shrewd and a stalwart friend. Dolly earned her keep if you invited her to 'make up numbers', a well-known role for widows. She would charm and entertain monosyllabic, depressed old codgers, discuss breastfeeding with lactating mothers or weigh in to the political foibles of the present government.

Dolly had sewn up the local branch of the Heart Foundation; she *was* the Heart Foundation. The local hospital had state-of-the-art equipment, thanks to Dolly and her cohorts. A diminutive sinewy little lady, with her brown curls and not a grey hair in sight and a still pretty face, Dolly led an apparently busy life. She was ideal for initiating Enid into the mores of widowhood.

'You always seem so busy and cheerful,' said Enid, with envy and admiration.

'Oh no, I'm not. There are days when I'm on my own, Enid, and I just stare out of the window and wish and wish that Freddy was back here. Well, not exactly Freddy, but someone. Mind you, I was a good bit younger than you are when he died. Cancer – it took six ghastly months. At the time I kept willing him to die and get it over with. You hear about people devotedly nursing their partners. Quite frankly, I hated seeing Freddy decompose before my eyes; he was quite revolting – emaciated, pathetic. Talk about euthanasia! I'd have willingly put plastic over his head, only I knew it was "not done", like cheating. Honestly, I would have killed him quite happily.'

They were eating chicken casserole and Enid was looking forward to a second helping. Widowhood seemed to mean bingeing in other people's houses and mortifying the flesh in her own. She put her knife and fork down and she sipped some wine and drew her confused thoughts together.

'Did you still love him?'

Dolly was contemptuous.

'*Love*? You mean all those exhausting feelings adolescents go in for? Of course not. Don't be ridiculous! No, Freddy and I had fused into a kind of "for better and for worse" soup. You know, like carrot and potato purée. If these kids could see what marriage is like after thirty years they might choose more carefully. I know it's an heretical thing to say, but Enid, one spends more time out of bed than in. There's a lot to be said for the French and their discreet love affairs. It keeps the mystery going and gets the shelves fixed. Just think of Mitterrand; I don't suppose Madame M sat at home waiting for him every night. I hadn't loved Freddy for years; I was completely bonded, though. Like some more casserole?'

'Please. Oh, Dolly, I don't know if I can tell you, but I spent last night looking at old porn movies Gerry liked to watch.'

'Just Gerry?' queried Dolly, with one eyebrow raised.

'Oh well, I can't say they had much effect.'

'My dear girl, you're an optimist. The libido finds bereavement heavy going. But cheer up; if you promise not to breathe a word, I'll tell you something.'

Dolly began her story.

'This is real, cross your heart and hope to die stuff.' Dolly paused and Enid leant forward.

'After Freddy died, I was very down in the dumps and Olivia and Andrew socked me a cruise. Three weeks round the Mediterranean in September. I have to admit that I went straight out and bought several diaphanous shirts and a glamorous evening dress. I'd never been on a cruise. It was pretty frightful, plastic opulence, right down to those little umbrellas they put in cocktails. It was all keep-fit, beauty parlours, quizzes and a second-rate cabaret. As for the people – lashings of loot, but very common. Well, to cut a long story short, a Scottish marketing executive for a biscuit firm picked me up – "Mr Shortbread", I called him. I never gave it a second thought; I was in his bed before you could say Jack Robinson. Luckily, we both had enough sense to call it a day – only in our case, a night. And do you know, Enid, I don't regret it at all. It's not something I tell everyone, but I have absolutely no regrets.'

'Dolly, you didn't! I wouldn't have the courage – I mean, I would insist on having the lights off. I can't imagine anyone finding me attractive enough. If you're growing old together these things don't matter, but left on one's own with sagging boobs, grey hair or even no hair, wrinkles, varicose veins and haemorrhoids, sex really doesn't stand a chance.'

'Enid, men are like beasts – a whiff of sex and they don't notice, believe me.'

Enid was sceptical. All the same, Dolly painted a picture of widowhood which was considerably less drab than the received wisdom Enid had in mind. With that subject out of the way, they reverted to gardening. Dolly had created a delightful terrace with large pots and a pleasant muddle of trailing plants.

'Mind you, I talk to the damn things the whole time, rather like Prince Charles and his trees; we're both probably lonely. I'm too lazy to take the garden that seriously. I keep it weeded, watered, and I shove little pills in the soil. God knows if it does any good. About three or four times a year I sit out in the evening and feel how lovely it all is. It's times like that when I miss Freddy most. It's a funny thing, but you can never tell when suddenly you are going to come face to face with, in your case, Gerry. Just the other day, I was buying some vegetables and there was a large swede that looked the spitting image of Freddy. Honestly, it was like seeing his skull lying there! At first I welcomed him. I needed him. But after a while I realised I had to stand on my own feet. That cruise helped.'

Enid stared at her scuffed shoes and wished she had worn a smarter pair.

'Gerry's all over the house still – clothes, toiletries, a desk full of bills. Most of all, I hear him talking, that gruff disparaging voice, taking the piss out of everything we hold dear. That's why I didn't give him a Christian funeral. The vicar was a dreadful chap, so sincere; I knew that Gerry would not just turn in his grave but positively leap out of his coffin and berate me for allowing it.'

'You take my advice, Enid. However unconventional Gerry

was, you have to live your life your way. He's dead. Adjust to being more yourself. Don't waste your time and emotions thinking what he'd like. He's dead, get it? He's dead. It's a mantra you must repeat.'

He's dead. Dolly had made it sound so matter-of-fact. Dolly had put spice into widowhood, warm food and wine into Enid and had provided comfort for her grief.

'Enid, what exactly did Gerry do?' Dolly paused with a spoon of apple crumble poised ready to eat.

'Do you know what I told the vicar? I said he was a spy. For all I know, it might be true. His office was in a drab building just off Trafalgar Square. There was an elderly temperamental lift and an adenoidal lady known as "The Cow" by everyone; her real name was Moona. Gerry used to say that he imported badger bristles from China to make shaving brushes.'

'Are there badgers in China?'

'I don't know. There is a delightful man called the Brig. He's the one who spoke about Gerry in the crematorium. Anyway, he's an old friend; I once asked him if Gerry was a spy.'

'And?'

'Well, he was charming – said that Gerry was a special person and he was sure to make a success of his trip to Ulan Bator. He added that I mustn't confuse confidentiality with melodrama.'

'Ulan where?'

'Outer Mongolia. Gerry said he was arranging for a supermarket to import mare's milk; apparently Tolstoy swore by it.'

'Tongue-in-cheek?'

'He was there a couple of months. Said that it was a dump, full of Russians who lived in decrepit railway carriages. There were also hopeless hotels with lousy food. He said the locals smelled, and many still lived in yurts, which I gather is a kind of tent. I mentioned the mare's milk; he hadn't a clue what I was talking about. I don't know. John le Carré is as near to spying as I've got and Gerry wouldn't fit comfortably into any of his books. I'm really none the wiser. I gather that the Brig was his mentor, but I'm not even sure the Brig had ever been in the army. But there can't be many jobs that take you from Paraguay to Minsk with only enough time to change your underpants. If the truth be known, and I suspect it never will be now, the Brig was right. Gerry was doing confidential work of some kind. Is that spying?'

'Maybe he was involved in industrial espionage?'

'More likely he was an esoteric cog in some machine of government. He was never well paid. He'd dash off at the drop of a hat, or rather a telephone call, and I can hear him now: "Edie, I'm off. Just a couple of weeks, Sri Lanka. Tea, that's the name of the game. Is my lightweight suit clean?"

'And I'd drive him to the station with a battered briefcase and a holdall. He'd kiss me, there would be a sparkle in his eye and, whatever he was off to do, he was mighty pleased to be doing it. I would return to Sal, Sophocles and the cat, not believing a word about tea. He's never kept anything back; on the other hand, perhaps he kept back everything and just spun stories. I don't know.'

Dolly was pensive.

'Of course, we are the wrong generation, aren't we? I mean, nowadays you and I would have a career, be teachers or solicitors. I'm the queen bee of the Heart Foundation. You'll have to find something, Enid; it doesn't matter what, but make it a heart and soul commitment. You'll never regret it.'

On that serious note, and the apple crumble having been finished, Enid felt tired. She thanked Dolly and drove home.

Who was the Brig, really? thought Enid as she drove. He had loomed so large in their life, yet remained totally enigmatic. You couldn't call him Gerry's boss exactly; he was more a father figure, always dressed immaculately, with a kind eye and a smile hovering over his lips.

He was like God, if he existed, Enid decided, before starting to cry again.

Next time she'd leave a light on. A homecoming in the dark was too depressing, especially if one's been crying. It had been always Gerry who stumbled through the dark and found the light by the back door. Enid stumbled, but less nimbly than Gerry had; a milk bottle clattered and she stubbed her toe against a step.

Last night she had remained in her pants, bra and dressing gown. Surely there must be something she could wear till she got to the shops. She found a warm shirt of Gerry's and felt a degree of comfort, but guilt too; this was not forging a life of independence.

But then I've never been independent, she reflected. I'd have been divorced years ago if I'd shown a shred of independence.

Oxfam couldn't have been more offhand about Gerry's shabby old clothes.

'Oh no,' said a blasé voice, 'we don't touch stuff like that. Our second-hand shops have only the best.'

Enid felt angry. How dare they turn their noses up at handmade shirts, albeit with frayed collars? The Boy Scouts were wonderful; the man called her 'love' and assured her that even socks were welcome. But Enid could use his shorts and hankies as rags for polishing. There was one jersey Douglas might like, and, if she turned up the new dressing gown, it could be ideal for her – warm and body-hugging, though a little drab.

If the truth be known, it smelled just a little of Gerry.

Then there were cufflinks; studs for an evening shirt, guaranteed not used over the last twenty years. There were ties, braces, a couple of belts and a photograph of a smudgy-looking dark girl. Enid looked at her; she had no idea who she was... funny, though. This left a bag of foreign coins, endless boxes of matches, several key rings and a wallet.

It was constantly time for a cup of coffee. Clutching the radio, Enid stood for a moment before going downstairs. The room looked bigger, impersonal. She had systematically ousted Gerry and he was no longer there. Well, that wasn't quite true. All the same, it quite frightened her how easy it had been. Were we all just trousers, shirts and undies at the end of the day?

She still hadn't done a proper shop, and for lunch she was driven to eating a tin of rice pudding she kept handy for the twins. It was rather soothing, she liked it. It was just at the end of lunch when she was washing up and the news was on the radio when there was an item about widows.

That's me, she thought facetiously, and almost at once dissolved into tears.

It wasn't so much the death of Gerry but the dreadful status of being a widow. A penniless old bag shuffling along at the back of life's queue, derided, despised and pitied by charities and government ministers. A far cry from Dolly's Mr Shortbread, Gerry's videos and the way Enid was determined to lead her life. Enid's determination was rather like a ten-year-old wanting to be a train driver – utterly sincere, but lacking that necessary 'oomph' which converts aspirations into reality.

'The trouble with widows is that they are culturally nipped in the bud by the welfare state,' burbled the voice on the radio.

Silly owl! What a specious thing to say. However, it made Enid feel better, as though she was taking part in the debate.

All the same, it was comforting when Sal rang and did some 'nipping in the bud'.

'How's it going, Ma?'

'Dolly was wonderful, but returning here wasn't much fun. When you think of all those years when you and I were left on our own…I never gave it a thought. I've mucked him out – five plastic bags. Oh! He had a very nice, almost as good as new, sweater. I'll bring it over for Douglas.'

'Bring it over on Sunday and spend the day with us.'

A generous gesture, but did it have to be Sunday? It seemed to Enid an eternity away. It was Gerry who was meant to be in eternity, not her. Eternity was spent going through Gerry's papers. Petulance and paranoia would sum up the two main piles. There were stiff letters demanding facts and figures from the council, something about dustbins.

There was a protracted correspondence about trains and another about felling perfectly healthy trees to provide a pavement next to the school. Gerry's presentation and grammar, that public school experience he could never throw off, impressed Enid with its hint of Latin texts, its rigour in argument. Was that the reason he bustled off to Lima, Peru, in a hurry? Just to produce reports written in clear, declarative prose only for them to be shelved in some dusty vault?

At last it was Sunday. She filled up with petrol and bought a couple of packets of sweets for the twins – not that bribery had much effect, nor widowhood, come to that.

'You're a widow, Granny, Mummy says so,' observed Beatrice, standing in the doorway, her stomach stuck out and her thumb jammed in her mouth. The child just stood there, so that Enid had to squeeze passed.

'Ah! But what kind of widow? A merry widow? A sad widow, a silly widow, a randy widow?' She hadn't meant to say that.

'What's randy?'

'It's a secret, really, someone who likes lots of kisses and cuddles.' Already Enid had misgivings.

'Granny wants to be a randy widow,' said Beatrice later at lunch, with a piece of lamb half in and half out of her mouth.

'Don't talk with your mouth full,' said Douglas, who was fussier about such things than Sal.

'Beatrice, ssh, that's our secret, remember?' Enid could have crowned the beastly child.

'By the way, don't do Pa's papers on your own. If we're going to unearth some juicy scandal, I want to be there, Ma. No, seriously, it's one thing to laugh about it here but quite another to come across a photo or something.'

'But I did, in one of his pockets – a smudgy blurred photo of a girl.'

'And you've thrown it away?'

'Yes, I mean no. It's in a plastic bag full of rubbish. You want me to empty it?'

'Don't you think you'd better? Doug, what do you think?'

Douglas was a big hunk of a man, solid, comfortable and blessed with common sense. His late father-in-law he treated with good humour. He'd regarded Gerry as unreliable; cantankerous, with a good brain he didn't do much with. A love-child was more than possible but he really didn't feel it was Enid's job to go looking for it. It was probably all years ago. All the same, it would be as well to be prepared.

'Better find it if you can; you never know.'

'Never know what? You think he might have a little bastard tucked away? I don't think I'd mind, really.'

'What's a bastard?' drawled Beatrice.

'Are you going to get another Grandpa?' asked Sophie as she scooped some ice cream into her mouth.

'She's too old,' said Beatrice, answering her grandmother's question.

'But it doesn't matter because she might have a little bastard. Tommy is a little bastard. His mummy calls him that all the time.'

'Beatrice is right,' said Enid, 'I'm probably a little long in the tooth.' She ignored the mention of 'bastard'.

After lunch, of course, they insisted on peering in Enid's mouth before exclaiming that her teeth were yukky.

'I don't want to know.'

Douglas returned to the farm. A cow was calving. Sal found a programme all about wild animals and there were still some sweets left, so the twins were silenced for a while.

'How's it going, Ma?'

Sal stood there, a strong young woman with warm, friendly features apart from her prongy teeth, a kind wise eye and a wisdom that comes from caring.

'Oh, you know. I make extravagant plans in the morning; kip after an improvised lunch; I really must do a proper shop. Do you know, I ate a tin of rice pudding I keep for the twins the other day? The evenings are horrible. I'm so used to Gerry being rude about the television – now I have to do it myself. I know it's ghastly but I can't concentrate enough to read or do embroidery. I go to bed far too early, sleep for an hour or two, then lie there thinking how awful life is. Life was Gerry. I was totally dependent on him because that's the kind of marriage we had, you know. With him away so much it was what he wanted, trusted, could always rely on when he came home.'

'It's early days. You'll find a pattern that suits. I do wish we could send you away for a while. Do you have any friends with villas in Spain or somewhere?'

'Don't be silly. Gerry didn't approve of people like that. As you know, Dolly had me to dinner. I thoroughly enjoyed myself. I don't want to vegetate nor do I want to go to Spain particularly. I'll dig out some old friends, try and get a social life going. Dolly swears by voluntary work. I'm sorry, Sal. Am I leaning too much on you?'

'Not at all,' said Sal briskly.

But she was, wasn't she? Enid drove home feeling rather sorry for herself. Sal had always been a brick. Even as a tiny baby the roles had been reversed. Sal had grown up to be a handsome girl, despite those terrible teeth, even though Enid had spent a fortune trying to straighten them. Now she had her red-raw hands from life on the farm with twins to manage as well. She had gone to art school, spent four years puffing dope and reading Kerouac. Inevitably she needed to find herself, so Enid and Gerry had encouraged her to go to India for six months, where she found dysentery rather than the meaning of life.

She met Douglas in a pub. Chalk and cheese, they were. There was Sal, all long hair, bare feet and bangles, while Douglas was already responsible for a farm. Douglas had inherited it in his mid-twenties. There were 500 acres and a bad-tempered foreman who prefaced everything with, 'In your uncle's day.' His uncle also left enough 'dosh', as Sal described it in those days, to make life bearable. Sal gave up dope and put down Kerouac; she said farewell to her brushes and had the twins.

Sal had flowered briefly, far too briefly. Enid adored her with all the attention of an only child. Now, after Gerry's death, however much she tried to give Sal her space, part of her wanted to cling. After all, clinging was all she knew about. How can anyone forge a successful independent life after a lifetime of clinging?

I mustn't, she told herself as she drove home. She's got her hands full as it is. She mustn't end up like me. I can't cope on my own. All I know about is being Gerry's wife.

Self-reliance was easier said than done. The house seemed so unfriendly; the cat looked at her with disdain. Even though no one could want to check through the rubbish for a torn-up photo, Enid did just that, and found four torn pieces of photograph. She sellotaped it together and took a longer look at the smudged girl.

I don't even know if I'm looking at a child or a young adult. Anyway, it's probably a complete red herring, someone's daughter who Gerry had been fond of...

But with the word 'fond', the genie was out of the bottle. How fond was fond? And anyway, Gerry never carried a photo of Sal with him. What if it was some passionate affair years ago? Enid couldn't get very excited about an affair years ago, and yet it nagged like a sore tooth. She wanted to know, particularly since Douglas had made an issue of it.

That night the photo hovered uncomfortably before her closed eyes – the dim features of a dark female, smudged and too indistinct to be more than an enigma. Surely, if she had been a glorious affair, he would have wanted something more memorable than a smudge. Who would want to keep such a lousy photo? Enid tossed about in indecisive discomfort.

There were other more important matters to fill the following days. The letters of condolence had to be answered. Determined not to use the hackneyed phrases that his friends had used in their letters, Enid found herself searching her rusty vocabulary for sentiments that were far removed from her iconoclasm. Yet as she answered she created a new Gerry, the one she would be living with from now on. He was more benign, cleaner, less mud about the house, and no scrambled eggs.

Sophocles took to Gerry's chair; Enid occasionally asked his opinion about a television programme. Outside, the daffodils waved their last, the hyacinths followed. The birds looked busy and tweeted in different sharps and flats every morning. Leaves appeared, weeds appeared and Enid found herself on hands and knees coaxing the plants and repelling the weeds. She found some weedkiller from last year, only in her mind the year was divided into before and after Gerry's death. She attacked some nettles and felt better. If Gerry could die, so could the nettles.

The Boy Scouts had been as good as their word and had even taken Gerry's old shoes. They smelled and were clearly down at heel. The bank manager had spent nearly an hour explaining the modest finances Enid now had to live on. His unctuous manner and gobbledygook banking terms annoyed her. She fidgeted, longing to break free and begin her life on a pittance. How different it all was to the romantic chic when they were first married and Enid waved away money for ideals. It was that idealism that brought them together. Gerry never called it that, but Enid had believed it.

'Now, we are always here to be of service, Mrs Tanner.'

Enid wanted to say 'Bullshit' but escaped from the bank without saying anything. The whole experience had been humiliating. The manager had made it clear it would be his assistant from now onwards.

Michael, her solicitor, had steered her through the formalities of Gerry's death. There was a small element of that in the wording of the will that needed clarification. It was now over to Enid to start her new life. She left his office feeling she ought to make some resolutions.

Resolution number one: she wouldn't ring Sal unless it was really important. Resolution two: she would stop telling everyone in shops that she was a widow. It had been rather embarrassing the time she bought her two nightdresses. The indifferent assistant had been told that Enid had never worn anything in bed but now she was widowed she felt she should. As the assistant said to her mate, Beryl, 'Honest, Beryl, she must have been all of sixty! Well, I ask you, would you want to see all those wrinkles getting into bed beside you? Disgusting, I call it. Mind you, they get all these ideas watching telly.'

Dolly rang frequently those first few weeks and invited Enid to the cinema. The film was about a child who had fallen off her horse and been taken by her mum to visit a horse whisperer. It was very long and not much happened. The best part of the day was in the jolly pub afterwards, where they drank a pint and chatted to a couple of gormless young men who were looking for girls and a good time but were being sidetracked by these two old 'biddies'.

'Come on, show us how you pick 'em up,' said Dolly, egging on the boldest of the two.

'You know – a bit of the old whatsit.'

He wriggled a little and thrust his hand through his ginger hair.

'Yer catch their eye, see, that does it,' said his companion, looking at the floor.

'Do you buy them a drink?' asked Enid.

'No, 'course not,' said the ginger chap. 'We're only out for a laugh.'

The two women left them staring at their beers and wistfully hoping for some giggling girls to materialise.

'Bit like us, poor devils, looking for something that isn't available,' observed Dolly. 'Cocoa and a hot-wotty bottle, as we used to call them – sorry love, that's us.'

'I've chucked out those porn tapes and I can't afford a cruise,' explained Enid, apropos of nothing more than a lengthening silence on the way home.

'Don't worry, Enid, you're doing marvellously. Still get the weeps?'

'And how! It's that bloody chair that does it. Gerry died in his chair. It's part of my three-piece suite. I get spooked looking at it. One of the twins sat in it the other day when I was babysitting. I hit the roof. The poor kid thought I was bananas. I tried to explain that's where Grandpa died, but you know what kids are like. "Where's the blood?" she kept asking.

'Anyway, I keep thinking of moving it, swapping it with another chair. I can't afford to change the covers on the complete suite. If I did that, then I'd never know which chair was his. Oh, I know that's a contradiction, but then so many things are these days. Sometimes it makes me cry with frustration. Just a chair, but it makes me cry. The other day I saw some lilac blossom. It looked so beautiful, I just started crying about that too. No one can claim Gerry is – I mean, was – a lilac blossom-type man. There I go again. Daft, isn't it?'

Enid didn't mention the state of the house – how over the weeks it still harboured Gerry, despite ritual endeavours to oust him; in the cellar, rummaging for a bottle of wine, in the bathroom where a collection of out-of-date pills lurked, and even in her desk where Gerry had dumped some papers.

Almost every morning in the post came more letters as she tried to make order of his life and affirm his death. All these could bring her to tears but Dolly wouldn't want to know. To think how she had told Sal how easy it was to throw him out with his rubbish. What she hadn't realised was that he'd creep back. Even kind, supportive friends don't really want to hear such things. The doctor is too busy, one's relations too embarrassed.

Then the black crows from the cremation flapped into action, their feathers shining with sanctimony, their beaks snapping malice. Gerry's older sister, Eleanor, was the first to summon Enid. She and Gerry would stay with Eleanor and Henry for a very short weekend every year. Gerry would squirm with irritation as his older sister patronised him. She had married well and was rich and bossy, as well as magnificently self-righteous.

'The trouble with you, Gerry,' she used to say, 'is that you lack judgement. Why you have to go gallivanting round the world at your age, I really can't think. Most people grow out of that kind of work. I suppose that you've failed to get promotion, that or your eternal need to save the world. So adolescent!'

'That's not fair,' Enid would interrupt. 'Gerry does very important work that he's not at liberty to discuss openly.'

Eleanor would look scathingly at her sister-in-law. It was the same every year. The words changed but the meaning remained the same.

'Why do we go?' Enid would say as soon as they were out of earshot. 'She's so busy being grand and patronising us.'

'Bet she doesn't have as good a sex life!' boasted Gerry, face-tiously.

'There you go…*so adolescent*,' mimicked Enid, before adding, 'shut up! You're incorrigible, *and* a liar. It's once weekly with you, and no marks for guessing how you spell weekly.'

It was a poor joke and unfair. Now she was on her own. Weekly could be spelt any way you like. If the phone rang, it was for her. No hiding behind that excuse that he would ring back or she'd have to consult him. So when Eleanor telephoned, Enid felt like a butterfly about to be pinned down for posterity.

'I've left it several weeks so you could pull yourself together. I know what it's like. Invite someone just bereaved and they either drink all your drink or sit in their bedroom all alone. The staff can't get on and everybody is put out.'

'Far be it that I should put you out.' It came out petulantly and Enid's voice rose slightly.

'You know full well what I mean. Now, why don't you come the weekend of 1 May?'

'That's a long weekend; the Monday used to be Labour Day.'

'Well, Henry and I don't believe in this left-wing rubbish. You can go home on Sunday night.'

Enid was grateful. She thought, Thank God! but said, 'Would Saturday morning be easier than Friday for my arrival?'

'I always think one night only is a waste of clean sheets. No,

Friday about six will be perfect. I imagine you'd rather not meet people yet, so it will just be us.'

How simply frightful, thought Enid as she replaced the phone. Dolly did warn me. She said family were the worst. So why have I been so gutless and said 'yes'?

Enid was bored of being a widow – bored of eating cornflakes for breakfast, lunch and supper because she couldn't be bothered to shop for herself, bored of mucking out the house so that Gerry could be exorcised. Anyway, it didn't work. She was fed up with legal documents, with banks, TV licences and MOT certificates. She was tired of writing letters thanking people for their condolences. She was ready for a bit of fun, not a weekend with an irritating sister-in-law. But it would have to do.

'Aunty Eleanor! Rather you than me,' chortled Sal. 'What are you going to wear?'

'Exactly what I wore last year. If she notices, she can show generosity and give me some hand-me-downs.'

'But you're small and dumpy and she's tall and ethereal.'

'At our stage in life we're all shapeless.'

'Maybe she'll introduce you to a sexy widower.'

'Are you joking? She's told me that it's just them, as she's sure I would prefer being quiet and on my own.'

'Pull out all the stops and flutter an eyelash at Uncle Henry. Must fly – the twins are doing the washing-up; there's an awful lot of soapy water sloshing about.'

The phone went dead. That was resolution number one being broken yet again. There had been no need to ring Sal.

Enid drove over to Oxfordshire, ticking off the names of the different towns till she came to more exacting instructions. It was a bright cold day with a piercing wind, chilling to the marrow anyone foolish enough to poke their nose outside. At the service station where Enid stopped for a coffee and a revolting bendy biscuity thing, women wrapped scarves round their hair-dos, children huddled in their anoraks and pieces of paper whirled round the car park before being trapped in a fence where they would remain for the rest of the year. Enid wished she could remember who wrote that doggerel about 'I wish I loved the human race' etc.

She did, however, remember Dolly's word about never turning down an invitation and, with grim determination, hit the road again.

'Turn right off the Bicester road; after half a mile bear left then take first right and look for stone wall with an imposing gate. Not that one is supposed to say such things about one's own property nowadays. Anyway, you already know it; you've been coming here for years.'

What Gerry's sister didn't add was that the imposing gate led to a drive through parkland with a stunning old pile of masonry at the end of it. She didn't mention the fine trees, the leaves of which had been trimmed by the cattle to an exact height, nor the ha-ha and cattle grid which the car rolled over as it approached the house. She didn't need to.

After all, Enid had seen them all before on an annual basis.

Enid drove through the imposing gate and the familiar knot of envy tightened in her stomach.

'Don't be such a silly owl, my girl. You know that Gerry turned his back on all this, and quite right too.'

On that note, said rather than felt, she swung past the front door and drove round to the back where dogs were kennelled, logs stacked and familiar friends greeted.

Henry appeared in immaculate tweeds. He was a stylish character but not very bright. He had been blessed with money and good looks but few brains, just enough to chair the local branch of the Country Gentlemen's Association and practice his private hobby, which was to harass the ramblers, whom he saw as a communist conspiracy. Seriously, it was his life's ambition to have the ramblers exposed as communists.

Even when communists became out of date, Henry still harassed them. Even when the government gave them the right to roam he still harassed them. The 'Right to Roam' Bill he blamed on the bishops in the House of Lords for going soft in the head and not upholding the 'rich man in his castle' ethic. Not that Henry would know an ethic if he stepped on one.

After driving a couple of hundred miles Enid thought she could greet her brother-in-law as she liked, so, climbing out of her car she declared, 'I'm exhausted.'

'Not surprised – you ought to have come by train.'

'Have you any idea of the cost?'

He had no idea so he changed the subject. He was just organising for some arthritic crone to take Enid's case up when Eleanor swept into the hall.

'Forgive me, Enid, how rude of me. I've just come back from a Red Cross meeting, county level. We're running a "do" at Blenheim in a couple of months. I see Margaret has got your case under control. I've put you in a single room. I hope you don't mind. It's difficult to know which; some people just cry out for a double room but I felt sure that you would be perfectly content in a single one. The bathroom is just down the corridor.'

It's not meant as a slight, Enid told herself.

'You know me, I don't care a damn where I sleep. A "do" at Blenheim…that sounds madly glamorous. Are you taking a large party?'

'It's a real bore, but we have to go. Now, I expect you'll like to wash your hands. We'll be in the study. Come down when you're ready.'

The study was full of William Morris fabrics, Thorburn prints and heavy Victorian furniture. There was a Labrador, a whisky decanter, copies of *Field* and *Country Life*, potpourri in the large Chinese bowl and a bookcase of unreadable books. Nothing had changed except the absence of Gerry, who would have sat clasping his whisky and brewing up some pretty purple prose about the landed gentry which he'd tell Enid later in the privacy of their own room.

Henry asked tentatively about Enid's life without Gerry.

'Bad business, bad business! All that gallivanting abroad, I shouldn't wonder.'

'Yes,' agreed Eleanor, who was fiddling with the flowers.

'I always thought there was something fishy about staying all that time in India; after all, we'd left. Who on earth did he find to dine with?'

Harry went not exactly abroad but to Scotland every September, stalking. It was as far from home as he was prepared to go.

Enid replied that a stroke could happen to anyone, which was a perfect opening for Henry who then regaled her with every stroke he had come across. There was the keeper who keeled over on a grouse moor. Lord Bateman collapsed on the croquet court. Mind you, he was also blotto. There was that pig lady at the County Show and, finally, Henry dug up a retainer who, in Henry's youth, had dropped down dead carrying the drinks into the drawing room.

Enid listened politely. Then it was Eleanor's turn.

'Of course, you are used to being on your own. I mean, Gerry was away a great deal, wasn't he?'

'He had retired a few years before his stroke and over the last few years I don't think he was away a single night.'

'Funny, you know, he was always bloody-minded, even as a boy. Anti-establishment, one calls it nowadays. I think you were very brave to take him on.'

Enid looked at Eleanor's profile. There wasn't a glimpse of Gerry to be seen. He had turned his back on his family – easy to see why. This couple were social dinosaurs. The rest of Gerry's family were just the same. His other sister, Blanche, had also married money, nouveau riche money – a neo-Georgian house with proper central heating, a genial husband slightly more tolerant of the ramblers but a pillar of 'nimbyism', the Tory Party, and an advocate of corporal punishment. He was a popular surgeon, private practice only.

How had Gerry survived with two sisters, both with money and married to more money – the unacceptable face of inheritance?

Dinner was dominated by the tinkling of silver and a curious discussion about female judges. For some unfathomable reason Henry didn't think women should be judges. Even Eleanor, hardly an enlightened feminist, told him he was an old fool. On that note, they retired back to the study where an unprepossessing cupboard revealed a television. They watched a social drama about a family with eight children; a father in prison and a mother caught fiddling the welfare. Of the eight children, five were well on the way to emulating their parents' lifestyle.

'I blame all this on do-gooding claptrap,' said Henry.

'But, you ass, this isn't real. It's just some drama,' replied his wife, adding, 'you can't have jolly programmes about stately homes all the time. Do you remember *To The Manor Born*, Enid? Well, Henry thought he had died and gone to heaven. He adored it.'

'Didn't think much of that greengrocer chappie.'

The conversation dragged a little. What had seemed quaint prejudices at the beginning of the evening were now small-minded irritants from people who wilfully turned their backs on a contemporary society.

A single bed is so very narrow when one is not used to it. Enid lay in the dark and juggled all the thoughts that tumbled into her head as a result of staying with Henry and Eleanor. It always came as a surprise that her grumpy old monster had started life amid this kind of nonsense. As Gerry had said occasionally, 'Too many silver spoons in the mouth and you can't communicate properly.'

She knew what he meant. All the same, he'd been reared in a world of servants, in a large old house with a garden boasting a cedar tree, tennis court and an asparagus bed, a mother who wore hats and saw the children briefly, and a grandfather who had been gassed in the 1914–18 war and was never himself again. At this point Gerry had shuffled like an old man, saying, 'What the hell do you want to hear all this crap for? Sentimental rubbish, all best forgotten.'

But Enid did want to know all the crap, especially now. Why did Gerry turn his back? Was it only because of some zealous desire to change the world? Perhaps he was just another kind of failure, like Henry. Both suffered from idealism, searching for a perfect world with no ramblers for Henry and no rich landowners for Gerry. It was just too easy to accept Gerry had given away all his money, but coming to stay here opened all the questions Gerry had never answered.

The next morning Enid helped Eleanor in the garden. As they snipped and tied back exuberant plants, Eleanor inquired about Enid's finances.

'That nasty little cremation you had for him can't have set you back much. By now you must have some idea about your finances.'

'The nasty little cremation, as you call it, had nothing to do with cost. If you must know, the curate, who would have taken the service, wore white socks and spoke with a hideous accent which was Birmingham and London suburbs rolled into one. I was not prepared to send Gerry on his way with that accent ringing in his ears. I'm damned sure you wouldn't let Henry go to the ringing accents of the great unwashed. Even I have my standards, Eleanor.

'There, that makes me as much of a snob as the rest of you. I suppose Gerry would have been furious with me, but I don't care. I know you didn't like the service. I don't suppose anybody did and I certainly didn't like it much either. It's difficult to know what to do for the best. Gerry wasn't a Christian, he wasn't conventional like you. He was a rum character, an elderly dropout in many ways.' There was a brief pause. 'I've got enough, thanks. Money isn't the problem, anyway.'

Eleanor paused from her snipping, her arm up in the air like someone in the classroom wanting to say something.

'That explains the poetry. The trouble with all this nonsense about not being a Christian is that it's rather like not being a member of the AA – very inconvenient; not that Henry or I go to church regularly – nothing like that – but Henry carries the wreath of poppies on Armistice Sunday. Gerry was made to go when he was young.'

It sounded exactly like potty training. He was expected to do many things when he was young, just as Henry did.

Enid remembered clearly when Henry, many years before and, after a little too much wine, had made her weep with laughter with stories of what he had to do when young. From opening his bowels between eight thirty and nine, no other time counted, to family prayers every morning...including the servants who trooped in to listen to his father reading from the Bible. Then there was nursery tea, with nanny presiding over the teapot, the whole scene an anally retentive nightmare.

Being beaten at school was such a regular activity that Henry, in a rare bout of humour, described it as just another subject, hands on!

'Henry was never in the army, was he?' asked Enid, wanting to change the subject and concentrate on the here and now.

'He was in The Blues; he won't go abroad now. He's dubious about the water and suspicious of goats – or is it donkeys? Hold this branch back while I tie it to the wall – it's prickly, be careful.'

Eleanor held a piece of twine between her teeth and hummed a tuneless noise as she fixed the miscreant branch.

'I always feel that peace and quiet heals the mind. I can potter in my garden for hours. After lunch I thought you'd like a real treat, a lovely kip. There's nothing like a sleep in the middle of the day to bring back memories of Tuscany, red wine, hot sun. Sadly, not with Henry! I could never get him over the Channel.'

Enid pricked up her ears. The silence was poignant enough to suggest that Tuscany might have been the scene of some sublimated passion. Good on you, Eleanor! Let's face it – she certainly didn't look the object of passion now, with a large gardening pinny, a floppy hat and flower basket – her fine features etched in vellum-smooth skin and her blue eyes dimmed with myopia.

The last thing Enid felt like doing was going to sleep in the middle of the day. She wanted to explain this to Eleanor during lunch, a revolting meal of macaroni cheese. Henry was, as usual, being paranoid about ramblers. He was sure they would make a point of trampling over his rolling acres this particular weekend, dedicated as it was to the workers of the world. It was their woolly hats that enraged him most. He leapt up throughout the meal to grab his binoculars and glare balefully out on his rolling acres for signs of woolly hats.

White socks, woolly hats and dreadful accents – the working classes are, indeed, taking over, thought Enid facetiously, before being booted upstairs for this great luxury – a sleep she didn't want. She grabbed several copies of *Country Life* and sat by her bed on an uncomfortable chair pretending to buy an estate; it palled pretty quickly. She looked at the few books beside her bed, hoping for Jeeves to come to her rescue. He wasn't there. Instead, there was a military book about the Great War, a novel by Margaret Drabble, and *Other Men's Flowers*, an anthology of poetry by some old general or other. Enid did not want to read any of them; her concentration when it came to reading was still poor. Dolly told her not to worry. It was just a spot of depression. It sounded like damp. Enid thought about what she would really like to do. She wanted fun, something to happen – like hunting ramblers with Henry, or finding some caravans parked on his land filled with New Age people. Henry would go apoplectic.

Enid allowed herself to imagine a group of men with matted hair, filthy clothes and eyes spaced out on dope; around them were women in tattered Indian-style fabrics, shawls and welly boots clasping grubby children, while clinging onto their skirts were older kids with hostile eyes. Mongrels growled and played with a dirty sanitary towel – Enid was proud of that little piece of imagination. Henry would go into reheat.

She stood by her bedroom window, feeling like some Gothic heroine, trapped in the castle. She stood there for what seemed like ages. The ramblers and New Age travellers faded away. Reality was here and she was stuck in her bedroom, being polite and having a dose of peace and quiet.

'This is so bloody boring it's like being in prison!' she shouted loudly and, as she spoke, tears welled up and she began to weep.

She wept for her Gerry as she had never wept before. She wept for him being the odd one out, escaping this way of life – the one who wasn't a success in his family's eyes, who did something slightly secret and dropped out of the comfortable upper middle-class way of life; no hunt balls, no Henley, no engraved writing paper, no grouse, rarely a DJ – and Enid didn't mean disk jockey, either – and only a few lousy memories of Latin irregular verbs learnt in some monstrous building, cold, uncomfortable and hundreds of years old.

'*Our younger brother who never really made it,*' she could hear Eleanor saying, adding her own silent testimonial:

'Poor love! He loathed his public school, didn't like hunting and thought the people who did it were awful. On the other hand, he wouldn't shoot – thought they, too, were awful. He simply sat around reading the *New Statesman* and God knows what else. Daddy was at his wits' end. Gerry just turned his back on his background – didn't want to know. Went to some provincial university – Reading, I think it was – and then disappeared – quite literally. I think it was India, somewhere hot and smelly. He came back and married some pleasant girl, if you know what I mean – perfectly nice, but not out of the same drawer – doctor's daughter – not very well connected unless you're interested in the NHS. Gerry worked for some government outfit – faintly confidential – badly paid, of course. His own inheritance was spent on drains – in India, I believe. They've been living in India without drains for hundreds of years. Why he should suddenly think drains were the answer, I don't know. He ended his life wearing shabby clothes, reading the paper cover to cover for something to do. He achieved nothing. He didn't even have a decent burial.'

Enid wept even harder. It wasn't true and he wasn't like that. Anyway, Eleanor had missed out Sal. Didn't she realise that he thought it all wrong, the privilege, that myopic world he was born into? He had more courage than the rest of them; after all, he had deliberately opted out. He had a social conscience – Enid could see him in his chair, hurling misanthropic abuse at the television set. When she first met him he had been an optimist…until he started seeing his contemporaries becoming successful: 'Whose arse has *he* been licking?'

Gerry hid behind the secrecy of his job. Meanwhile, Enid felt a toothache in their marriage as it drifted into numbness. No love, no hate, no interest, no future – but clinging to each other for fear of drowning in the awful mediocrity of the lives that they had deliberately chosen – lives fed by irritations, the nearest thing to love in many marriages. Now, there were no irritations, no dirty loos, no trousers put out to wash with the pockets still bulging with coins, keys and mysterious pieces of paper. There were no more meals for two eaten in silence, no longer his choice only on television. Enid wept harder than ever. The silly old sod! Had he been brave and taken risks involving him in skulduggery of one kind or another? Was he a real spy? Now she would never know – just as she could never explain where his private income had gone. That drains nonsense was bullshit. No, it had disappeared before she married him; that was all she knew.

'Does it matter?' he had asked her when they were engaged. No, it didn't. Enid didn't mind two hoots, not in those brave days. She was mildly curious about how much he had given away and to whom, but he replied mumbling about India and Enid could well imagine him wanting to alleviate poverty. That is why he wanted to marry her; she cared.

The weeping grew less. She started to pack because she wasn't staying here. She wasn't going to remain imprisoned in her bedroom with its tasteful green wallpaper and interlined curtains in lieu of proper central heating. She carried her case down the stairs. She didn't want to creep away and in a way she needed the confrontation. Eleanor was found back in the flower bed.

'I'm sorry, I want to go home.'

'You what? But you can't, I've got Dover soles for dinner.'

'I can't handle it. All this peace and quiet, it gives me the creeps.'

'Don't be so silly, it's what you need.'

Eleanor stretched up to her full height and walked slowly towards her sister-in-law.

'It's just a case of a chip on the shoulder, isn't it?' You can't bear the reality that Gerry never came up trumps, turned his back on all this and died leaving you nothing. You're not a weeping widow, Enid, you're a green-eyed monster.'

'I'm jealous that you and Henry can still have sex…'

'Have sex? After the Dover sole?' Eleanor looked aghast.

'I must go, I'm miserable. I hate all this solitude. I'm sorry.'

Enid fled to her car and drove off, leaving Eleanor still muttering about those Dover soles.

Three

What do long-distance lorry drivers think about hour after hour? Do they invent stories, imagine sexual encounters, stand on rostrums at political meetings, or pick their noses and listen to the same musical beat on a trip from Southampton to Aberdeen? With only a modest Ford to steer, Enid had plenty of time to think about Eleanor and Henry, their ivory tower and their sex life.

Only she didn't, she thought about her Gerry. No one ever used the word 'spy'. It was too exotic. Enid saw Gerry as some kind of Queen's Messenger, flying round the world with diplomatic communiqués clasped to his bosom. However, there were months when he didn't fly abroad, when he came back from the office full of spite and malice about his colleagues.

'That silly prat, Humphrey, do you know what he did? He ordered a kissogram for his wife's birthday, I ask you. Apparently an out of work actor turned up and gave Mrs Humphrey the works – and I mean it, the real works.'

'Did that cost extra?' asked Enid, her imagination quite excited at the idea.

'He's a stingy bastard – I wouldn't have thought so.'

'That's an idea. Why don't you give me one?'

Gerry had given her an old-fashioned look instead.

Enid's imagination remained with that kissogram. That's an idea; she could order her own, in the car right now. She dressed herself carefully, as carefully as you can while driving a car and fantasising about kissograms.

Her hair would smell of the avocado and honey shampoo the twins had bought her for Christmas. But she could hardly wash her hair in the middle of the M1, could she – imagination or no imagination? She would wear that pretty blouse which showed her bra, but couldn't make up her mind between the well-cut black trousers that showed her crutch or the longish skirt that disguised her roly-poly tum.

The doorbell! Just a last-minute dab of scent – she hadn't got any, but once again her imagination came to the rescue.

The M1 is a grim example of already out of date modernity. Enid swung the car into the middle lane and did what everyone says you shouldn't. She sat there. Lorries swished around her or trundled along in the slow lane. A car full of Sikhs clung to the slow lane, their turbans giving a vivid splash of colour to the car's interior. Behind her swung out a van hell-bent on delivering pigs, frozen pigs, but already Enid was imagining the doorbell…

A man of about thirty stood there. His expression suggested that he had been just about to scarper when the door opened. He did the decent thing and smiled.

'It's Enid, isn't it?'

'Yes,' she murmured.

Surely I can do better than 'yes'! It was an irritated thought. A large sports car was driving far too close behind her.

Enid decided that the kissogram bit was not what she wanted. She wanted sex with a man, pure and simple. In her fantasy she switched from kissogram to telephone sex, where men and women could telephone for a partner the same way you order a taxi.

This time she wouldn't say 'yes'. She would try a different opening.

'Hi, come on in.'

He would come through the door and then put a gentle hand on her arm. 'We're going to have fun this afternoon. My name's Josh…'

No, it didn't work. If he said something as daft as that she would run a mile. The fantasy faded. It didn't work and, anyway, the traffic was too heavy.

Was she jealous of Henry and Eleanor? Not really. Gerry had deliberately turned his back on that way of life, not on the people; in truth, he was rather fond of his sisters. No, it was the excess of everything that offended. A house with twenty bedrooms for two, and down the road a house with two bedrooms for God knows how many, but possibly twenty. Not only that – look at those benighted ramblers who made Henry so angry! All they wanted was to be free to walk through the countryside. Enid could see them, bobble hats and stout walking shoes, a couple of grey-haired whiskery ladies, maps swinging round their necks in plastic sleeves, a fierce young man who knew his rights, and a couple of gentle souls who saw the flowers and trees and wanted people to love each other…

While back in the dining room of Enid's fantasy, with the curtains drawn and the silver tinkling, Henry suddenly bellowed, 'They'll insist on portaloos, sandwich kiosks and every tree labelled. Who do they think I am, the National Trust?'

'No, dear,' murmured Eleanor. 'They are the kind of people Gerry liked to know, do you remember? It wouldn't surprise me if Enid didn't have friends like that. Although, I must say, even if Enid hasn't the manners to stay for a Dover sole, she has her standards. Did you know the reason Gerry went to oblivion rather than heaven? It was because the curate turned up with a simply dreadful accent. I quite understand. Poor her! It must have been dreadful, but I do wish she wouldn't fight being a widow. Do you know what she said? She was jealous of us having sex.'

'Having *what*?' exploded Henry, the ramblers forgotten.

'I know – perhaps that's why Gerry died. I mean, Sheila told me of a friend of hers who had a priest friend, an Irishman, who came over here for rest and recreation. He died while you know what.'

This talk was too much for Henry, who had to drink a glass of Chablis.

Meanwhile some nifty driving was called for. A large lorry was hogging the middle lane and forcing Enid to drive faster than she liked, fantasy firmly forgotten till she had whizzed passed the pestilential gallon-guzzling beast – politically, Enid was vaguely green about lorries – and no wonder!

The spell was broken.

Eleanor would never know anyone who knew anything as risqué as a bonking priest. Anyway, Enid realised that she'd gone too far, trying to fuse reality and fantasy; they never fitted and her fantasies were always being destroyed by the introduction of reality.

Reality was far more prosaic. After she left, Eleanor went back to her gardening; she puzzled over that extra sole. They didn't have a deep freeze, nor a microwave, come to think of it. No, their kitchen was aggressively 1950s, with an ancient Kenwood mixer to prove it. She decided to cook the extra sole – more than they needed, but she could throw it out with a clear conscience afterwards.

But why had Enid suddenly departed? All this nonsense about not liking pèace and quiet! Enid was reliable. Gerry had made a very judicious marriage even if – and here an Eleanor prejudice came unbidden to the surface – she was only a general practitioner's daughter. Eleanor paused to snip back an exuberant creeper hell-bent on re-rooting itself. She continued to think, this time about her deceased brother.

She could see him in his grey school shorts, socks already slithering down his legs and an expression of sullen belligerence on his face. Later she saw him in ill-fitting grey flannels and a shapeless jacket hunched over George Orwell. He was nuts about Orwell.

During dinner one evening, he had asked what the different servants they employed were paid.

'Not much,' said Papa, grinning, as he continued to eat his trifle; it was trifle, wasn't it? Eleanor's memory was not what it used to be.

The family always assumed that Gerry had become something in intelligence. They also assumed that he was pretty pink politically – too pink to get on. 'Can't trust the buggers', and all that. No one could imagine what people in intelligence did except sit in gentlemen's clubs and ask discreet questions of other gentlemen who had been posted abroad – just in case by some ghastly mischance a paedophile might be about to cause a diplomatic incident in China.

The glamorous, fictitious image that Gerry could have perilously risked life and limb crawling on his belly through mud, only to be captured and tortured, was completely beyond their comprehension.

'He didn't feel comfortable with us, nor apparently does his widow. All the same, I do think Enid should have had a Christian service for him. Surely there are some vicars left who speak the Queen's English and wear proper socks.'

The world was becoming incomprehensible. She and Henry were relics living out their privileged lives in stultifying boredom. They had children, stuffed away in equally grand houses: a daughter forever looking for original Georgian curtain material, and a son who married the only daughter of a pathetically grand but mildewed family whose house and gardens were open to the public. Henry and Eleanor's son was just a high-class jobbing gardener.

It was no wonder Enid couldn't stand it.

Concentrate! Coming off a motorway requires cool nerves. Enid slowed down before seeing a hitchhiker standing by the side, thumbing a lift. He had an army canvas bag with him. Snap judgement – it's more fun having someone to chat with than driving alone. She slowed down and unwound her window.

'Coventry?'

Why not? She couldn't work out the mileage. Anyway – wasn't sure where Coventry was – it was where Lady Godiva hung out, wasn't it? Actually he could have said 'Glasgow' and she would have probably said 'Yes'. She was in that kind of mood – the kind that moves from the mind to the pit of one's stomach.

'Sure,' she smiled. 'Put your bag in the back and hop in front.'

Forty-ish, receding hair, good figure still, with a pleasant face etched with experience. Soon Enid had learnt that she was travelling with an ex-sergeant who had left the army to become a National Parks ranger. Why Coventry? His car had broken down en route to staying with his sister; he had to collect it.

These brief details gave a skeletal idea of what he was superficially like. However, Enid was lonely, wanted the company and didn't relish going home to an empty house. She asked about his work as a ranger. He was a good communicator, knew about the flora and fauna he was protecting and was despairing about the ignorance of the people visiting the parks. His voice was soft like moss and, as he spoke, he gave an impression of his job, a sense of woods, tumbling streams, warm sunny banks. He beguiled her with imagery of the wild countryside. She drank his words in. They filled her with a gentle pleasure. He lived alone in a small cottage, lighting a fire every evening and listening to the radio. No, he didn't have a television.

Later she was to admit over the phone, 'Sal, I'm so ashamed. I must have gone nearly a hundred miles out of my way, but he was well worth it – pure Lady Chatterley, if you know what I mean. I just can't remember that game keeper's name.' She paused.

'Anyway, Henry and Eleanor were so stuffy. The idea that Gerry and Eleanor were siblings is sometimes utterly bizarre. I know I'm pathetic, but I funked it. If anyone else invites me to enjoy peace and quiet, I'll throttle them. As it was, I burst into tears and fled.'

'Ma, you are silly. One moment you're extolling the virtues of wild woods and rangers writing poetry by moonlight and the next you're bolting from your sister-in-law's attempt to provide you with peace and quiet.'

Enid snapped. 'It's not the same thing; you know it isn't! That hitchhiker was so comforting. It wasn't sex; I didn't whip off my knickers in a lay-by. It was just being with a lovely man.'

'Well, I think you might have to come to terms with the fact that, from now on, you're not going to find many men in your life. Never mind, Ma, it's not the end of the world. I must fly. The twins have found a dead mouse and want to know what's inside it.'

If Sal didn't understand, no one would, or at least, perhaps Dolly might? She dialled Dolly.

'Dolly, he wasn't Mr Shortbread exactly but I picked up a hitchhiker yesterday and it was like having a gentle affair. He worked as a countryside ranger or something. He told me all about his job and how he lived. He wasn't married and, just for a while, I fantasised that I'd go back with him.'

'My dear girl, you're not safe to be let out on your own. Do be careful – picking up hitchhikers could be dangerous. I mean, you hear stories of them whipping out knives and things. It looks as if you could manage the "things" but I'm not so sure about the knives. Weren't you going to stay with Gerry's rich relations?'

'Yes, I did, but all that peace and quiet – it spooked me. I fled.'

Dolly was busy; she was just about to go out when Enid had rung. Frankly, she wasn't interested in Enid's flights of fancy on the motorway. God knows, it was difficult enough to keep one's own head above water without having a friend drowning beside one. With a brisk farewell, she rang off – felt guilty, but what the hell!

That left Enid suspended with a phone in her hand. Who could she tell now, how could she explain that she had turned round the car and driven home in a cloud of happiness? A man, a very nice man, had been sitting beside her. His smell, just faintly of bracken, had attracted her. His voice, no rasping accent, just a northern burr, had led her into an entrancing world of wild countryside. She imagined herself walking quietly by his side, noticing what he saw, always a step or two behind him. As for his cottage, she wanted to cook his tea, lie on his bed, feel his body slide in beside her. The fantasy repeated itself, over and over again.

'Oh, for God's sake, grow up,' she told herself angrily.

The radio was doing its best to distract her and providing an excellent programme about whether pagans should be regarded as belonging to a mainstream religion. However, Enid wasn't listening. She sat still, mindlessly staring into space. Neither Sal nor Dolly were interested in her experience. Why should they be? It wasn't that she was missing Gerry, but she sure as hell was missing something. She went outside and took a slow meander round the garden with Sophocles. There were many shiny shoots, quivering spears of pale green, a great many weeds and some alpines in full flower. Yes, it was starting to be lovely, but that particular day Enid had no ability to enjoy it. Indeed, she barely saw the flowers. Food was still a problem too; she simply hadn't got into the pattern of buying meals for herself. Chocolate biscuits and some salted peanuts do not a meal make. So she then had an apple and finished with some cereal.

What next? One can't go to bed at twelve thirty in the morning. Well, why not? So she did. She slept a wilful sleep, stretching out the waking up for as long as she could. Before she went to sleep she once more buried herself in the fantasy of her lovely man, only this time he looked and felt like her Gerry. She couldn't explain it even to herself, but Enid still seemed totally incapable of living as an independent person. She saw herself only in terms of other people, never as herself.

She paid for it. She found herself scrubbing the kitchen floor, the first time it had been thoroughly cleaned since Gerry's death. After that she made herself a coffee and sat in introspective gloom. Sal was out. She mustn't overdo Sal. Remember resolution number one? Dolly had been a little offhand – probably had other things on her mind. Who else could she phone? What if it was to invite them to a meal? Sunday lunch, two couples and roast lamb. She turned it over in her mind – not very appealing, not without Gerry to stir the platitudes and challenge the obvious.

The first people she telephoned were mildly over the top, not so much in their greeting but the tone of voice they, or rather she, used.

'How are you doing? We've been meaning to get you over but you know how it is, time flying and all that jazz. It must be such a difficult time for you; I mean, so much to do. I must admit I haven't a clue about wills, probate and all that stuff. All the same we'd love to come. One-ish?'

Enid put down the phone; she had done it, no getting out of it now. Already carrots and dauphinois potatoes swam into her mind, as well as treacle tart – standard favourites.

It appeared more people had been thinking about her; most gratifying.

'We've been thinking about you. I must say, you're very courageous to start entertaining so soon. Just before one?'

'I've had to do more than think. I'm the one who's had to lift the phone!' muttered Enid. 'All this thinking about me – where has that got me, for God's sake?'

This time she thought about what she would wear – trousers and a vaguely glamorous top. Shit! She hadn't got one and wasn't prepared to spend the money. All right, she'd wear a thinnish jersey with a scarf flung casually round her neck, and it would probably slither in the soup but *tant pis* – whatever that meant. Some people were scarf-friendly. The wretched things hung lovingly round their necks while others, like Enid, offered the hand or rather the neck of friendship only to be spurned. She sighed; it was bound to fall off.

When you add together the wine and food, the house cleaning, flowers and a visit to the hairdresser, it was an expensive couple of phone calls.

That Sunday was sunny, but with a shrill wind. Enid had done all the housework the day before, laid the table, dashed off to the hairdresser and then done the cooking. Now she felt relaxed as she waited by the window to watch her guests arrive. The sitting room looked horribly tidy and unnatural. Come to think of it, someone would have to sit in that chair. Would that make them next? It was a silly, ghoulish thought. The flowers looked like the bought ones they were – stiff, with dreadful green foliage which resembled bracken stems. A car turned into the drive. Sophocles began to bark.

It was over an hour before someone had the courage to mention Gerry's name. They had drunk their sherry. Mike sat in that chair – a picture of health – then they had trooped into the dining room. Enid leapt up and down to serve the food and open bottles of wine so that Sam and Mike had little time to talk to her. Instead they discussed slow trains, very slow trains and no trains, which was a fair description of their local service.

'Why don't you do something about it?' she asked petulantly.

'Come off it, Enid, I'm a thinker, not a doer. I'm also a specialist. I write about economics, not about late trains.'

'Well, why can't you write about the economics of inefficiency, Mike?'

'Because, quite simply, it is more than likely that it pays to run slow trains, just as it pays to build motorways to a relatively low standard and then maintain them at great inconvenience to everyone.'

It was Mike again who first mentioned Gerry.

'Do tell me, Enid, how did you choose Gerry's final farewell poetry? I didn't know he was a Shakespeare buff, or that he liked Auden, for that matter.'

'Gerry wasn't a complete ass, you know,' retorted Enid. 'He didn't leave any instructions about his funeral or whatever. I tried a C of E service but the whole thing just stuck in my throat. The vicar had such a ghastly accent. So I went for the simple service for the non-believer approach.'

Mike's wife, Sybil, spoke. 'There really isn't any way to commemorate a life of someone whose views on religion are vague and frankly of little interest. I mean, we had the same problem with Mike's sister, who died of cancer last year. We ended up with a hotchpotch of poetry and tasteful prose, like you did for Gerry. Frankly it didn't seem to work.'

Then it was the turn of Sam's wife, Jane. 'Sam's having the whole works, aren't you, darling? We've been feckless friends of Christ's over many years and paid our dues, so the least we can expect is a bloody good turnout this end and for St Peter to vacuum the red carpet that end.'

Sam turned to Enid. 'Hasn't the lack of ritual, like wearing black – that kind of thing – made it very lonely, scooping up the remains after a death as though nothing has happened?'

'It's been very lonely, yes. I'm not sure wearing black would have helped. The postman twigged and the nice lady in the bread shop heard; how, I don't know. She pressed my hand and said how sorry she was. I suppose years ago, with big families, ritual would have been very therapeutic for the widow adjusting to her new role, but our whole attitude has changed. I mean, I still do the housework, pay the bills. Frankly, I miss companionship more than anything. This is the first proper meal I've eaten in this house since Gerry died – that's three months. My life was geared to the notion that I existed to maintain Gerry's existence. Even when he was away, I was waiting for his return, as if that was a role in itself. I know all those bra-burning ladies would despise me, but they are probably clever women. Don't get me wrong. I'm not a total ass, but Gerry never asked me to work and Sal was enough to fill my time. After all, neither Jane nor Sybil have ever worked. Comfortable middle-class women like us didn't. Now it's all different and they do. His death has challenged my existence. I feel I don't really have one, not yet.'

Quite suddenly, and apropos of absolutely nothing that was being said, Enid announced, 'Mellors!' rather loudly.

Then she said, 'Sorry about that. I've been trying to remember that name for ages. It's been niggling in the back of my mind. Gerry would have known at once, that's the problem. I'm so stupid without him.' Her voice wobbled. Her guests studied the pattern on their plates and Mike put his hand on her arm.

'Steady, old girl, you're with friends,' he said, and with clumsy kindness tried to change the subject.

'Talking about Gerry being away, do you have any more idea what he did?' Mike had been dying to know for years.

'He was a kind of spy, I suppose. The Brig didn't give much away, did he? No, Mike, I don't know, nor do I know whether I'd tell you if I did. The whole point of confidentiality is that it is exactly that. I'm part of the conspiracy too, if you like – waiting at home with my knitting.'

'Did you really?' asked Sybil.

'You mean knit? You are a snob! What's wrong with knitting? Pruning is OK but knitting is out. What is it people say? "Giving women something to think about while they talk." Come on, Sybil, grow up. We don't all own Georgian houses and Labrador dogs with tapeworm. I cannot see worming the dog is in any way socially superior to knitting. I've made a veritable legion of nasty, shapeless jerseys, most of which poor Sal has had to fling out for the jumble without offending me, and all this before I became a widow.'

'What now?' asked a suitably chastened Sybil over coffee, while the others were entertaining each other with horror stories about holiday plumbing abroad.

'Do you really want to know? I would like to meet another man.'

'At your age!'

'You're being ageist, Sybil. I'm not saying that it's likely to happen, but it is what I'd like. I come from that way of life which only values women in relation to what they can do for men, unless one is a career woman, which sadly I am not. I know it's awful, I know I shouldn't say it. I realise that it's my attitude that has brought about women's lib and I'm the first to champion what they've done. But I'm too crushed and damaged by the old system to thrive under the new. It's like bound feet in China. You can turn modern Chinese women into athletes but, for their grandmothers, it's too late.'

'But would you want a sex life?' Good old Sybil went straight for the jugular, no nonsense about being sidelined by bound feet.

'Why not? A good bonk would put roses back in my cheeks.'

'Yes, it might, but you're no spring chicken, love – that's the problem.'

'You're right. I'll probably get involved in some charity and the nearest I'll get to a man will be driving incontinent old codgers to their hospital appointments.'

All the same, the lunch did it; the ice was broken. Enid was back in circulation.

So Enid started her career in making up numbers. She went to several ladies' lunches and began to wonder if she ought to wear make-up; everyone else did. They managed pristine hairdos of the bouffant variety, cheeks blushing from an application of 'Eternal Spring' or other such bloody silly names, eyelashes à la Cartland and lips coated in the wet look. The over-fifties really shouldn't wear the wet look. They wore white silk blouses, big bold costume jewellery and well-cut tweed skirts over spreading hips. As for their conversations, they were heavily fortified with brand names Enid had never heard of. Colefax and Fowler was old hat. Anyway, you leave that kind of thing to your interior consultant. Really, Barbara Simpson, who had invited her to this curious social gathering, was putting on airs. Married to a gynaecologist, she had appeared at dinner parties to be an acclaimed mouse, hanging on her husband's every platitude. When asked once by Gerry whether he would practise euthanasia, her husband had leant over and replied, ignoring his wife, 'Bumping off old ladies is more difficult than you think.'

His wife had chipped in, 'Simon would never do anything to risk his reputation.'

'He never thought of thinking for himself at all, and now he's the head of the Queen's Navee,' quipped Gerry, adding, 'bowd-lerised *Pinafore*.'

'That's not fair!' snapped Barbara, missing the point and feeling a little out of her depth over 'bowdlerised'.

'I don't suppose it is,' retorted Gerry.

So it was surprising that Enid had been invited to this ladies' luncheon but not so surprising that she accepted, remembering Dolly's dictum: a lonely widow, floundering for a role, flounders in some pretty frightful places.

Dressed to the nines, in Enid's case about 7½, the ladies had arrived at twelve thirty at the surgeon's home, a large white house in a smart suburb of Harrogate. A waiter offered a champagne cocktail. There were tiddly bits as well, to munch if one was a little nervous. Then they trooped into the dining room and ate a pretentious lunch with coriander, sun-dried tomatoes and ginger trying to disguise some poor old chicken. At the end of the meal, when Enid was totally bemused and wondering for the umpteenth time why on earth she had been invited, her hostess stood up and introduced a speaker. It was a con. Enid was fodder for a promotion – a health clinic at the modest price of £900 a year all-in.

She was livid. Now she was on her own she was apparently fair game for every exploitation going. Who did Barbara think she was? Never, never would she accept another invitation from her! When she got home she kicked off her uncomfortable high-heeled shoes, her skirt, blouse and petticoat. Then she lay down on her bed and wished she was Piglet, when he felt the need to roll in mud after a gruelling bath given him by Kanga. As Gerry might have added, 'A A bloody Milne!'

In the ordinary course of events, to recover from such an occasion Gerry would have watched her wrestling with the nettles, digging deep for the docks and pulling away the chick-weed. He would have lobbed caustic comments, been downright rude and she would have forgotten the whole damned incident.

'Health bloody clinic, I ask you. Typical!'

'Edie, you missed some nettles, old girl.' She could just hear him.

But, on her own, there were doubts. Were lunches like this how women survived? Those who hadn't already been called to other things – the check-out counter at Valueprice, or to be a junior partner with Smug, Smug and Simper? Even her Sal, knee-deep in cow shit and twins, had a purpose. Next, Enid sought her therapy among the nettles but, without Gerry, there was much sighing and little resolution. Finally she sat, muddy boots and hands, reading the local paper.

There it was, staring her in the face – a plea for volunteers.

'Come on, old girl, have a bash.'

'Oh, shut up, Gerry; go back to being dead and leave me to make up my own mind.'

They needed friends at the local home for young adults not

capable of living in the community. Well, anything would be better than those ladies' lunches.

She arrived with the same trepidation reserved for the dentist. In a small room smelling of all-pervasive cabbage, someone called Lizzie explained what the volunteers were expected to do – 'the impossible' was how it was succinctly described. Lizzie then took Enid round the home for twenty or so young people. There was a curious pomposity about it all, with swimming described as hydrotherapy and almost every activity reduced to the stilted language of the Social Services. Enid was being asked to 'relate' meaningfully to one youngster in particular. She was introduced first to Shirley, who explained about Adam. Listening to Adam's background, it seemed quite clear that he had so far managed to escape any of this 'relating' lark in his life.

Adam was in the day room. Why, oh why, they couldn't call it the sitting room, even the lounge? Who the hell has a day room in their home? Adam looked like any student doing some home-work. He sat at a table covered with paper and coloured pens, all marshalled into neat piles. He didn't look up. 'Too busy,' he said. Adam was not composing a letter to his MP or bank manager. He was tidying up the pens and paper for those who wanted to use them. None of the young people could read or write. Some drew weird shapes with 'buttercup' written underneath by some staff member trying to placate an unquiet mind.

'This is Enid, Adam. She is going to take you out to lunch.'

Now the twins at this point would have set up a howl of indignation followed by some nifty negotiation over sweets before they clambered into the car. Not so Adam – he took his punish-ment like a man.

She had been told that he was a tall, handsome young man who said little and didn't read or write. Indeed, Adam did very little. Catching him tidying the paper and pens was near to a miracle. Usually he mooned his way through the day with an expression of mystic divinity. Asked if he would like to go out to lunch with Enid, he had nodded – a tenuous form of acceptance. But, frankly, the staff were at their wits' end to boot him out. The records – funding depended on the records – required each young person to be 'befriended'. The busy ladies on the committee required it, not that they volunteered.

In the car he studied the dashboard, then said, 'It's quite complicated, isn't it?' Or rather, Enid thought he said that. She wasn't totally in tune with his speech.

Back home, Enid handed him a bottle of ketchup to put on the table. Apparently he refused to eat anything without it. He shrank away, yelping as if in pain. She had handed it to him the wrong way. Their meal was quiet. Enid made several statements but Adam didn't reply. He simply stared out of her window, chewing. Suddenly, towards the end of the meal, he turned to Enid and without looking at her said, 'I must watch television. They do dreadful programmes when I'm not looking.'

'They do those when I am looking,' smiled Enid, but Adam didn't want to know. He stood up and ambled towards the sitting room. Enid nipped ahead and turned on the set, leaving him there while she cleared up.

'Let's go for a walk,' she announced briskly, having finished the washing-up.

Adam looked up, his face creased with concentration.

'Muddy shoes.'

'Never mind, Adam, muddy shoes are usually a sign of a lovely walk.'

Adam shambled after her reluctantly. Enid stopped to show him some narcissi lurking in a sheltered place under a cherry tree.

'Aren't they beautiful?'

'It's nature,' replied Adam darkly, as if nature should be banned. After that he lapsed into silence all the way back to his home. Asked by Shirley, his care-worker, if he had enjoyed himself, he replied, 'We saw some flowers.'

Shirley and Enid decided that he probably meant it as a compliment and another lunch was called for.

Adam might have seen nothing, but Enid couldn't help noticing that the greeny spikes had become lupins, delphiniums and irises. Meanwhile the weeds looked on, sneering at Enid's attempts to destroy them.

Her social life wobbled like a newborn foal on spindly legs.

Everyone likes to come in useful. Enid was no exception, so when some respectable friends rang in a panic she leapt to the rescue. Their son, Guy, had turned up unexpectedly with Paul, a boyfriend. They were having a lunch party. The two boys really wouldn't fit in, and their friends were elderly and not used to that kind of thing. On the other hand, they wanted their son to feel at home and bring his friends home (separate rooms, according to the boys). It really was rather difficult but they knew Enid was – well – sophisticated and probably feeling a little left out of things what with Gerry's death. Would she like to be a brick?

Brick she certainly was, with Pyramus and Thisbe on either side making love through her ineffectual barrier. It was not an occasion to 'come out'. So while the respectable end of the table tub-thumped for Europe, with one noisy exception, the lovers also in not so sotto voce voice brought Enid up to date with smart gay London.

'We all went as Romeos, Casanovas, Abelards, any great historical lover. You've no idea. We were so beautiful in doublet and hose and just a hint of a ruff – what a turn-on!'

His companion leant over, 'There was a minor scuffle when a couple of Romeos made a beeline for the one and only Lord Byron. My dear, you have no idea. One Romeo ended up with a black eye while Lord Byron locked himself in the john and had a good snort of coke before he emerged.'

It did indeed sound like quite some party. Enid learnt about the fringe theatre. They both directed. Guy was about to tackle Ibsen in Gateshead by producing Ibsen's *The Master Builder*.

'They're in touch with Norway. They understand the underlying melancholy.'

Who 'they' were wasn't clearly defined. No doubt a handful of souls shipwrecked in Gateshead did yearn for Ibsen, but to suggest that there was enough angst in Gateshead to sustain *The Master Builder* for long was absurdly optimistic. Guy's friend, Paul, was taking round the country a contemporary Indian play about a girl who is driven from her community because she refuses to marry the man chosen by her family. Was there another man lurking in the shadows? Enid asked.

'Good God! No! That's Laki for you. He would regard another man, as you put it, as being every bit as bad as the guy chosen for her.'

'There are Indian lesbians, presumably. Why can't she be one?' suggested Enid. Why not indeed! She had got it in one.

'You know, you fellows are damn lucky in many ways. I mean, you're free to pick up partners when you need to. I'm recently widowed and my age rules out pretty well everything. But I'm not totally past it.'

'Saucy, saucy!' Guy rolled his eyes. 'A respectable lady like you!'

'You're right, don't tell anyone!' Enid bent her head conspiratorially. 'It's hell, being single.'

'You tell me!' said Paul. 'I tried it for three weeks once.'

'It's not only sex, it's companionship. You know, watching crap on television because the other person adores it – bickering over what kind of coffee to buy, and not leaving towels on the bathroom floor.'

'Are you on the Net?' asked Paul.

'That sounds like advanced computer studies.'

'Six-year-olds have no trouble,' Paul assured her.

'No, I'm not on the Net, as you put it.'

'Pity, there's a possibility down the drain.'

The three luncheon guests shared a contemplative silence, so much so that the host (Guy's father) looked across the table at the three and said, 'Angel passing over!'

'The silence is just to catch my breath,' said Enid.

After everyone had left, Guy told his parents that Enid wanted another man in her life.

'But he's only just dead. Anyhow, look at her age,' said his mother.

'Only you would regard four months as a short time. I regard four days as devastating.' Guy looked dramatic.

'Daddy has made Mummy pregnant,' announced Sophie from the back of the car.

'He did it with his willy,' added Beatrice.

'He...' began Sophie, only to be interrupted by Enid, who really didn't want to hear the facts of life while driving the twins to swimming.

'Did you remember your swimsuits today?'

But it was a waste of time.

'They swim you know, just like us.'

'What swims?' asked Enid, listening with half an ear.

'The sperm,' replied the twins in unison.

'Bet they can't dive in the deep end!' Enid was hoping that might put them off the scent.

There was a pause before Beatrice replied, 'Mummy doesn't have a deep end.'

The twins were looking particularly frightful, Enid thought. Beatrice was wearing a repulsive pink slide. Her hair lay lank and scruffy except where the slide had gathered it up in a severe bunch, making a plain little face even plainer. Sophie was no better. She favoured a bobbly thing holding most of her hair in a ponytail. However, there were enough straggly ends for her to have one dangling in or near her mouth. Sal had bundled them in T-shirts and faded summer shorts, with anoraks to accommodate the English climate, before retiring to her bed to feel sick in peace.

Enid parked the car and walked, while the twins skipped and leapt, to the ticket office. It was strictly understood that the twins were having a lesson and there was no need for Enid to get wet. Only if the lesson was cancelled would the girls be too young to swim unaccompanied. Just in case, Enid had brought an elderly shapeless costume.

Being a granny can be tough at times, particularly if you have an image problem. The lesson was cancelled. There can be nothing more conducive to feeling old and doddery than creeping round the shallow end trying to keep your hair dry, stomach in and breasts above the knee caps. Enid thought about her crinkly arms, flabby thighs and wrinkled cleavage.

Any wishful thoughts about the future and Mr Right were put on hold and made considerably worse when Beatrice looked at her with the withering contempt of childhood and announced, 'You need ironing!'

Fuck you, thought Enid, who replied, 'I'm permanently creased.'

Then there were the sweets. While the wet bundle of towels was thrust into Enid's arms, an argument broke out about how many sweets were in each packet.

'That's not fair,' bleated Sophie. 'I've only got nine in mine.'

'Yes, but yours are bigger,' explained Enid, joining in.

That was a mistake. The twins first sulked then broke out into a rip-roaring battle in the back of the car. Seat belts were unfastened, swimwear used to throttle each other and the sweets tossed on to the floor. They lunged and grabbed each other's hair, grunting and squawking as Enid ineffectually yelled at them to shut up and sit down, gradually descending to language such as, 'If you little fuckers don't sit still and shut up, I'll stop the car and you can walk.'

She was as good as her word and stopped about a hundred yards before the farm, turfing them out and making them walk.

'This is the last time you get pregnant, my girl. They've been hell,' she announced to a whey-faced Sal.

The twins arrived back, speechless with indignation at their grandmother.

'Granny made us walk! She's horrible and she needs ironing. She's old and crinkly.'

'She's boring and won't let us have more than one packet of sweets.'

'And she's strict. She yelled at us in the car. She called us "fuckers"!'

This litany would have continued had not a cartoon on television saved the day and left Enid and Sal to peace in the kitchen.

'How do Catholic women manage, year after year? No wonder you only had one,' said Sal, wearily.

'Well, I had several miscarriages before I had you and, quite frankly, when the doctor said one is enough, I was inclined to agree with him. I'm sorry, love, I'm a useless granny at the moment. I know I'm meant to feel wanted and loved but I don't. I feel a kind of last resort, clumsy old thing. I've lost my touch since Gerry died.'

'Don't you dare talk like that. It's bad enough having a little mistake without you walking out on me. Anyway, you're a smashing granny. I need you to have them on the twelfth for the weekend while Douglas and I creep off on our own for a couple of days. Please, Ma, they know you well enough to grumble about how awful you are.'

Enid drove home in a pensive mood. How right Sal is! That about sums up all relationships, she reflected.

Enid mulled over her daughter's words. She wasn't applying them to the twins, more to Gerry, with whom she found herself increasingly irritable. His selfishness in dying was high on her list – and before he'd fixed that tap! The mower had been left in a terrible state and she still hadn't found that expensive set of spanners. As for his desk, there were stacks of papers she hadn't had the heart to sort through.

Now she had further reason to be disappointed with herself. She needed ironing, she was a crinkly old mess. It's bad enough being a widow but, with your faculties in need of a service and little hope of repairs, widowhood has a lot of detractions.

Having laid the twigs of disappointment, followed by the coals of irritation, Enid had stoked up a fire of misery by the time she reached home. The house was bleak in the soft summer air, the sitting room stale and the kitchen horribly silent. In deep melancholy, Enid drifted through her house. The frightful twins no longer liked her, Sal was involved with her new pregnancy and no one had rung. She found a bottle of wine, uncorked it and slumped in front of the television. She still didn't buy proper meals, so she ate shortbread and some prunes.

While she ate she built in her mind a wobbling, festering pile of miseries till at last the tears began to ooze – then pour – from her eyes. At first it was all her fault. She hadn't bullied Gerry to go to the doctor for check-ups. She had been rude to his family, pretending she was independent, in control, fun to be with and all that shit, but it wasn't true. She was lonely, unhappy. What's more, nobody cared. Sal wouldn't be pregnant if she really cared about her. As for the twins saying she needed ironing, it wasn't just ironing – ironing wouldn't do anything. No one, there was no one! Why bother? (The bottle by this time was empty.) She wasn't going to be a nuisance; she could take the hint.

A fog of despair swirled in lazy dizziness. She made her way like a blind person up the stairs to the medicine cupboard and with great care swallowed half a bottle of tablets before tottering off to bed, hoping to float off to an easy death.

They were, unfortunately, Gerry's pills for when he was constipated. You just try taking fifteen cascara-based pills, a bottle of wine, a fair number of prunes and a large dose of self-induced misery. Enid ran out of loo paper, kitchen roll and was reduced to greaseproof paper, which didn't flush very easily. Her bowels felt as if they had shot down the loo. She definitely overtook Sal in the advanced stages of labour when it came to contractions.

For three days she lay either on the cold bathroom floor, moaning, or she moaned in her bed. She drank water but ate nothing. She didn't dare to answer the phone for fear of yet another bout. She was smelly, disgusting and dreadfully sorry for herself, quite frightened and weak as a kitten. What was worse, she couldn't tell anybody. She was so ashamed of herself. Sophocles and the cat sulked downstairs. They did other unmentionable things downstairs as well.

The exorcism was painful and disgusting, with nothing but cornflakes to eat. Enid scrubbed, washed and flung the windows open to let the fresh air flow round the rooms and round her self-respect. She shook her newly washed hair and muttered, 'How could I?'

At last she could face answering the phone.

'Where have you been? You gay old thing! On the razzle?' It was Dolly inviting her to an auction of some really lovely antique furniture.

'Outside our league, old girl, but you never know: household effects often include dustbins and brushes. I got a wonderful electric bed-warmer at one of these sales that my electrician tells me is about as safe as a Russian nuclear reactor.'

'Do they auction lavatory paper?' asked Enid.

'They were the kind of people who still used that old scratchy stuff, the kind that tickles the haemorrhoids.'

'That'll do, let's go.'

Dolly arrived looking quite stylish, with a whiff of glamour – but then she was always better dressed than Enid. She hadn't sunk into a cheap cotton skirt and top with shapeless 'cardy' and comfortable sandals, as Enid had. Her hair had bounce, as well as a pleasant shade of nut brown quite unknown in the real world. Her face was leathery but like chamois leather, with just the texture to polish the car. Her breasts were well above the Plimsoll line. As for the rest, it did at least look packaged properly.

She arrived at Enid's house a little early. Enid studied her from her bedroom window. She wore eau de Nil trousers, well cut, and a chunky cardigan in roughly the same colour over a silk shirt, with a casual scarf draped round her neck. Enid was green with envy when she saw that scarf. For years she had tried to drape a scarf elegantly round her neck but it ended in being tied in unbecoming granny knots. Sometimes she wore it loose so it slithered off into wet muddy pavements, or tucked into her cleavage, where it wriggled out, flapping into whatever she was eating. Occasionally she wore it back to front like an absent-minded Girl Guide. Whatever she did, the bloody thing refused to produce that casual elegance Enid longed for. She had dozens of the wretched things, piled in a drawer. At one point she thought of making a patchwork quilt with them, only she was even worse at sewing than she was at tying scarves.

'Hello, Dolly, you look smashing as ever. I've checked the map; it shouldn't take long.'

The peeved cat sulked in the kitchen with the dog while Enid locked the back door. Sophocles didn't come because Dolly's car had a strict 'no dog' policy. Off the two women went, Enid to replace lavatory paper while Dolly needed a pair of old-fashioned kitchen scales.

Why am I doing this? Enid kept asking herself. After all, I'm not that interested in antiques, not like Dolly. This isn't me. I must take a pull, not just swan off in any direction. I must find my own. I want sophisticated romance. I want to meet an eccentric, unusual character with just a hint of money. Money is so useful.'

Dolly prattled away easily. After all, she was doing something she liked, that she knew about, in a world she was comfortable with. Enid sat in a sulk, wondering why she had agreed to go on this expedition. It was typical, people inviting *her* out to do what *they* liked. Nobody ever thought what she might like to do.

'You're very silent.'

'Am I?' Enid sighed like a thirteen-year-old.

'Come off it, what the hell's up?'

'It's your bloody trousers and scarf. No wonder you picked up

Mr Shortbread! Don't you think that I'd like to feel attractive again? How do you think I feel, being patronised like this? Driving across the countryside to some bloody sale just to see furniture I can't afford and in the vain hope that something I can is going for a song.'

'Grow up, Enid. I don't spend my waking hours wondering what I can do especially for you. I am simply a friend, someone who is prepared to let you join me in what I want to do. It might have been stout boots and walking in the rain, church fonts, buying another pair of trousers at eighty quid a go. I realise that you rarely go above thirty quid. It looks like it too. Get this straight, Enid, you're not as poor as a church mouse, it's just that you're as mean as one. All right, you're frightened of being on your own, but isn't it time you lashed out on something, established your own identity? For Christ's sake, stop whingeing and trying to ruin the day for us both.'

After that both women drove in strained silence.

The field next to the house had been made available for parking. Already several large cars or vans were ready to carry off the loot. 'The Larches', as the house was called, didn't appear to have any trees by that name, but it had an aggressive, mock-Tudor ugliness. Outside in the courtyard were various garden implements laid lovingly in a row. There was a mower, an ancient Ransom, rakes, forks and spades with a clutter of secateurs, and other small hand tools. There were galvanised buckets, sieves and balls of twine and rolls of wire. An elderly wheelbarrow was upturned beside an equally elderly deep freeze cabinet.

'I hope they've remembered to empty it. Think of the stink if you got that home and some putrescent sausages flew out.'

Stink was very much on Enid's mind, along with petty grievances. They bought a sale catalogue with indignation as well as money.

'I think it's outrageous. I mean, you never have to pay at the local auction sales.'

'It keeps out the riff-raff,' announced the pert blonde who was in charge of the catalogues. 'Anyway, twenty pence never harmed anyone.'

Enid muttered something about a fixed income, but Dolly's

eye had already spied a really rather lovely games table with delicious inlay in holly, walnut and rosewood.

'Bet the old dears were stingy with the heating. Look, there's little or no damage.'

Already, Enid was forgotten. She just mooned along in the background.

'It was just one old dear, according to this, said Dolly, reading out the details. 'A Miss Hermione Scailes who was the late deceased. I can just see her – last of an honourable line of Scailes, with a photo of her fiancé still by her bed – the Great War, you know – one of the old school, a little sherry before lunch and seed cake with her tea. Probably wore pink silk lingerie and played a vicious game of croquet.'

Then Enid clambered out of her reverie and added, 'Scailes. I wonder if she was any relation of Poppy Scailes, who married David Kernick – you know, the solicitor.'

'Never heard of him.' Dolly didn't want to play the 'who knows who' game.

'Not many springs left in those chairs. I like the chintz, though. There's nothing like a nice old-fashioned chintz.'

'But the size!' said Enid. 'You need a huge room to take that suite as well as that pair of enormous bookcases.'

'Sure, but many people have that kind of money and choose to live in that kind of house. Not everyone is a penniless widow.'

Enid pretended not to hear that one. They walked round peering at a mahogany dining table with a dozen Chippendale chairs, including two carvers and a hideous sideboard. There were splendid beds from Heal's, a chandelier from Spain and a clutch of standard lamps. There were at least three different dinner services.

'One for the nursery, one for the kitchen and one for the dining room,' intoned Dolly.

'What about breakfast?' asked Enid, who suspected Dolly was in some obscure way cheating.

'There's the tea service too – rather pretty. Where's the tea-pot?'

They hunted a teapot down in the silver section along with a clutter of fancy tableware, the canteen, four candelabras and endless napkin rings, all tarnished. They admired the damask tablecloths, the table napkins, the linen, blankets, towels and fiddly things like tray cloths. The ornaments were good quality Staffordshire, Meissen and Crown Derby, nestling among the sentimental flotsam of a lifetime – a model of a foxhound, several contemporary china horses, a piggy bank, some rather revolting glass characters and a humble wooden owl with all the hallmarks of having been made at school. Yet all this was but to touch the surface of the items for sale.

There were the handsome wooden towel rails, fire tongs and endless fenders, and a charming fire surround with a leather seat to warm the bum on a cold day. There were large washbasins with generous jugs, wooden chairs galore, embroidered stools, elderly bathroom scales, mirrors ranging from distorted for shaving to distorted for elegance, with an elaborate gold frame. In the kitchen were pots and pans, basins for puddings, Pyrex for everyday, chopping boards and a mountain of obscure implements and yes, there were the scales, elderly, chipped and paint flaking, but with most of the weights intact.

'What number?' asked Dolly.

'916.'

'They're exactly what I want, but I can't stay here that long.'

'Leave a bid, go on, have a go.'

'We haven't found your loo paper. Don't you want to leave a bid on something?'

'Love to, but I promised the bank manager I wouldn't.'

The two women stood by the scales. Neither had a clue how much they were worth. Actually, both were out of their depth. Auctions are places you go to with your man. Oh, there are formidable ladies who spend thousands of pounds before slipping away in their chauffeur-driven Rolls. Or the professionally beady-eyed ones who run successful antique shops. Dolly and Enid didn't fall into either category.

'I wouldn't have any idea how much,' she confided to Enid.

'You mean you don't know whether it's ten pounds or a hundred?'

'Do you?'

'Not a clue, but we've come all this way. I'll do it for you.

That way, you can blame me. Let's make it ten pounds.'

'Ask about the scratchy bog paper,' said Dolly, after Enid had handed in her bid to an enigmatic gentleman in a well-worn suit and greying hair.

'Is there any scratchy lavatory paper in the sale?' Enid asked.

He looked up. 'I know exactly what you mean. No, there isn't. I don't know if it's made any more.'

'They have it in some gentlemen's clubs still – prisons too, I believe,' said Enid.

She and the enigmatic gentleman shared a comfortable silence. He seemed pleasant – a little younger than her. He really needed a new suit and a snip to the ends of his hair – it was a little too long. The silence ended in a conspiratorial glance. They both smiled at the same time. It might not have been the kind of investment the bank manager was thinking about, but Enid was certainly thinking of making an investment of some kind. She was investing in the fantasy of meeting a new man.

They stayed for the first hundred lots, noticing the ease at which the auctioneer plucked out of the crowd of people hundreds of pounds. Just a wink, a nod, a hand momentarily held in supplication and it was all over, the bidder noting the price, and on with the next lot. But Enid wasn't concentrating. She was looking for the man in the shabby suit. He wasn't there. But his image was clearly visible in Enid's imagination.

She met him again as they were leaving. At once she imagined she had bought a pretty Pembroke table, deftly missing out on the obvious, like its price.

'Hello,' he said in her imagination. 'That's lovely – better than loo paper.' He smiled. 'Let me give you a hand. I reckon more damage is done in a car ride home than in the hundred years before.'

Enid agreed as they eased it into the car. They stood by the car, calmly looking at each other.

'By the way…' He faded, she faded, the Pembroke table faded. He'd been too young, his suit too shiny and his hair just a little too sleazy. Enid found herself concentrating on a large gong on a stand, which was well over £200, and going strong.

'Have you had enough?' asked Dolly.

'I think so.'

As they made their way out they met the man in reality yet again, still sitting at his table. Enid shuddered. It had been a narrow escape.

Why did she do it? It was as bad as being a teenager. Here she was, a recently widowed woman, fantasising about the most unsuitable men.

When they had started the return journey and Enid felt her bad behaviour earlier had been forgiven, she tentatively raised the subject.

'Do you ever,' she began, 'daydream about...well...warm, comfortable images, like men, for instance?'

'Do I ever!' replied Dolly, as they turned into a main road.

'I mean, still?'

'Of course I do. There is a permanent need for the comfort and companionship of a man. I'm not, never was, a career woman – never had a job to sublimate all that stuff. But don't worry, Enid, you'll get used to it. Look at me. I bowl along nicely, thank you very much.'

There was a silence.

'Did you fancy a bloke there?' asked Dolly,

'Kind of, but it was a narrow escape.'

'They usually are,' laughed Dolly.

That evening Enid ate some cereal and a banana while watching television. She noticed three dirty bowls and four mugs, two with banana skins in them, surrounding her chair. She was fast becoming a slut – a slut thinking about nothing but men. They never tell you that in the textbooks. Ravenous hordes of middle-aged ladies searching for a man are a frightening thought, admitted Enid, as she dragged herself off to her lonely double bed.

Sal was looking tired and drawn. She was not yet thirty, but this unplanned pregnancy was making her worn out. Enid tried harder than ever not to lean on her. Her hand would hover over the phone then drop on her lap.

No, I mustn't...

Just occasionally she would get through and then feel obligated to say, 'Why don't I have the twins for the night? Give you a break?' Very sensibly, Sal always said, 'Yes.'

Enid would stand outside the school, the years peeling back to when she stood there for Sal – the same smell of grubby bodies, the same shoelaces flapping round, the same pieces of paper that need signing for a school visit; the other children too – the same fat boy bullying the younger ones, the same beautiful child with blonde hair, the same prongy teeth, the same plain child bossing the others and, in the corner, finger in mouth and legs twisted one over the other, the same sad child.

The twins would take a running jump.

'Granny, can we buy sweets?'

'I want Kit-Kat.'

It was the same, 'What do you say?' followed by a surly 'Please.' Enid would steer them to the shop where little fingers would touch and take anything they could.

'Beatrice, put that down, I didn't say you could take Sellotape. Anyway I've got lots at home.'

'Have you tidied the house yet? Mummy says you're becoming a slut.'

'I live on my own and I can keep the house any way I like – and it's rude, young lady, to tell your grandmother she's a slut.'

'Do you like living on your own?' asked Sophie.

'No, I don't, I find it very lonely.'

'The thing is, with the new baby, we won't have any room for you.'

'Are you pleased about the baby?' Enid asked.

'Well,' began Beatrice, her head cocked to one side and her hair draped round her face, 'I don't know. You see, Mummy says it will come out of her wee. They will wash it, won't they?'

There is a lot to be said for gooseberry bushes and storks, and very little for the truth. Enid remembered telling Sal everything one needs to know about babies, only to find out years later that Sal thought it all a pack of lies anyway. Did these sophisticated winsome creatures understand it all?

While sitting in the bath with endless rubbery creatures, Beatrice asked Enid, 'Where are you going, Granny?'

'Nowhere, pet. Now clean your face.'

'But if you let go, you must go somewhere.'

'Who says I'm letting go?'

'Mummy says you've let yourself go since Grandpa died.'

It hurt. It stuck. Enid turned her head so that the children couldn't see tears welling up.

Fuck her, she doesn't know what it's like! Nobody knows what it's like. What's the point?

'Life is about day-dreaming, waking up and despising yourself.'

Enid sniffed before lifting the two wet bodies out of the bath and soon had them tucked up in her spare room. She had kept some of Sal's old books and soon was deep into *Winnie the Pooh*. Outside, the summer light softened and the birds called out that the day was ending. In her garden the weeds flourished and a mole had taken residence near the hedge and created a veritable pyramid park. In the house the dust gathered. A wash was clocking up its fourth day in the machine. The rubbish bin had begun to smell. There was another banana skin by the television. Where had the brisk 'Begin as I mean to go on' attitude gone?

Where indeed? Enid felt disgusted with herself. Frankly, it wasn't as if she and Gerry were madly in love or had been closeted together without a break for years and years. It wasn't as if she had had an exotic, stimulating life and it had suddenly disappeared, like the proverbial carpet beneath her feet. Enid saw herself as a fairly ordinary widow. Husband had died, income had shrunk, house seemed too big, friends were few and far between. Family was no longer particularly interested. Everyone had moved on while she appeared to have sunk – but instead of without a trace, with a trail of banana skins and empty coffee mugs.

As Adam said at lunch the following Sunday after a stroll round the garden, 'Those moles; very messy, you know.'

'I know, Adam.'

'I don't watch television with banana skins at the home. It's dirty.'

He didn't say much more that Sunday but watched with total concentration some highly technical programme about snorting whales while Enid cleared up all the mess and plumped up the cushions. He was irritated by her efforts to clear the room and sighed several monumental sighs.

Later, after she had returned him, a care worker telephoned to say Adam hadn't enjoyed himself. Enid felt awful. An embarrassed flush suffused her face as she stammered her apologies for the state of the house. It had nothing to do with that; he had complained that he had eaten strawberries two weekends in a row. At the home they weren't allowed to serve the same pud two weeks in a row. It was against regulations.

While Sal bulged, Enid waned. The summer dragged grey clouds across its stage. Adam ate chocolate mousse, apple crumble and lemon meringue pie for pud, and Enid ate the remainder during the week. Adam confided that he was autistic – would Enid please be more understanding? He didn't like the way she moved things around and hated it when she touched him.

The twins disappeared with their parents to wave buckets and spades in Cornwall. Enid was mildly miffed that they didn't invite her.

I mean, I know they want a family holiday – but I'm not such a drag, am I? Yes, she was. She knew she was, too. Everything seemed so dreary. Gerry wasn't really that much cop, but they had rubbed along happily – Gerry in his bumbling, irritable way. Enid let what energy she had evaporate in the summer cool. The flowers she had looked after with modest care in the spring now were dying of neglect – the same neglect the weeds thrived on. The mole hadn't liked the garden and had disappeared back into the field. Only the pyramids remained. Inside, the dust rested lazily on every surface. Scum collected round the bath. Clean clothes were flung on her chair in her bedroom, dirty clothes ditto. Enid watched old films filled with heroes from her youth. She collected the banana skins and mugs only when Adam appeared; otherwise she did nothing. She thought a great deal, though.

She thought a great deal about sex. Her libido had gone into hiding at first. Gerry had made sex a minimalist activity over his last few years. Enid hadn't really minded; she was used to the dear old thing – if that is what he wanted, so be it. But where had that left her? She turned over and over in her mind the injustice of being a conventional housewife. They had enjoyed a compatible sex life for many years, though his trips abroad broke the rhythm.

But sex had fused into so many of the gestures and habits of their life. Sex was stroking his hair as he sat watching cricket; sex was nestling his bum into the curve of her body in their big double bed, especially when it was cold. Sex was the mock grabbing of his genitals when she wanted to tease him. Sex was his body smell when he slipped into bed after a bath. Sex was licking an ice cream and catching his eye. It was also oral sex, when he would regain his strength and his libido, raring to be off like the olden days, only to soon lie panting for breath. She thought a lot about that.

That bloody Viagra stuff! It's just for men – typical! And don't tell me about vibrators. I don't want any mention of the damned things.

Not that anyone was likely to mention them. Could friendship ever replace that level of intimacy? Not that she had many friends. So she heaped misery on misery, introspection on introspection, and found another banana and took it back to bed.

The cat was furious. It was fed irregularly and never so much as had a hand lain on it from one day to the next. Its coat was becoming matted and it was generally neglected. If it could have telephoned, it would have rung *Pet Rescue* and complained. So would Sophocles, whose daily stroll was more honoured in the breach. As it was, the cat spent most of its time by a beech hedge that housed a late nest of fledgling blackbirds, while Sophocles lay supine just inside the kitchen door, hoping to jog Enid's attention. They were doing just that when the postman arrived. He rang the bell.

Four

'What the hell,' grumbled Enid, slipping Gerry's huge dressing gown over one of the famous nightdresses. She felt a little embarrassed to be still undressed at eleven on a warm summer's day.

'Registered, love.'

He held out a pencil. The postmark said 'India' and it was addressed to Gerry. They didn't know anyone in India, not after all these years. She had a strong desire not to open it. She was frightened that it would cause her effort, emotion and concern. She held it warily before putting it on the kitchen table. She would get dressed first; it would be like putting her armour on. But first a cup of coffee – which, by this stage, meant rinsing out a dirty cup. Enid procrastinated for a good hour before taking a knife and slitting the envelope open.

'*Dear Daddyji,*' it began. Enid stopped there.

Daddyji, Daddyji! Who the hell...?

She continued to read, '*Mumsi is distraught...*'

Aren't we all, thought Enid, sourly.

'*You always said you would give me a dowry.*'

'That's more than he gave Sal,' she found herself telling Sophocles, who had almost given up hearing Enid speak.

> We need it now. Ran is quite white. Oh, Daddyji, I do want to be married before I get any longer in the tooth.
>
> What has happened? It has taken bloody ages to find you. A dark horse, that is what you are. Do you remember? It was a dowry or Oxbridge – those dreaming spires. Funny! I can never find it on the map. How do you say it? Thanks for small mercies? This dowry business is serious. I mean it, so please cough up, as you say.
>
> Your loving daughter, Vijaya

Enid reread the letter slowly, aware that a fire was stoking up in her stomach and its flames were already licking her imagination, above all her admiration for her Gerry. So he did have a secret! Bully for him – the old boy had balls after all! All that badger bristle nonsense was just a jolly for a bit of leg-over.

Oh, Gerry, why didn't you tell me? It's marvellous! It's so funny, can't you see?

Later, having read it for the umpteenth time, Enid quietened down. She still thought it very funny but an inkling of all the repercussions was beginning to dawn. Still, this beat eau de Nil trousers at eighty quid a pair any day of the week.

Enid heard her heart banging away. She couldn't think very clearly. Gusts of half-formulated questions flew across her mind. What was crystal clear was that Vijaya must have her dowry and find out the mystery of Oxbridge. That stood out as imperative. Mumsi could wait. But she must let them know that Gerry was dead. She looked at the address, Mumbai – wasn't that Bombay? Sal's pregnancy pushed the excitement away. She couldn't simply gallivant off to India with the dowry. Anyway, what if the groom wanted camels and goats? Or more likely a sports car, something like that. She wanted to share all this astonishing news – but not with Sal, not yet. She dialled Dolly.

'I must tell someone before I burst,' began Enid. 'Guess what! It looks as if Gerry had a double life.'

'So what? You've always implied that.'

'Yes, but another wife, and a daughter called Vijaya who wants a dowry.'

Dolly whistled. 'That's quite something, Enid. What did you say the name was?'

'It's Indian; they live in Bombay. The mother is just "Mumsi". Vijaya writes about a dowry because she wants to marry someone who is white.'

'My dear girl, this'll cheer you up. I hope you're going.'

'What about Sal?'

'Have you told her?'

'You're the first.'

A telephone silence is different from an ordinary silence. In this case Dolly assumed Enid would speak next while Enid thought the reverse. The silence stretched further and further.

'Doll, are you still there?'

'Then invite the newly-weds here – that can be the dowry.'

'Do you think I can? I mean I wouldn't know what to do with them. I suppose I can reveal the mysteries of Oxbridge. Anyway, I couldn't afford the whole trip; perhaps I could pay for them once they are here.'

'Don't be so short-sighted! There's Gerry's pompous family for starters. I bet you haven't seen the Tower of London recently, and you can always book them a tour of the Highlands. There's nothing like five days of pouring rain in Scotland to cheer one up.'

'Do you think there will be legal complications?'

'And how! Indians are terribly litigious. Look, Enid, this is just what you need. Forget do-gooding.'

'I can't forget Adam. Everyone has forgotten Adam.'

'Sentimental crap!'

'Don't be like that about Adam. He's important to me.'

'Sure, Enid, but are you important to him?'

'That's unfair! This India affair is terribly exciting but, when it's over, I'll need Adam.'

'There you go again. Well, you know best. Don't you dare have Vijaya to stay without inviting me to see her!'

Typical of Dolly, she had just made the whole thing a big adventure. That's why you rang her, you silly cow, Enid told herself.

Dolly was made of more perceptive stuff than simply goading her friend into some crazy family adventure. As she sat down and thought about Enid's astounding news she realised that there was a terrible flaw in Enid's reaction. Yes, in one sense it was an unexpected drama and poor old Enid was definitely bereft of excitement in her life. But surely, if only moderately, Enid would see this as a kick in the teeth and, with a daughter like Sal, teeth were a sore point.

She phoned back.

'Enid, are you all right? I mean, now the shock is over, you must be feeling pretty pissed off.'

'Oh no! You see, Dolly, I can't be cross or jealous. Gerry would hate that.'

'Enid, listen, Gerry is dead. What Gerry would have thought

doesn't matter now. It's what *you* feel that matters now.'

'But you don't understand, this is Gerry's daughter. He'd be furious if – well – if I let him down.'

Enid put the phone down and stood still, concentrating on a middle distance somewhere well out of focus. As she stood there a groundswell of tears built up and overflowed, trickling down her face, silently but relentlessly. It was several minutes before the sobbing started and even then she didn't dare face what she was weeping about. She refused to see the callous, selfish behaviour, the betrayal and disloyalty. Her Gerry had done this to her, her Gerry, the idealist who had turned his back on his family's stultified background and chosen a career involving confidentiality. Was it all a ruse so he could get some leg-over? Where did his money go? Surely not to… No, no, he was an idealist, he was her Gerry – hers, not some Mumsi's, whom she didn't even know about till today.

It took a while to put the genie back in the bottle and suppress the truth that was rapidly confronting her – an hour spent vacuuming the house, as though that would help her come to terms with the letter.

Now she must tackle Sal. There was a reticence – unusual for Enid. Sal was tetchy; coming to terms with her little mistake was taking it's time. Enid worried about how she would take the news of an Indian half-sister. It was the kind of news better broken in person. She phoned her and asked if she could come over.

She bowled through the stubble fields. A plough was already out and turning the rich chocolate soil while seagulls whirled and swooped. Already the first signs of autumn lurked in the leaves, the undergrowth and the sweet blackberries. Sal was starting to show; one of Douglas's shirts hung over her belly. The twins were wearing pants and T-shirts. They appeared to be sloshing water and sand together in the sandpit. Beatrice was sitting on her hunkers with a can for watering flowers, pouring a steady flow of water onto some complicated sand construction. Sophie, on the other hand, looked up on seeing the car.

'Hello, Granny; the baby has started to kick.'

'How exciting! What are you and Beatrice playing?'

'Oh, the usual, you know.'

She took a bucket, filled it with more water and poured it in one dollop onto Beatrice's sandy edifice whereupon Beatrice let out a piercing yell and kicked her sister. Now they were both letting out a piercing yell.

Sal put her head out, saw Enid and said, 'Hello, Mum, now look what you've done! They've been playing beautifully for at least ten minutes.'

'I gather from your resident midwife that the baby has started to kick.'

'Don't! Beatrice is already kicking up a fuss because we've told her she can't watch it being born.'

'I suppose,' said Enid grimly, 'there is nowhere we can speak in relative privacy?'

'You must be joking! I'll put on a video and see if that will do it.'

The girls were thrilled to watch a video at such a forbidden hour. Beatrice was suspicious. 'You want to get rid of us, don't you?'

'Yes,' added Sophie. 'You and Granny want to discuss the baby in private.'

'Too right, she knows more about babies than you two,' said Sal, as she handed out forbidden fruit in the form of a packet of crisps each, adding that she and Granny would be just in the kitchen.

A cup of milky coffee for Enid and just juice for Sal.

'Coffee tastes foul still. What's up, Mum?'

'I got a letter – from India – or rather, it was addressed to Gerry. It appears to be from a daughter, Vijaya. Look, here it is.' Enid handed over the letter.

Sal read it slowly, her lips moving over the words. She didn't say anything when she finished, just looked with concentration at the middle distance – obviously a family failing. She looked up from her reverie.

'Wow! Mumsi sounds a bit of a drip…all those years just waiting for Pa to turn up. You're going to invite Vijaya to stay, aren't you?'

Oh, you wonderful, generous daughter – no wonder I love you to bits, thought Enid. Aloud, she said, 'Yes, it's a question of when. I mean, I don't know if or when you'll need me with the baby.'

Sal yawned, throwing back her head and stretching every facial muscle she had. She looked remarkably like one of Douglas's heifers.

'It's due about New Year's Eve. I hope you'll give a hand over Christmas – pantomimes, things like that. Perhaps we could share the cooking; it's just us, so we can cut corners. Afterwards is anyone's guess. Why don't you invite her next spring? She's right, Pa was a dark horse. How do you feel about it, Ma?'

'It's really cheered me up, to tell you the truth.' (Oh, yeah!) 'I mean, probate and all that went relatively smoothly. You know, I've been feeling pretty down with the boredom of life on my own. It's no good saying that I must learn to stand on my own two feet. I don't want to. Life on my two feet is deadly, quite frankly. But this letter is like an offer for bionic legs and that makes my two feet a very different story. I can't afford a real dowry but if they can afford the fare, I think I can manage the rest.'

'What if it's a hoax?' Sal looked at her mother straight in the eye.

'You mean I pay the money for the dowry only to find Vijaya doesn't exist and the loot is spent on some dastardly plot? I did wonder if I ought to ring the Brig.' A longish pause followed. 'You're not cross, are you, Sal?' whispered Enid.

But it was a twin who answered. 'Sophie keeps eating my crisps.'

There is nothing like a six-year-old standing with a protruding tummy, grubby as hell, moaning about crisps, to bring everyone back to reality.

'Tell her she won't get any sweeties after lunch.'

Sophie appeared at that minute, looking every bit as grubby.

'I only ate more 'cos Beatrice said I could.'

'You made me say you could. It's not fair!' wailed Sophie.

Sal turned to her mum. 'I'm letting myself in for this all over again. I must need my head examined.'

'It's not twins again, is it? asked Enid anxiously.

No, it wasn't.

Enid was still appalled but said nothing. Sal would slip further and further away into her world of 'Whoopsie-daisy-never-mind'. Her original, lovely Sal – apart from those dreaded teeth – would be relegated to motherhood and some voluntary work during her most creative years. What a waste! A lead lump of depression sat heavily on what had been her wildly exciting news.

If the truth be known, the boring baby nonsense lurked for several more days till Enid pulled herself together and became positive about the dear little bundle. She bought some needles and a knitting pattern. It did the trick – so much so that she felt able to write back to India as well.

Dear Vijaya

I am sorry to say that I have some bad news for you. My husband, Gerald Tanner, died at the end of February. He had a stroke. Apart from a blurred photograph of a young lady, there is nothing in his papers to suggest he had another family.

Now, if Gerry promised you a dowry, I will do my best to help. Would you accept as your dowry a visit here with a trip round Scotland? There is no way I can afford the airfares, I'm afraid. It won't be possible till next spring because our daughter, Sal, is having another baby in January.

Can you tell me more about Mumsi – where she met Gerald – and about yourself and Ran? I am Enid and I married Gerry thirty years ago. We have an only daughter, Sally.

Please write back. I'm interested and very curious about you and Mumsi. I enclose a rather bad photograph of Gerry and myself with our granddaughters, Beatrice and Sophie.

It wasn't really what she wanted to say. She wanted to throw open her arms and gather the whole new bundle of problems and complications to her breast. She wanted to welcome Vijaya like a daughter, Mumsi like a sister. She wanted to plunge headlong into wherever the letter took her.

Where reality is sparse on the ground, fantasy takes over. She imagined the beautiful Vijaya living in a large, elegant villa. It would have to be garden level. No Indian fantasy was complete without a veranda with tropical vegetation with Rikki-Tikki-Tavi scuttling in the bushes and the sinister Nagina coiled under the shed. Enid loved reading Kipling to Sal when she was young.

Vijaya lived with her mother, Mumsi – an unsatisfactory name, but Indira was the only other one Enid could think of. The villa had little furniture, just cushions and joss sticks – perhaps not, that's more like phoney India in Wimbledon. Well, if not joss sticks, a smell of spice and sophistication. Mumsi was probably a semi-invalid – bad arthritis or possibly hepatitis. She just drifts elegantly through the fantasy waiting for her Gerry to arrive. It made Gerry much more attractive! Vijaya was the bright spark. After a good secretarial school she had bubbled to the surface and taken a job in the media where, in next to no time, she was a PA to the director. Having disposed of Vijaya fairly satisfactorily, Enid returned to the villa and wandered dreamily through the garden.

Soon it was Adam's day. Adam was pleased to see Enid. He asked to sit in the back of the car, as the Queen always sat in the back. When they got home, Enid suggested they walked round the garden. Adam shuffled beside her as they admired the late summer flowers, the ripening apples, the plums and pears. After a while Adam became bored. Who wanted to look at flowers when he had something far more interesting? He unzipped his flies and drew out a pink, taut erection. Enid turned round; she had been warned.

'Adam, your willy is private. Put it away. I don't want to see it.'

He grinned and giggled, giving it another stimulating stroke.

'Adam, you are going straight back to your home if you don't put it away this minute.' Still he just stood there, giggling slightly. Whatever she did, she mustn't touch the damn thing. It would give wrong signals, apparently.

'Adam, do you want ice-cream with lunch?' He wasn't listening. He was absorbed in masturbating.

'I'm going in the house to get lunch. You can't come in till you're properly dressed and you've put that away.'

Enid walked towards the house. Behind her she could hear Adam's giggle and the occasional bleat of alarm at being left by himself. She was mildly scared. What if he wandered down to the road and someone saw him? What if he followed her into the house? She couldn't lock him out. What if he grabbed her? She nervously banged pots and pans around with one eye on the door in case he arrived. After a while she was sufficiently anxious to go into the garden to look for him. She couldn't find him. Really worried by now, she ran out into the road. It was empty, dusty and curiously dangerous. She started calling him. 'Adam!' She repeated his name as she retraced her steps to the house. Surely he hadn't gone in the house? Panting with anxiety, she opened and slammed the doors. He wasn't there.

She found him sitting in the back of the car, rocking gently. His penis was put away but telltale signs of semen were round his zip. She was relieved and angry.

'Adam, it's lunchtime.'

Adam wanted to be difficult. He didn't like the food and ended up eating peanut butter sandwiches and chocolate biscuits. The usual diversions like the television failed completely.

'What do you want to do?' she asked irritably.

Adam looked at her with that expression in his eyes that indicated he was on a different planet. Reaching Adam was never easy, but right now it seemed utterly impossible. Enid felt useless – she'd better ring the home.

She left Adam trying to tune the radio while she telephoned from the hall.

'Is that Oak Lodge? It's Enid Tanner here. Adam is spending the day with me. He unfortunately masturbated in the garden this morning. He won't eat lunch and doesn't want to do anything this afternoon.'

'That's Adam for you,' said a cheerful voice. 'Try not to let him get his penis out. Once out, nothing short of a bomb will interrupt him. Don't worry about lunch. He'll eat when he's hungry. Try to interest him in something really complicated. He's mechanical, is our Adam.'

He sure was! Tuning the radio was one thing, but Adam had found a screwdriver and was taking the damned thing to pieces. It already lay in several parts, the circuit board sprouting wires. Adam was enjoying himself; at least it was a diversion from earlier antics.

Why do I do it? she asked herself as she drove away from the Oak Lodge later that day. Her radio was never likely to recover. Adam's wanking habits frankly rather disgusted her. All this hands-on voluntary work was rather more than she bargained for.

As she cleared away the radio she found herself putting it all in a box for next time. She hadn't solved the conundrum, but there would be a next time. The Adams of this world were too vulnerable for the fickle fancies of ladies like herself. She had agreed to befriend him and befriend him she would. It mattered, possibly more than Mumsi and Vijaya mattered.

That letter – Enid's reply – was posted and Adam safely bundled back in his home. Enid was once more at a loose end. She tugged at the weeds disconsolately, snipping and pulling at the straggly ends. Loneliness is such a persistent companion. It followed her round the garden, hovered round the telephone, prevented her from cooking, distracted her from picking up a book or some embroidery. Worst of all, loneliness is jealous. Play bridge? No way! Loneliness wouldn't like it. Nor would loneliness let you join a group, show some initiative. Loneliness likes nothing better than to sit you in a chair and goad you into tears.

'It's over six months,' said Enid as she wiped away her tears. 'I mean, why aren't I back on my feet?'

Enid was not one for praying; not believing in God, she didn't see her problems in terms of religion. She saw them as an institutional injustice. Widows were extraneous.

Damn it! Men can hobble to a brothel and spend an hour fantasising that they are still alive.

Enid was invited almost as a matter of course to Sunday lunch at the farm.

Douglas listened to his mother-in-law bleating like one of his sheep. The bleat was continuing long past its sell-by date. Enid was becoming a bore. So long as she stuck to the children or was speculating about that letter from India, she was OK. But allowed to talk about being a widow and the old ewe bleat would begin.

'Why don't you start an agency for older people wanting companionship?

'How do you mean?' The bleat had stopped.

'You know, these lonely heart advertisements; you could start a specialist one for the over-sixties.'

'The trouble with that is that men cheat. At sixty they can still pull a woman in her mid-thirties – not so vice versa.'

'I still think that women like yourself who are pining for companionship would do well to group together – with men too, if you like.'

'Douglas, you miss the point. I loathe women-only activities, all dressed to the nines with libidos shrieking out for their vibrators. *Yuk!*'

'Enid, as your son-in-law I can say this – you are rapidly becoming a bore.'

'Well, who the hell wants to go on the over-sixties coach trip to see the Christmas lights or whatever?'

All the same, it set her thinking. So the following Sunday she bought some papers and a copy of *Time Out*. She read through the ads for sex, friendship and making dreams come true. It was a little like buying several pounds of truffles and eating them all at once. She read through with prurient curiosity. No one claimed to be pug ugly and as dull as ditch water. Everyone was anxious to proclaim their slimline figures. Many wanted good conversation, and to 'go out' played a large part in their lives. It was in almost every respect exactly what Enid also wanted. Her figure wasn't up to snuff, though. But, having started life a bit of a mouse, now she was a doughty arguer – if that passed as conversation – and would gladly go out so long as it wasn't in a bus to see the Christmas lights. Piss off, loneliness! Enid was going to advertise.

It would have been more honest to have simply advertised for Gerry to come home.

Before she began composing what to say, she couldn't help noticing that the house was a complete tip. Months of neglect had laid a smell of stale toast over the house. That and coffee mugs with a scum of green growing on the surface added to the neglect. She rinsed the wash that had been done days ago in the machine and then piled in some of the grubby clothes that had lain forlornly on the floor and over the chair. The kitchen was coated in a veneer of grease. Summer insects had buzzed querulously and then expired on their backs. The whole place was utterly disgusting. Enid could see a wagging finger admonishing her. Was this a home she'd want to bring someone back to? Perish the thought! She'd set to at once. Armed with Pledge, the Hoover and a bucket of hot soapy water with a large dollop of disinfectant for wiping painted surfaces, she opened windows, dusted away cobwebs and wondered how much it would cost to get someone else to do this job.

She had to feel good. It was no good writing how smashing she was if she palpably was not. That meant washing her hair – no point in overdoing it – she wasn't due to have her hair cut. She ran the bath and stood naked in front of the mirror, just as she used to for Gerry. Only he really didn't care two hoots what her body looked like, bless him. It wasn't a pretty sight; it was lumpy and dumpy without an iota of sex appeal.

If only you could see me on the inside. All I want is to live again, touch, feel, argue, share and even love again. Frankly, looking at herself standing there in the bathroom, all her flights of fancy seemed pretty remote. The Christmas coach tour loomed.

'No thank you!' she shouted out loud.

Clean, and if not exactly beautiful, she was ready. She sat down and composed her advertisement.

> I'm sixty, a widow, nothing special to look at. I just want some-
> one to fill that gap. I'm interested in most things. I just hate being
> a widow.

She read and reread it over and over again. This was no act of fantasy; she was deadly serious. Poor Enid! However much she longed for Mr Right to step through the door, there really wasn't room for him till that philandering old bully had been finally put to rest. Now, with Vijaya hovering in the wings, that wasn't likely to happen.

Adam's weekly outing came round again. Enid was mildly put off by his escapade the previous week. The radio certainly hadn't recovered, so she decided they might do some gardening together. She bought some daffodil bulbs and hoped Adam would enjoy planting them.

Adam looked at her with his blankest of expressions on being told they were going to do the garden. He sat beside her, seat belt done up, and halfway home he announced it might rain. But it didn't.

Enid showed him how to plunge the bulb planter in the earth

and then drop in the bulb. She showed him again and again.

'Your turn,' she suggested.

He shook his head and waved his hands around. He didn't want to get his hands dirty. So Enid continued to plant the bulbs and Adam continued to bend down enthusiastically watching what she did. After a while she stood up and stretched.

'I'll get lunch. I've made a casserole, Adam. Do you like casseroles?'

He nodded his head vigorously.

'Do you know how to whip cream? Look, here is a whisk and here's the cream; you see if you can whip it.'

Whip it! Adam almost produced a pat of butter.

'Wow, Adam, you sure can whip cream!'

He was thrilled by this new accomplishment and very disappointed that Enid didn't have more cream to whip. The buttery mess he had made he insisted on eating with the fruit salad before going in to the sitting room to watch telly. She found him a little later, rocking to and fro while mouthing some mantra. He was watching football.

'What team do you support, Adam?'

'The blue ones.'

As neither team was wearing blue, Enid could only assume that it was some other team. However, her complete ignorance of anything to do with football precluded further conversation. So she picked up a book and began turning the pages. After a while Adam stopped watching and began tugging at her sleeve.

'What is it, Adam?'

'The daffodils, I want to see the flowers.'

'They won't be out yet. It will be next spring when they flower.'

He looked disappointed and angry.

What was the point? Oh, never mind.

He didn't speak again that day. Enid drove him back feeling profoundly guilty. She should never have involved him with the bulbs, but it was so difficult getting it right with Adam.

His worker was reassuring. Adam could be great but he was as stubborn as a donkey when he felt like it.

'What kind of future does he have?' asked Enid, as Adam

disappeared into the home to watch, no doubt, more television.

'Don't ask that. It doesn't have any meaning in Adam's life. He learns various social skills and can communicate at a very modest level. He's clean, warm, well fed and protected from the unkind world he lives in – meaning his mother. She couldn't cope, became angry and disappointed and then rejected him. You can't blame her. She didn't actually physically abuse him, just neglected him.'

'Excuse me asking, but why do you do this kind of work?'

The girl smiled. 'I'm waiting to become a nun.'

Enid drove back in anger at poor old Adam, who never harmed anyone, being some kind of religious comforter to a sanctimonious chit of a girl who wanted to give her emotions, virginity and God knows what else to God.

If Adam had been furry, cuddly and cute, he'd have been re-homed in next to no time. Remember *Pet Rescue*? Enid could see Gerry now, roaring with laughter at some vet operating on a bat with toothache, or watching with incredulity as five sheep found a happy home, with not a hint of lamb chops. Armed with a mug of coffee, they would sit side by side, as kittens, cats, dogs, geese and canaries had their toes trimmed and their psyches smoothed, before 300 excited mums rang to offer a loving home. The 'would-be' nun could cut Adam's nails and his hair, get him a new pair of trainers and pop him on telly and bingo! No one would ring. No one would care a toss.

'Not even me, if I'm honest,' Enid said to herself.

So Adam faded till next time round. Vijaya faded for a while too – Enid had little faith in the Indian postal service. But that advertisement would be out tomorrow. As if expecting a horde of randy lovers to breach the fence and head for her bedroom, Enid pottered away a complete day of shifting flower pots just a little to the right and picking up rubber bands and, using an old ashtray, made it into a rubber band bowl. While doing these minor tasks, her imagination created the kind of pornographic material the police complain they have to watch. She picked some of the gravel from the drive off the grass where the twins had put it when playing some game. She was about to clean out the porch when the telephone went.

'Enid, I'm so glad I've caught you. Merry widows are so difficult to pin down – they're always gadding around.'

'Hello, Jane…that's bullshit!'

'What about dinner, Thursday week?'

'Great – very smart, smart, or clean jeans?'

'Do you still wear jeans?'

'They get increasingly metaphorical, but I can produce a pair.'

'Well, I think smart will do; round about eight?'

It was enough to produce a tuneless hum. Enid upgraded the fantasy pornography and made sure the porch was spotless in less than no time.

Eating was still a problem. One knife and fork laid out on the table, one carrot and a blob of fish – it looked so disgusting. Mixed nuts and dried fruits were her favourites, but Enid munched her way through anything that didn't require effort, the cooker or much washing-up. The only exceptions were Adam or the twins, with one or two limp dinner parties that she had tried to pretend were an answer to that blank space.

'Birthday or something?' the postman asked, as he handed over fifteen letters to Enid.

'My goodness, it looks like it!'

She took the bundle into her kitchen, kicked the cat off the chair and sat down. She suddenly felt shy, or at least sheepish. What had she done? Part of her wanted to turn the clock back – not send that ad. She must have sat there about fifteen minutes. She had replaced Adam's wreck of a radio with a small portable one; it produced a tinny sound but she rarely listened to music. She began playing games. She'd begin opening the letters the next time someone said, 'I have to say'. It was one of her pet hates. She waited and waited; a comedian was talking about depression. Can't comedians talk about anything else? Then a lady banged on about chimpanzees. She made them seem such ideal companions that Enid toyed with the idea of acquiring one as the answer to her problems, until she heard their lavatorial behaviour was unreliable.

'Yes, got it!'

She heard the chimpanzee lady say really clearly, 'I have to say the present guidelines stink.'

'Stinking guidelines!' Now she could open the top letter.

It turned out to be an invitation to a fundraising auction for Riding for the Disabled and had nothing to do with her advertisement. The next was from a faith healer who suggested Enid became reconciled with God. She enclosed a price list for this reconciliation business. The next came from an elderly lady trapped in an old folks' home who wished her well. She remembered vividly feeling just the same after her husband died. At last, a letter from a man – a pretty desperate man, by the sound of things. He wanted a housekeeper. Another man – this one was living in his car – his wife had chucked him out of the house. It was inevitable that some elderly stud had got hold of Viagra pills and wanted to try them out. Several more women wrote as kindred spirits. Enid was feeling disappointed till she came to a letter at the bottom of the pile. It was from a retired teacher in the Midlands. She had for some time been thinking of starting an agency for older people to date each other. She pointed out the problem of finding men; they all were looking for the younger woman. Had she tried the Net? Enid sighed. It was a really sensible letter, mirroring almost to the word what Enid had envisaged; but, seeing it written out, Enid's heart sank. They were all missing the point, and she couldn't put the point into words. So there they were – all those letters, all that excitement, all that disappointment. It was the same the following day – a few cranks, some well-wishers, and a couple of men whose needs were obscure and probably nasty. She had almost given up when yet another letter arrived.

It was from a young woman doing a PhD on the effect of hormone replacement therapy on the post-menopause libido. She had included a list of questions as long as your arm. Enid read through the list and couldn't help feeling that it would take an intrepid lady of sixty-plus some nerve to answer such questions as number eight, headed, 'Your orgasm', followed by: 'a) single or multiple; tick the appropriate box, b) length of time to climax: five, ten or fifteen minutes, please tick…' And so it went on, relentlessly probing the quality, quantity and stimulus needed for these feats of geriatric endeavour. At first Enid hooted with derisory laughter. She might claim to be a liberated widow, pining for another Mr Wonderful, but this questionnaire was a far cry from her fantasies – about as far as the gadgetry in the average sex shop is from most people's sex lives. Who filled in such questions? Who felt comfortable with that level of question? It was like those porn films Gerry liked – fine for a while, but not where she was. She wrote a short letter to the young woman and tried to explain that she had a gaping hole but the questionnaire didn't help fill it.

It had been exhausting – all those letters, all those crazy, crackpot, wacky, sad letters. It was the overwhelming sadness that hit her. How can one hope to find an instant alternative to the relationship that's taken over thirty years to build up? Gerry hadn't walked – he had shuffled. Where could she find a shuffler? Enid wanted a shuffler. She wanted that smell, a smell that was Gerry's. She wanted a calloused hand to creep over the sheet and simply caress her flank. She wasn't going to get it.

Out loud, she found herself saying, 'We're all catching that coach to see the Christmas lights. It isn't what we want. It's just a bloody patronising gesture, thought up by the smug elderly who still have a man in their bed.'

She imagined the letter writers clambering on board the bus – the nasty little man clutching his Viagra; another, a little grubby after months spent living in his car. A very decrepit old lady, but with all her marbles intact, being inched in by a pert nurse. The PhD researcher turned out to be the driver and, diverting everyone from those lights, took them to visit a sex shop first.

Sex shops, if you've never seen one, are rather like hardware stalls filled with little gadgets the purpose of which escapes you. However, this is a fantasy sex shop. There are no creepy men to take your money. Just look – that decrepit old lady with marbles intact is propped up on a chair with her head half buried in what looks like pink hot-water bottles with pubic hair. Several other ladies are looking at bondage gear, with whips, handcuffs and leather pieces not unlike a horse's bridle. Frankly, to some of them it looks exactly like a stable's tack room and Enid feels sure they are asking where the twisted snaffle or drop noseband is. The man who wanted a housekeeper is looking at the dildos. Enid can't help feeling he was a narrow escape. A lady of ample proportions waves one threateningly at some sour old man who dives for cover, only to find himself face to face with videos of grossly fat ladies masturbating. It is a 'something for everyone' shop. An old lady is thrilled with her napkin ring in solid stainless steel. Her neighbour explains the basics of gay sex. The man next to her overhears and cheers up. You can come out at any age, in Enid's fantasies. The old people shuffle round and, picking up a pink fist, look mildly quizzical. The same neighbour whispers something and the pink fist clatters to the ground. The man, who is even more cheerful, picks it up. An absent-minded lady has bought several pairs of flimsy crotchless pants. Has she noticed? Of course she has! She'll wear them at her coffee mornings. 'Real badgers' hair' announces a plastic-wrapped little number – what on earth? But the fantasies are fading. They clamber back into their coach clutching several inappropriate bulging packets. The old lady waves her new hot-water bottle with its gaping rubber vagina and away they go to see those Christmas lights, bless their hearts. What the WI make of their purchases when they stop for tea, Enid's imagination is not prepared to speculate.

The ad hadn't worked, had it? All that excitement and nothing to show for it! Did real people really meet their partners this way? Was it because she was old – a widow – that the gaping hole (no – not that hot-water bottle) remained? Enid reminded herself yet again that it took thirty years to long for that calloused hand to stroke her thigh, but she couldn't quite believe yet that it had gone for ever, for ever and for ever.

Enid stumped off to the garden and hacked away at some overgrown plants. Autumn was ruthlessly killing off flowers that till recently had glowed with ruby-red vigour. Now the first frosts had frozen out life and left a tangled mess where a plant had flourished. Enid cleared the mess and any weeds while thinking how gardens were hell for analogies, especially in the autumn. Death and dying – it was worse than a hospital.

The phone rang and she sprinted to the house in order to get there before the caller rang off. It was Sal, moaning that she was exhausted.

Enid was pleased to be distracted from her garden in its death throes but the twins were a heavy price to pay for getting away from the melancholy. She drove over and found her daughter looking like a beached whale.

'Sorry, Ma, I'm knackered. Could you have them overnight and drop them off at school tomorrow? How a working mum with children handles another pregnancy, I just can't think. By the way, heard any more from India?

'Not yet, love. To tell you the truth, I've rather put it out of my mind. Actually, I've been taking Douglas's complaint that I'm becoming a bore seriously.'

'Oh lor! What have you been up to?'

'I placed an ad in *The Sunday Times* saying that I was a widow, sixty and lonely.

'Ma! Did you have to?'

'Yes, I think I did. It didn't work. I won't bore you with the replies now – some other time. Do you want me to pack the school clothes?'

'I'm going to be an angel in our play,' announced the far-from-angelic Sophie.

'I'm a shepherd,' added Beatrice.

'Well, I'm more important than you,' said Sophie tactlessly.

'No, you are not. You're just a soppy girly angel. I'm a shepherd. I can hit you.'

'Why can shepherds hit angels, Beatrice?' queried Enid.

'Shepherds are boys – only Miss made us take a name out of a hat thing. I got shepherd and Sophie got angel. God is a girl – Angela; she wears glasses.'

'She smells; her dad is a mender,' said Sophie.

'What does he mend?'

'Roads and things.'

Enid found these forays into the world of six-year-old twins quite riveting. She could see some politically correct young teacher determined to challenge the biblical orthodoxy. 'God is a road mender's daughter' seemed as good a start as any. She wanted to probe further, but concentration time was up and the twins were busily discussing Guy Fawkes, the next excitement in their lives.

'He wanted to blow up the Houses of Parliament.'

'Don't we all,' said Enid, dryly.

'Where are they?' asked Beatrice.

'In London,' replied Enid.

'Mummy says we are going to have a bonfire and fireworks in the field. London's a bit too far to go,' said Sophie.

They tumbled out of the car and headed towards the biscuit tin, leaving Enid to gather their clobber and bring it into the house. At first they wanted to paint. No sooner had Enid got the paints out than they changed their minds. Beatrice wanted to play Junior Scrabble and Sophie wanted to watch *Blue Peter*. Enid sat on the floor and put out the Scrabble board. Beatrice changed her mind and decided to watch *Blue Peter* as well. Enid cleared up the Scrabble – then slipped away to get their tea. She had injudiciously made them a wobbling jelly. After the fish fingers she produced the jelly. The phone rang. Would she like to go to a fund-raising dinner at the end of November in aid of a cancer charity? There was a whoop of joy from the kitchen. Enid didn't want to go in the slightest but said 'yes'. The noise from the kitchen was like yelping pups. Enid arrived back to find the jelly being hurled round the kitchen. The twins were ecstatic and shrieking with joy.

It took Enid well over an hour to clear up the kitchen. How many women, and particularly older women like her living alone, have to mop up jelly in order to feel wanted? There must be some way of scrambling out of this pit called widowhood. Later, with the twins asleep, she sat in front of the television, unable to concentrate on any of the programmes offered, and felt sorry for herself.

Where was she going wrong? Surely by now she should be over Gerry? But if truth be known, it wasn't Gerry, was it? He had been her lovable old thing, riddled with eccentricities – not to mention downright faults, possibly leaving her to mop up a bigamous marriage. He had stranded her between the privileged background he had rejected and a middle-class smug world he railed against.

It's all very well for you, Gerry. You could take off whenever you liked. Hole up in India with Mumsi and Vijaya. What about me? Her imagination whirred.

What about you, you stupid cow? If you think mooning about sex and mopping up jelly is any way of filling that gaping hole you bang on about, just think again. Get out, join the WI, or are you too sophisticated? Oh dear, oh dear – thought about an Open University degree? The annual summer bash is legendary. You can't face reading Milton on your own? Come off it! You wouldn't understand Milton if your life depended on it. It's just some kind of nappy disinfectant to you. As for sex, Adam masturbating is as near as you are likely to get. So forget it, you wrinkly old bat – you're on your own; now grow up.

The twins are in bed. Enid is pushing the iron with great ferocity. Not that there is much ironing with none of Gerry's shirts, hankies or well-worn trousers. Ironing finishes and, still full of self-pity laced with pull-yourself-together kick-up-the-bum, difficult at the same time. Enid sits down to an evening's television. There is a situation comedy, a 'des res' among programmes – with a wife with pert tits and a whiplash tongue after a day in the office being a high-powered executive. A wet, weedy house-husband bleats about the whites not being white enough. Should he change the brand of soap powder? There are two children straight from drama school and about as unconvincing. Press another button – football. Press another button – a game show.

'For twenty points, bringing your score up to sixty, can you tell me how many wives Henry the Eighth had?'

'Stands to reason, doesn't it? – eight!' suggests the beaming, strapping hulk of a man. Press another button – a car bonnet is open, a man in overalls is talking to another who looks suspiciously like a well-known racing driver and they are discussing camshafts. Press again – a cowboy lurks at the back of the veranda. There is the pounding of hooves and a posse of half a dozen more cowboys arrives. Our guy by the saloon door manages, with a modicum of effort, to wipe out all six. And so to bed. No doubt the strapping hulk would put that quotation down to Mae West.

Eventually next day arrives. There is a letter from India.

Enid held it at arm's length and invented a myriad of trivial reasons why she couldn't open it. At last she decided that the only way to read it was upside down. It would take time to work out what was written. It wouldn't come as such a shock then. She read:

Dear Enid Tanner

Mumsi had her suspicions. Ran is doubled up with curiosity. Your honeymoon suggestion is spot on.

Daddyji dead! Well I never! Mumsi and I have done a lot of crying but, with all his comings and goings, we are progressive. We knew at heart there was 'a you and Sal' knocking around somewhere.

I guess I am your stepdaughter.

Vijaya

Upside down, it took a while to read the letter. Mumsi, Ran and Vijaya seemed to have accepted Gerry's death. The letter didn't say enough. How old was Vijaya? When did Gerry meet Mumsi? How did Mumsi survive financially? What caste were they all? Enid had only the vaguest notion of caste and what it meant. Vijaya hadn't sent a photo. Enid wanted to know if the blurred photo she had in her desk was of Mumsi. She would compose a letter tomorrow – suggest a definite date for the honeymoon; only, didn't Indian marriages have to wait till an astrologer gave the go-ahead? Enid was full of muddled notions about India. Were they vegetarians? Was Vijaya a virgin? How progressive was 'progressive'? Gerry had spent several years there before they married – was that when he lived with Mumsi? He would never talk about his time in India other than the odd disparaging remark. His description of eating shrimp caught in the Ganges was enough to make one throw up.

'Granny, don't you ever listen? I can't find my reading book. Miss gets furious if we lose our reading books.'

Enid was delighted that she could get rid of the twins very soon. A little twin went a very long way. She drove back from dumping them at school with the sudden realisation she had forgotten the highlight of her week. She was going out to dinner.

It was Sam and Jane who had invited her to dinner. She would drink just one glass of wine, as she was driving. Enid promised herself she wouldn't mention the letter. She would have to think of something else to say about herself. There wasn't anything –

nothing interesting, anyway. But had there ever been anything? Frankly, no! When Gerry had been alive, Enid's life revolved round his so completely that in many ways she'd atrophied. There are thousands of sad, lonely women who have allowed themselves to be sucked dry by men as sad and inadequate as themselves.

Tonight will be different. Turn the page to a new beginning!

It was raining. The mud clung to Enid's high heels. Rain plopped on her newly washed hair. A drop landed on her nose, which had been powered – and the car didn't start. She went back into the garage, found the spray and opened the bonnet. She sprayed the leads, getting a large splodge of grease on her coat, mud on her tights and filth on her hands. She was late, wet and muddy.

'The car; it wouldn't start.'

A lady Enid didn't know observed, 'That's why I keep a husband, just for those occasions.'

The tactless cow!

'That's why I'm looking for another husband – for car maintenance and keeping me warm in bed.'

A little risqué – she hadn't yet been introduced. Then she was – and, as usual, couldn't remember anybody's name. They trooped into the dining room before she had even been offered a drink; a sure sign of being in disgrace.

'Bet you can't remember my name!' He smiled engagingly.

Enid laughed, 'Got it in one! Can you remember mine?'

'Yes, I can, as a matter of fact. I had a great-aunt called Enid. She was rather splendid – nursed in the 1914–18 war. Her boyfriend was killed right at the end, so she never married. She ran one of those public school charities in the East End. I used to go down to her centre in the holidays and help out.'

'Patronising, wasn't it? I mean the young gentry seeing how the other half live.'

'Very. Do you think that matters?'

Their conversation drifted cheerfully back and forth. She still didn't know his name, what he did or whether he was married. She got through to the end of the evening without any useful information about him. Every time her neighbour on her other side engaged her in conversation, an invisible rubber band sprang her back to whoever it was. She learnt about being a young public school boy, flung into the depths of East End culture. He still had a friend from those days, a butcher called Al who had become a Labour councillor.

'I thought butchers were essentially conservative,' said Enid.

'Quite right. They are; so's Alf. He sent his lads to City of London – a private school. But Alf is a realist. He wanted to help his community, particularly the new immigrants. There's lots of friction between the different groups. The Labour Party was the only power for getting something done, although now I gather the Lib Dems are as strong.'

'I thought the East End had weird, nasty parties like the British National Party.'

'They do. Alf's had graffiti on the walls and threatening letters and excreta through the letter box. And his kids have been beaten up.'

Now it was End's turn. 'Whoever it was' wanted to know about her – not those dreary details about name, address and phone number. He wanted to know her opinion. Enid, whose opinion-making skills had shrivelled to nearly nothing, struggled to put into words the half-formulated views she found lurking inside her.

'Do you know…' he said, smiling over the coffee, 'do you know my name yet?'

'I've been too embarrassed to ask.'

'It's Mark, Mark Everington.'

It wasn't until she was safely in the car that Enid could begin to romanticise about her evening or, to be specific, about Mark. It was lovely to feel really in touch with a man again. She had taken for granted the confidence she felt with Gerry at her side – bellicose old thing; he'd grumble down one end of the table while she chirruped away the other end. Being a widow was different. It was no longer necessary to keep half an ear cocked. Chirruping had disappeared too. It takes confidence to chirrup – ask any canary! But tonight she felt for the first time since Gerry's death that she was an attractive woman, that she could still attract attention in her own right. What really had made her evening was Mark asking her opinion.

He wanted to know my opinion. What I thought! I haven't had a public opinion for years – just those inside ones. I have those two-a-penny. As for his looks – he had kind, shrewd eyes set in a pleasant face, which was a little leathery. He was almost stout; not wobbly fat but firm fat – 'chunky', that was the word. Actually, he was lovely.

Next day, whistling outrageously out of tune, Enid got cracking on that letter to Vijaya.

Dear Vijaya

There are so many questions I want to ask you and Mumsi. Could I ask for a photograph? I found a photo in one of Gerry's pockets. Could it be of you? Gerry left very little money. I am so excited that you and Ran accept my invitation to spend your honeymoon here. Let me know the date of your wedding. I thought I would book you a short trip round the Highlands of Scotland. Is three weeks about the time you expected to be here? Did you know that Gerry belonged to a very grand family?

(It wasn't really true. He didn't come from a very grand family, just a family who thought themselves very grand. Let's face it, that is an entirely different matter.)

Please let me know if there is anything special you want to do and write back with more news of Mumsi, where you live and what you do. I know nothing about India.

Enid

She continued to whistle, then picked up the phone to Eleanor. Give her the shock of her life, she hoped. Henry answered. He was polite. She refrained from asking if he'd shot any ramblers recently. Then Eleanor came to the phone, with a Dover sole still in the back of her mind.

'Eleanor, your brother appears to have been a bit of a lad.'

'Have you found out something?'

'Only that he has a wife and child in Bombay. His daughter is coming over here for her honeymoon. Can she come and stay with Aunty?'

'Oh God! What is she called?'

'Vijaya.'

'I'm bowled over! I don't know what to say. Do they want money?'

'Vijaya wrote asking for a dowry. I replied that Gerry was dead but I was willing to give her, for her dowry, a honeymoon over here.'

'Unnecessarily generous of you. I don't know why, but people on limited incomes are inclined to be generous. It's self-explanatory, in a way. Do we really want her here? I mean, we don't know what she's like.'

'Kith and kin,' said Enid tartly.

'I suppose you're right. OK, put us on the itinerary. Incidentally, how are you managing? Not run out on any more weekends, I hope?'

'Chance would be a fine thing!'

'Well, I did tell Maud what happened and she said she'd leave it for a bit.'

'She has – a very long bit.'

Eleanor ignored the waspish tone of voice and asked after Sal and the twins. Another on the way – how exciting for Enid! Enid retorted that only someone without grandchildren close by could ever say that about a baby.

'But it will make you feel wanted. Isn't that what you crave?'

No, it wasn't. Enid rang off. Some loving creatures might enjoy every moment of their grandchildren growing up, but not Enid. Why were women of her age bundled into the nursery or, alternatively, given a packet of seed, a trowel and told to garden… or made to see those old Christmas lights with the over-sixties? There was more to life, wasn't there? She began to whistle again.

Sophocles wasn't best pleased with this widow business. It played havoc with his routine. The walks had petered out to the occasional trip round the lanes, with not a hope of a rabbit. His food arrived sporadically and he couldn't find a place to lie where Enid didn't trip over him. But the last day or two had been a real improvement. They had taken the car and gone for long meaningful walks on the moors without his lead.

Five

Mark rang about a month later, just before Christmas, to ask her if she'd like to go to a concert. If the truth be known, she had already forgotten about him, added to which Enid was completely unmusical. She was stunningly unmusical. But could you keep her away from that concert? Not on your life! Opportunity knocks and you bloody well run for it.

'How marvellous! I'd love to. Where did you say?'

Sophocles had an even longer walk and the tuneless whistling went on and on. Who could she tell? If she had been fifteen, there would have been a best friend. Even in her twenties there were parents who might listen. But now there was nobody. Sal would snap and tell her to be her age. Dolly would either be a green-eyed monster or, like Sal, snap at her disparagingly. There was only one person left; she'd tell Adam.

'I think I'm in love, Adam,' she said at lunch, a little melo-dramatically.

'You should go on that programme – *Ricki Lake*. They are always in love on that programme.'

He was right. Enid watched it carefully for the following week. The first time she saw it, there were six really fat young people sobbing their hearts out and asking for help. A jolly faggot waved his magic slimming recipe. The tears flowed even harder as one by one they admitted no one loved them.

'Try being over sixty and a widow,' Enid told the television set.

The following day another six women wanted to find their first loves. Reconciliation and all that were slightly spoilt by one half of this 'true love' business being married to someone else, while another fellow looked aghast at the idea. The following day was more complicated. It was another six women whose hus-bands were sleeping around – more tears, more reconciliation, more love.

'You know, Adam, you were absolutely right. I watched *Ricki Lake* last week. It was a good idea of yours.'

But Adam wasn't interested; he didn't say anything. After lunch she asked him if he would like to decorate the house for Christmas. She showed him the small tree she had bought.

'Not much,' he said, taking the box and looking at the tinsel and decorations. He meant it. He kept hiding the decorations and putting the tinsel behind the sofa and chairs.

'It's meant for children. I am an adult.' He spoke very resentfully.

Sal was waddling round with varicose veins and backache. She invited Enid to see the famous nativity play with God the road mender's daughter. The hall was packed. Miss Roberts played a selection of carols and there was a hum on the far side of the curtain, which, when it reached a certain pitch, was greeted with a huge '*Sssh*'.

This had happened three or four times before the headmistress stood up and explained that the play had been created by the children themselves. Up went the curtain and the play began.

Mary and Joseph wandered unsteadily into the middle of the stage. Mary announced that her legs were killing her. Could she have a cup of tea? Joseph replied that she was meant to ask for somewhere to stay, not a cup of tea. She then said that she was coming to that because she thought she was having a baby. There was a shiny door with 'The Ritz' written above it. Someone was giggling on the far side. Joseph opened the door, which nearly fell off its hinges.

'The wife is having our baby,' he said in a pleasant Yorkshire brogue.

'So what? My missus has had twelve,' Sal groaned.

'We want a bed to have it in,' continued Joseph.

'Well, you can't! I've got the Leeds football team staying here.' There were lots of yah-boo noises off stage from Newcastle supporters.

'You can 'ave t' shed. My ole man keeps 'is pigeons there.'

'*Coo!*' roared the chorus off stage.

Accents having slipped once more into broad Yorkshire, the

pace quickened. The interior of the shed looked very snug.

Mary said 'Ouch' very loudly and asked for some hot water, which arrived in a watering can.

Joseph faced the audience and announced that it was half a boy and half a girl. The audience leant forward; this was serious stuff. Enter God, in a white sheet, who explained that she also was neither a girl nor a boy.

'Must run in the family,' hissed Sal.

God carried on about how important the baby was, when there was a loud knock and a side of the shed nearly fell over.

'We are shepherds,' announced Beatrice. If she'd said it once, she'd said it a thousand times at home. The shepherds were dressed in jeans, tweed jackets and flat caps. They were meant to wear green welly boots but that message hadn't got through. Instead they wore a variety of highly coloured wellies. The overall effect was pretty eccentric.

'Urps,' said some lad or other, clapping his hand over his mouth. 'We forgot to mention the star.' He turned to the audience.

'You see, there was this star – much brighter than the others. We wanted to find out what it meant, and all that.'

A buzz went through the parents. Was this part of the play or was Roy extemporising? But back to the story…

Several sheep and some cows had arrived and were sitting cross-legged by the shepherds. One or two were waving at their parents. Face-paints and thick woolly sweaters with tights were worn by both sheep and cattle. The cattle had horns – or were they Jacob sheep?

A star had arrived a little late in the day. It was held aloft by means of a bamboo pole.

A bright light showed up on the other side of the stage. It looked like the gypsy scene out of *Carmen* but was in fact the kings. A pretty tacky crowd of kings they made. Their teacher was obviously a staunch republican; the kings were dressed in dinner jackets and crowns – or an approximation of. The head king looked at the stars and told his colleagues they ought to go to the shed but first buy a present. Gold, frankincense and myrrh had been translated into a box of chocolates, some smelly soap and a bottle of scent. There was a quick change of lighting and a return to the shed where Jesus had been laid in a wicker basket. The kings shuffled forward and handed over their presents to Joseph and Mary, who looked a little bored by now. Then lo and behold! Standing on top of a ladder, looking clean and almost angelic, there was Sophie, dressed in an old petticoat of Sal's.

'Thank you for watching our play.' She drew a deep breath, 'It's a play about today. That is why some of us wear today clothes, and why girls play parts usually played by boys. It's meant to make you think.'

The piano played several chords and everyone sang 'Away in a Manger'.

Sal and her mum waited for the budding thespians to change into their clothes and come out into the playground.

'I was good, wasn't I?'

'So was I,' said Beatrice.

'You were both wonderful,' said Enid, carefully.

They drove home. It was already dark and Christmas lights twinkled everywhere.

'Do you feel a little like Mary?' Enid asked her daughter.

'After that play, I assume I'm giving birth to some transsexual person who is going to grow up to be a staunch republican. I don't think there'll be any extra stars knocking around and I don't think I'll need a watering can full of water at any time. Nor am I prepared to make do with a shed.'

'I don't know why, but Christmas is so hyped these days that it can only be an anticlimax. Do you remember last year? We dragged Gerry along and he fell asleep! The twins were furious with him. You know Adam? Well, I invited him to decorate the tree. He hid the tree stuff and shoved tinsel behind the chairs and then told me rather pompously that he was an adult and decorating trees was for kids. I was put in my place, so to speak.'

Enid didn't come in. She dropped Sal and the twins and then drove home – just a flicker of independence. Sal probably never noticed. It was a start, like not phoning. Enid wanted to give Sal all the space she needed over this baby.

Anyway, Enid had other things to think about. The concert was tomorrow evening. She had left it late, but was determined to buy something special. After all, she had done all her Christmas shopping and didn't need any booze this year. She'd spend the booze money on a dress.

Harrogate is a very appropriate town for dispensing hospitality. She has a penchant for bright colours. Her shops are expensive and stylish for the older woman. Harrogate is a town that appreciates Noel Coward and adores Alan Bennett; where one wears make-up, carries a spare pair of tights in the handbag and ends the day having coffee – at Betty's famous tea rooms, of course. It is comfortable. Handsome people do the crosswords and argue about felling trees. And one can buy coriander all the year round.

Enid sighed. It seemed ridiculous to dress up in order to buy a dress. Who cares what she wore? But Harrogate did.

'Did you see that, Carol? Honestly! In this day and age, there's no need to go around with safety pins keeping you together. I mean, if you're overweight, go to the gym.'

Carol was overweight. She never went near a gym so she grunted. Her friend continued, 'At her age you have to make just that bit more of an effort. She can't have been a day under sixty-five. It's the menopause – it can make them very depressed. They lose all interest, you know.'

Carol knew all too well, and she wasn't a day over thirty.

Enid had put on the skirt she'd worn at Gerry's 'do'. It was a good quality skirt, or had been. It was about ten years old – a long time with middle-aged spread. Anyway the safety pins only showed when she fastened it in front of the beastly gossiping assistant, who took one look and told Carol.

Enid looked at rails of dresses. There was only a handful in her size and of that handful there were usually only one or two she'd be seen dead in. Then there was the price. So it took an age to pin down what she wanted or, rather, was prepared to be seen in. For nearly a hundred pounds, Enid found a blue fine wool dress that barely went in at the waist, had a pretty neckline and a fairly full skirt.

Hair was washed and nails filed neatly, a hint of make-up applied. It was left over from the seventies in an old sponge bag. Then a dab of cologne – everyone knows you can't go wrong with cologne. Enid didn't have enough money for shoes; so her old black Louis heels would have to do. She gave them a good rub. As it was winter, it was necessary to bundle into a warm coat, shove a scarf round her head and find her gloves and a hanky – some kitchen paper would have to do.

The concert was held in the long gallery at Effingham Hall – known locally to some as 'Fuck 'all'. Without resorting to Christmas baubles, the interior was a delight with banks of holly and poinsettias. The lighting was focused on the magnificent ceiling with frolicking nymphs and Pan chasing each other round bacchanalian scenes, interspersed with fronds of ivy and imitation vegetation. Enid craned her neck while looking for Mark.

She met Mark in the hall. 'About as gauche as a fifteen-year-old,' he was unkindly to proclaim later on. Certainly she felt as if her knickers were about to fall down, as if she were in some slapstick farce. What if she got his name wrong? It was Mark, wasn't it? Would they shake hands, kiss or just bend at the waist? Had her mascara smudged? Did she snip the price tag off the dress? *Panic*!

Mark saw her first. As he said afterwards, it looked as if she was auditioning for *Brief Encounter*. He dined out on their evening for weeks afterwards. There was too much of a crush to shake hands, so she let out a little yelp and apparently said, 'It's you!' He reassured her that it was, and steered her to their seats.

'Isn't it beautiful?' said Enid, craning her neck yet again.

'I hope you like Monteverdi?' said Mark.

Enid didn't know who Monteverdi was but guessed he was probably the composer. Wasn't he one of those early guys whose music all sounded alike? Didn't he write songs for men with very high voices? Let's face it, she hadn't a clue. But a lifetime of being unmusical had taught her some native cunning.

'Yes, I'm not that keen on Stockhausen. He always sounds as if he's dropped some iron filings. I find the twentieth century a challenge at times, but the early stuff I love.' Phoney is as phoney does – Mark wasn't fooled for a minute.

The music began and Enid didn't listen to a note. Her whole body was tuned to the pleasure of being dressed up and sitting next to an attractive man. She found herself thinking about the proximity of his penis to her. It started quite innocently with fond memories of Gerry. The fond memories became fonder memories. Next she wanted her nipples to be taut but they failed to comply. She undressed slowly in her imagination, then undressed Mark. That took her till the interval.

'Would it sound the same in some municipal hall, I wonder?' said Enid. She held her glass of champagne high and looked at the bubbles.

'I don't see why not,' retorted Mark. 'Have you noticed how when you ring banks and similar places they put you on hold and play the 'Four Seasons'? It sounds like the 'Four Seasons' and, by God, it is the 'Four Seasons'! They play it throughout the country.'

Four Seasons? Enid did some quick thinking. She knew she ought to know who wrote the beastly thing.

'That's the one that sounds as if the needle's got stuck in the groove, isn't it?'

They chatted on. Enid, although out of her musical depth, kept well afloat when it came to the chitchat of life. Soon they were sitting down again and, sure enough, an earnest young man with a receding hairline sang several songs about his true love. Enid tried to listen to the words but it was impossible to hear them. She surreptitiously looked round and noticed the different expressions on the faces in the audience. She spent the rest of the concert inventing words to fit the expressions like, 'I'm dying to have a pee' – all perfectly harmless and, some might say, an improvement on the first part of the recital.

After the clapping had died down and the audience were moving to the buffet supper in the great hall, Enid suddenly said, 'Vivaldi!' Mark smiled and said, 'Quite right.'

The buffet supper was wonderful. Gastric juices flew, greed's eyes popped out of her head – with dislocated eyeballs all round. There were huge platters with cold meats, new potatoes glistening with an olive oil sheen and salads mixing flowers, fruit, nuts and greenery. There were pea pods tossed in a dressing and haricot beans nestling in a bed of leeks and baby carrots. For the following course there were black chocolate gateaux quivering in cream, mandarin oranges soaked in Cointreau and a slippery smooth crème brulée.

'Where does it all come from?' asked Enid. 'I mean, half the vegetables and fruit are out of season.'

'They're flown in. It probably takes no longer for a plane of strawberries to get here from Kenya than it does for some spuds to trundle down from the Borders.'

Mark handed her a plate. 'Roughly what you want?'

'Exactly what I want.' They smiled.

It was a terrible squash and difficult to hear each other talk. Enid smiled at one or two people she knew, mostly women on the ladies' luncheon circuit, who barely concealed their surprise at seeing Enid there. Or were they looking at her smart dress? Mark, too, nodded and spoke to any number of people.

Inevitably, Christmas became a subject. What was she doing? Enid explained that Sal was about to give birth and she would be left with the terrible twins. Enid found herself describing the twins and some of their antics. She gave a graphic description of their nativity play, starting with God the road mender's daughter.

Mark laughed comfortably.

'You know,' he said, 'we still feel very uneasy when we're challenged on gender issues. Don't you think so?'

It was those last few words that got to her. Once more, he wanted her opinions. Gerry didn't want other people's opinions. He didn't love Enid for her opinions. No, she didn't challenge his prejudices or require him to be honest with himself. She accepted him, warts and all. Not like some women who are real wart removers – very painful they are too, with acerbic tongues and whiplash retorts – real harridans from hell. Here was a man asking her to have an opinion about gender issues. Did she have an opinion? Wasn't her life itself a statement? Born a girl, with a peep at a boy round about six – how could she compete with that thing? Education was no help. It ended in a secretarial course; a secretary who couldn't spell – that is what she was when Gerry found her playing tennis. She married without an opinion – at least, not about marriage. Loving didn't seem much of an opinion, not like, 'Should female circumcision be banned?' Anyway, her enigmatic knight had had all the answers. She admired him for that and grew to feel really secure with the often surly and unpopular opinions he growled out in public. In a curious way,

Enid felt that to have an opinion was to betray Gerry, to make a mockery of her thirty-three years of married life.

'I don't know if I have any strong opinions about gender issues.'

'But you must, if not for yourself, for your granddaughters.' Mark was persistent.

'I'm delighted for them to be major generals, firefighters or take the top job at the UN. I suppose I'd be less happy if they married money and disappeared into Harrods, if you know what I mean.'

'What if they had the same kind of life as you?'

Do I detect an attempt to make me emote all over the crème brulée and admit that I've led a wasted life? Enid thought angrily. Really! This is no place to bare breasts. Well, not in that kind of way, or whatever I'm being asked to do.

She looked Mark full in the face.

'You know, you are an intellectual bully. So was my husband, come to think of it. Can't I just enjoy the concert and this delicious food?'

He smiled the smile of a charming man who knows it. In a moment of perception rare for Enid, she realised that he was bathed in his own conceit. She found herself talking pleasantly for another hour – just easy conversation. It was for her a kind of debriefing as she withdrew what emotion and fantasy she had invested. It had been another narrow escape and, this time, the real thing, not a fantasy.

She drove home after a friendly farewell – no kiss on the cheek, no lengthy grip of the hand. It had been a lovely evening for someone as unmusical as her. She had behaved like a teenager about Mark. Can't women of her age behave like that? But common sense had prevailed. There were no fantasies on the road back. Sophocles welcomed her warmly. The cat wasn't there, as he was out gadding. She locked up the house, made herself a cup of tea to help the crème brulée and then calmly, cheerfully and by now sleepily, went to bed. No one need know what a fool she had nearly made of herself but Adam.

Mark's view of the evening was mildly malicious, as well as funny. He amused Jane and Sam by telling them that Enid was about as sophisticated as a fifteen-year-old and totally unmusical. She looked really elegant and had made a great effort. Had she been married to a bully? She seemed deeply reluctant to venture a serious opinion about anything. Mark went on to say that Enid was typical of that generation of women who were never encouraged to develop their intellect.

Jane then told Enid what he had said. She added that Mark was a dear and such fun. He'd never married and never been short of a woman on his arm.

'*Yuk!*' That was Enid's response when she put down the phone. How dare Mark ring up her friends and gossip about their evening together! How bloody patronising of him to say she looked really elegant. As for all that business about opinions, he should ask her in the bath if he wanted opinions. She was full of them there. It was a salutary lesson. Enid still wanted a man, but not any man. She still wanted her old curmudgeon.

Christmas arrived, with only a few Christmas cards. Let's face it, she hadn't sent any either. Adam's decorations had been redone by the twins who came over to give Granny a hand. Granny was sad.

'Why are you sad, Granny?' asked Sophie.

'Christmas is the season for loving. I haven't got Grandpa to love, so I feel lonely.'

The twins looked at their grandmother thoughtfully.

'Like when Mummy and Daddy go away and leave us?'

'Yes, poppet, something like that.'

'We love you and Baby Jesus loves you.'

'Gosh! I'm lucky. Now, who is going to help me make some mince pies?'

Wonky mince pies are all part of Christmas. The twins made a great many, leaving an indescribable mess for Enid to clear up.

The great day dawned with the cat sicking up a large amount of what was probably dead mouse. Enid took Sophocles for a wet and windy walk. No one was about. The rain dribbled down on the track making rivulets in the soft, sandy surface. Gusts of wind shook the naked branches and the world looked cold. Enid thought about all that Baby Jesus bullshit. She started with her few facts of biblical knowledge – an angel telling Mary she'd have a baby. What a wanker! Christmas was just a mid-winter opportunity to have a piss-up.

That bloody skirt again! With the safety pin leaving enough room for a real blow-out. She drove over to find Sophie and Beatrice tearing open their presents, breaking several and complaining that they didn't like others. On being told by Sal that any they didn't like could be sent on to poor children who didn't have presents, Beatrice observed, 'They are boring. Bet you poor children find them boring too.'

Whereupon Sophie asked, 'Does Father Christmas go to poor children?'

'Anyway, he doesn't really exist. It's just Daddy.' Beatrice had sussed this for real. She saw her dad putting the stocking at the bottom of her bed.

'Oh, I know that,' retorted Sophie. 'But do poor dads give their children stockings?'

'Not Muslims and Hindus, people like that. They believe in different things.' This profound sociological debate was brought to an end with an 'Ouch' from Sal, followed by, 'Bugger! My waters have broken. I've started.'

Douglas slid back his chair and said, 'OK, we're off. You can manage, can't you, Enid? I'll have to get back for feeding. I've given everyone Christmas day off.'

'Can't the twins and I do that?' Enid had images of herself tearing round on a tractor.

'No.' It was said with particular finality.

Roger failed to make Christmas Day by ten minutes. Pink, wrinkly and with a piercing yell, he arrived home the day after Boxing Day. Roger Gerald Weatherman had a shock of black hair and appeared to be mouthing obscenities a lot of the time.

'Mummy says it's wind,' announced Beatrice, who was clutching him like a rag doll.

Enid had gone home to feed the cat and, after a few hours' sleep, arrived early enough to give the twins breakfast and stayed in a state of desperate, overworked boredom till their bedtime. Far from forgetting, she remembered all too clearly the aching tedium of looking after young children – the frightful food they liked to eat, the concentration span of a matter of seconds, the pleas that she played Junior Scrabble and did demandingly dull jigsaw puzzles of horses' heads leaning over the gate. Then there were the muddy winter walks for the dogs, for the grandchildren – traipsing over rutted wastes with gloves half on, snot dribbling down nostrils and a perpetual wail about the injustices of this world.

'Mummy lets us stay in and watch telly in the winter,' moaned Sophie.

'Yes, she does, and she lets us have sweets,' added Beatrice.

'Then why did Mummy suggest we all go for a walk?'

'She only meant you and the dogs.'

'Mummy has a lot on her hands with Master Roger. I gather he makes a great deal of noise all night.'

'Do you think he was properly cooked?' asked Sophie.

'What do you mean?' Enid hadn't quite cottoned on to what Sophie was getting at.

'He's so skinny and floppy. He can't do anything.'

'You just wait. He'll be a damn nuisance in next to no time. Now, come on, girls. Let's get home for lunch.'

Enid was booted out on New Year's Eve. Sal's milk had settled down and Roger was sleeping better. The twins wanted their mum back and Enid realised that both she and Sal had had enough. As for Douglas, she sensed that a little went a long way with mothers-in-law. Or perhaps she was just being ultra-sensitive. Her house was cold. The decorations looked tawdry. The cat was indifferent. Only Sophocles seemed pleased to be home.

The New Year dawned raw, wet, grey and filled Enid with despondency. She mooned round the house, remembering Gerry only a year ago, spluttering about a leaking downpipe. She still hadn't fixed it. She remembered him glaring at the television. Some presenter had had the temerity to suggest that it wasn't always possible to rely on Arab politicians to tell the truth.

'Who the fuck does tell the truth? White Anglo-Saxon public school arseholes? Really, it's such crap. Edie, what's for supper? No more mince pies, I hope. I hate the bloody things.'

She had worked herself up into a maudlin state when the phone rang.

'Hello?' There were several clicks and buzzes before a cautious voice inquired whether Enid Tanner was there. Yes, she was. It was Vijaya.

'Happiness for the New Year, Enid. I am bubbled over with excitement.'

Enid laughed. 'Vijaya, how wonderful to hear from you. Oh, Sal had a boy a week ago.'

'The pitter-patter of tiny feet and all that. Now look, this honeymoon business, Ran and I are very excited. We marry on 4 April. Can we fly over on the tenth? We long to look at Shakespeare's cottage, Windsor Castle, Oxbridge and Reading Gaol.'

'You'll have to write it down. I'll never take it all in. How's Mumsi?'

'Oh, well – you know. She still finds it difficult that Daddyji is dead.'

'Tell her I feel the same way.'

'Doesn't time fly! I must go. I will write soon. Lots of happiness, Enid.'

The phone went dead. Enid found herself whirling around like a dervish. It took several moments before she fully absorbed the phone call. She then did something off the cuff, a spontaneous act to verify what was happening. She rang the Brig.

He was there to take the call in his greenhouse, with rooting powder in one hand and a cutting in the other. There was a mobile phone handy. He hated the beastly thing but they were adamant – it was moving with the times. The Brig wasn't too happy with moving with the times unless it was at a snail's pace.

'Enid, my dear, how lovely to hear from you! Everything settled down now?'

'Not really.' She told him of the letter, the dowry, the second letter and now the phone call.

'My dear girl, any more strange letters and you send them straight to me. Now, you say this girl is called Vijaya?'

Enid added the bit about Oxbridge, Mumsi, and the bridegroom Ran. She also explained that she was going to pay for the honeymoon.

'Look, my dear, I think I'd better come over. We don't want you getting out of your depth, do we?'

The Brig drove over in a squeaky-clean car that clearly wasn't the tip on wheels most people run around in – but then they provided it along with that beastly phone. He eased himself out and then stood, dressed immaculately, with a sharp frost all round him. The grey ice gripped. The lawn, with its cold congealed roses, looked particularly chilling, while his camel hair coat, over rich brown tweed, gave a touch of warmth and reassurance.

Enid had vacuumed the sitting room and worn that skirt. She could just feel the safety pin. The Brig had that effect. She had made coffee with cups and saucers and some shortbread – homemade and just a touch overcooked.

She poured the coffee and offered him a shortbread.

'Thanks for coming, Brig. You did say—'

He cut her short. 'I meant it, Enid. Gerry was a special chap, not a great one to be bound by convention or respectability – the kind of constraints the rest of us live by.'

'Brig, what exactly did he do?'

'One way or another, Gerry did a fine job. He wasn't a great one for drawing attention to himself. That was his great asset. Oh, I know he could be tetchy – not one for licking boots, anything like that. But he's left you a comfortable pension, Enid. He was one of those indispensable people who could be relied upon to show complete confidentiality. Believe me, that is a rare attribute these days. You only have to read the papers. People simply can't keep their mouths shut. Mothers going out to work; now, you never fell into that trap. I put a great many of the nation's ills down to that – and comprehensive education. I have nothing against a comprehensive intake, socially speaking, but the garbage they teach!' He shook his wise old head.

'He always told me that he had deliberately turned his back on his background, that after Reading University he went out to India. I suppose that is when he met Mumsi. Do you think he married her and then committed bigamy with me? Honestly, tell me, did you know about this Indian business?'

The Brig put down his cup of coffee. Achingly slowly, he collected his thoughts before saying, 'Vijaya, you say – not in the first flush of youth. Yes, Enid, I do know about her. I think you'll find Mumsi is really "Savita". I think you'll find that Gerry and Savita met when he worked in India after he left Reading. Gerry didn't marry Savita, but he made over to her his entire personal fortune. She's a wealthy woman. Don't go overboard on this dowry business.'

'Weren't her family horrified? I mean, I always thought Indians were very straight-laced about these things.'

'Savita came from an artistic tradition. She's – how can I say it? – more sophisticated in many ways than you, Enid, and richer. I don't think you need feel any responsibility there. Vijaya, I gather, is quite some "gel", as they said in my day. Do be careful, Enid, I don't want you to be trapped by your naivety. Spontaneous gestures can end in tears.'

The Brig felt he had said enough. He asked about probate, as if it were a smelly old dog, and her income and probed gently into her social life. Enid told him about Adam. She added that a widow's lot was not a happy one. It was lonely, boring and, worst of all, emotionally barren. The Brig belonged to the school of thought that preferred rooting powder to emotions. He also believed that behind every tiresome man there lurks a good woman. Here was one going spare.

'What you need, my girl, is another husband.'

'I tried that. I advertised for a man in one of the more respectable papers. All I got were nutters and randy old men who had been buying Viagra.'

'Dear me! Why don't you take a cruise – or a holiday studying Greek artefacts? Much more suitable!'

'With my pension? You must be joking!'

'Just a thought. Are you sure you couldn't afford a cruise?'

He drove off into freezing fog. Enid watched him go. She suddenly realised that the bloody man still hadn't said what Gerry had done all those years, apart from his antics in India.

'But then, that is typical,' she decided.

She sat in the twilight. It really was a miserable day. She was not thinking about Savita and Vijaya – that was all too complicated. Instead, she mulled over the idea of a cruise. She remembered Mr Shortbread. That wasn't what she wanted, was it? Sophocles rested his head on her lap and looked at her with large sincere eyes.

'It would be Greek artefacts and Etruscan vases with some provincial professor trying to pay off his overdraft,' she told the dog. That, too, wasn't really what she wanted. She shuddered at the idea of being herded with a group of earnest tourists hell-bent on learning all those complicated Greek names.

'Dave, what was the name of Agamemnon's wife? You know, the one who's lover killed him.'

'Clytemnestra, dear.'

'They all sound like nasty diseases to me.'

'Really, Beryl, this trip has cost us a small fortune. You might concentrate a little.'

Beryl was. She was concentrating on Marcus, a retired head-master with a roving eye. They had rummaged round the nether regions of Piraeus together and drunk ouzo while Dave had elected to visit a dig.

God – I mean Brig – you've got it all wrong! I just want to fill that yawning gap left by Gerry and made draughtier still by the status and role of a widow over sixty. Drinking ouzo with a clapped-out schoolmaster isn't the answer! I want someone to fix the downpipe, make me laugh and come to bed with me. The phone went. Enid picked it up without enthusiasm.

It was Dolly asking her if she'd be willing to help organise some entertainment for the over-sixties. One of her Heart Foundation ladies had asked her if she knew anybody. There had been two scandals the previous year, one when the old dears were taken for a day out in London and marched round the Tower, while several committee ladies made a beeline for Harrods and bought designer dresses on expenses. There was also the affair of Cecil – just don't ask about Cecil! After these two disasters, the committee had all but fallen apart.

'The way you dress, Enid, I don't think you will pose a risk by visiting Harrods. But honestly, Enid, the poor old loves are fed up with trundling round the Dales on a mystery tour with an annual outing further afield. They want something with more fun than that.'

'Line dancing! Can't they do that? It certainly went down well on *The Archers*. As you know, Dolly, I loathe fund-raising. But if I'm just being asked to spend it, that's a different matter. Who else is on the committee?'

The first meeting of the volunteers took place round a dining room table. Not a man in sight, which seemed a pity. Enid caught the Chair's eye – or was it Chairman? – so difficult to know these days.

'What, no men?' she asked facetiously.

'It's so difficult,' bleated the Chair, a solid lump of woman with too much make-up and bright red nails. 'We have tried, haven't we, girls?'

'We had Cecil for a while. He was an absolute dear – drove a bus and knew exactly what the pensioners wanted.'

'And?' coaxed Enid.

'Well, it was all a little difficult. He liked cross-dressing, if you know what I mean.' The Chair was breathing deeply.

'He would drive the bus in a variety of ladies' clothing but used to wear the same jaunty hat every time. It was very stylish with a feather – or rather several feathers. It looked like those hats worn by Germans in lederhosen.'

'What was the problem?' asked Enid, intrigued by the idea of a transvestite bus driver whizzing round North Yorkshire with a coach-load of elderly ladies.

'He insisted on using the ladies' loo.' This came from a pursed-lipped lady at the end of the table. After she had spoken there was a knowing nod.

'You mean you kicked him out because he peed in the ladies'?'

'Not exactly. There was a question of insurance. The police advised us and social services got involved.' The Chair was puffing importantly. The remaining ladies practised rectitude with hands folded, buttocks taut and expressions of tight-lipped sanctimony.

'All the same,' persisted Enid, 'what about the over-sixties themselves? Did anyone ask their opinion?' No one answered her.

The Chair, Wendy, was a busy lady who was active with the local Soroptimists. Wendy really was overweight, with heaps of eye make-up, several bangles round her wrists and large flashy rings on her podgy fingers, as well as her bright red nails. Now, with Cecil out of way, she wanted the formalities to start.

'Ladies, look at your agendas please. Item one, new members. It looks as if Enid Tanner needs no introduction. We look forward to working with you, Enid. We're all very informal here. I must also welcome Rose Hepburn.' The Chair paused and smiled at a mousy lady sitting the far side of the table, 'and Ally Smith.' Again, her eye swivelled round to catch another mousy lady with a faded perm who gave a simpering smile. The Chair rattled through several items with a brisk disregard for the niceties of democracy before coming to the meat of the agenda – next year's special outing.

'Nowhere near Harrods this time,' declared a severe lady in a blue suit.

'That is all behind us,' reminded the Chair.

'A trip to Paris for a couple of days,' suggested Janet, who was the treasurer.

'What about the food? I can't see our old people tucking into snails and garlic.'

'Why ever not? They would love it.' Gillian went camping with her husband and two boys. They spent their holiday money on grub and regularly dined off snails and garlic washed down with a local red.

'I think we mollycoddle them too much. We never give them a chance to experience new things.'

The Chair wanted more ideas.

'A coach tour of beautiful gardens,' suggested one of the mice. 'The National Trust has some lovely places.'

A spirited conversation took place about the best time to prune buddleias. Janet reminded everybody that the old people had been to Newby Hall the year before. The highlight had been a ride on the model railway.

'Why don't we link up with Saga and take over a holiday village out of season?' This was Janet's contribution. The next suggestion was Amsterdam, preferably with the tulips thrown in. Wendy turned her ingratiating eye on Enid, who launched herself.

'Frankly, all these suggestions are about being sixty. Why don't we give them a real treat that no one would associate with being over sixty?'

'We've tried the Big Dipper. Some of the old men like it, but the women won't touch it.'

'What about the Chippendales?'

'You mean furniture?' asked someone whose name Enid couldn't remember.

'Not exactly.'

'Then what are the Chippendales?' inquired Janet, whereupon Wendy murmured, 'Through the Chair,' but no one took the slightest notice.

'They are a group of young men who cavort around and make the old feel a little younger. If we throw in a slap-up meal, serve decent wine and generally make sure there is nothing tatty or cheese-paring, it's less work for us than gadding around Paris or Amsterdam, and it really will take everyone out of themselves.' As she spoke she could feel animosity growing from the Chair. Presumably the Soroptimists didn't go in for the Chippendales.

Cautiously, like tortoises creeping out after their winter sleep, the ladies round the table mulled over Enid's idea.

'I don't understand what these Chippendales do, exactly…'

'Well,' began Enid, who had never seen them, 'they are a first-class male act.'

Gillian let out a piercing yell.

'*The Full Monty*, of course! That'll cheer them up. You're so right! We play safe and bundle these old dears into coaches to visit places they have no desire to see and never give a thought to what they'd really like. I think it's a great idea.'

Then one of the drearier women spoke – the one with a floral blouse done up to the neck and half-covered by a shapeless cardigan. Her hair had a DIY look about it. Never judge a book by its cover!

'I took my old mum to see it. She thought it was wonderful. I think it's a terrific idea.'

'Isn't that the film where they show their bits and pieces?' asked Wendy, resigned that her command was slipping fast.

'That's right,' answered Enid. She was surprised that the Chair hadn't remonstrated with her.

'You mean their you-know-whats?'

'Absolutely.'

'You bet! I'm all for it.'

One of the pursed-lipped ladies wasn't to be persuaded, however.

'I don't think it's very nice, myself. I wouldn't want my elderly mother to see anything like that.'

'Who are you to decide what your mother should or should not see?' said Enid, glaring at the woman.

'My mother has led a very quiet life. She would be deeply shocked by men doing – well – behaving like chorus girls.'

'That is just the point,' said Enid, throwing caution to the wind. 'If you've lived in a cardboard box all your life, it's never too late to get out.'

Something had happened. The dreary women round the table metamorphosed into chattering, squealing girls, excited about the idea of seeing the Chippendales. Subconsciously, they felt their breasts levitating and their private parts come to life. They patted their hair and started to preen, while those with husbands were already fobbing them off in their imaginations on daughters-in-law for the evening. The widows – there were three – felt constraints loosen too.

Enid was surprised. She never for a moment thought that her preoccupation with needing an emotional life was one shared by other women. The Chippendales hardly made an emotional life, but they were a damn good start.

It had been the anniversary of Gerry's death and an excellent way to spend it. Was he starting to grow cold in his non-existent grave?

The Brig's visit didn't go unnoticed either. It was his statement that Savita was richer than she was. She knew that Gerry had no private income – any more than she had. They accumulated the odd piece of furniture over the years and several portraits of deadly dull Tanner forbears. But Gerry had no time for investments beyond a pension scheme for Enid. They lived their married life within their income. After his death, she was left enough to run a car and keep the house going, with a modest amount over to lead a comfortable life. It was all she expected. But Savita was a rich woman. All the years she had been married, or whatever, Savita had lived in luxury with her daughter. What arrangement had Gerry and Savita come to? Had he told her that he loved her more than anyone else in the world? Had he swooped back from time to time, repeated his love and kissed his child before flying back to her and little Sal?

The more she thought about it, the more apprehensive she became at the prospect of meeting Vijaya. She regretted her generosity.

All the same, I've said I'll do it. And do it I will – well, up to a point.

It was soon after that she slipped on some ice. It was on the way back from a walk with Sophocles. The snowdrops bowed their heads to the frozen wind. The daffs stood green, cold and unlikely to ever blossom. Catkins shrivelled in the cold and the robin fluffed himself out and sulked. Enid had noticed all this – but not the sheet of ice.

Her ankle yelped silently and then lay inert, radiating great dollops of pain, which prevented her from moving.

'Shit!' she yelled. You never know, even the Queen might sink to that level if entirely on her own. Philip certainly would, alone or not.

Sophocles scampered back and licked her face.

'Oh, fuck off, you beastly dog. I think I've broken something.'

Agonisingly slowly, she dragged herself to the back door. It took at least ten minutes getting the key in the lock and another ten manoeuvring herself to the telephone. She felt sick, cold and frightened. The ankle ached and throbbed.

It seemed like hours before the ambulance trundled up the drive. And when it did, all she could think of was Gerry.

'I can't leave the dog. I'm all on my own.'

A kindly man telephoned Sal. He passed the phone to Enid.

'I'm sorry! I think I've broken my ankle. It's Sophocles, I can't take him to hospital. If I leave the key under the dustbin, could you collect him?'

'You owl, of course I will.'

The pain was still there but, surrounded by skilled people, it wasn't quite so frightening. But it all took an age. There was a long queue of fractures, mostly among the elderly. There was no way Enid could walk, but she was booted out after six hours and handed over to Sal.

'It's so humiliating,' whined Enid.

Beatrice and Sophie were delighted to play doctors and nurses. Enid was very tired and in a certain amount of pain, but she allowed herself to be subjected to her temperature being taken with a pencil. She put the fear of God in them by explaining that on the Continent they used a thermometer up the bum. Bang goes that camping holiday in France!

'Er, I'm not going there. It's disgusting!'

They wound a bandage round Enid's arm, put a pirate's patch over her eye and gave her a shot of medicine – a nasty mixture of cold coffee and Ribena with a dash of tomato ketchup. Worn out by these attentions, Enid fell asleep before supper. She stayed there a couple of days before Sal and she agreed that she'd soon be beyond her welcome.

'It's the driving, Sal. No driving, no food – it's living in the country.'

Sal stocked up on the basics while Roger lay like a pink Mars bar in his cot beside Enid. By now, the snowdrops had shaken off the frost. The daffs were touched by yellow and the catkins flapped in the wind. Sal and Roger drove away and Enid felt a lump in the pit of her stomach.

'What have you been up to?' It was Dolly on the phone.

'I've broken my ankle.'

'I don't mean that. I mean your idea for the over-sixties. You've got them all in a tizz. I heard from Rose – she plays bridge on Tuesdays. Can I come? I've always wanted to see the Chippendales. What did you say about your ankle?'

'I fell on some ice and broke it.'

'You should have telephoned. You'd better come round for a meal. I'll fetch and deliver – don't say another word. Tomorrow do?'

Meanwhile, Enid watched with glee a peach of a row over Gerry's favourite programme, *Pet Rescue*. It was on the news, talked about by those who talk about everything. It even made *Any Questions*. Basically, what had happened was this: three kids –

goats, that is – were at an animal centre ready to be adopted. Mr and Mrs Chaudray and two little Chaudrays, all dressed in Indian clothes, arrived at the centre to adopt the goats. Yes, they had a lovely paddock with shelter and a fair amount of experience with goats. They were turned down as not suitable people. The animal centre suspected they ate goat. Quite rightly, the Chaudrays were incensed and took their case straight to the Commission for Racial Equality. The uproar that followed was quite extraordinary. There were several bandwagons. The animal rights contingent were adamant – goats before Indians. There were several radical Muslim groups who took offence at being told their rituals were cruel and disgusting. Why shouldn't they execute goats? After all, we executed turkeys at Christmas? The Chaudrays were in fact vegetarian, but no one bothered to ask them that.

Enid sat with her leg on a stool and followed the row with great enthusiasm. She watched with fascination the pundits mouthing platitudes. Even poor old Salman Rushdie was asked his opinion. He appeared with the editor of *Goat Breeder*.

Gerry would have loved it. It was on occasions like this that she missed her own special old goat. She could almost smell him in the room, such was her longing to have him back with her.

Dolly was kindness itself. She cosseted Enid and allowed her to bore her with the accident – one of little interest, let's face it.

'We widows have to stick together, Enid.'

Do we really? thought Enid with a shudder. I don't want to stick together with other lonely widows. It's just a form of invisible purdah which I loathe.

'Have you heard this row about *Pet Rescue* and the kids?' asked Enid.

'Yes, I have. I can't see what the fuss is about; goat is delicious. Think of all those benighted rabbits that are made into pets and kept in tiny cages. If that isn't cruel, I don't know what is. Do you know that they'll soon be using pigs' hearts in organ transplant surgery? The antivivisection people are up in arms, but I really don't see why.'

Dolly prattled on. She was no lonely widow. What was her secret? Enid asked herself. She looked round at the warm friendly kitchen where they sat. Dolly had a son in Canada with two children. He couldn't come running if she broke her leg. It then struck Enid that the big difference between them was not the detail of widowhood itself but where their lives were at the time of bereavement. Dolly's husband, Frank, had toppled over from cancer when he was still a successful, busy man. They were both still on that roundabout called success. When Gerry died, he'd been retired, put out to grass. As for Enid, her life had never got started, really, and had certainly not reached the dizzy heights of personal success. She hadn't noticed, with her all-encompassing grumpy old Gerry, that she too needed to grow and become personally confident and successful. Now he was gone. There was this blank section called 'experience' which he hadn't encouraged her to fill. And now there was very little time to fill it.

Hobbling to the front door, Enid received a letter from India that required her to sit down before reading it. After all the revelations, you never knew! Vijaya wrote a long enthusiastic letter. She quite understood about the dowry not including the airfare for herself and Ran but Enid would sock them a trip round the Highlands. Vijaya wrote that it didn't matter at all, as they had pots of money.

Pots of money! Enid was alarmed.

'We are very sophisticated,' the letter continued. 'Not like the peasants who came over and now live in England. No, no we are very different. Who wouldn't be with Daddyji for a father?'

'Do Daddyji's family live in a castle?' the letter asked. 'He used to tell me all about passing the port and the ladies leaving the gentlemen at dinner. I want to see a green baize door. I gather they are now pretty rare.'

'He never told Sal anything like that!' Enid was starting to feel jealous of this new family that had sprung from Gerry's loins. It was the first time she allowed herself to recognise that a green-eyed monster lurked in her breast. Pots of money, green baize doors – this was all the stuff that Gerry held in contempt. He'd spat it all out, along with the silver spoons, and she had loved him with no money, no green baize door and no silver spoons. Enid had believed he'd given his fortune to a deserving cause abroad, not to some floozy who bore his child. Gerry was letting her down in death. Part of her wanted to cancel the whole business of

Vijaya, but it wasn't in her nature. She'd see it through.

No one would call Enid exotic. She was still pretty in a care-less way. She was warm, friendly and practical, but knew nothing of the cash register, the office pecking order, a rush job or even how to use a computer. After school she went to a finishing school: not a smart one in Switzerland, rubbing shoulders with minor aristocracy, but a minor one in Bournemouth with daughters of prosperous farmers – or doctors, like her dad. She played tennis, learnt how to iron a man's shirt and to lay the table for a dinner party. God, what useless rubbish it was! That is what Gerry found attractive. She had been taught the drill and had turned her back on it.

She could almost hear herself saying, 'Honestly, Gerry, we had to hold a handbag, a pair of gloves, a glass, a stale biscuit with something nasty on it and a ciggie – if we admitted to smoking. Then this lady with a squeaky voice would say, "Now girls, when your husbands are invited to receptions, you are their precious pearls at their side."

'I know how to prevent a ladder in my stocking from sullying my pearl status. Don't you think the whole thing is nonsense, Gerry?'

As their relationship developed, so Enid's uncouth naivety grew – not so much into confidence as into dependence.

'Don't change, Edie, always remain the same.'

She had. That was her tragedy. In her sixties she had the sophistication of a twenty-year-old. She was intelligent, thoughtful, caring and beached like a whale while life swam on. And the Vijayas were coming to taunt her, or rather she was letting them taunt her.

While clearing out Gerry's dressing room in those dreary weeks after his death, Enid found an old album of wedding photos. She brushed off the dust and sat on the edge of her bed. There was only Sophocles to talk to, whether he listened or not. Talk to him she did.

'What a frightful hairdo! Of course, bouffant was all the rage – and that eye make-up! Yuk! Come to think of it, I probably still have the eye stuff in a bag somewhere. Mummy made me wear that veil – something to do with a great-aunt. We bought the dress at Selfridges, in the sales. I remember Eleanor was rather shocked I hadn't had it handmade. There, look at Gerry. He never really changed, did he? Mind you, it was his own morning suit – the kind of pompous rot he was all against. Good heavens! Look, there's Andrew, our best man. He's dead, I believe – something nasty. And Mummy and Daddy, looking every inch the successful doctor and his wife. Gerry's parents were rather sniffy about the whole business. They didn't think I was quite out of the right drawer. Funny, isn't it? I mean, the Tanners were very snooty about the blanc de blanc and there's me chucking out the Rev. Weatherall because of his accent. Nothing really changes. It doesn't make sense, does it, Sophocles?'

Nor does it make sense to invite your husband's bastard daughter to stay when you're screwed up with jealousy and strapped for cash, Enid thought to herself.

It's not that she's Gerry's bastard. It's the money and the life-style. I would have liked just a bit of it, so that I could have been frivolous just once in my life.

Am I making a mountain out of a molehill? It became a ritual question every time she found herself thinking about Mumsi, Vijaya and Ran. Part of her was intrigued to find out more about Mumsi, about her affair with Gerry and how far it ran parallel with her own marriage. She kept trying to remember anything he had said – any smell on his clothes, snippets of tickets, or just anything – but she couldn't. So she imagined what reality couldn't provide, namely their sex life. When he found out she was pregnant, did he say, 'Darling, I love you and will care for you and your child for the rest of your life?' It wasn't his style. But apparently it was exactly what he did.

All this was over thirty years ago. Vijaya was certainly a bit long in the tooth to demand a dowry. As for Mumsi, had she lived the life of an outcast all these years? Living from visit to visit, bringing up her daughter. It didn't work. Not even an Indian could endure that. So Enid would try again, but knowing absolutely nothing about India didn't help.

The spring brought out the old routine – digging the garden. Enid found herself with secateurs, fork and trowel. She snipped and dug through the border. With great daring she started the lawnmower and was compensated with that wonderful smell of new-mown grass. The inside of her house was given the equivalent of a short back and sides. It wasn't a particularly nice house, a 1920s barn style, painted white. She paid great attention to the spare bedroom. She didn't want Vijaya reporting back that it wasn't up to snuff.

Wendy, the Soroptimist, rang to say the Chippendales were booked for next November but there would be a meeting to fix a summer programme. Did she have any more bright ideas?

All in all, Enid told Sophocles, she hadn't let the grass of widowhood grow under her feet. But silently she had to admit, as she climbed into her cold double bed dressed in her nasty nightie, there was still that damned hole in her side that needed attention. She wanted to describe it more accurately – an emptiness? No, it felt more physical than that. Was it pining? Not really, not for the Gerry who died, anyway. Maybe she was pining for the Gerry that, somehow, didn't happen – the Gerry who wanted to change the world and ended up propping up the bar; the Gerry, born into privilege, who turned his back and then regretted it; the Gerry who married beneath himself and then had a secret mistress.

'Gerry, you are a sod to do this to me!' she protested.

Six

For the twins' birthday party, Enid offered to pay for a bouncy castle. It was a blustery day of scudding skies, with a sharp wind and bright sun. The bouncy castle was bright blue and wobbled in the wind. The twins were wildly overexcited and ran round waving plastic swords and wearing helmets. They had eight friends coming to their party. Before any of their friends had arrived, they whacked Enid on the bum and told her she was dead.

'Cos you're a wicked, evil witch,' explained Beatrice.

'So what if I am?' grumbled Enid, who felt a little aggrieved, having paid for the bouncy castle.

She retreated to smile at Roger, who had just begun to make appreciative noises.

'Who's a good little boy?' she repeated over and over again, while thinking, What a bloody silly thing to say.

The first to arrive was Darren. He pushed Beatrice over and grabbed her sword before he had even entered the house.

'He's a bit of a handful,' was his mother's parting shot.

Two monosyllabic girls arrived. They stood, tummies thrust forward and thumbs stuck in their mouths. One of them, Sharlene, piddled on the bouncy castle. That was before Darren found the power plug and let all the air out.

Enid served jelly. Darren began it: he threw some jelly at his mate, Simon, who giggled and retaliated. Soon the air was thick with jelly and Enid had some in her hair. She retired to the sitting room – out of bounds – only to be told by Douglas that she mustn't sit down; her backside was also covered.

'Why are you hiding in here while your wife and I put our lives at stake with that lot?'

'Someone must survive and it doesn't look as if it is going to be either of you.'

Barely! Enid crept home, dishevelled and alarmed at the antics of the young and ready for a hot bath.

Eleanor was next to challenge Enid's equanimity. She rang about Vijaya's visit.

'They'll hire a car, I suppose. No one goes by train these days, more's the pity. Henry is rather worried about food…'

Enid interrupted her. 'Lay off Dover sole, just in case.'

'But cook doesn't do curry. Maybe they are vegetarians.'

'Vijaya is rather keen to see the family castle. I thought you and Henry could be the next best thing.'

'Henry isn't very good with foreigners. He thinks we were wrong to give up India.'

'Eleanor, I wish I could be a fly on the wall. You must ring and tell me how it goes. Incidentally, have you heard from Blanche? She's having them for one night only. They're busy doing something or other.'

'Not just something or other. Patrick's giving a very important paper.'

How typical, thought Enid. Gerry's sisters lived in a world of superlatives – never big, rarely bigger, but almost always the biggest – and failing that, the best. Even after all these years, Eleanor could, with a swift turn of phrase, make Enid see herself as the doctor's daughter who married the brother who never quite made it. They had accepted Mumsi and Vijaya, one felt, because an Indian mistress is a considerable improvement on a mistress whom Gerry might have had – some ghastly common lady who wouldn't know how to hold her knife, had peroxide hair and spoke with an accent straight from Ealing Broadway.

Decidedly jittery by now, Enid convinced herself she needed a new skirt to meet the flight from Bombay. She plunged into the bosom of Harrogate and emerged with one of those pale brown, straight summer skirts. Throwing caution and the bank manager to the wind, she then bought a pair of low-heeled comfortable shoes. There were enough daffodils in the garden to fill a vase for the sitting room. As Gerry loved to point out, Eleanor and Fiona both had drawing rooms. Why didn't they call theirs the lounge? Just to take the piss! She filled another vase for the bedroom.

Enid had prepared a simple quiche and salad with fruit and cheese. There was a bottle of God knows what for a fiver in the fridge. And off she drove for four anxious hours.

Heathrow must be the most dehumanising place on earth. It is almost as if the powers that be have deliberately designed somewhere which could be anywhere and ends up being nowhere. After parking in some expensive disembodied concrete building, smelling strongly of pee delicately scented with just a touch of vomit, Enid lost her way a couple of times trying to find where to meet passengers from Bombay. Even the signs and instructions were written in gobbledygook.

The terminal – or was it an exit? – anyway, the place to meet people and take them away, was teeming with excited children in iridescent coloured dresses, their hair already wriggling out of the bright ribbons tied earlier in the day. Proud fathers were dolled up in the Indian equivalent of the Sunday best, while plump mothers shimmered with jewellery. There were some indigenous people. They looked like hen pheasants moving among preening cocks. Enid's new skirt couldn't compete among the elegant saris. Enid was deeply regretting the whole escapade. She was very angry with Gerry for doing this to her. A light flashed on the board. The Air India flight had arrived right on time.

Enid's anger had flared up in her stomach. She wanted a lavatory and to faint and needed to breathe deeply all at the same time. She galloped to the loo, which was blessedly close, thanking the guy who designed 'nowhere' for getting something right. When she returned, she had at least one orifice less to worry about. The passengers were arriving. Several whey-faced, crumple-suited gentlemen with briefcases and expense accounts melted into the morning light. An elderly couple with a mountain of luggage waddled towards the taxi sign. A couple of unaccompanied children were enveloped in a gigantic hug. No parent would waste that amount of emotion – must be Aunty from Southall. More and more families trundled through Customs, with mountains of luggage, to be greeted by relatives and hip-hopping children. The sounds of excitement lifted the decibels. A glamorous film star posed for the cameras. Where were they? Enid anxiously looked around – had she missed them? A couple about the right age stood tentatively with their brand new luggage. Enid moved forward.

'Vijaya, Ran?' They looked straight through her. Enid was

embarrassed. She stepped back. Another flight had landed from Jakarta. Indonesians meeting people had joined those already waiting like Enid. She was worried – no – she was in a panic. Where were they? The Indian parties moved off. The shy couple made their way to the taxi rank. The businessmen had long since disappeared. Standing in the hall was just the ravishing woman who was posing for the cameras, wearing skin-tight jeans, cowboy boots and a sweater with beading round the plunging neckline. She was stunningly glamorous, in Enid's provincial eyes, and impossible to place. Even her age seemed anywhere between twenty-five and forty. Beside her was a blond god straight from the Norse sagas. He was at least 6'6", with curiously pale blue eyes and swept back blonde hair. He dressed with that casual elegance reserved for the international chic. This pair, or rather the woman, was now being interviewed. Enid watched. She was very professional. After a while the interview finished. The photographer and journalist, both Indians, moved away and the only passengers left from the Indian flight were this couple. Enid's heart thumped uncomfortably as she shyly approached them.

'Enid?' It was Ran who spoke before grasping her hand in an act of deep sincerity, as practised by world leaders meeting before the television cameras. Then it was Vijaya's turn and a deep embrace straight from that scene in her latest film when she meets her long-lost mother. The photographer and journalist were still there.

'Just my Aunty,' muttered Vijaya. They left.

'I'm sorry, I must have missed you. It's my career, you know.' Vijaya tenderly released her.

'I'm so sorry, Vijaya. I just didn't think. I mean, having your photo taken and everything – you must be very famous. Did you have a good journey?'

Five more 'I'm sorrys' and they reached the car. Despite a visit to the car wash, the car looked shabby, elderly and cheap. It was. Ran folded himself into knots and sat in front while Vijaya clambered into the back, filling the car with an overpowering perfume. Enid said, 'I'm sorry,' once more, this time for having to drive for four hours on the M25 followed by the M1. But her passengers assured her that the M25 and M1 were too wonderful for words. They were quiet, apart from sudden excited observations.

'I didn't expect to be interviewed as well.'

'You looked beautiful, as always, Vijaya. Didn't you think so, Enid?' Ran spoke with an Indian lilt.

'What was that all about?' asked Enid.

'Didn't I tell you in my letters? I'm an actress. That is why we live in Bombay. My agent decided that Heathrow was a good place to be photographed for my fans, especially the ones living in England. My latest film is coming out shortly.'

Enid heard what the glamorous creature said but, knowing she had another four hours behind the wheel, decided with determined concentration to put it to the back of her mind. To be frank, it didn't always stay there. All too soon she found herself thinking, A film actress! They must be rolling in it. What am I doing paying for a film actress and her godlike husband to visit England? It's a sick joke, that's what it is. Gerry, you're a monster!

'My gollygosh! Just look at the size of that lorry. We have enormous lorries as well, but ours aren't as clean. The roads are very dusty, with potholes.' Vijaya pressed her nose against the window. Enid rather wished the photographer had caught her like that.

'Isn't that a Roller? Our friend Gupta has one, doesn't he, Vij?' Ran watched the silver Rolls float passed.

'Did Daddyji ever have a Roller, Enid?'

'Not his style. Gerry wanted to castrate people who drove them. It was part of his social programme if he ever stood for Parliament. This is Gerry's car. Cars really didn't feature much in his life, not as symbols, anyway. Rolls-Royces stick out as a symbols of wealth and achievement. My Gerry didn't have wealth or achievement.' Enid had just a shade of misplaced triumph, almost hysteria, in her tone of voice. Let's face it, her reply was over the top.

Why had she referred to him as 'My Gerry'? Did she suspect that Savita had known a successful, man-about-town Gerry? A Gerry with money in his pocket, while she had stayed loyal to a clapped-out wreck of a man who was belligerent, lonely and a failure, whatever the Brig might say. She wanted to stop the car –

there, on the side of the M1 – drop them off and drive away. She didn't want her relationship with Gerry probed by this glamorous couple. She didn't want them to sneer at her home, constantly asking if Gerry did this, had that.

The next best thing to turfing someone out on the motorway is to take them to a motorway service area. They pulled into Watford Gap services and Enid suggested they had a cup of coffee and possibly something to eat. They lined up with trays, Ran and Vijaya delighted and curious about everything from cornflakes in tiny packets to blueberry muffins. Ran ordered a huge breakfast. It was ten minutes inside the time breakfast was served. Most people would have encountered dark looks, but his piercing blue eyes must have done it. Vijaya was more modest. She wanted croissants and picked out one of every kind of the little jam pots available.

'They're cute.'

Enid ordered a coffee and sourly paid the bill. What the hell was she letting herself in for?

'Ran, I'm dying to know – where do you come from?'

'India.'

'Really! I don't mean to be rude, but you look like a Norse god, and I don't think I'd go to India to find a Norse god.'

'Why ever not? India is very progressive. Everyone lives there.'

'I'm sure you're right, like America. But where did your parents come from originally? Were they Norwegian or something?'

'Enid, it simply doesn't matter – but if you must know, he was a master mariner, sailing oil tankers. My mum died when I was three. He was away at sea at the time. Anyway, after he heard, he scooped me up and took me to India, married his girlfriend and that was that. In progressive India it is unimportant. You English still have hang-ups about where people come from, but we don't. So, which side of the railway line were you born, Enid? Isn't that what the English think?'

'In the signal box! Anyway, I don't know if that is true about most Indians. We see on our television sets riots because untouchables want to go to university. You have a Hindu party dominating your politics. You go into reheat over Kashmir—'

'But Enid,' Ran butted in, 'Vijaya and I, we're above all that nonsense. We're media!'

Enid felt a strong desire to take a hairbrush and whack him on the bare bum with it. The arrogance! The sheer bloody poppycock! Well, he should get on well with Henry. They could go rambler hunting together.

Enid decided that if she was to get them home without further confrontation she'd better shut up and choose something less controversial to chatter about.

'I'm longing to hear all about the wedding. I hope you've bought some photos. What did you wear, Vijaya?'

Vijaya spoke with a silky smooth voice that rapidly developed a sulk.

'A beautiful dress, of course.'

Enid added, unnecessarily, 'Over here people wear all sorts of weird things – from parachute outfits if they are getting married mid-air to diving suits. You name it, they wear it.' As she spoke, she was thinking, Three weeks with this prickly couple gallivanting round the country – Gerry, why did you do this to me?

They weren't really that bad – in many ways they were worse. As for Enid, she was far too curious to be too censorious. She was a bit like a tiny reed warbler with a cuckoo in the nest. Ran and Vijaya both slept for the second half of the journey and arrived in North Yorkshire to an April deluge, with rain bouncing back off the hard surfaces, pouring into the gutters and causing rivulets in Enid's drive.

It wasn't just Enid who was feeling tired and awkward. Ran and Vijaya ate the quiche in silence but didn't drink the wine. They didn't drink alcohol.

More's the pity, thought Enid, who would have liked the excuse.

'I'm pooped. I'm sorry, Enid. No way can I be the life and soul of the party. Not till I've had a good sleep.'

'Well, why don't you go upstairs? Do you want to go as well, Ran?'

They sloped off to bed and Enid did wonder if sleep was the only thing they had in mind. After all, they were such a beautiful couple and newly married.

She rebuked herself soundly. None of that!

It wasn't going as she imagined. They didn't appear as exotic as she expected. Indeed, in many ways they were even more exotic. That film business, she hadn't expected that. What did they call it? The media business, the same kind of jargon the Beeb kept banging on about. The jeans had thrown her, as had Ran's blond good looks. They were so very foreign – well – different, anyway. Vijaya's speech was peppered with outmoded expressions and Ran delivered his over-polite answers in that sing-song style. But Enid's prejudices didn't last for long and, once they woke, the three were busy chattering like jackdaws.

'Stop, stop, stop!' pleaded Enid. 'I am also bursting with questions. You must remember, Vijaya, that until you wrote to me, I didn't have a clue that you existed. Incidentally, when did you last see Gerry?'

'He came to stay with Mumsi and I just after I started my first job. I worked for a small film company making advertisements. Mumsi was in seventh heaven. I have never seen her so happy. She hired a cook specially to make his favourite dishes. I was rather grumpy, I'm afraid. I didn't like sharing Mumsi – not with this funny old Englishman. I knew he was Daddyji. He was very kind. It was then he offered me a dowry. I remember him saying, "Vijaya, you are a very lovely girl. One day you will want to marry. I will make sure you have a dowry." And look what a special dowry it is – staying with you, visiting Shakespeare, the Queen's palace – or is it castle? Mind you, Ran and I have been living together for three years. I must show you a photo of our little Rani. He's two and a half. Mumsi adores him; she says he has the same ears as Daddyji.'

The same ears? How dare he have the same ears! Anyway, why didn't anyone mention this child before? Thoughts flashed through Enid's mind.

'A dear little boy. How lovely! Yes, do show me his photo.' It was as near simpering as Enid was prepared to go.

A photo of a fat lump of a pampered little boy was thrust in her hands, followed by another – this time sitting on the lap of a beautiful woman of her own age in a sari.

'Is that Mumsi?' Enid stared at her rival. She imagined Gerry's leathery old cock beavering away under the sari. The scene was rather disgusting, so she tried to imagine beautiful young love when he first went to India – furious copulation under one of those fans pulled by some diminutive, half-starved little boy. That was better, but the half-starved little boy was a mistake. She replaced him with electricity. All the same, the fantasy was rapidly becoming something straight from the *Kama Sutra*.

'Has she worn glasses long?' Enid didn't need them except for reading. 'You should have told me about Rani. He could have come with you.'

'Oh my God! Not bloody likely. Anyway, Mumsi dotes on him. She has him while I'm at work. I didn't want Daddyji to think I didn't need a dowry. That's why I didn't mention him.'

Conniving bitch! Typical of today's young – fucking furiously at the first opportunity, completely wrecking my image of India. No sari, no face gently hidden under a veil, no red spot in the middle of her forehead – or was that for Brahmins only? Thoughts bubbled and exploded through Enid's head.

'Are you a Brahmin and all that?'

'I am the bride of Thor, the Norse god of war, as well as a computer doctor. My Ran is very brilliant, you know.'

Ran laughed. Yes, he was a doctor. He had a doctorate in computer systems – McGill University.

'Bombay might have bullock carts but it also has computers. I have my own business – 500 people working for me. We are all over India – very progressive. I am the major software business. I work all hours.'

'Do Indians mind that you are white?'

'Enid, I am Indian. I speak Hindi.'

'What about Mumsi? Does she have a job?'

'Mumsi is famous in India. Her image is all over garages and cafés. Well, it was. Now she is retired. She gave up working about twenty years ago. Very famous actresses never really retire. Now she wears saris and has never been seen dead dressed like me. She has a column in a film magazine for women with problems. She doesn't write it – writing isn't her thing. Mumsi is very shrewd, isn't she, Ran?'

Enid's head was bloated with undigested images and information. These two bizarre creatures under her roof were systematically destroying any patronising role she had cosily created for herself in her imagination. Enid had created a relationship with Mumsi and Gerry that she could understand and sanction. But the idea of giving all his inheritance to a successful actress was very difficult for Enid to accept. It was put securely to the back of her mind.

'How did you two meet? I mean, I thought that India was still a country where marriages are arranged.'

It was Ran who spoke. 'You haven't met Aunty Jamila. My God, no! Aunty Jamila is a real character. She runs a hospice. She is not Mother Teresa, no way. How do you say? Fingers to one God. Aunty prefers lots of little gods. There are shrines two a penny in her hospice. Aunty wanted a computer for her hospice. God knows what for, but she says the sick and dying like modern equipment. Anyway, I had to donate the computer and Vijaya cut the ribbon. Aunty Jamila lets anyone who wants to die come to her hospice. She has hundreds of babies – left behind babies. Those babies are so stubborn. They just will not die. So Aunty Jamila lets them go to an orphanage that helps them survive. She makes Mumsi help raise money. She is bully, bully, bully! She made us marry: "Look at your poor mother," she says. No disrespect, Enid.'

Enid had anticipated a quiet day with dinner at Sal's – a day when she could reconcile Gerry's fortune seeping away into the coffers of the dying and those bloody babies refusing to die. She had not anticipated Vijaya telephoning her mother and son for one of those totally inane telephone conversations.

'Rani, Dani, do you miss Mummy?' was multiplied by ten expensive minutes.

'Mumsi sends her best regards and asks if you have a recent photo of Gerry.'

There is something about breakfast at eleven that spoils lunch at one. Enid was damned if she was going to serve avocado pear and Cornish pasties for lunch, not after the orgy of muesli, toast and coffee which she found herself clearing up at eleven thirty. She suspected that avocados were two a penny in India, but hoped Cornish pasties were a rarity. Lunch was just Cornish pasties and put back an hour. Afterwards she suggested to her guests a walk with the dog. Only Sophocles wanted to go, so she left the photograph album open so they could look through it. She hadn't expected Vijaya to nick just about the only decent photos of Gerry. She only found out later. China tea was the next problem. They weren't used to it and did she have any proper Indian tea? No, she didn't.

'It's casual,' Enid had said. Vijaya wore a slinky floor-length black dress with a scarlet flower in her hair. She looked glorious. Ran had a silk roll-neck shirt with a casual jacket. He looked like a successful media giant. Enid wore her blue light wool dress. Poor Sal! She wore a well-washed purple cotton top over a pair of pink trousers.

Good manners precluded everyone from knowing how disappointed they were with each other – except the twins, who hadn't learnt about good manners yet.

Beatrice began with, 'You smell like a tart's knickers. That's what Daddy says when Mummy wears perfume like that.'

'Beatrice, really! Don't take any notice of her.'

'Well, he does say that.'

Meanwhile Sophie tackled Ran. 'If you live in India, why don't you look Indian?'

'My mummy and daddy came from Norway. Have you ever heard of Norway?'

'No, does it have a capital? We do. It's London.'

'We do, it's Oslo, and we have a king.'

'Then why live in India?'

'Better weather, and the women are beautiful.'

Charm gets you absolutely nowhere with seven-year-old girls.

Dinner was more of a question and answer session. Sal found out how Gerry had met Mumsi.

'Mumsi was an actress. She was very famous. She was asked to appear in a small film for Family Planning – no money, but big prestige and donations to the cause. Gerry was the person negotiating. The rest was history.'

What did her family think? 'You mean about me?' said Vijaya. She went on to explain.

'There was one hell of a hullabaloo. But my mother's family were very modest people – poor, uneducated – and your father's money was not to be sniffed at.'

'And history is now repeating itself with little Ranji?'

'No way! Ran and I are sophisticated. We work. Ranji has a modern future.'

Sal couldn't help wondering if her children were having a modern future. Somehow, going to school with the Darrens of this world might make them streetwise, but it could hardly compare with the International School in Bombay or whatever place they were going to send Ranjit. Sal felt very provincial and dowdy besides her father's other child. She also felt pretty sour about the money. We won't mention the teeth.

'I went to India before I married Douglas. I loved it. Gerry understood, I think: crowded buses, filthy bazaars, skinny children everywhere, wonderful train journeys over hundreds of miles of flat, flat landscapes. I loved the quaint English everyone spoke and the remnants of our imperial past, like cemeteries, hideous bungalows and museums full of mouldering Victorian relics. We went up into the mountains. We met Tibetans; they were lovely people. Best of all I loved the shabby beauty of it all and the laid-back ineptitude.'

Vijaya flashed her eyes. 'Well, really! Would you want to live your life in laid-back whatever it was? My God, I don't. I want to be modern and make good money, not all this bullshit you talk.'

She was quite agitated. 'I wear chic clothes and go to modern parties. Ran and I live in an expensive air-conditioned apartment.'

She waved her arm round the entirely conventional farm-house dining room with three of Sal's paintings as the only touch of modernity.

'You are very traditional. You like looking backwards. Daddyji always said that the trouble—'

'While fucking your mother!' interrupted Sal, with a snarl. Even the trifle froze.

There was a stunned silence. Enid couldn't help thinking how Sal had occasionally blown a fuse like this as a young girl. Luckily, Vijaya's hide was like a rhino's.

'For goodness' sake! Be sophisticated. When Enid offered me a dowry, I knew she was sophisticated.'

'She offered you a dowry because she assumed you had little money, little opportunity to better yourself and would appreciate a break.' Sal's voice was brittle, nastily polite and could explode again at any minute.

Vijaya listened, her head faintly cocked to one side and a smile stretched across her face. 'And now you find the boot is on the other foot.'

How true, how true, even if the level of anger had silenced the rest of the table! Douglas had been discussing sorghum strains which can withstand drought. Ran was frankly bored and ignorant, but people with such good looks can usually get away with it. Enid had been listening with increasing alarm at the two women's acrimony. It wasn't what she had planned. However, Vijaya was absolutely right. They were the poor relations harking back to gentility, while Ran and Vijaya grabbed not only cash where they could but were determined to lead the good life as well. They were trampling over India's age-old customs and despising Enid's world also. What was it Gerry called it? 'Import-export, my foot!' That is what he had called it.

Surely the British Government didn't pay every time Gerry felt like a leg-over? He must have done something else as well as wallow in the comfort of his own money. Enid reflected, When I think how I've skimped and saved all my life to have this thrown into my face... Gerry, you're a bastard! But she didn't say a word. She smiled her finishing-school smile, ate her trifle and felt mildly queasy.

They drove home in a sombre mood. Vijaya tentatively suggested that Sal was jealous. Why, she couldn't imagine. After all, she had Daddyji as a real father, while Vijaya and Mumsi had to make do with him once in a while. At least Vijaya didn't point out that Sal looked like some raw-boned peasant beside her beautiful half-sister. Only Enid was allowed to think that – and consume herself in flames of guilt afterwards.

It was overwhelming confusion that made Enid toss and turn that night. Gerry and she had based their marriage on mushy values about changing society for the better. He had climbed out of his ivory tower and invited her to join him. She had done so willingly – all for a lie, apparently. It wasn't whispering sweet nothings into Mumsi's shell-like ear; it wasn't the damp little bundle, now a stunningly beautiful actress; it wasn't even relegating poor old Sal into a blonde lump with rabbit-like teeth – all that she could accept. After all, Gerry had been difficult. Didn't the Brig tell her that? What she couldn't forgive was the money – just giving it away to some beautiful woman, while she had scrimped and saved to maintain a way of life. *Why did I bloody bother?* She fell asleep before the answer.

The hired car was bright red, spotlessly clean and included an excellent map. Ran and Enid drove into Harrogate to fetch it. Ran was going to do the driving, even though Vijaya made a point of explaining that she drove as well. Their tour would take them to Stratford and Oxford – but don't make a joke about Oxbridge, Vijaya would not be amused! She had been embarrassed to find out her mistake. Then there was Aunty Eleanor and Aunty Fiona and a tour of the Highlands before returning to Enid and, after that, Buckingham Palace on their way back home. Enid was paying. She had whittled it down to petrol for the tour. That was quite sufficient. They could pay for their hotels. In the light of what she'd learnt, even the petrol was far, far too much.

She waved them off on a chill April morning with Vijaya wearing leopard-skin trousers clinging to everything she'd got, with short suede boots teetering on high heels, together with her leather jacket and its huge fur collar. Ran looked like the hero of an advertising film – hot on looks, but short on dialogue.

Sophie was absolutely right. The sheets smelled like – well – 'a pair of tart's knickers' was one way of describing some exotic perfume. She changed the bed, threw away the flowers and dusted the room. All the time she kept berating herself for being such an ass. Gradually she began to change her tune. Poor Gerry! Begetting this exotic, beautiful creature who was untouched by the sensibilities of either culture – neither Indian nor British, just rich and vulgar. Ran, was he any better, with more money, more success? Just a parasite, really, living off the heaving humanity of India. He wasn't a Norse god, just a modern, money-grubbing, successful man. They both belonged to the world of 'think of number one, play hard, make oodles of money and you'll succeed'.

Enid felt violated. Her values, her integrity, her offer to pay the dowry had been made into some big joke. She broke rule number one and rang Sal.

'Honestly, Mum! What was Daddy doing begetting that thing? She's so un-Indian! They both are. Indians are lovely with beautiful manners and charming to talk to. The educated ones are far more cultured than we are in many respects. But that couple – what kind of values do they have? Money, money, money! She made me feel such a dreary, provincial nonentity. Thank God Daddy's dead, that's all I can say. If you come across any more of his little mistakes, you're not to touch them, please.'

'Sal, I feel terrible about it. What will Eleanor and Blanche say? I invited them because of Gerry. There isn't an ounce of the Gerry I knew in her. I thought she was going to be funny and easy to get on with, like when I first got in touch with her. But now she's here in those ridiculous, expensive clothes; it makes me look so shabby and silly.'

'Quite frankly, Ma, I thought they were both odious. We might not be flash and rich, but Dad and you gave me a good home and my lot does all right. She's not like anything I met in India, anyway.'

Enid felt better after talking to Sal. It sustained her for several days. She had just finished tidying the house quite unnecessarily and was priding herself on the way she handled her husband's bastard child when the phone rang. Even before she picked it up she knew it spelt trouble. It must have been the angry tone.

'Enid, how *could* you!' It was Eleanor. 'That young madam is outrageous. As for that tall blond husband, why do the Indians allow it?'

'I gather he is Indian, that's why – rather like being black as your hat and a judge over here.'

'Are there any?'

'I rather hope so. Gerry would have been happy enough. It would have vindicated all those letters he wrote to *The Times*.'

'Don't mention my brother's name to me. He's got a lot to answer for. Do you know what that flibbertigibbet of a girl had the audacity to say to me? She said that we were relics – like Maharajahs, but without any money. If we had money, we would give the house a face-lift. I ask you! She said that to me! As for poor Henry, do you know she said that it was people like him that made the Indians throw the British out. That was until she met Bertie. Tiger skins are in great demand in India. You just can't get them, apparently. Well, that little minx thought she could take Bertie back in her luggage… "I'll pay you far more than he's worth."'

'For a moth-eaten old tiger we've always called Bertie!'

'As for what she wore – her bedroom literally stank.'

Eleanor puffed and pontificated for a further five minutes. She questioned Enid closely about Vijaya, suggesting that she must be a usurper.

'I can't believe she's my niece. I mean, she is nearer to me as a relative than you. You can disown her, I can't. You're not thinking of inviting the mother over, are you?'

'You're just like Sal. She's spitting chips about her. I wonder how Blanche will manage?'

Not much better.

'How could you have lumbered us with that frightful couple? Do you know, she told our dear friend Jeremy, a retired doctor, that England was completely out of date in medicine? That doctors only come over here because they can't get into America? She then went on to say that private medicine in Bombay is as good as anywhere. When I mentioned the poor and needy she just dismissed them. She said it was only tourists like us that notice them and make them into a problem. "I never see them, nor does Ran. After all, you don't notice your quaint old houses, do you?" Honestly, Enid, are you sure Gerry is her dad? She's awful.'

'I'm sorry, Blanche, you're not the only one. She's just not us, let's face it. She left me feeling dowdy and dull, as if Gerry had had an exotic life to balance his deadly dull one with me.' Enid's voice began to shake. Tears were not that far away.

'Well, I think it's disgraceful. She's our guest – and so rude! If any other little Gerrys turn up, don't invite them over. I always thought all that travelling abroad was dangerous. Well, you've learnt the hard way. By the way, do come and see us. We are none of us getting any younger.'

What have I done? The tears welled up, then dribbled, warm and wet, down her cheeks. Enid felt horribly used. Vijaya and Ran were frightening people, with their good looks, their glamorous clothes, her perfume and his penetrating blue eyes. It wasn't just those things. They themselves were so superficial. And their arrogance! They felt they could walk all over the earth. Isn't that what the British had done for hundreds of years? Were we really as insensitive and alarming as they were? Enid wandered to her window and reassured herself with nodding daffodils, like little old ladies in yellow headscarves discussing with vigorous enthusiasm some spicy act of hanky-panky. They might have told her they were rich and didn't need her pitiful largesse. They might have said they had a child, that of the two of them only a quarter was Indian.

They are the new age of success – the international smart set – all nightclubs, cocaine and screwing anyone they can for money. Poor old India! Enid tried to tweak a sense of proportion into her distress and alarm. She supposed that India was big enough to take it. It had enough history to tether it firmly. It was a wise old country, steeped in traditions and educated enough to despise this bubble of luxury, or so she hoped.

It went further than that, didn't it? What did it say about Sal and Douglas? They were the same age, tied to the soil and steeped in their culture. They quietly went about their lives as magistrates, county councillors or in similar roles. Sal was involved in a local arts festival. Douglas was a school governor – it was a start. Don't say Ran and Vijaya and their ilk would ride roughshod over Sal and Douglas! Enid began to cry again. She could just imagine a time where the Rans of this world bought up the land and turfed out Sal and Douglas. The twins would be thrown aside and little Rani sent to Eton. She could hear Gerry roaring with anger at the social injustice he saw all around him – but wasn't he the cause?

A parcels van whizzed up the drive and spun expertly to a halt. Out jumped a man in a natty uniform.

'Tanner, that's right? Big parcel from Scotland.'

Enid wiped her wet hands and frowned before a knot of dread twisted itself in her gut. She stepped forward to take delivery of a large box.

'What do you think it is?'

'Luckily, ma'am, my job is to deliver the damned things, not guess what's in 'em. The only guessing game I'll go in for is one of those telly jobs with lots of money.'

He drove off at a pace which might frighten the police and certainly alarmed Enid. It wasn't the only parcel. Several others arrived at breakneck speed. Enid carried them up to the spare bedroom.

Wendy rang. There would be a meeting to discuss the entertainment programme. Could she come?

She was there in her new skirt and a top nicked from Sal who couldn't wear it with her big breastfeeding boobs. Enid felt that the social needs of the over-sixties would prevent her dwelling on the outrages of her guests who seemed hell-bent on buying up the Highlands.

'Ladies,' began Wendy, her eye make-up a dazzling emerald green and her figure wrapped in a russet red tent. 'We have our gala evening well in hand, but there are another four occasions when our older friends like to have an outing.

The faces round someone else's dining-room table looked as if they were bursting, not necessarily with brilliant ideas – more with a corporate anxiety.

'I think we should take to heart what Enid said last time and make our activities more fun and not so patronising.' Bless her heart! It was Doris who spoke and she wouldn't recognise fun if she stepped on it.

Janice gingerly put up her hand as though she was at school. 'It's all very well, but some of our old folk need help with walking.'

'So does Stephen Hawking,' retorted Gillian.

'They enjoy visiting TV studios. Why don't we arrange that?'

'Do we have to trudge round Emmerdale Farm yet again? Can't we ask to see some other sets. I mean current affairs – programmes like that?'

'That's an idea! They do lovely teas afterwards.'

'Is wine tasting something they'd enjoy?'

'They'd get tipsy.'

'So what? They're not driving home, are they!'

'I know!' said Sheila, a lovely, warm, friendly lady with just a suspicion of a twang and a plastic handbag. 'What about getting them to act as mannequins for a fund-raiser, wearing designer clothes particularly for their age group? Just think of the fun of wearing smart clothes and swaggering down the catwalk.'

'What about those who can't walk?'

'Clothes that flatter the wheelchair.'

'I feel sorry for the blokes.'

'If they have their wine tasting and the outing to the TV studios… Anyway, male models are all the rage.'

The ladies plied their wits, juggled priorities, while all the time they ruthlessly assessed each other's clothes, accents, weight and hairstyle. They sighed with indecision. They sighed with satisfaction when a decision was taken. Then they all went home.

Would Vijaya ever do that for the halt, the lame and blind in India? What was it about her that riled and threatened her relations?

The spare room was piled high with trophies from Scotland. Enid didn't feel inclined to put a second vase of daffodils in the room. She had learnt about putting flowers in visitors' rooms at that dotty finishing school in Bournemouth.

They drove back late on Thursday. The evening had set in. Enid was gritting her teeth.

'Cooee, we're back and just about pooped.' Vijaya teetered into the sitting room and collapsed onto the sofa. Ran was just behind her.

'Honestly, Enid, Scotland is just something. Those castles and huge parks! Edinburgh is dishy too. I bought yards of tweed.'

'Whatever for? You can't wear it in India,' snapped Enid.

'You'd be surprised.' Vijaya rolled her eyes. 'We bought some lovely glasses with gold round the edge – have they arrived? – and a dear little bird. What was it, Ran?'

'A grouse.'

'That's it. It's stuffed and looks cute.'

Over a chicken casserole Ran explained that his Norse relations had conquered Scotland and how Shetland still had distinct Norwegian features.

'But I thought you were Indian,' said Enid irritably.

'Vijaya and I are tomorrow's world,' said Ran pompously.

So you keep telling me. You are just like nasty fascist thugs as far as I'm concerned, thought Enid venomously.

Later, when the couple had retired, Enid rang Dolly.

'You said you wanted to meet them. Now's your chance – tomorrow night, and God help you!'

'Oh lor! You mean we have to eat chicken korma sitting cross-legged on the floor?'

'That's what you and I do when we pretend to be Indian. They whoop it up with dancing girls—'

Dolly cut in. 'What, you and I, too? That'll be a laugh.'

Over breakfast at eleven – now the regular time – Enid mentioned Dolly.

'I've asked an old friend of Gerry's and mine to supper. I know she would love to meet you both.'

Vijaya assumed everyone loved to meet her. Ran, too, was a born peacock.

'*Come and meet Gerry's little bit on the side*,' mimicked Vijaya, trying to speak the Queen's English and then giggling furiously.

'No, Vijaya, that's Mumsi. She is the little bit on the side. You are living proof of it.' Enid sounded pompous.

Vijaya looked Enid straight in the face, quite unnervingly. 'You don't appreciate us, do you? You wanted me to swan around in saris looking demure and being eternally grateful for your generosity. You know, Enid, my father was really rather pathetic. Look at you and Sal – you're not rich, successful. I don't suppose you can bend anyone's ears.'

Bend anyone's ears? Enid had a bizarre vision of herself standing in Ripon's main square on a busy Saturday, bending ears. But ssh, Vijaya was still talking.

'He led Mumsi and then me to believe that he was somebody. Eleanor and Henry, now, they have been somebody. They even have a tiger skin – proof of their imperial past – but not now. Even they are left behind. In India, if you are left behind, you are nobody.'

'You do keep banging on, don't you?' murmured Enid in a sotto voce voice spoken with a stiff upper lip manner. She needn't have worried. Vijaya was in full flood and not listening to a word.

'Aunty Blanche – now, she is better. She had a coffee morning for me while Ran looked round the hospital – a proper private hospital and hellish expensive. I had Rani in a place like that – state of the ark.'

'I think you mean "art",' murmured Enid.

Vijaya looked at Enid for a minute then said, 'We have proper investments. You just have a pension.'

'I think it's rather vulgar to talk about money.' Enid's voice had risen like dough, while inside she prayed, *Just go away and take everything you stand for…*

There was supper to organize. Vijaya was not the type to ask, 'Can I help?' The way Enid felt, she would have asked her to plunge her elegant hands into scalding water! As it was, she left Vijaya and Ran chirruping over their goodies from Scotland while she banged bad-tempered saucepans in the kitchen.

Dolly arrived, full of curiosity. Blow me, if it wasn't the eau de Nil trousers – very elegant! She shook hands, took a glass of sherry and then sat down beside Vijaya. Enid retired to more clattering in the kitchen.

'I knew your father well. What fun it must be to see his home.'

'See his home! Bombay was also his home. After all, he kept his slippers there. You mustn't patronise me.' And here Vijaya gave Dolly a playful dig in the ribs.

So Dolly very sensibly tried patronising Ran.

'You are like a Viking god with your blue eyes and fair hair. Have you two been taking us by storm?'

'Storm? What storm? We have been visiting the family.'

'And were you impressed?' said Dolly, already smarting on her friend's behalf.

'We thought that Gerry was really grand. Maybe his relatives lived in a castle, but he wasn't grand! He was very ordinary. Just "import-export". I ask you!'

Dolly didn't want to hear this gratuitous piffle. Instead she watched Gerry's daughter with fascination. Her friend had been 'had' by this elegant, dusky girl with her bangles, her scent and her arrogance. That's the telephone for you and those quaint, ill-phrased letters. Poor old Enid, with her muddled preoccupation of 'must do the right thing', now lumbered with this cuckoo. Meanwhile Miss Success was explaining that everybody had to have a pad in New York.

To think I've managed all these years! thought Dolly, increasingly bitter for poor old Enid.

Enid tip-toed into the room. The meal was ready. She had been listening.

'Not everybody has a pad in New York, Vijaya, just the kind of people you choose to like and know. You and Ran mix in a very small world, you know. All that money…' Her voice trailed off, leaving just a hint of envy.

'You are so serious, Enid.'

'And the rest of the world? Particularly those who don't have a pad in New York, as you say we should?'

'Can get stuffed!' Vijaya laughed a metallic, theatrical laugh, her head thrown back and her arms flung gracefully in the air.

'Just joking!' She stood up and everyone watched her walk towards the dining room, her thighs gliding and her head slightly thrown back. There wasn't a shadow of doubt she was hypnotically beautiful. No sooner was she sitting by Dolly than she continued, 'Aunty Jamila is into good works and saving the poor. What's the point? Save one, and there is always another! That is what is wrong in this country. Everyone has been saved and now everyone is poor. So sad! What makes me so puzzled is how someone like Daddyji could give all his money to a girl like Mumsi and then live like this.' She waved her hand disparagingly round Enid's room.

'Do you ever think of anything else?' said Enid, but she smiled. 'You know it is regarded as rude to mention money in company.' But Vijaya appeared not to hear.

'I mean, Mumsi has servants and a villa by the sea. She is chic, elegant and has a gentleman friend who also showers her with money. What a talent! Well done, Mumsi.'

Enid and Dolly caught each other's eye.

'You know, Enid, the word that sums up this place – quaint,' announced Ran, bestowing it as if it was an accolade.

There is so much to be said in favour of good manners. There was to be no unseemly punch-up here. Vijaya spoke – or rather told – Dolly all about smart shops in Bombay, while Ran treated Enid to international management theories, or something like that, for she was up and down a great deal serving the food. But that didn't stop him from talking.

Finally, the evening drew to an uneasy close. Then Enid walked Dolly out to her car.

'That couple are about as much in sympathy with our cosy middle-class world as you and I would be in Benidorm. No, it's worse. You see, poor old Gerry was a link. How could the same man beget Sal and Vijaya? How could he shift all that loot and hand it to a spoilt actress? I can't hate him now. He was too old, too irascible by the time he died. I suppose he adored her. Why didn't he leave me?'

'Don't be daft, Enid – he adored you. Married to those values he wouldn't have lasted five minutes. He probably worked his way through the *Kama Sutra*, got bored and import-exported his way back to you.'

'Where does that leave me? In reduced circumstances back in the Dark Ages! Do you know what that bloody girl had the audacity to suggest if I want to make an extra bob or two – entertain Indian visitors to England. Apparently they would find my house quite "dinky", whatever that means.'

'I have a friend who does that – lives in a damp Elizabethan moated house. They have guests from all over.' With that, Dolly drove off into the night.

'I couldn't, simply couldn't,' muttered Enid, as she did the washing-up on her own.

The grouse, tweed, glasses and the complete works of Shakespeare were sent by courier. It cost a fortune. Vijaya packed her suitcase and then bellowed down to the sitting room for Ran to come up and pack his. Enid had been listening to Ran talk about computers and the market in India. He spoke of villages barely blessed with electricity which were being hurtled into the computer age, their veiled women clustered together in walled seclusion watching hard porn while their menfolk sat under a tree in age-old tradition discussing politics.

'What is going to happen, then?' asked Enid, her mind furiously trying to imagine these retiring, uneducated women suddenly exposed to raunchy, naughty and probably very crude sex.

'Keep ahead – that is what is going to happen. Keep ahead and you make money. After sex, what will these women want to find out? How to avoid babies, that is what. I tell you, Enid, porn will do more to educate women about contraception than all those "do-good" projects.'

Enid looked at the blond god with his lilting Indian accent. She knew nothing about Indian mythology but wondered if the Northern invaders had brought with them tales of pale princes. She could well see Ran playing such a role.

'Do you finance these porn films?'

'Of course; the market is insatiable. But it is just – how do you say it? – a sideline. Providing software for India's growing industry, that's me.'

'What will you do with all your money, Ran? Do you want to collect paintings, build beautiful palaces, go into politics?'

'Politics? Don't be silly! Politics is for noisy men with opinions. If I want politics, I pay for it. If I want to break the law, I just pay for it. If I want to impose my law, I pay more. Money is the only voice that carries – what is that wonderful word you have – I know, *clout*, Enid. Vijaya and I are young, beautiful, rich and powerful. Your old man was a nothing, but he created this beautiful goddess. Vijaya is like a balloon. She has sailed above you, out of your reach.'

'Ran, you lazy bugger! Get up here and pack your clothes.' Vijaya's voice had the melodic quality of a raucous whore – or so Enid thought. She was becoming decidedly prejudiced. Having heard Ran discussing his power and success, Enid felt masochistic enough to ask Vijaya her views. Vijaya liked nothing better than to air them, so she sank into 'that chair' as Enid still saw it.

'How many more years will you continue to make films?' She looked at the fine features with the sulky mouth and flashing eyes. She marvelled at the cascading black hair and willowy neck without a sign of rough, hardened skin. There was an uneasy stillness about the limbs spread over the chair. Vijaya was certainly not here to stay. Thank God, thought Enid.

'So long as I'm beautiful and desirable. Mumsi worked till her forties. I want another couple of babies. Mumsi should have had more babies but she was sentimental about Daddyji. I will never be sentimental, never.'

'Not even about your babies?' Enid watched Vijaya carefully.

'Not even about my babies. You see, Enid, being successful is bloody hard work. You know nothing about success, nor did Daddyji. He was just sentimental about Mumsi.' There was a pause. 'I don't think he was about you, you were his working wife, you might say. But, look at you. You never reached for success. He never did. And your Sal will spend the rest of her life cooking for a farmer. My children will be taught how to reach for success. Being sentimental won't teach them.' Vijaya frowned and the beautiful face became old and tired, much to Enid's delight.

Would the smell of perfume ever leave the car? Vijaya was once more in her skin-tight jeans with her suede coat, with its soft fur collar, belted at the waist. She wore her casual-look make-up and carried that capacious and expensive Gucci handbag. Ran wore the open-shirt casual look with some medallion or other resting on the V of his neckline, where just a sprinkling of hair framed the golden medallion. Enid wasn't to be outdone. She wore her new skirt with a smart new shirt and jacket. She was pleased to be seeing the back of her guests, but apprehensive that the journey would be exhausting for her. They drove for a couple of hours before Enid insisted on a pee and a coffee. Eyes turned and men ogled Vijaya as she walked through the service station. Ran, too, looked oddly out of place, his blond good looks as incongruous as Vijaya's dusky, striking image.

It was while queuing for coffee that a nasty little incident happened. A big bull of a man with a tired little woman in tow jostled Vijaya's tray with the coffee.

'We know what you are. Wearing those clothes don't change anything.' He was angry, suppressing his violence while at the same time lashing out in the only way he felt was left to him.

'Don't, Bert, leave it!' his sad wife pleaded.

Vijaya stood with the pale coffee sloshing over her tray. Under fire she looked quite magnificent.

'You silly little man! Just look what you have done.'

People looked up, staring at Vijaya and the furious-looking man. Ran put his tray down on a flat surface, walked up to the man and said in his best Indian accent, 'Got a problem with my wife?'

'Yer should stick to yer own!' the man spat out, almost snarling with anger.

By now the other people were concentrating on the drama, twisting in their chairs and silencing whatever conversation they were having.

'But I have. We are both Indian.' Ran was courteous, in control and not in a mood to quench this scene, baiting peasants being listed among his hobbies.

'Then why ain't she dressed like one? And why are you white? You've no right to be white. It ain't normal.'

'Thank God for that! Of course, we aren't normal, as you put it. My wife is a famous Indian actress and I am a very rich businessman. It is you, my dear sir, who are normal. God help you.'

The finer points of philosophy sunk slowly in and the man reluctantly turned away, muttering.

'That's what comes of encouraging them,' was Vijaya's comment.

Enid, who had done her best to disown everyone during this little scene, gathered her troops and found a table. The stares continued. Then one by one a small group of autograph hunters shuffled towards Vijaya. Vijaya flashed her dark eyes and beamed at the various people.

'Please, miss, do you make films over here?'

'My friend goes to see Indian films. Can you sign your name?' So it went on. Embarrassed, gauche and utterly ordinary, the little queue produced pieces of paper, napkins or diaries. At last they were free to drink their by now tepid coffees.

'It is a tyranny to make everyone the same. There can be no hope of progress, no success if people like him have his way.' Ran shook his head.

'You might like success,' said Enid with just a touch of severity, 'but those of us who, as you and Vijaya constantly point out, are not successful, see success as quite threatening. He's not the only one who expected Vijaya to wear saris, or you to be a real caste Indian. You know, Ran, it does turn everything on its head.'

'Maybe, one day, if you are rich enough, you will come to Bombay, Enid. There, you will experience a city full of vitality – lots of crime, lots of success, lots of poverty – lots and lots. It is alive, thriving, dying and beginning all over again. Not like this fusty, dusty little place with mean men. Enid, we are the future. You are ancient history.'

'And there was I, dreaming of the Taj Mahal, ancient Mogul forts and villages untouched by the twentieth century – a land of teeming millions, mostly living out their lives according to a timeless tradition.' Tongue in cheek, Enid was delighted when they rose to the bait.

'How romantic – how do you say? What bullshit!' announced Vijaya.

Enid was so glad the honeymoon was over.

Buckingham Palace was inevitably a disappointment. The guards stood in the wrong place and there was not a corgi in sight. The Queen very sensibly was washing her hair or clipping her toenails. She certainly wasn't giving a conducted tour of her home. Nor was Prince Philip swearing at the troops. Indeed, he wasn't even swearing – probably cutting his toenails too. After that came the highlight of the trip for Enid – booting out this frightful couple at Heathrow.

It was Vijaya who put Enid's mind at rest when she announced that Mumsi was the height of sophistication and elegance, rarely wearing the same clothes twice – a dig at the new skirt bought to welcome them and worn pretty well every day since. Vijaya continued with stiletto-like precision and tact to point out that dowdy old Enid would have nothing in common with Mumsi, apart from having been fucked by the same man many years ago.

It was 'the many years ago' that enraged Enid. 'Not so many where I'm concerned,' she muttered.

'It's not that I'm not really grateful for this honeymoon. It has been quite an adventure. But at the end of the day I go back to our sumptuous apartment, servants and the lap of luxury while you crawl into your little house and potter round the garden because you can't afford a gardener. You would feel very ill at ease with us.'

They parted with a stiff kiss, Vijaya keeping an eye for a possible fan to emerge for her autograph and Ran standing like the Nordic god he undoubtedly was. Enid scuttled from the scene, paid a small fortune for parking her car, and got the hell out.

Seven

Whew! A narrow escape! But from what? It was well past Luton before Enid could allow herself to think about Vijaya. When she did, it was just a dribble. Enid didn't want to be swamped, even if the back of the car did retain the cloying scent she used. Daddyji's sperm had certainly found its way into a bizarre world. Was it one he felt comfortable in? What had that bloody girl said only the other day? Something about him leaving his slippers in Mumsi's house. For slippers, read sperm, she thought, sourly. Nor was it the only sour thought to accompany her home. Outside the turn-off for Nottingham, Enid found herself totting up the cost of her misplaced generosity. It totalled somewhere near £2,000. Damn it! Her car wasn't worth that. At the junction with the M18, Enid started to become enraged with Vijaya's patronising attitude towards her Sal. Sal wasn't the most beautiful girl in the world – her teeth had always been a problem – but Douglas had been a solid, worthy find and Sal had settled down to be a lovely mum and sturdy partner. So, their house was a little scruffy, with scuffed carpets, torn covers on the sofa, plastic toys breeding quietly under the chairs and burnt saucepans. Funny that! Sal always had a burnt saucepan on the go. She also had the dogs' and cats' bowls, the twins' painting gear, the washing, drying and ironing plus a pile of farming magazines and the telephone with endless pieces of paper with cryptic messages written down. Then there was the sink, which was empty for about ten minutes in every twenty-four hours: the cereal packets, a huge fridge with magnetic letters spelling some naughty word or other, and a hole in the lino where Sal had dropped a hot casserole. So, what was wrong with that?

Then Enid started on another tack, remembering a conversation from a few days before. Vijaya had made a disparaging remark about peasants.

'What's wrong with being a peasant?' Enid had said. 'I thought

Ghandi wanted to create an India where the peasant was revered. You know, Vijaya, maybe I choose to be like the untouchables.'

Enid wasn't very clued-up about caste, but she knew that 'untouchable' was a buzzword that caught the attention.

It had set off a tirade.

'You know nothing, God damn it! After all those years in India, you people know nothing. You can choose to be rich, successful, even powerful, but you do not choose your caste. Mumsi's family was not rich but they were from an acting caste. I am an Anglo-Indian. I am not proud of it, but it is fact. You choose to do the garden because you are poor. You could never be untouchable. I wouldn't eat with you if you were.'

Luckily Ran and Vijaya had wanted to visit Castle Howard that afternoon. They had seen the TV serial, *Brideshead Revisited*, from Evelyn Waugh's book. Enid had lent them her car, as the hired car had gone back, and reckoned on at least a couple of hours rolling in some metaphorical mud to restore her equilibrium – or rather, doing the gardening.

'I imagined Daddyji living somewhere like that,' confided Vijaya, who had enjoyed Castle Howard.

'We all imagine living somewhere beautiful like that. What about you, Ran?'

'Live way out in the country with only cows for friends?'

But now, driving home, Enid was very tired. She drifted between the reality of the A1 with its thudding lorries, filthy, littered hedgerows and air polluted with diesel and petrol fumes, the flow of images and remembrances floating through her imagination. Tiredness became exhaustion as she swung the car into the final lap of the journey. At last her home was there, pleasant, unassuming and perfectly comfortable. But was it? Didn't it just reflect the muddled limitations of some silly old man? She was too tired to follow the train of thought.

It took Enid, Sophocles and the cat a couple of weeks to make the house scruffily comfortable again. It took Enid a couple more weeks to bring the garden to heel. By now it was high summer. Baby Roger could lie on a rug and admire his toes. The twins were hunting Smarties in the garden while Sal and Douglas were spending the night in London. No cucumber sandwiches, no

Pimms, no new-mown grass, no thump of a tennis ball, none of that – just Granny trying to keep the three occupied and peaceful till lunchtime the next day – that time-honoured mixture of annihilating boredom and tiredness that accompanies enthusiastic grannies in harness.

'Granny, you know those brown and white people you had staying, did they come from the same place?' Beatrice was licking the chocolate off a digestive.

'Yes. India.' Enid tickled Roger's large fat belly and received a lovely 'coo' for her pains.

'But why were they different, then?'

'They weren't, love. They were just the same, boringly the same.'

'But, Granny, they were different colours.' The chocolate biscuit had transferred itself to Beatrice's shorts, T-shirt, nose and hands.

'Oh, that! Well, you are a different colour to Sophie now, with all that chocolate over you. Colour has nothing to do with it, love. Never judge a person by their colour. It's unimportant. No, that couple were rich, successful and beautiful. That's what they had in common. They both lived in India but could have lived anywhere, I reckon.'

'But Mummy says they were relations.'

'Yes, they are, kind of.'

'You're not rich, successful or beautiful, are you, Granny?'

'No, love, I'm not. But, do you know – it doesn't matter. That's the lovely thing about it.'

'Oh yes it does! I like being top of my class. Only Sharon usually beats me.' The fierce little face, surrounded by wispy, messy hair tinged with chocolate, stared at Enid who looked away. It was all too painful. The child was right.

By the time Sal and Douglas had arrived to collect their brood, the damage to the house and the garden, the mess in the kitchen and the almost tearful exhaustion felt by Enid were obvious for all to see.

'Oh, Mum, it's too much, isn't it?'

'No, it's not. I've loved having them. You know that.'

No one doubted that Granny loved having them.

Sure enough, the moment they were out of sight, Enid began to cry, not that she knew what it was she was crying about – the beastly Sharon beating Beatrice, probably.

Vijaya sent not only an airily funny letter thanking Enid but enclosed a photo presumably used for her fans. She did indeed look ravishing and, once more, Enid felt torn with possessive loyalty for old toothy Sal and admiration for this other product of Gerry's sperm.

She thought a great deal about his sperm, where he shoved it, when and if there were other results running around. Not just his sperm – after thirty-something or other years, she assumed she knew something about him – from his scrotum to his balding pate, not forgetting his gnarled toenails. Apparently she had been wrong. Oh, there were bits and pieces she undoubtedly did know, but dig inside that grumpy old head and he was a mystery. What the hell did he think he was doing? Relieving hundreds of years of imperialist guilt with one ecstatic jerk in the depths of a glorious make-believe creature!

She thought bitterly of all those years when she had assumed he had given away his personal wealth for some ideological statement, only to find that he had used it to fund some beautiful actress and her little bastard, *his* little bastard. Not just that! He pops over whenever he can to dip his wick, wear his slippers and make extravagant promises about dowries. But did he really love her, or was Savita – Mumsi – simply part of his hang-up?

She tried explaining all this to Adam – as well as remembering not to give him strawberries twice running. Adam listened politely and then delivered his verdict.

'Nine o'clock watershed, that's when they have that kind of stuff.' He was absolutely right. She should never have confided in him.

Adam had lasted with her the year. His worker had left for God and given Adam a portrait of the Virgin Mary. He told Enid that the Virgin didn't show her tits. He would have preferred a portrait of a woman with tits. Enid found a postcard of one of Picasso's paintings of a woman with tits everywhere. Adam took it back with him. It was his pride and joy till it was confiscated after he was found masturbating all over it. There had been a further slight hiccup when Adam produced a packet of 'Velvet Touch' condoms and blew them up so that they whizzed around Enid's kitchen making rude noises. Enid remembered the golden rule and told him it was inappropriate behaviour.

'So what?' he had replied, quite rudely.

Determined to do something with Adam apart from feed him or ask him questions till it was time to go home, Enid taught him chess. It was a resounding success, subject to certain rules. The first was that Adam had to win, the second was that no game should be longer than ten minutes and, finally, there had to be a little licence about cheating. But week after week he asked to play chess. Enid knew nothing more about Adam than she had the first day. He lived in a world with no past, no future. His new worker was a jolly lass called Kate. No nonsense about God with her. He was perfectly bright, full of unrelated facts which he would produce like a rabbit out of a hat, but totally unable to connect anything. Not that it mattered to Enid, but she did wonder if coming out to lunch with her had any meaning for him. She put the question to Kate.

'You'd be surprised. He's been on about Indians. You've had some relatives over. He's seen a photo of some fabulously beautiful woman who is your cousin or something. That's made some impact.'

Enid couldn't help thinking that there had also been a photo of Sal and the twins in the sitting room even longer and he hadn't noticed it. But that was just sour grapes and she wouldn't really want Adam round the twins – not with his sexual interests. So the Sunday lunches continued. As Dolly pointed out, 'It makes you lay the table and cook a proper meal.'

The over-sixties were champing at the bit for their outing. However, wires had got crossed to such a degree that they inadvertently were about to become the invited audience for a TV debate on the age of consent, chaired by Claire Rayner. As one executive admitted, 'There's been a monumental cock-up!'

It was to the clatter of milk bottles and the latest scandal-sheets dropping on the doormat that the old people gathered round the bus station waiting for their coach. The public lavatory was a good gallop from the bus stop, so Sheila was kept busy carrying the incontinent in her car to the imposing edifice in the town square which doubled up as war memorial and lavatory all wrapped up in one. The toilet at the bus station didn't open at that hour. Mrs Jessop flushed her incontinence pad down the loo by mistake. The chemist's was still shut. However, our Sheila hadn't been a girl guide for nothing. Back at the bus stop, a large lady was complaining about her shoes. She hadn't worn them since Christmas and they hurt like hell. Sheila drove her back home. The shoes were changed for bedroom slippers and they were back in time for the coach.

'Where are we going?' asked Bertie Simpson. He liked to slip away to a pub, given half a chance.

'It's one of those mystery dos. We'll be driven to Scarborough to watch the rain, mark my words.' Annie Tolson clasped her capacious bag to her equally capacious bosom and scowled.

''Aven't you 'eard? It's a TV studio. I 'eard them two ladies talking about it.' Mary came from Watford and, after thirty years in North Yorkshire, still had her aitches and glottal stops in the right places.

A groan went up – not Emmerdale Farm yet again! The teas might be good but the flimsy scenery didn't pass muster. As Amy said to her friend, Carol, 'It shouldn't be allowed, not with all them regulations and things. My house is better built than that place.'

They were off. The coach swung onto the A1, avoiding all signs to Scarborough and instead following all signs to Leeds. As Les, who was a bit of a wag, observed, 'Those who belong to the flat earth society, get ready to jump.'

The ladies – as opposed to the women – sat together, warily eyeing their charges for signs of imminent death, vomiting or waterworks. The bus had a natty little loo.

It was then that Wendy, the Chair with bright red nails and loads of eye make-up, dropped the bombshell.

'I think there's been a muddle. It says here that the invited audience is expected to participate, according to their expertise, in a debate about the age of consent.'

Expertise? The ladies looked alarmed. Mrs Cole had fallen

asleep. Her teeth wobbled as she breathed. Could she be regarded as an expert? After all, she had produced ten children. And just look at old Reg, hunched up like a garden gnome. Did he have anything to say about teenage bonking?

'I think they've muddled us up!' Wendy's voice had a touch of hysteria about it. But ladies aren't ladies for nothing. They'd face the challenge.

'Don't tell them till we get there, then they won't have time to panic,' suggested Sheila.

'I don't think they'll panic. Do remember, Sheila, these people are all sentient beings. They have the vote, pay council tax and I don't suppose there's a virgin between them.'

'What about Miss Kitchin? I'm sure she's still a virgin.'

The ladies nattered on. They were clearly apprehensive. The women and what few old men had come along snoozed, chatted or stared at the world over the edge of the flat earth they knew and understood. The bus swung into a car park.

A bevy of lovely girls, bird-brained but with clipboards, met the bus with beaming smiles. TV studios are dead nuts about security; everyone had to have a tag. No umbrellas were allowed, and all handbags had to be inspected.

'It's me rights! Me and my umbrella go everywhere together.'

'I'm sorry, madam. It's the rules.'

'Bugger rules! What does a flibbertigibbet like you know about rules? Do you think Winston Churchill won the war sticking to rules?'

With irrefutable argument like that, what can a flibbertigibbet do? Ada and her brolly were allowed through.

It did cross the mind of Janice, the senior girl among the welcoming staff, that these old things were a curious audience for the live debate. But Janice knew it wasn't her job to decide on audiences so she just continued to process the queue, peering into handbags, making out badges and, where possible, confiscating umbrellas.

The group shuffled from security to lavatory and into the small studio.

'All this way to see a show you can get on your telly.' This statement was accompanied with a significant sniff.

'You've got it wrong, Martha. *We* are going to be on the telly. We have to ask questions and that.'

'Like what?'

'Well, do we think it's a good idea…'

'What's a good idea?'

'Sex and that.'

'Chance would be a fine thing,' came the truculent answer.

The bigger ladies – everyone was a lady here in the egalitarian media world – were squeezed into their seats and there was a great deal of shuffling with coats peeling off in the heat of the lights in the studio. Some ladies were already mumbling suitable questions about the age of consent. Others sat down as if they were about to be electrocuted.

Excitement rises. Claire Rayner arrives with three men. Someone taps the microphone. One of the men speaks.

'Good afternoon, welcome. Oh my God!' There is nothing for it – he continues to explain to this audience of grey-haired, beady-eyed audience how the debate will be conducted. He stresses the necessity of a balanced approach and…would the audience please refrain from interrupting speakers? Finally, would every speaker please say what organisation they represent? Then it was over to Claire. The three men were showing signs of great alarm. The one who was speaking left his seat and almost ran out of the studio.

Five minutes to go. A colossal fuck-up! Someone had invited the over-sixties as the audience for the debate on the age of consent! No doubt a bemused party of experts on sex were being given the spiel about some soap or other before being given a slap-up tea.

Lights started flashing. The monitors picked up our Les picking his nose and Mrs Peabody having a snooze. Mostly it focused on beady-eyed old people waiting for their moment of glory. The cameraman desperately panned across for some younger 'experts'.

'Bloody hell, mate! You've got a right bunch of OAPs here. You sure they are the right lot?'

Someone whispered to the Chair. Claire chuckled, 'Well, that's a turn-up for the books. Bless 'em, they'll do you proud. Just watch.' She tapped her microphone and away they went.

For a dizzy half-hour, quite by mistake, the over-sixties were encouraged to have an opinion. And have it they did. Amy Harrison was the first to speak. She wasn't quite sure what age and what consent she was meant to be talking about but she realised it was to do with sex. Mr Harrison had died many years before and Amy had felt left out of things.

'It's all very well banging on about when they start. Kids play at that kind of thing from the word go, if you ask me. It's the other end that worries me. Why should they assume we're not interested just because we're over sixty? It's not fair.'

There was a murmur of agreement. Several heads nodded, including Bertie, who was having a kip. Sandra put up her hand. A young lady scampered over with a microphone.

'My name is Sandra – Over-sixties Club. I was sixteen when I had my first. In them days we didn't have no contraception and that. I might have ended up Maggie bloody Thatcher, like, if I hadn't had ten kids! Sex and babies aren't the same thing, are they? I mean, cut down on babies and these kids are safe enough with sex. I say teach them about contraception. Leave babies out of it.' Sandra had made, for her, a very long speech. She was slightly tearful at the end and sat back, quivering with emotion.

Woman after woman, and occasionally an old man, spoke with strong emotion about their early gropings, their initiations into sex, their trapped marriages, their large families and handicapped children. But, above all, they spoke about the lack of control over their lives. As Carol explained, 'Carol, Over-sixties. The age of consent is at both ends. When we were young, we weren't meant to know or do anything till we were married. Now we aren't meant to know, and certainly aren't meant to do, if you know what I mean. I tell you, Claire, if that audience out there thought we were still interested in sex they'd run a bloody mile. No ages of consent, that is what I say.'

Several said that being fiddled with was really horrible but the age of consent did little to stop fiddling. The same with rape. It happened all the time. Having them short skirts and bare midriffs didn't help.

A brave man admitted having sex at thirteen and standing up to avoid pregnancy. As he pointed out, with a packet of condoms he'd have been able to lie down. 'Age of consent – what does that mean to a couple of sexually charged kids?' he asked.

Miss Kitchin spoke next. She introduced herself and the Over-sixties Club. She announced she was a virgin and felt that it was more than likely she would remain one. It was a perfectly acceptable state. She had held interesting jobs, been able to buy herself a small house and thought young people should be encouraged to see it as an acceptable alternative to – and here she pursed her lips before saying 'bonking'. Cheers greeted her contribution.

The next speaker was the diminutive Mrs Black.

'Mrs Black – Over-sixties. Age of consent, my foot! What those busy-bodies don't understand is that even babies play with each other's bits and pieces. What's the harm? Plenty of young lads do it – very young, like – and girls. Tell 'em not to make babies, tell 'em what to do, where to go, an' that. It's not the sex that matters, it's the babies.' It was a message repeated over and over again.

'Ron White – Over-sixties. Has no one read their Bible? Sex is a gift from God. You don't open presents before Christmas Day. The age of consent should be like Christmas Day.'

There were a handful of old codgers who basically thought the whole business rather disgusting and several more who completely got the wrong end of the stick. There were a couple of randy pensioners who thought it was a government plot to stop their sex lives.

'Just when they've got that pill to keep the old pecker up,' as Charlie so beautifully put it.

Claire summed up. She stressed how privileged she'd been listening to the views of older people. The programme wasn't quite as advertised, but she felt sure that we were all the wiser to have the opinions of older people who aren't usually heard or understood. She stressed the tolerance shown by the older people and suggested that if there was a lesson to be learnt it was to include older people in discussions on all topics in future.

Enid, in her best skirt, had sat near the front flanked by two old ladies. She was almost weepy with admiration and solidarity for the dignity and honesty displayed as the old people painted their sex lives, with the grim toll of unwanted pregnancies and the rigid veneer of secrecy covering every aspect of sex and reproduction. She shuddered at the problems any homosexual might have experienced. The old people had made one point over and over again. They wanted to make sure that never again were young women faced with unwanted pregnancies.

'The trouble is that trendy social workers tell these bloody girls that it's their *right* to have some damp little bundle. What about the damp little bundle's right to a decent home?'

It was all a little close to home for Enid, who found the image of the beautiful Vijaya leering at her.

Enid shook her head like an old horse trying to rid itself of a wasp. Was she the unwanted curse in Gerry's life? Had she got the whole business cockeyed? She couldn't answer. She was better off thinking about the old people and their opinions.

She noticed two changes in the bus on the way home. The first was with the old people themselves. On the journey home they chatted like magpies, prodding their fingers into their neighbour's chest to make a point, cupping the hands to impart some juicier snippet. The other change was with the organising ladies. They dropped their patronising manner and those terms of endearment which equally demeaned the old people. Something had happened. There was a respect in the air and, by the time they reached Ripon, everyone felt they had an opinion worth hearing.

The television company's public relations department was in uproar. The national papers were thrilled:

SEXY SUSIE SAYS SEVENTY IS NOT TOO OLD FOR A BIT OF THE OLD
WHATSIT

or:

GRANNIES VOTE FOR SEX, IT KEEPS THEM YOUNG.
SHY RON HAS SOME ADVICE.
KEEP IT UP, GRANDPA.

The bus station in Ripon is no place for looking your best after a hard day's outing. But the press were there and they wanted their pictures. Mrs Black's great-niece had a hair salon nearby and she was dragged out from *Brookside* to open up and titivate the ladies and gentlemen to be photographed. It was a riot, a ball: cameras clicked and the elderly preened. Afterwards, the TV company socked them all a Chinese and no-one got to bed before midnight.

It caused a stir. Even Enid was drawn into the debate and interviewed by the local paper. The reporter, an elegant young lady who was destined for greater things than rural gossip – or so she thought – bounced out of her blue Golf and silenced Sophocles with a tuck under the chin.

'Mrs Tanner?'

It was a warm day. Bees were already droning in the border and the lawn needed mowing. It was a day that made it a criminal offence to stay inside. Enid had made a jug of fresh lemonade.

'You don't mind being out of doors, do you?'

'Not at all. It's so lovely it seems a shame to be working.'

Enid sat composed on the old bench with the reporter beside her. The reporter's name was Serena. Enid suspected she was privately educated.

'I gather you've been trying to get the over-sixties extending their interests?'

'Yes, I have, but the visit to the TV centre was nothing to do with me; it was a genuine mistake.'

'But you are pleased the old folk had a chance to put their views?'

'Do stop using the term "folk". I'm sure you'd hate it if I called you "young folk". But of course I'm pleased. If those old people had been in the House of Lords, or what's left of it, everybody would have listened to them. Elderly bishops, ex-MPs long past their sell-by date, arse-lickers and the rest can pontificate, but if you're old and ordinary, you are usually booted out from what you've been doing, and from then onwards the chances of anyone listening to your opinion about anything other than the weather is nil.'

'But sex…' began Serena.

'Particularly about sex. Can you imagine what it is like to lose your sexual partner at a time of life when you haven't a hope in hell's chance of getting another? Can you imagine what it is like being the butt of sexual jokes simply because you are old? Can you honestly say you haven't patronised and ridiculed someone simply because they are old? Would you expect the Queen to have an opinion on the age of consent? I bet you would – so why not the over-sixties?'

Enid rattled off her questions before sitting there ready to take the flack. She rather wished she hadn't mentioned the Queen. It seemed most unlikely that the Queen did have a public view on the age of consent.

Serena was getting used to passion about pigs, pylons and dog shit, but sex in North Yorkshire seemed pretty matter-of-fact. She asked Enid if she was a feminist.

'I suppose so. I don't really know what it means. I'm that generation which didn't bother with slogans like that.'

Enid had run out of steam. There was something inhibiting her from telling the truth. She resorted to the lemonade and tried coaxing Serena into revealing her views on the age of consent.

'But you haven't told me yours yet,' protested the reporter.

'I think it's a daft concept. Two randy kids can screw like bunnies at eleven or twelve. But having babies, now that is totally irresponsible. Having sex with someone young and vulnerable, if it's genuinely consensual, I don't know. If it's a question of power – that is wrong. There are so many cases of marriage with night-in, night-out sex, quite sickeningly loathed by the woman, with no redress…and we lock up some gormless idiot who has done no more than screw some willing-to-be-screwed scrawny maiden. All I know is that the whole idea of the age of consent at one end affects our attitude at the other.'

Enid had said too much. She was out of her depth, she didn't know what she was talking about. What would Vijaya say if she could see her now? Probably sneer and say only the beautiful, only the desirable had a right to discuss such matters. Enid was neither beautiful nor desirable. She was a widow in her sixties, having buried her husband who, bastard that he was, had lived a double life with a film star. Poor Enid began to cry.

BONKING GRANNY SEEKS PARTNER was one of the headlines. As Dolly observed, 'You can't keep a good woman down. Enid, you're rapidly becoming an icon for the over-sixties. This means a completely new wardrobe, proper haircut – and your face could do with some help. It's those whiskers on your chin.'

Led by the hand, coaxed and bullied by Dolly, Enid found herself with nail polish, moisturiser, a glamorous swept-back hairdo which cost fifty pounds and, too embarrassed to mention it, she bought some saucy undies.

'It isn't me,' bleated Enid.

'It's not you, Granny,' said Sophie, slowly walking round her grandmother.

'Ma, what have you been up to?' Sal, in contrast, had the lank unwashed look. She hadn't started on the whisker syndrome yet. She wore no make-up. Enid didn't want to think about her knickers, for there are some things that are strictly taboo, daughter's knickers being one of them. Let's face it, Sal looked a cheerful mess. Roger lay propped up on a towel covering several filthy cushions, gurgling and waving the egg whisk, his clothes well-washed hand-me-downs.

Douglas came into the kitchen and gave Enid a kiss.

'A sex bomb mother-in-law, what about that?' He laughed. 'Want a hand, Sal?'

It was a world Enid understood, a world of hard physical work, a belief that your values are the right values – they must be right – the hard graft and the educational standards the children must strive for. Saving, always saving, for a holiday, a new tractor, a pair of shoes. They must be right, otherwise what's the point? A brief flowering, a dizzy freedom, hard grind and it begins all over again.

Enid stood in the middle of the kitchen, her family all around her and shouted, '*Stop!*'

She put up her hand. The baby began to cry and immediately Sal scooped up the bundle.

'Sal, I'm sorry.' Sal looked warily at Enid and asked what for.

'Getting it wrong. Why shouldn't you lead the life of Vijaya? After all, she is your half-sister. It wasn't really Gerry's fault. I know now. It was mine. I haven't taught you how to have fun, how to be a beauty queen to yourself.'

'Are you off your rocker? How the hell could I be a beauty queen? Apart from anything else, I haven't the time or the money, and I certainly don't have the motivation, not with teeth like mine.'

'But I should have insisted you wore those horrible braces. You refused and I hadn't the heart to make you.'

Douglas clasped Sal and the baby, nuzzling his wife's neck. 'You're *my* beauty queen,' he told her.

'Give over! Anyway, I must get lunch.'

'Granny, are you trying to be a beauty queen?' It was Sophie.

'Granny is off her rocker, if you ask me.' Sal stirred the gravy.

'Are you?' It was Beatrice this time.

'Do you know about butterflies?' asked Enid.

'Kind of, they start out as an egg – like Roger did.'

Sophie added the next phase. 'I know, I know. They become caterpillars and eat and eat. Then they hide in a chrisamus, something like that.'

Beatrice finished, 'They come out of the chrisamus as a beautiful butterfly.'

'That's pretty good. It's a chrysalis. They wrap themselves out of sight till they are ready to be butterflies.' Douglas loved it when his family produced nuggets of wisdom.

'I want my Sal to be a butterfly, not a drudge,' whined Enid.

'Oh, for God's sake, shut up. All this nonsense has gone to your head,' snapped Sal, trying to carry young Roger and serve lunch.

'No, Sal, I won't shut up. Why should you end up a washed-out wreck with years ahead of you? Why should you lose your looks, your figure, yet retain a frustrated libido?'

'Yours might be frustrated but, I assure you, mine isn't. Now sit down and shut up.'

She was pissing up a rope. Enid ate in silence with a veneer of a sulk. Well, Sal had tried to warn her.

Granny was booted out early. She hadn't the right shoes for a walk and so was sent home.

Sophocles was furious. He had little time for swept-back hairdos, moisturiser and elegant shoes. He liked walks, disgusting smells, bitches and his grub. Now he had to sit in the back of the car and listen to Enid moan.

She didn't moan for long. There was a pile of letters from women trapped in a lifestyle that did little or nothing to massage their egos. Farmers' wives, with red-raw hands, up at five milking cows; wives who booted out their men before getting the children off to school. Then they were off to work for a day of endless repetition – shop, home, tea, telly. There were sad letters from devoted daughters and even sadder letters from defeated women raped years before and still feeling soiled and ashamed years later. There were the wives pushed aside for mistresses, mistresses waiting for wives to drop down dead, and divorces that took women from the frying pan and hurled them into the fire. Then there was money – never enough – with wives sourly making ends meet while pampered girlfriends strutted around in their finery.

That rang a bell. It was Vijaya all over again. Enid did her best, she wrote kind letters with simple generalities. She was tentative, modest and scared at the level of pain the letters revealed.

'Dolly,' she rang, ' I know it sounds awful, but I just can't answer all of these on my own. Any chance of mortifying the flesh on smoked salmon and a bottle of Chablis, then you giving me a hand?'

Dolly came like a shot. Remember her advice to Enid after the funeral? Never turn down an invitation.

Enid brushed her hair and changed into something smarter than jeans. She had learnt that much.

She still wore those awful nightdresses, climbing into her double bed with just the radio for comfort. Lying there after a hard evening responding to the pent-up emotions of the women who wrote to her, Enid's head spun in a kaleidoscopic mixture of anger, elation, self-doubt, yearning and an itch. There was a desire to move, struggle and fight the emotional dead-end Gerry had pushed her into. Or was it she who had done the pushing?

'I know,' she said aloud, 'I'm going to move! I'm going to buy a house for myself. I'm going to begin again. Gerry can't stop me.' She sat up in the dark; the radio was droning on about the shipping forecast – Rockall, Malin and all those boring bits of rock only mariners know about.

She raised her voice, 'Gerry, do you hear? I'm off. All that bullshit about loyalty – forget it. It's getting me nowhere.' She snuggled under her duvet and, very soon, the weight of loyalty lifted. She slept deeply, dreaming about flailing limbs.

Next morning she told Sophocles what she planned. He was licking his private parts, making a disgusting slurpy noise.

'What do you think, old boy?' He didn't bother to stop his ablutions, so she shrugged and asked the cat instead. Cat gave her one of those looks which have a 'drop down dead' stare built into them.

Animals can be so unsatisfactory.

She rang an agent who advertised in her local paper. A Mr Potter would come over the next day.

It's appalling what one takes for granted. There was that piece of string holding up the cupboard which Gerry was going to fix – was it ten years ago? And the cigarette packet jammed under the door to make it shut; he hadn't smoked for the last six years. The curtain rail in the downstairs cloakroom had come adrift months ago; she still hadn't fixed it. The light had gone in the corridor; she hated fixing lights. What a shabby dump it was! The garden had been nearly cleared for the winter. There were just a few frosted plants curled and withered to mush, droopy nettles and overgrown raspberry canes with some bulging, slug-ridden lettuces. A huge marrow sat like a spaceship in the vegetable patch, its belly a veritable housing estate for destitute slugs. Enid made herself a cup of coffee and sat in the kitchen remembering when she and Gerry had bought their house.

He had just returned from Peru – 'Hot and smelly'. They were living in a small but delightful terrace house – two-up, two-down – with a tiny bathroom. There was no central heating, no washing machine and a fridge which made so much fuss and bother, clanking away, that Enid often thought it was easier not to use it. Sal was a damp bundle.

'Come on, Edie, I want something better for us.'

'But can we afford it?' Enid could see herself frowning slightly.

The Old Barn was built between the wars, someone's idea of a rural retreat. The 'barn' bit was phoney as hell – just some exposed timbers. It had a large kitchen garden, several flower beds and a patio which appealed to Gerry's inverted snobbery. It was the first thing he told his sister, Eleanor. 'We've got a patio! What about that?' Later, in case Enid had missed the point, he added, 'Eleanor will know we've definitely come down in the world – a patio is living proof. After all, she has a terrace, while we're reduced to patio status.'

'And a lounge? What about going whole hog and putting a cocktail cabinet in the lounge. I'll tell her that too.' They had roared with laughter. But even Gerry balked at the lounge and insisted it became the sitting room. Had she seen the joke, Enid asked herself, while all the time that tart in Bombay was whooping it up on Gerry's inheritance? Enid had been curious to start with, naive and sympathetic, till Vijaya spilt the beans about Gerry's fortune. Now she was heading towards bitterness and jealousy. That cow! Enid had been prudent and careful all her married life – only to find that that cow had got in first. Gradually her resentment turned to Gerry.

'You bastard! How could you do it?' That was why she wanted to move. She wanted to begin again without Gerry's duplicity rammed down her throat.

Mr Potter seemed very young. He had bad spots, a loud tie and a clipboard. He walked into the sitting room, mumbling square footage as he did so. He mumbled throughout the house, occasionally changing his tune to, 'The wiring; it will need complete rewiring. Some rising damp there. What about a damp course?'

He walked round the garden, peered into the garage then sighed over his coffee. Never a good time of year to sell. The market was stagnant. He would do his best, but he couldn't promise much. How much, was what Enid wanted to know. Mr Potter gave a figure per square foot. Enid was none the wiser.

'Just tell me how much – or words to that effect?' Mr Potter sighed a great deal more, looking at her with such melancholy it was neck and neck who would burst into tears first. Mr Potter gave a figure, immediately retracted it and they were back at the rising damp. Sophocles joined them. He stood, tail slightly wagging, staring up at Mr Potter, who bent down and started patting him.

'He's lovely. A Highland, isn't he?'

'Do you have a dog?' asked Enid.

'It's difficult, being out all day. No, I have gerbils.'

'Oh, how lovely! I've often thought I would like to own gerbils.' This was a downright lie.

Half an hour later Enid had learnt that Mr Potter hated being an estate agent and really wanted to be an RSPCA inspector but was turned down because of his asthma. Yes, he watched *Pet Rescue* whenever he could. At this point Enid remembered how she and Gerry used to watch it and felt terribly guilty at selling the house.

'You know, Mrs Tanner, it doesn't always pay to move.'

'I know, Mr Potter, but there are times in life when you have to get out. I need to start again.'

'I'll do my best. Quite frankly… I – I'll be in touch.'

The following Sunday, for want of something to say, Enid told Adam she was planning to move. The news was greeted in silence. After about five minutes Adam asked if Enid had done her Christmas shopping. He had. She asked him what he had bought. It was a secret, apparently. When they got back to the house, Adam, who was no cold weather fan, said he wanted to look round the garden. He walked round with great solemnity but no words. Over lunch he said little apart from expressing the opinion that Brussels sprouts stank like Billy, one of the youngsters in the home. Enid had heard them described as smelling worse than that. 'Like Daddy farting' was Beatrice's description.

'Shall we play chess, Adam?'

He sat opposite her and put the pieces out with meticulous care. He was allowed to start. Pawns cautiously moved forward. A dashing knight started prancing, only to be struck down by Enid's bishop. Adam disliked losing pieces. He would contort himself into knots, flail his arms and shout, 'Oh no!' When in a real rage he hurled the board to the ground and Enid had to shuffle round on her hands and knees finding the pieces. But today he concentrated. Enid made sure he won. Usually he was ecstatic, but not today. He sat silently, switched off from chess, Enid, everything.

Mr Potter and Enid decided to put the house up for sale after Christmas. It gave Enid a chance to get the Christmas decorations out of the way and Mr Potter a chance to enjoy Christmas without Enid breathing down his neck. There was one place Enid hadn't had the guts to clear out after Gerry's death and that was the attic. 'Guts' was the wrong word. It was very difficult to get into the attic. There was a special ladder which was heavy and difficult to elongate and retract. She lugged the unwieldy thing into position, gingerly climbed up and pushed open the trapdoor. A fusty, musty smell met her as she clambered through the opening – bat shit, she suspected. A weak light filtered through the attic, enough to show the outline of a trunk with Gerry's name. Enid thought of the television programmes she had watched with skeletons, dead bodies and other nasties lurking under the lid. She lifted it, peering inside once her eyes became accustomed to the gloom. She found some cricket pads and old school reports.

'Tanner dreams too much'; 'Tanner must overcome tendency to lose concentration'; 'Tanner thinks strong views are the same as knowledge'… Tanner this and Tanner that. Enid read on. She agreed with his English teacher, chuckled at the bad-tempered comment from his history teacher, sympathised with several others, and was amused at his housemaster's report:

> Tanner is independent to a point where it is a liability. He must learn that this is neither a home nor a community run for his benefit alone. He proclaims profoundly left-wing views. It would be as well that he reads and learns what he is advocating. God help us if he goes into politics.

Enid struck out.

'Well, he didn't! He joined some hush-hush enterprise, went off to India, gave away his fortune and spent the rest of his life a grumpy old man without much money, peering over his shoulder at his well-heeled relations.'

Her voice meant nothing in that attic, with its harsh tone and waspish delivery. She let the lid snap shut. It didn't; it let out a squeak of protest and slowly creaked back into place. Next was a pair of skis with bindings at least forty years out of date. A chair with a broken leg leant lopsidedly against a very nasty bamboo table that her mother had given them when they first got married. There were several paintings of splendid Tanners who had not

194

given away their fortunes; however, they seemed universally plain and the frames were ghastly. Enid had begun this search of the attic with a certain dread – the dead body syndrome. Now she was rather sad. It was a dull attic representing a dull life – his life and hers. Well, what about her life?

'I'm sixty-plus and I haven't even started,' she murmured.

They always proclaim that the nativity play is about the start of something and, sure enough, it was time for the nativity play all over again. This year Beatrice was the innkeeper and Sophie a wise man. They came over for the day to help Enid decorate her house.

'You're such a grouch, Granny.' The little girls peered at her tree decorations and tut-tutted at the paucity of tinsel, paper chains – and where was the fairy for the Christmas tree? They drove over to Ripon and spent what Enid considered a fortune buying a revolting fairy with a simpering expression and a white nylon dress. On her back was stamped 'Made in Hong Kong'. The twins, with unerring bad taste, chose some frightful baubles for the tree. On the way back they rehearsed their parts for the nativity play.

'Granny, I speak first. I say, "'Allo, 'allo, 'allo, what can I do for you?" Then I say, "Sorry, mate, we're choc-a-block, but you can have the stable. There's plenty of straw and there's a manger for the nipper."'

There was a certain amount of shoving before Sophie began her part.

'I'm very wise, see? And I see this star. "That is most interesting, let's find out more." These wise people go down to the manger in Bethlehem and when they see the baby, I say "That is a very special little person and I shall give her some frankincense."'

Enid noted with satisfaction the feminist contemporary theologian was still at the helm in their primary school.

A couple of days later she sat with a bonny bouncing Roger beside her on Sal's knee and watched the performance. Mary looked pretty glum about the whole business. The donkey waved enthusiastically at his mum and a tree was overcome with stage fright. Enid tried to remember when she last went to the proper theatre; Gerry wasn't interested. It always came back to that – Gerry this and Gerry that. She remembered the housemaster's report and a well of bitterness stayed in her throat.

All I seem to do is go to crap nativity plays even though I think it's a load of junk, or make up numbers with other middle-class bores like myself so that the table looks even. Or I cart old people round stately homes, many of whom spent a life of servitude working in some grand house and swore they'd never, never again set foot in another. Oh, I comfort my conscience with poor old Adam and that's about it. Sixty-something – and years, boring, uneventful years, married to some old fart who was absent-minded about where he left his money and his sperm. If I've ever had an original thought, I've lost it. If I've ever felt confident enough to do something, that nano-second soon passed. But ssh, the nativity play is about to finish...

'So, everybody, our Christmas message to you all is, "Fight for what is right". That's what Jesus did.' The speaker was a very plain tall girl with glasses, dressed in a boiler-suit several sizes too big.

Too bloody late! thought Enid. Anyway, I don't believe in all this Jesus crap. But all she did was smile – she didn't mouth a word. Later in bed she finished the sentence by adding, 'Nor anything else.'

Christmas Day was spent eating dry turkey, underdone roast potatoes, mushy Brussels sprouts, lumpy bread sauce and supermarket pud served with Douglas's brandy butter, followed by the washing-up. It was revolting and Enid felt very guilty even thinking it. After all, Sal had put her heart and soul into cooking the meal. Afterwards Enid tried to assemble a stable for Sophie's toy pony. Douglas disappeared to feed some heifers and Roger stuffed his mouth with wrapping paper while Sal did a quick sketch of the children engrossed in playing with their toys.

'Do you often get the paints out, Sal?'

'Not often enough, but I've got my daydreams. You know the large barn that is full of clapped-out machinery? Well, I want to convert it into an art centre – get a grant and do it properly. I don't want to start doing it commercially till Roger begins school, but don't you think it's a good idea?'

Enid almost found herself shaking with jealousy. Why wasn't she twenty years younger? Yes, it was a wonderful idea and would lift Sal out of the kitchen sink. Sal was better than foul Brussels sprouts, better than the dried turkey. Sal used to be fun – full of wacky artistic ideas – all blonde hair, teeth and energy. Now she was off again, bless her heart. But the green-eyed monster didn't like it one little bit. She couldn't tell Sal; all she could do was beat a hasty retreat home.

Christmas was over and done with when the phone went. It insisted on being answered; an urgency permeated the room. Enid, frowning, lifted the phone.

'Mrs Tanner?'

'Yes…' She said it with drawn-out exaggeration. Her spirits sank; was it that awful Vijaya?

'It's about Adam. We thought you would want to be told. He burnt himself to death.'

'He *what*?'

'There'll be an enquiry. He's not been himself the last few days – very withdrawn. Last night he poured petrol over his body and set fire to himself, Mrs Tanner. It was ghastly; there was nothing we could do. He was wrapped in a fire blanket but it was too late.' Whoever was phoning her was reduced to sobs.

'Oh my God! You know, when he was last here, he was not saying much and fingering everything. You don't think it was because I'm selling my house?'

'We're going round and round worrying about what triggered it. It's impossible to know with someone like Adam. He didn't have any visits over Christmas. Many of them go home, but not Adam.'

'When's the funeral?'

'There will be a coroner's inquest first, but I'll let you know. Oh, Mrs Tanner, he so enjoyed his visits to your house; it was the highlight of his week.'

And where he got the matches, decided Enid, after she had put the phone down. She was shaking and had to make herself a cup of coffee before she could begin watching the television again. She saw limbs dutifully entwined and lips pressing their fleshy moistness on other lips; moans and lusty noises accompanied the bodies, but it was wasted on Enid. She was wracked with guilt. She had supplied the matches. He had been fingering them the last time he came – on the unsatisfactory visit, when he had said little and fingered the house as if he knew it was the last time. She knew he had taken the matches because she had looked for them that evening and not found them. The small Christmas tree and the attempts to introduce Christmas cheer looked cold and inappropriate. Enid found herself going over and over the incident of the matches.

Poor Adam, with his quirky mind and crazy insights – often spot on, in their way; his pomposity, like the time he complained about too many strawberries; his resolute inability to relate to her or to anyone, despite his quick wit and cunning; his inflexible routines: where he sat, what Enid must do – like her seat belt. Adam would rather die than let someone drive without a seat belt. And sex – she wondered if he had ever made love. No! Those were idiotic words to use about Adam: 'Ever had sex with a woman?' The Adams of this world had a role to play. They were important. We just don't treat them with the respect they deserve.

Enid saw the pernickety, fastidious young man who taught her not to be frightened of people who are different, to delight in what they give, however quirky. With Adam, it was often his reply to some question Enid had asked him. Love, relationships, Christmas presents, what to eat – Adam had an answer. But why, why, had he killed himself? Part of Enid blamed it all on herself. It was moving house, wasn't it?

Don't be so melodramatic, chided a more balanced side of her brain. *Adam wanted to, that is all.* There was little autonomy in his life, far too much overprotection, little stimulus. He wasn't slow or stupid. He was different – something that is threatening and misunderstood; a challenge few people accept; while many, like Enid, cock it up – or thought she had.

How was I to know moving would be so dreadful for Adam?

Enid and Sophocles wandered the muddy lanes. It was a sad Boxing Day with weather to match. Enid was obsessed by Adam's death, blaming herself over and over. She had even rung to tell them that he had taken her matches and she also blamed herself because she had told him she was moving house.

'Nonsense!' they reassured her. Life was about accepting that people move house. Adam knew that intellectually. But chew on it she did, working over and over her own insensitivity. She tried the 'If only' syndrome and applied it to the number of times she gave him strawberries before he complained. Like Adam, Enid knew intellectually that people don't actually set fire to themselves because they have too many strawberries six months before. But, like Adam, Enid's hold on reality was distorted – in her case, by her grief. She wept down the phone to Sal, to Dolly, to one or two comforting old stalwarts – and they, to a man, said the same thing once they had put the phone down.

'She never did that when poor old Gerry snuffed it,' or words to that effect.

The coroner's court was stuffy, cheerless and had a great many middle-aged men padding around. It wasn't petrol. Adam had used lighter fuel – six tins of the stuff. He stole it from the workshop where, to while away the time, he made useless things no one wanted. The instructor had noticed that a tin or two was missing, but that was several months before.

Before he knew I was moving, Enid told herself. Having taken on the mantle of guilt, she felt curiously let down that her scenario was more melodramatic than it was accurate. She was asked about the matches and said she had found some missing just before Christmas. The appropriate verdict of misadventure was brought in and there was only his funeral left.

Apart from three members of staff, there was one woman in an anorak and Enid. What Gerry had been denied, Adam had in rich abundance – a vicar with a frightful accent and genuinely frightful socks, not so much white as tartan. There were prayers galore, a brief speech about how much Adam had enriched other people's lives – 'Hear! hear!' And everyone trouped out to 'dust to dust' and down he went, rather gingerly, into a hole draped in phoney green grass.

Afterwards, Veronica, a member of staff, asked Enid to meet Adam's mum. They shook hands. She was a gaunt, bony woman wearing a thin cotton dress under the shabby anorak, plimsolls and no stockings. Her lank hair was pulled back by a slide so that her bony features stuck out in a face raw with cold.

'Hello, Mrs Lamden. I'm one of Adam's friends. He came over once a week.'

Mrs Lamden said nothing.

'He was such a character, a really special person.' Still the mother stood there, her eyes warily flicking to and fro. Poor love, she must be frozen, thought Enid.

'Would you like a drink or something before you go back?'

Veronica, the cad, claimed another appointment, leaving Enid with this unprepossessing creature. Mrs Lamden and Enid walked in silence from the cemetery along a neat street with a touch of prosperity in the front gardens and parked cars until they found the Brown Heifer. Enid pushed open the door and an all-embracing beery fug enveloped them. Several faces swivelled and then returned to their beer, their thoughts and their privacy. Enid found a table with a menu.

'What would you like, Mrs Lamden?'

'Double whisky.'

Well, at least she speaks, thought Enid, as she looked at the sad, cold, tired and surly woman.

'I'll order the food at the same time. You would like something to eat, wouldn't you?'

Mrs Lamden flipped through the menu before asking for burger and chips. Enid found lasagne and thought she'd drink a beer. She gave the order and brought back the drinks.

'Do call me Enid. What's your name?'

'Name, name, name! It's always yer bloody name,' declared Mrs Lamden, and she gulped back the whisky in one. 'Any chance of another? I'm perished.'

Enid asked for only a single measure this time round. Mrs Lamden knocked that back, observing as she did so that a single measure wasn't what she'd asked for.

The lasagne and burger arrived. Mrs Lamden tucked in with her knife and fork held with pathetic gentility.

'Tell me a bit about Adam. What was he like as a kid?'

'Barmy, that's what. Them doctors and people were forever testing him.'

'You must have been very worried.'

'Knackered, not worried. The little blighter didn't do this, couldn't do that, trips to the hospital, special schools – you don't know the half of it. Well, I said, if they want him so much they better keep him. The money spent on that kid – it's disgusting. You have to be nutty as a fruitcake to get any sympathy these days. There's my Adam having dinner with you every Sunday. What about me? Bet I wouldn't get asked!'

The whisky was loosening her tongue. Mrs Lamden was bitter. She was also getting drunk.

'I did ask for a double, you know. I asked you for a double. I suppose you know best, they all know best.'

'Here it is, Mrs Lamden.' She was right; Enid had taken it upon herself to change the order to a single shot. All the same, if the woman wants to get drunk after her son's funeral, why shouldn't she? So a double it was.

The next double whisky was knocked back in one. Now that colour had suffused the cheeks of Mrs Lamden, her pale blue eyes focused on Enid.

'A lady like you wouldn't 'ave a clue. Ever been on benefits? Do you know, my room is so fucking damp I can wash me bloody hands by wiping them down the wall. Now, Adam had a lovely room in that place, all his meals taken care of, pocket money. I ask you! *Pocket money* for that great nut! You 'ave to be loony these days. Fancy letting 'im 'ave matches an' the like. Mind you, it's no great loss, is it?' She paused, as if finding some new grievance.

'I did ask for another double, didn't I? Now if Adam had asked… as I said…it's daft buggers that get the help these days.'

Mrs Lamden's features had reddened, her eyes were angry pellets, her voice softened to a maudlin purr.

'You think the world of them when they're born; then the yelling starts. Got on me nerves, all that racket.'

'Did you have a husband to help?'

'Wot ya think, lady – me, the marrying type? No, lived with me mum till she kicked us out – it was the bloody crying. Housing got me somewhere. Then they started: "'Ave you done this, 'ave you wiped yer arse? Does baby smile?" Fucking baby was too busy yelling to smile! There's another word they never stop using: "Does baby relate?" No! Baby doesn't. Baby is bloody nuts. Lucky ole baby, he never knew the half of it. Ended his bloody life having dinner – oh, pardon me, *lunch* – with some la-di-da lady who gives him matches. Mind you, I don't s'pose you thought he'd burn himself with them. What about that shot you owe me?'

This, Mrs Lamden, is the last thing you are going to get out of me. You are a very nasty – I suspect alcoholic – wreck. Enid smiled pleasantly as she composed these thoughts and handed over the whisky.

Mrs Lamden threw back the whisky and prepared to tell Enid her life story. Enid suspected this and invented a dental appointment.

'It's the dentist – I must go.'

'You 'aven't got the fare back, 'ave you?'

The last sight of Mrs Lamden that Enid saw was this shabby figure looking round the pub for further comfort and a source of drink. She must have found them, for in the local paper the following week was the account of Mrs Lamden who, much the worse for wear having drunk the money to get her home, had broken the windows of the home for disabled youngsters in Lion Place. In another part of the paper was an account of Adam's funeral. Enid tried hard to tie the two events together but it didn't fit. Still, it made for an unusual Christmas – a counterbalance to the inedible Christmas dinner and Sal's chance of a breakout from the tyranny of domesticity. The next thrill was the Chippendales.

The over-sixties were a little vague about what the Chippendales were. But the prospect of a knees-up at a swanky nightclub in Leeds had done wonders for the local hairdressers and produced from the wardrobes some fabulous outfits.

'They are a group of dancers who do erotic dancing for women.' That is what Wendy told her bathroom mirror. After all that bravado from months ago, she was feeling a little ambivalent. Despite the publicity and Claire Rayner's plea that the old should be included, they weren't.

Like the rest, Enid had also been washed, set and brushed to an unusually elegant shape. She wore her blue wool. In front of her mirror she admitted she hadn't a clue what the Chippendales really did. She only hoped they didn't go too far.

The ladies – we are all ladies now – and gentlemen clambered on board the bus. Mrs Thompson sat next to her friend, Ada. Mrs Thompson had a halo of blue curls and was wearing a scarlet top with sequins draped over her capacious bosom. Ada's hair was severely straight, snipped to perfection. She favoured a dark blue dress. She was a beanpole of a woman and carried her years well.

'Well, Ada, what do you think – them Chippendales?'

'To tell the truth, Doris, I thought they were furry things from America. My Iris says it's all the rage – wiggling their privates and that.'

'They never! You mean we're off to see some what-have-yous? Well I never, whatever next! Mind you, Ada, why shouldn't we? After all, we pay our rates same as everyone.'

Then there was old Reg and Margaret. Reg was a little deaf. He lived with his daughter and went over for a couple of hours every day to see Margaret. She still managed on her own but the stairs were getting her down. Reg was buttoned up in a tweed jacket, pullover and nice warm shirt. Margaret had on her best skirt she'd bought ten years before when her Ernie got married.

'Button up warm, Reg. You don't want any problems with your chest.'

'Do you know what we're going to see, Mags?'

'You'll see soon enough. It's cavorting boys wiggling their bums.'

Reg looked with incredulity at Margaret. 'At our age?'

'Why ever not? Come off it, why shouldn't we have a bit of fun!'

'Speak for yourself. Now, if it was topless women I'd be as keen as mustard,' he croaked cheerfully.

There were several ladies who were confused about Chippendale. They had mostly been in service in their youth. Several more thought they were off to the cinema to see *The Full Monty*. Enid and the other committee members going with the coach reassured the confused and encouraged an element of ooh-la-la among the saucier ladies. There was a difficult moment when Sam Tolson announced he could save them all the bother and show what he had instead.

'No you can't – I didn't bring my microscope!' It not only brought the house down but put Sam in his place. The other old gentlemen sensibly kept quiet. There was a sparkle of anticipation as they drove into Leeds. The conversations about onion sets ceased, shoes were eased off during the journey and were eased on again; the bright lights flashed and there they were.

As Fanny Fisher said, it was really grand, with red plush, fancy lights and powder rooms. That was just the start. There were round tables with ever so fancy table napkins, crackers and little pats of butter. No sooner had they sat down than waiters poured out some champagne – on the house. There was prawn cocktail, roast turkey, pavlova and coffee with petit fours. The music throughout had been gentle fifties. Then, suddenly, it changed to much rolling of drums. The curtains parted and – *wow*!

The Chippendales rippled their muscles, jerked their pelvises, cavorted and rippled round the stage before descending to the tables and rotating their pelvises right in front of the noses of these happy old people, who hooted, laughed, cheered and shrieked the evening away.

'Laugh? I haven't seen anything like that in years.' Annie was still laughing as she boarded the coach. There was much mirth and showing off in the coach on the way home.

'Don't you give me that nonsense! I don't believe for a moment you and Mr T pranced around like that. For one thing, the neighbours would have complained. That house of yours – you can hear your neighbours breathing.'

'They did complain. We'd go down to the hollow on warm evenings and do it there.'

'You never! Ben and I did the same thing when we were living with his mum. Fancy that! All them years ago! It's different now. They do it everywhere – even seen them do it in the back of the car. I ask you!'

'It's good to be reminded, though. I mean, most of the time we're treated like we don't know nothing.'

The over-sixties arrived home entirely satisfied by their evening out. As one of them said to Enid, 'They don't think it matters any more, but its part of you till the day you die.'

It had been a success. Enid drove home contented with the

choice of entertainment. She had been right – old people don't want to be shoved out to grass. Days of passionate sex might be long over, but memories linger and the indignity of being treated with as much sexuality as a headless chicken should be over. Yet, slipping on her nightie reminded Enid who she was. There would be years ahead of her – years and years with Sophocles, Sal and the grandchildren. Adam wasn't there and the over-sixties were hardly a full-time commitment. Basically, she was back where she started when Gerry died. Maybe selling the house would change things. Well, would it?

Mr Potter arrived with several couples. The standard pattern was for the party to ring the bell, when Enid would let them in and then follow Mr Potter, who conducted the tour. But the couples would behave in unexpected ways. They would peer out of the window before asking if flying saucers had been seen in the area. Another couple asked if the principal bedroom faced east. Another was very keen to build a darkroom for photography in the bathroom. Enid pointed out there was only one bathroom. Some were hell-bent on knocking rooms into each other. Others wanted to pull the kitchen apart, change the fireplace, build a conservatory, raise ceilings, expose more beams – and everyone wanted to decorate it. Enid took it all personally. She would see them out, shut the door and summon Sophocles for a conversation.

'Really, it's intolerable! What's wrong with the spare room? It's always been like that. I simply tell visitors to bend their heads. People have too much money. They watch telly programmes about decor and all that crap, then buy some unassuming house like this and try to make it into a suburban nightmare.' The conversation continued as Sophocles and Enid pounded the path for their daily walk.

Then the day arrived. It was pouring with rain. Enid had a cold and there was a smell of burnt toast in the kitchen. The couple were in their thirties and had a child of about four in tow. Mr Potter began intoning the virtues of the dining room. The child pointed to some crumbs and ketchup on the table and said, 'Err, yukky-yuk!'

'Yes, well, if you have twins about your age to a meal, these things get overlooked.' Enid stared with loathing at the child.

The parents were sufficiently embarrassed to launch into repetitive apologies.

'I'm ever so sorry, Mrs Tanner. I don't know what's come over Geraldine. Really, I'm ever so sorry. It's such a pleasant room too – not too big, if you know what I mean.'

The sitting room – which they insisted on calling the lounge – was bright and sunny, apparently – a little difficult to judge in the rain, but there's nothing like optimism. As for the kitchen, the husband reckoned he could, with the help of a little DIY, make it good enough for one of those dreadful faggots who cook on telly – only it seemed he was on first-name terms; the 'dreadful faggot' bit was Enid's interpretation. The twins had left several one-eared teddies, a duck and some books in the spare room. Geraldine was mightily impressed and said she'd like to come to stay.

Let me get out first, thought Enid, sniffing into her handkerchief.

They put in a bid later that same day. Apparently there was no 'chain', a term new to Enid, but she gathered this was good news. It was somewhat on the low side and Mr Potter felt he could squeeze a little more out of them. He made it sound like a blackhead on the nose.

It was too much to expect such good news not to be balanced by a dollop of bad. Cat had been off colour for several days. It had refused to go out and sat with accusing eyes and limp tail, breathing shallow cat-like breaths. Off to the vet they went. He was a nice young man, far too young to be a vet – just as that nice Mr Blair was far too young to be Prime Minister. The vet lifted Cat onto the couch, or whatever they call it. He thumped and bumped the old thing, took its temperature, listened to its heart. He straightened up, stethoscope round his neck.

'Mrs Tanner, this old cat is worn out. His heart isn't working properly and he's too old for any intervention. He'll die in a day or two.'

'Put it down. I can't face nursing it. It's had a good life. I don't want it to suffer.'

She watched the vet fill the syringe. The cat had closed its eyes already. It was simple, quick and painless.

Enid paid at the reception desk. Then, in the privacy of her car, she brewed up a terrible fantasy of the over-sixties having a day out at the vet's. It would be too easy with those fatal syringes. She imagined directives from Whitehall in times of crisis, war and famine – particularly famine. Hadn't she read somewhere that the agencies working with famine leave the old to one side? Enid felt the gut fear that life from now onwards was just a waiting game for death. She drove cautiously, as if expecting the State to haul her over to the kerb and remove her licence. She would be the target of well-meaning, raincoat-clad professionals, ruthlessly divesting her of any autonomy before throwing her into a home where everyone was too busy to listen, to encourage, to care, where Sal would find the journey just too much and the twins had flown the nest. By now the scenario was so bleak, Enid allowed tears to trickle down her cheeks. She wondered where Cat was now and decided that he was deep in the heart of some incinerator. And the soul of Cat, where was that? Souls weren't things Enid thought much about. She was well aware that cats didn't have souls, but what the hell was it then that she, according to the rules, had but the cat lacked? From there, it was an easy leap to Gerry.

Those eyes, faithful and accusing with Cat, not quite so faithful but every bit as accusing with Gerry. She could still see him, dribble down the side of his mouth. She wondered what he was about to tell her when he died. Probably another bleat about his health. He was a bore about his health, insisting on plasters, pills and Vick. He swore by Vick, using it to clear his nose, ease his arthritic knee, sooth bruises and as an infusion for sinuses. Enid thought about poor old Gerry's soul. The more she thought, the more she hoped that Gerry hadn't been blessed with one.

Gerry had changed slightly over the couple of years since his death. His duplicity, for starters, had caused another facet to heave into view. If nothing else, she had found out that he had sired a staggeringly beautiful daughter. Let's face it, he had sired another who was not unlike a rather amiable horse. Then there was his job. If he'd been rolling in it, one could assume he was part of some international scam, but a modest income, a great deal of travel and anecdotes, entirely omitting any factual information, still left several question marks. Enid clung to the conviction he had been a spy, a very humble one – none of that MacLean, Philby nonsense with accounts at Fortnum's for the marmalade. No, Enid was sure that, in his humble way, Gerry had turned his back on hunting and Boodles for a world of anonymity. Where did that leave his soul? Nowhere, was the only possible answer.

Given the vast amount of thinking that goes on in the car, it is surprising that there aren't more crashes, and even more surprising is the fact that anyone arrives home at all. The cat's blanket was the first thing she saw in the kitchen, so she threw away the repellent thing.

'It's just you and me, now,' she said, looking sternly at Sophocles.

The squeezing of the metaphorical blackhead worked and contracts for the house sale were exchanged. Enid went over to lunch with Sal. The twins were growing up. They no longer ran to the car – just lifted their heads and gave a preoccupied greeting. But little Roger would totter up, covered in muck and grime and allow Granny to lift him. Today, however, given the juicy news that Cat had been put down, the twins were more forthcoming.

'Did it mind?' asked Beatrice.

'Cat wasn't comfortable. I expect it was a relief.'

'Why don't we put people down?' enquired Sophie.

'It would be too easy. Take me, Sophie – I'm getting old. Let's say Mummy found that I was becoming a nuisance. Bingo! She would have me put down.'

'Then you wouldn't be able to come to lunch.' Sophie looked pensive.

'But Granny, suppose you were really old and in pain, what then?'

'I don't know, pet, I don't know.'

'I do, God will take you when he's ready. Father John at church told us that when Billy's daddy died of cancer.'

'Do you believe everything Father John says?'

'Of course; Father John knows the right answers about God. It's his job, like Daddy knows about cows.' There was a massive silence – the kind of silence that requires unseen hands to prevent it falling on their heads.

'What do you know about, Granny?'

'I know about nothing. You know that as well as I do.'

People who know about nothing are destined to lay tables. Enid laid for lunch and played peek-a-boo with Roger, who was easily pleased.

'Are you sure you're doing the right thing? I just don't see that moving at your age makes sense, Ma.'

'Please, Sal, we've been over and over it. I just feel that I must do something that's for me. Gerry is over, or nearly over; he's yesterday's news. I must move on. Then there's Adam's death and Cat being put down. It's a bundle of laughs, isn't it?'

Douglas fixed his all-weather eyes on Enid.

'I sent three hundred lambs to the slaughter last week, and we're not moving house. You do talk a lot of tosh, Enid.'

'Fuck that, Douglas! You don't understand.'

'Not in front of the children, Enid. I'm sure swearing is very therapeutic at your age – gives you a nostalgic sense of being sixteen, not sixty; but I'm old fashioned. I don't like it.' So Enid glared.

Sal interrupted, 'Douglas has been asked to be a magistrate. Isn't it lovely?'

'That's typical, isn't it? Choose people who are so damn square, haven't a bloody clue, and want to wrap everyone in their sanctimonious self-righteousness.' Enid pushed back her chair, stood up and in a tremulous voice said, 'Fuck, fuck, fuck! I'm off.'

Sal and Douglas looked at each other, raised their eyes to heaven and heard the car roar off.

'Wow!' said Sophie. 'That was like Brookside.'

'Granny was very cross, wasn't she?'

'Granny has a lot on her plate,' said Sal primly.

'Not enough to do, if you ask me,' grumbled Douglas.

'Don't be too hard, Doug. She's had a tough two years, what with Vijaya and that lad she saw dying like that. I just wish she could get away, stay with a friend. You know what will happen. She'll move and after a year be back where she started.'

'Hardly, if she's sold the house. Now, look – I know she's your mother, but I don't want her or anyone swearing like that in my house, especially in front of the children.'

'Don't worry, Dad, we know what it means. It's the same as sex. Granny just shouted *sex, sex, sex*.' Beatrice waved a piece of roast beef on the end of her fork as she mimicked her gran.

'You keep out of this! Granny was very naughty to say words like that; they are naughty words, do you understand?'

Sal was very uncomfortable. Douglas was right – Enid shouldn't have challenged him. She seemed so genuinely enraged at the news of Douglas becoming a magistrate...but why? Douglas was kind, sensible and popular in the village. Sal had looked forward to telling Enid the marvellous news that she had got planning permission for her art centre. Now there was something she could do – get the centre up and running. It would take a while and raising the money was going to be a challenge. Enid could help with the fund-raising.

What a far cry from the dizzy days of art student values to the sober, sensible, methodical development of this rural attempt at art appreciation. Enid knew which Sal she preferred and felt duly guilty. But help with the fund-raising was exactly what Enid didn't want to do. That was exactly why Enid drove home the first five miles shouting, '*Fuck!*' She knew it was childish. She knew she was showing off. She also knew it was a cry for help, not that anyone was going to hear her. It was a kind of relief, though. She telephoned Dolly when she got home.

'Dol, it's Enid. I need a shoulder. How is it you've got your act together and I haven't yet? Sal and Douglas sent me home for behaving badly at lunch. I said "fuck". Actually, I said it several times.'

'When are you going to grow up, Enid?'

'Growing up means growing older. That means even more options closed to me. There are pretty few as it is. Oh, I forgot to tell you, I've sold the house. You will come searching for my next, won't you? And Cat had to be put down.'

'Enid, do yourself a favour. It doesn't much matter what – an Open University degree or a part-time job, like those nice middle-class ladies who help out in National Trust properties. I don't know, there must be thousands of jobs out there you can do. Forget your smart in-laws, forget your life history – for what it's worth – and just go out and get a bloody job.'

The phone went dead. Bang went a long introspective phone call!

She thinks I've become a bore. She's damn right, I have.

Enid sat down rather heavily, an old lady's way of sitting. She looked round her sitting room, self-consciously noting the pictures, ornaments and photo of Sal's wedding. She looked at the apricot paint that had seemed so mellow, rich and warm at the time and now looked tawdry and dated. The curtains, too, were very expensive. Now the sun and years had dimmed the colours and given them a droop. A persistent spider had woven a complicated siege fort round the corner and caught several flies that had remained stuck for ages. Stuck for ages, that was it… What was worse? Any movement would be forward towards a future, a future of old age, more isolation, more whiling away the hours. Dolly was right, of course, but it isn't easy. Enid had thought about the Open University. The study weeks sounded fun. Maybe there would be a geriatric gentleman or two, but her motivation was alarmingly at odds with academic study. As for being a National Trust lady, she could just see it!

'Hello, Enid, what are you doing here?'

'I am one of the helpers, making sure you don't carve your initials on Sir Richard's tallboy.'

Sunday afternoon at four – no papers delivered, no cat to feed, no friends to talk to, nothing. Enid saw herself being sucked into the fucking, bloody over-sixties. Life, if you could call it that, would be Christmas bloody lights, scones with seedless raspberry jam and talks with slides on the architectural treasures from Afghanistan.

'Afghani – *where*?' would bellow Mrs Morgan.

'Somewhere in the Cotswolds, I think.'

'Coxwold – me gran came from there. She never mentioned no treasures. She was in service – miserable lot they were too.'

Twenty slides later there would be a pause; Mrs Morgan is confused.

'That weren't Coxwold.'

'Course it weren't. It's Afganiwhatnot; you know – where women wear them things over their faces.'

'Oh, I never realised. Fancy, there was me thinking it was Coxwold.'

Enid could see it all. First she would be in the ingratiating role, like she was now, choosing the Chippendales. Now, that was a success. But all too soon she would be on the receiving end – all the more reason to get some fun activities onto the agenda.

It was four thirty. That brief foray into fantasy hadn't lasted very long. Enid decided to daydream about her ideal house.

A 'bungy' made sense – what with stairs and getting older. It was as if one has never left the ground. Enid thought what her parents would say if she ended her days in a bungalow. They had bought a delightful cottage like an illustration for some Jane Austen novel. It had a well-dug kitchen garden and enough shrubs to promote privacy. Her father pottered comfortably in the greenhouse and took an active interest in conservancy. Right up till his last illness, he was forever putting up notices to warn drivers that frogs were crossing or helping fence off orchids. He built nesting boxes to attract shy feathered visitors. He dragged his wife to conservation sites in Norfolk, the Outer Hebrides, even down to Spain. Dad had been an utterly comfortable soul.

And her mum? Enid remembered her mother as a dull person. She had smart relatives and wanted to be up there among them. Her conversations were peppered with references to people and houses, both to establish her as a cut above the norm. She was undemonstrative but easy-going with Enid so long as she observed the niceties of good manners. John Betjeman needed to look no further for his fish knives.

Rose and Archie Fox were tickled pink when Enid got engaged to a Tanner. There was money in the air, but better still there was status; who knows, Enid might turn out to be the wife of a High Sheriff. Even in their disappointment, and Gerry was a real disappointment, they held to the chance that Gerry might return to the fold. As for that spying nonsense, Dr Fox was of the belief that Gerry was a bit of a bounder. God knows where he had squirreled away his money – he ruled out a leprosy mission. It was, as it were, the only cloud in their uneventful retirement. Dr Fox died of cancer of the liver. He died quite quickly in a hospice, with Rose and Enid with him. He had been in pain for several days and, as he said just before he died, 'A few more ospreys and we're there.' He was a twitcher to the last.

Rose hung on a while, got very muddly and became convinced

Enid had a title. She was bundled into a home and insisted the nurses called Enid 'Lady Tanner'. She made the staff refer to 'the lavatory' and refused to eat dinner at any time but six – she wasn't too happy about that either. Finally the faculties faded, and so did her bladder control. The last few months had her sitting on incontinence pads composing letters to the Queen about the pigeons that flapped and cooed in the courtyard outside the home.

After her parents' death, Enid mopped up their bits and pieces. She found some condoms among Archie's toiletries. Even at her mature age, the idea of her parents having a sex life seemed utterly disgusting. Distracted by the very idea, Enid imagined urgent buttocks thrusting themselves into the mysteries of her mother. Thanks to Shakespeare and all that she found herself murmuring, 'Out, out, damned cock!' But her father beavered away with gasps of breath and Rose's moans, till Enid found herself with her hands clasped against her ears.

Rose Fox had liked cooking, flowers and running local charities. She wore hats long after most women had stopped. She liked glossy magazines and would moan about being married to a provincial doctor – shades of Madame Bovary. She had a brother called Hugo, who was a colonel and lived in Germany for a number of years. If she met someone who was in the army, almost the first thing she would say was, 'Do you know my brother?' It was a weakness, but not a serious one. Rose so wanted to know and be known. But she was neither interesting enough to be known for herself, nor grand enough to be known for her family. Poor Rose, she was so full of aspirations. It was perhaps pertinent that she should end her married days living in a house reminiscent of Jane Austen; for, in their way, Rose and Archie had many of the foibles characters in an Austen tale.

When she was young Enid had had a nanny – why, she couldn't imagine. Her mother had little to do beyond longing for grandeur and had only the solicitor's wife for a friend. Enid went to dancing classes in a frilly dress, with the boys wearing white gloves. The whole thing was ridiculous. Then there was the kindergarten – Enid learnt that 'please' and 'thank you' were not enough to curry favour and that influence required more manipulative skills. After that, the nanny left and Enid went to Mrs Herring's, a vicar's wife who had twenty pupils. There she learnt 'There is a green hill far away without a city wall'. It seemed reasonable enough to have a hill without a city wall and Enid spent hours puzzling out what the problem was. Mrs Herring had 'readers' – books of remarkable dullness with characters like Pat who liked to bat and wore a hat and had a cat. If that was reading, why bother!

Enid's reverie would have continued if the telephone hadn't intruded with a raucous buzz.

Eight

'It's Cousin Jean.' Usually when you pick up a phone the raucous buzz ceases; this time it continued. Who the hell is Cousin Jean with an accent you could cut with a knife? Cousin Jean must have been expecting this reception.

'You haven't a bloody clue who I am, have you? I'm your dad's niece from Australia – Jean, Aunt Peg's daughter. I'm doing the Continent with my granddaughter, Josey. We're only in London a few days and I thought we'd have a little party of our friends and relatives over here. Any chance of you and Gerry and Sal putting in an appearance? I've taken a friend's flat in Kensington.'

'Steady on! You're my Aunt Peg's daughter. Of course, I remember now. It's been years. I don't think I even bothered to let Aunt Peg know. I was widowed a couple of years ago.'

'Well, that's a bit of all right. She's been dead these ten years. It's just that Josey is curious about her family and I thought I'd ring round on the off chance.'

How typical! thought Enid. Relations that one has hardly heard of and never met make a beeline at the first opportunity. Not only that, they invariably remember who begat and divorced who. So long as it's not another Vijaya creeping out of the woodwork – I couldn't bear it if I have to deal with Dad's wandering sperm as well.

Enid took down the address and time. Well, why not? She'd go up to London for the day. You never know, she might meet some distant cousins – ones her parents didn't approve of, for no better reason than that they had slipped over the tracks and lived on the wrong side of the world, to cap it all, successfully. However, after behaving so badly at lunch, she felt inhibited about phoning Sal, even though she had been included in cousin Jean's invitation – so inhibited that she never told her daughter about the invitation till after the event. Time – that was the thing; time the healer and all that.

Jean, daughter of Peg and grandmother of Josey? That left out Josey's mum; perhaps she did a runner? Enid, who rarely thought about her own family, was having a field day. She vaguely remembered how Peg had been wooed and won by a dentist who went out to Australia. Frankly, it was a bit of a relief. Having a dentist in the family is only tolerable if he practises in Australia. He ended up a professor, which is a darned sight more than her father did.

The nice blue wool dress, a hairdo and a dab of cologne; Enid peered at a mirror – handsome is as handsome does – something like that, anyway. She drove to the train and found a place to park riddled with broken glass. There are days, and this was one, when 'Bugger broken glass and to hell with it' is the response, followed by a guilty reminder that you still haven't filled out that AA membership form. She bought her ticket with difficulty.

'Now, if you had caught the earlier train I could have given you the Early Bird return. Mind you, if you had come here last Thursday, your Supa-Save would have been £10.27 less. On the other hand, there's the midweek discount, but not on this service. Why you don't apply for an over-sixties railcard, I don't know! Because, if you catch the 6.30 train and return on the 10.40, you have all that time in London and it's less than thirty quid. What about that for a bargain?'

'But I only go to London about once a year.'

The man gave a sigh that seemed to ask, who would pay his wages if everyone was as thoughtless and mumbled on like that about railcards giving you real value?

Trains for those who rarely use them are still frightening monsters, slithering into the station with hissing noises and other uproar. Enid clambered on and, with a sinking feeling, started to shuffle down the centre aisle to find a seat. There were the inevitable children wriggling and colouring pictures with dribbly, sucky sweets stuck in their cheeks. There were ladies of Enid's age, only tidier, with sandwiches and severe expressions, as well as young men in anoraks or ill-fitting suits cadging jobs in the metropolis. Not a seat in sight. Finally she found the smoking area, which engendered a corporate disapproval, with the stink of cigarettes clearly titillating the nostrils of the smoker. Two desperate men were already deep into their fags, clasping them as an alcoholic does his glass. But it was more than the fear of being ostracised that worried them. It was that other bloke. This other bloke sat just in front, opposite Enid, who grabbed the empty seat, slipping in and vaguely aware that the seats seemed particularly vacant in an otherwise crowded train.

The train drew out a mere ten minutes late when the character opposite lowered his copy of *The Times* and winked! He was stark naked to the waist, in just a loincloth, and sitting cross-legged on his seat. He had long matted hair and a tangled beard. Most startling of all, his toe-toes, as the twins used to call them, wiggled merrily just at the table level.

Good heavens! I've never thought of toes having body language, mused Enid, peering rather fascinatedly at the black hairs bristling on the top of his big toe, which twitched a merry welcome as she looked at the man, his belly button, his almost hairless chest and his matted hair. That was enough. Hadn't she been taught it was rude to stare?

'Namaste! What about twelve down? You look an intelligent lady.' He shook *The Times* and read out, 'The Greek lets the hairdresser get down to business.'

'Do you always travel like this?' Enid couldn't resist the challenge, adding, 'Probably the Duke of Edinburgh. He's a safe bet with most things Greek – well, contemporary Greek, if you know what I mean.'

'Doesn't fit. Something a little grander, I think.'

'What about Leonidas combing his hair?' A stroke of genius, that.

'"King of the Persians, beware! beware!" Lousy poem but perfect; only I thought he combed his own wretched hair?'

'But he did, that's the point.'

The character paused to see if the letters fitted.

'Which is more than you do.' It just slipped out. Enid bit her lip with consternation. What would her mother have said? Her mother was unlikely to travel to London with a half-naked man searching for crossword clues. Still, in for a penny, in for a pound.

'Don't your toes get cold?'

'No more than your nose.'

'What do the inspectors think?'

'Very touchy, very racist; there is nothing like bare feet to make people racist.'

In a perfect, flat Midlands accent, our friend provided a skit of the train guard requiring the offending feet to be lowered.

'"Excuse me, sir, please remove your feet from the seat." As I point out, it's my religion. I am a fakir. That gets them.'

'You mean you are a holy man?' Enid spoke with incredulity.

'Why not? There are holy men all over India, so why not here?'

'I can't believe bathing in the Thames is quite the same as bathing in the Ganges.'

'Absolutely right; our hearts beat as one.'

Enid's heart didn't care to beat as one. It was a level of familiarity that she didn't deem appropriate with a fakir.

'It might not wow them in the aisles but I always get a seat,' announced the holy man, observing Enid take a sneaking look at his toes again.

'You're a phoney and as opportunist as the Church of England,' said Enid severely.

'Away in a manger to you too,' chortled the fakir. 'Anyway, I'm on a fact-finding tour. Tell me all.'

'Certainly not, but I'll tell you about my Australian relatives – not that I know anything about them. They're over from Australia and have invited me for a drink.'

'At least they will be white,' murmured the fakir, unctuously raising his hand in benediction for this deliverance.

'You can't tell these days and, anyway, it really doesn't matter any more. After all, my husband's daughter is married to a tall white he-god and they swear they are Indian.'

'I swear I'm a true – but not very blue – Brit. I told the guard that. "More's the pity," he replied sourly.'

A fag-drenched, wheezing smoker observed Enid chatting away and felt compelled to say something. He leant over, beady eyes fixed on the fakir's podgy toes.

'Look, lady, you don't know where he's been, take it easy. I've got nothing against foreigners, but…' Here he collapsed with a wracking cough and Enid was secretly rather proud she'd found the seat she had.

'It was my father's sister, who married a dentist. I don't know them. They sound, well, full of bonhomie, if you know what I mean.'

'I don't care a Foster's!' This was spoken in an excellent approximation of an Australian accent.

'It's not fair. You can publicly speak in a vaguely Australian accent and no one cares a damn, but if I spoke in your accent I'd be accused of taking the piss and all that.'

The train sped through flat water meadows with motley cows, the occasional pony, a car dump or two, small industrial units, grim, cheap housing and a church in the distance…always a church in the distance. Enid looked up and saw it all. Had she gone too far? It was so difficult to rein back when having fun – and this was fun. There she was with her hairdo and cologne, her blue dress and, above all, someone interesting to talk to. That is what she could never fully explain. Gerry was interesting to talk to. God, how she missed it!

'It is a conundrum, is it not? But conversation closed.' I must finish the crossword puzzle.' Like a curtain pulled across the stage, the performance was finished. *The Times* was draped across his belly and the holy man was no more, save for those toes.

I should take trains more often. Frankly, I think this is better than those Chippendales, thought Enid.

Enid lolled against the window and allowed herself to meet in her mind's eye an assortment of lifeguards, beefy ladies and shrill yells from the suburbs of Sydney. The 'Bondi whoop', that's what she'd imagined. But before she could get embroiled in a 'barbie', *The Times* lowered itself, replete satisfaction covered the holy man's face and he scrambled for a rough cotton shawl that hadn't seen a washing machine for months.

'That's cheating.' said Enid.

'That's life. Anyway, never invite a beautiful lady out for a meal without any clothes on. Would you like to have lunch with me at your expense?'

'Why not? I've got my credit card with me!'

The water meadows had become rows of houses with neat gardens. Traffic whizzed along the roads beside them, sometimes faster, sometimes slower. The waste dumps proliferated, the industrial units grew and grew, buddleias sprouted in the sidings and old advertisements peeled off dilapidated buildings. The fag addicts squashed their cigarettes and looked morosely at Enid. No one likes to see a lady taken in like that.

Everyone loses their head once in a while. The symptoms are thinking it's a mystic dawn at King's Cross with heavenly or any other chorus singing full throttle. Just try to remember, you do not take offers from holy men, especially if they ask you to pay for them. And you most certainly don't invite them to meet your long-lost relatives in Cadogan Square. This is exactly what Enid did.

By King's Cross, it had become 'Fack' and, by the end of the taxi journey, his mendicant ways were obvious.

'What a beaut! Hey, folks! Here's Aunty Enid with her... er, gentleman friend...little brown job called Fack.'

Cadogan Square has seen it all but, when some winsome lass called Arlene opened the door and shrieked, it was possibly unique even for that smart area of London. Aunty Enid was prissily pissed and clinging to the arm of a beaming Fack.

'I'm your Aunty Enid, and this is Fuck.' Here she giggled a little.

'I mean Fack, F-A-C-K – fakir, get it? Now, who are you, deary?'

'I am Arlene. You all right, Aunty? I mean, we thought you were a widow.'

'A merry widow,' agreed Enid, with just a hint of a burp.

Lorna bustled forward with her hand apparently clenched like a knuckleduster after a shopping spree in Selfridges.

'Enid, dear, this is such a treat.' Her eyes swivelled over Fack. 'Our Abos go walkabout too.' She turned back to a vacantly grinning Enid.

'Can you hire them, just like we used to with the old kisso-gram? Well, Fack, if you're ever short of a date, just call Lorna. I think you're a sweetie. What part of India?'

'Leicester, I am a holy man from Leicester.'

'Leicester? Isn't that awfully cold? Our lot like to get back to the bush after a while. What do you think, Fack?'

Boy, did Fack have views! He knew considerably more about

the Australian policy towards Aboriginals than his hostess. Soon he was sitting cross-legged in his loincloth holding court. His listeners' comments rose and fell with sympathy or surprise – 'What do y'know?' – and an element of awe.

'Did you ever!' sprang from Cousin Jean's lips.

'She's a beaut,' he said, referring to the Queen. Fack was keen on the Queen. He had seen her sitting with that bunch of crooks she called her Commonwealth ministers. The Queen was not racist, not if she could sit with that lot of rogues.

'My cousin's ma came over to Australia as an orphan but she can't go anywhere – at least the Abos can go home.' It was Arlene again.

At the end of a perfect day and an even better evening, like any good entertainer Fack wanted to end on a good note – and what better note could there be than pointing out that, with Enid on his arm, they were going to do just what the Abos liked to do best – go walkabout back home.

Enid didn't think of herself as an ethnic totem and she was feeling rather sick. She starting crying and threw herself into the arms of some startled cousin sobbing, 'It's all right, my poppet,' possibly in commiseration for all those orphans shipped to Australia.

Fack then put in a plea for his own brand of walkabout holiness.

'A holy man cannot choose where to be holy. Just look at Jesus. Who in their right mind would have chosen to stump round Palestine? Lucky he didn't get his foot blown off by a mine. No, my friends. Our lot is the search for the infinite wisdom and God in all his guises is our guidance. He's done me proud today – a lovely lunch and now the delectable Enid and your esteemed friendship. I tell you, this holiness business is, as you lot say, a bit of all right.'

Lorna was confused.

'Naughties' were one thing, but talking about Jesus like that was going it a bit. Also, Fack was pretty brown, if you thought about it. Now she was as liberal as the next. All the same, she was a Prot, went to Church regularly Christmas and Easter, could take a joke and liked the old royals; and yet it just wouldn't be the same if that young Harry married a black, while here was Aunty, tiddly if you asked me, on the arm of a naked dago – European Union, he probably gets a grant. They say it's sending the old country to the dogs – to the dagos, if you ask me.

Fack had enjoyed himself considerably. He had, among other things, admired the ringed belly of a girl called Shirley while they discussed nudity and acceptability. Shirley was thirteen, the right age for serious talk.

Poor old Enid had ploughed her way through a begetting game quite as intricate as any biblical ones. Her Australian relations had splendidly vulgar names, including Clint. She wouldn't want to introduce him to Henry and Eleanor. But well-heeled they certainly were, with brains too. Shirley's dad was an academic and she already intended to study some women's issue or other.

'The hussy's flaunting her belly button at Fack!' shrieked some relative or other. To do her justice, Enid didn't make a fuss. As for Fack – he was, well, above such things.

Towards the end of the evening, Enid's queasy expression made Lorna realise that it was time for Fack to take her home. It was then that she made her offering to Enid – a kangaroo's testicle made into a pouch: so useful!

After the party, where friendships had burst, sparkled and died like fireworks, and visits promised like South American railway bonds, Enid and Fack stood on the street wrestling with drizzle. Enid had wasted a fortune on that meal and that, or rather those, taxis. It was time for reality. The tube it would be from Knightsbridge.

Wearing just a loincloth on a wet evening in Knightsbridge is perfectly de rigueur so long as it is a designer loincloth and worn by a woman. Even the latter can be open to question. Fack's grubby piece of cashmere somehow didn't meet the criteria, nor did his plump goose-pimpled shoulders have quite the mark of authenticity.

'Now, sir, it's a little chilly, even for fancy dress,' suggested a special diplomatic policeman used to the vagaries of the diplomatic community, as Fack and Enid lurched by several embassies.

'This isn't fancy dress. That's an insult. I follow in the exalted footsteps of Gandhi. By the way, this is Enid. She believes in me.'

Two people were being put on the spot. The policeman had been put through a thorough course on how to avoid observing blatant slavery, and was forever calling out the fire brigade when his diplomatic nose smelled roast goat sizzling over the remains of Louis Quinze chairs which had been reduced to embers in the centre of an Axminster carpet. He knew that Caracas was the capital of Venezuela, but was a little vague about Kabul – was it a country or a capital? Probably like Monte Carlo with no drains.

He had eyed Fack prancing along beside Enid and at once whispered sweet nothings into his radio.

'Zebra 2 calling – naked nutter and girlfriend approaching embassy. Nutter wearing just a piece of cloth and has filthy hair – middle-aged and possibly Indian.'

Like everyone else, the police are nervous of nutters. Honest to goodness criminals they know how to handle, how to intimidate. Murderers, drug addicts, drunks and dossers – no problem; but nutters, they are another game. As for 'friends of nutters' – they were just as bad.

While dilemmas coursed round the highly trained officer's mind, Enid was nursing too much drink and the astounding proposition of being told she believed in Fack.

Belief is dodgy at the best of times. It waxes at Christmas, waxes considerably less at Easter and sinks without trace the rest of the year. To be resurrected in Cadogan Square by Fack and a mere policeman was intolerable.

'I'm an atheist. I am moderately sober and believe passionately…' Here a slinky clean car purred up behind them. A man in a blue blazer leant out. 'Evening, officer; any problems?'

'This gentleman appears to have lost his clothes.'

'No, I haven't. I'm a holy man, we don't wear clothes. My whatsits are covered. What more do you want?'

'I met him on the train,' added Enid, offering a totally unnecessary piece of information.

But trains are the answer to everything with the police. If you can catch one in one direction, you can return the same way, can't you? It is an abiding disappointment to most highly-trained policemen that there isn't a train to the back of beyond, one way only.

'Hop in. We'll run you to the station. Leicester, is it?'

'King's Cross actually,' muttered Enid, who was starting to feel sleepy and who had resigned herself that Fack's idea of nothing included money.

'Mahatma Gandhi, so that's it, is it?' asked the driver.

'He stood by the King dressed like this – no bother.'

'I know. It's not fair, but there you are. Political, are you, sir?'

'Staunch Conservative. What are you?'

'We don't mix politics with pleasure, sir. Whereabouts in Leicester did you say, sir?'

It was Enid who answered.

'For God's sake, listen. We are going back to Northallerton. It's in North Yorkshire.' Enid never meant to say it. It just slipped out of her mouth. 'Fack's coming with me.'

It wasn't enough to be deposited at King's Cross late in the evening, where stationary trains still hissed from somewhere and where cold, tired, young boys ply their shabby trade for a night's kip and girls find that true love is illusory. The drunks have shuffled back to their boxes and only the tetchy public peer at the arrivals and departures.

Fack and the suave policeman discussed the finer points of Gandhiji's life. It appeared that this policeman knew more than just the capital of Venezuela, a bloody sight more.

Then the penny dropped. Blow me, if it wasn't Gerryji all over again. Had Gerryji spent all those years at King's Cross? Seriously, had Gerry at some level or other spent his life discreetly sorting wheat from chaff? Enid had to laugh. She wondered what Vijaya and Ran would make of Fack. Despite his grubby loincloth and preposterous figure, Fack exuded class, that symbol of survival for so many. He was obviously well-educated, convivial and had style and a shrewd eye. What more could you want? Money? They – the others, the common man made good – had that, and mighty vulgar they were. She thought contentedly how she had a bit – enough if they were careful. Obviously, Fack had none, or rather none that was visible, and intended to live as someone who had nothing. You had to admit, Fack had class. He could do *The Times* crossword. Enid was still rather tipsy, a little muddly and undoubtedly lacking judgement. What a day it had been! Picked up a fakir, got rather pissed with the far-flung Dominions and ended up – but that was the point; there was no 'ending up', just a very exciting new beginning.

Their policeman's friend in a blazer was already speaking over his phone as the train drew out.

'Nutters! He's doing a walkabout with a middle-aged lady – educated, politically sound, just daft. Born over here, I gather. She's silly; well, you'd have to be. Pity her lot when she arrives with him in tow. Her married name, I gather, is Tanner. He didn't give a name, apart from Mahesh; said something about what was Jesus's other name, then veered off the subject. International bomb squad they were not.'

Suddenly the phone went berserk, lights flashed, the train lurched and, in typical British manner, Enid and Fack slid into the night – after which the officer found he was nearer demotion, having let the wife of some clapped-out deceased intelligence officer disappear into the night with a sought after, fully-accredited millionaire nut.

Enid slept almost the entire way, a sleep that was shallow enough to fix on a single subject – where Fack could sleep; not on the train – when they reached home. The move was any day now and the house wrapped up in cardboard boxes. The spare room was awash with boxes full of clothes and memorabilia that had escaped Gerry's death. Not only was there not a sheet in sight, there wasn't much to be seen of the bed either. Sal's room wasn't much better. A bookcase had been taken apart and left on the bed, while the books teetered like wobbly tower blocks. That left... Here she tossed a little and her hand moved away a crumb that wasn't there. No, not yet – she mustn't. She grinned at herself – life in the old dog yet! What would Gerry think?

This torpid state was jerked into the reality of Peterborough, Grantham, York and finally their stop. A policeman joined the train at Peterborough, the discreet kind who just keeps an eye.

'Well I never! It's Enid, isn't it?' A tall lady in well-cut tweeds shot out a hand with military precision. Unfortunately the station lights were working properly. 'Bess Thomas – over-sixties club;

you remember?'

Enid didn't recognise her and even if she did, she didn't. Introducing Fack to her Australian relatives was one thing, but she felt tired. The fun had gone and Bess Thomas probably had no sense of humour. People with tweeds often don't.

'A little of what you fancy, eh? Nothing like practising what you preach, eh?' Bess dug her in the ribs. 'Who's this, a retired Chippendale?' So much for people in tweeds having no sense of humour.

'I think, Bess, you ought to know that this gentleman is a friend of my late husband.'

'No, I'm not!' declared Fack. 'I am a holy man wandering penniless for inspiration. This lady, Edith –'

'*Enid*,' hissed Enid.

'– has inspired me.'

It was not so much a battle of wills as one of those distinctly English skirmishes based on the unwritten attributes of loud voices. In the battle of Northallerton, Fack rousted the tweeds.

'You bet!' muttered Bess, who was cold and tired and not really interested at that hour in talking at length about the private life of some old codger like Enid. For Christ's sake, her own sex life was elusive enough.

Come the morning she would think differently and, by lunch, the telephones would whirr and purr with outrage coupled to jealousy, a coupling far more corrosive than any Fack and Enid might consider. For if the truth be known, Fack made himself comfortable on the sofa and ran up a fortune in electric heating in lieu of blankets. But Bess the tweed was already plotting her revenge.

Sal was wary. Ma wanted to bring over a friend who was staying for a while. Ma wasn't on staying terms except with her family – hardly friends, unless you counted those frightful Indians. Anyway, they turned out to be family, more's the pity. Perhaps an Australian cousin had leapt into her arms. It was those terrible soaps…swept proper values out of the window. Mum had more sense than to team up with some hobo from the bush wanting to go – what did they call it? – 'walkabout' round the old country.

Sophie saw the car first. 'Gran's arrived. She's got someone in the car.'

Beatrice took up the commentary. 'He's got no clothes on, has long hair and is brown.'

Sal let the Brussels sprouts slip and swore. She arrived at the front door just as Beatrice was asking Fack if he wore knickers or not.

'A mere nineteenth-century notion, my girl. Genitalia have been around longer than anything, even Adam and Eve. It's only you Christians that make a fuss about such matters. And, I'll have you know, it shows a deep lack of respect for my role in life. You would never ask your headmistress if she wore knickers, would you? Anyway, you shouldn't mention such subjects, especially in front of your grandmother.'

'Oh, she doesn't mind. She's that kind of gran.'

'But I mind, your mother minds and we are not chopped liver, you know.' Fack stood looking severe and rather intimidating.

The chopped liver spoilt the discussion. Neither Sophia not Beatrice could work it into further whimsical observations and retreated, if not in form, at least in spirit. Beatrice wormed her thumb into her mouth; her eyes looked like glassy beads. Next to her, Sophie squirmed like a belly dancer warming up. Fack was not used to children, that was obvious.

Sal kissed Ma and put her hot, red-raw, kitcheny hand forward for Fack. He smiled and cupped his hands before murmuring, 'Namaste.' The dogs were less than friendly. They growled their racist best.

Fack was not an inviting sight. He had this long cloth of coarse cotton firmly woven round his waist and through his legs, then slung over his arms or head. Weather and audience permitting, he wore in addition his cashmere shawl. Like Enid, he too had a pouch; his was made from the equally unmentionable parts of a sacred bull. He wore it on a leather thong round his waist and in it he carried a photo of Gandhi talking to the Queen Mother and a gold credit card, just in case. Fack was holy, but not that holy. He lived in fear and trembling of coming across a real bed of nails. His credit card was a pragmatic touch. He thought of himself as a cut above the hoi polloi holies, although he rather liked the idea of levitation.

Enid was telling Sal about the party in London while the twins watched in fascination as Fack removed their toys before sitting on the old, smelly, cat-ridden sofa, curling up his legs and retiring into some seraphic pose, his lips barely moving. When Douglas marched in, he stopped, turned abruptly to Sal and asked, 'Who the hell?'

'I can explain,' began Enid, laying an arm on Douglas's in supplication for a peace she felt was missing.

'We met on the train. Seven across, wasn't it, Fack – something about Leonidas?'

A deep, penetrating '*Ommm*' met the question.

'Well, it was all about Leonidas beating the shit out of Xerxes.' Enid paused, looked up at Douglas, clamped her hand over her mouth and rolled her eyes before saying a loud and deeply insincere, 'Sorry.' She added, 'I try so hard to observe the conventions of the conventional middle classes, but at times I just forget. If Fack did his hair, I think he would appeal more, don't you?'

Appeal more! With that puppy-fat body, squat head, no neck, bedraggled locks of shiny black hair with stern inroads of grey, and his legs – two spindly posts – holding it all in place? There was nothing appealing about this fakir sitting down to Sunday lunch. Frankly, he was downright revolting. Or so thought the distraught Sal.

When the floor has fallen out of your market, when prices for your stock have reached rock bottom, it is not the best of times to entertain a vegetarian to lunch. You begrudge every bloody pea he munches, every bean, cauliflower and sun-dried tomato. However, just wait a minute; this vegetarian turned out surprisingly well-informed about farming, government policies and the quandary Douglas found himself in. Fack still didn't eat meat – unless it was accompanied by very expensive wine – but at least he held forth intelligently, if a little alarmingly, on the subject near and dear to Douglas's bank balance. There was an authenticity that no one could deny. He might be a weird character but he was undoubtedly an intelligent one. There was an awesome thought that crossed both Sal and Douglas' mind that maybe Fack was utterly genuine. After all, why not? Is it so unreasonable that an educated Indian should, after a life of making money, find solace and spiritual enlightenment in the time honoured-role of a holy man?

During lunch there had been a certain amount of not-very-Morse code to the effect that Douglas would do his stuff in the sitting room while Enid helped Sal with the washing-up and the twins would amuse the young Roger.

'You don't know where he's been or anything,' began Sal in a hiss.

'Didn't know much about Gerry either, did I, till the other day?'

'That's not the same thing; at least you knew his family.'

'Don't be so square! What has his family got to do with it? Fack is what he says he is – retired from the busy world of wives, children, businesses – and now he's trying to lead a more spiritual way of life, shedding everything to give authenticity.'

'Bollocks! He is probably just a manipulative little money-seeking rat. Anyone can see that. He's found a sucker and is worming his way all the way to the bank – your bank. Or do I mean his bank?' A saucepan clattered.

'What's bollocks?' piped up a twin.

'Sssh! Ma's having a row,' admonished the other.

'Tell me.' Enid's voice was rising. 'Why is it a beautiful ending when a penniless, sweet-natured girl marries a comfortably off hero but a lousy ending when a lonely widow with a modest income chooses to befriend a holy man?'

'You know as well as I do!' A plate narrowly missed hitting the floor. A radioactive silence permeated the kitchen.

'Do you have sex, or does his religion prevent that? Incidentally, what is his religion?'

'Your mother's sex life is a private matter.'

'Since when?' snarled Sal. The twins were agog.

Let's face it, she was damned if she was going to tell Sal that she had cut the whiskers on her chin, changed the sheets and started using eau de cologne, but so far nothing had happened.

'What kind of values are you giving the twins, for Christ's sake?'

Frankly, as much as she loved them, Enid regarded the twins

as the epitome of depravity without any help from her.

Enid flung the grubby tea cloth on the floor. It had a faded and revolting floral pattern; last year's Christmas present from the twins. She saw her harassed daughter working her butt off against a background of Brussels sprouts nobody liked but were served just the same. Wasn't this what Gerry riled against and wasn't this what Fack was questioning? Fack had eaten plates of the damned things, metaphor or no metaphor. And to think her beloved Sal had once tossed back her blonde hair and stripped for peace – at Glastonbury, Enid thought it was. In those days, Sal had wanted to storm the citadels of smuggery with poetry, art and music, but had sunk, in a matter of years, into Brussels sprouts and narrow-minded bigotry.

'Sal, Sal, I could shake you sometimes. Can't you see? I'm just finding out if this super, eccentric guy who does the crossword in next to no time and doesn't require much valeting is the Mr Wonderful I'm looking for. My eyes are open, for God's sake! If I teach your beastly girls anything it will be to live with open eyes and open minds.'

'Live where? Not in the real world! Anyway, you know as well as I do, Mr Wonderful doesn't exist. You're damned lucky if you find a partner for the hard graft of raising a family. You are just a self-indulgent, silly old fool, hell-bent on making an utter ass of yourself,' complained Sal, as she swished the greasy water sulkily round the sink and dried her splotchy hands on one of Roger's T-shirts lying conveniently near at hand.

'Well, I'm moving out on Tuesday week.' Enid had caught the mood and was also in a sulk. 'I'm putting the furniture in store and Fack and I are starting straight away to look for something more appropriate.' An elongated silence followed. 'Until I find something—'

'No, absolutely not!'

'I'm disappointed in you, Sal. I thought you had a really open mind but you are just as prissy-nosed and intolerant as the rest.'

Enid's lip wobbled and a few tears ran slowly down her cheeks to meet some mucus that had time to emerge before she found a grubby handkerchief.

'I shan't bother you then. And since we're being honest, I

think the twins are ghastly, Douglas just a bore and you're rapidly becoming one too. I hate the lot of you.' The tears flowed noisily.

'Granny says she hates us. Let's hate her back,' whispered Beatrice.

'Yes, let's. She's smelly, grumpy and now has that grotty little brown man who likes chopped liver,' Sophie whispered back.

However, if the truth be known, Douglas and Fack had had a very interesting conversation about cutting out the middleman in cattle sales and dealing direct with retailers.

'Believe me, Douglas, it must make sense. You see, your produce is geared direct to a specific market—'

The door was flung open. Enid was no Sarah Bernhardt but she did her best.

'We are not welcome here,' she announced, sobbing copiously. 'I thought at least my daughter understood.' She made that rather nasty gulpy noise, like a car starting in cold weather.

'Let's get out of here. Come on, Sophocles.'

'But my name is Fack and I've been having an excellent conversation with Douglas – a delightful gentleman. You don't meet many like him down in Leicester.'

This provoked Sal into an exasperated outburst and she wailed tremulously as she stood peering over her mother's shoulder.

'How could you! He's virtually stark-naked and we know nothing about him.'

'Well, I like that! Doesn't that sum up all those awful people you had to your eighteenth birthday party? I don't remember Gerry and me making quite so much fuss.'

Enid felt strangely powerful. She looked up at Fack, who was obviously used to outbursts like Sal's. He beamed, his shrewd eyes not missing a trick.

'That's it! That is the difference.' Fack snapped his fingers. 'We British are an eccentric lot. Where else in the world would it be necessary to actually know someone, however tenuously, before you have them in your house? It's a form of restrictive social practice. No strangers here!'

However, there were only two words that were heard, words so intimidating, so abhorrent, that even Enid gave an impromptu squeak. They were 'We British'.

'We British', with Sophocles in tow, drove off, while Sal snuffed and sniffed a tearful account of the kitchen drama and Douglas reassured her that the 'fella' knew his facts and a thing or two about farming. The twins added their pennyworth. It was Sophie who spoke first.

'Perhaps he's Melchior come to see Baby Jesus and had a puncture; that's why he's late.'

'No, he's a funny man – like a vicar – but doesn't wear clothes. Don't cry, Mummy; he won't have any money for sweets but that doesn't matter, because Granny usually remembers,' observed Beatrice, adding, 'it was rather like *Eastenders*, only without the hitting.'

'He will be my news at school on Tuesday. Last week 'Arry told us all about visiting his dad in prison. Have you ever been in prison, Daddy?'

'I'm too busy farming, pet.'

'I bet Fack's been in prison. I think policemen don't like men undressed like that.'

'But is it a crime?' asked Douglas gently, more directed to Sal than his daughter.

It was Beatrice who replied.

'That's not the point. He's made Mummy cry.'

'What religion is he anyway,' asked Sal, adding, 'in India?'

'Does it matter?'

'When I was in India there were endless holy men, emaciated little men sitting cross-legged like Fack and murmuring their prayers, making their way to holy shrines. Some acted like medicine men in the local villages. They were quite safe but a little scary. I think I sketched some.' Then, guessing what Douglas was going to say next, she cried out passionately, 'It's not the same thing. It's my mother!'

Douglas gently wrapped his arms round his distraught wife. He cradled her head and wiped her eyes and took her chapped hands in his.

'Keep the door open, Sal. Remember, we've always told each other to keep the door open. You see, it may not be as phoney as you think. It wasn't in India. Why should it be here? I think you'll find that Fack is a very unusual man. Let's face it, your mum goes for unusual men.'

Nine

A sleek Rover purred into the drive already lined with ancient gardening tools, including a hand-powered mower too stiff to push let alone mow, several bent forks, some spades and blunt shears. There were boxes of twine, spray cans and cartons of elderly potions and powders for killing slugs and weeds and for encouraging growth in the roses. If the truth be known, Gerry hadn't been too fussed about what he used for which task.

The Brig got out a little stiffly. He wasn't getting any younger and, indeed, he had long retired from 'the business' and only undertook certain tasks for – for why? Finishing his own personal life's crossword, he supposed. He eyed the gardening tools and recognised at once the hand of Gerry.

'Good guy, Gerry. Yes, a splendid fellow! A little chaotic in his private life but then so are many of our best chaps, if the *Sun* is anything to go by.' The Brig was an avid reader of the *Sun*; so many of his chaps wound up there one way or the other.

He pressed the bell. It wasn't working but Sophocles was and he let out some hysterical barking from the kitchen. Fack was deep in his daily crossword while sitting on the most comfortable packing case. The Facks of this world don't leap – nor, sadly, levitate; they sink heavily to the floor. He opened the front door gingerly to see an upright, distinguished figure, hardly in the first flush of youth, standing there.

'She's moving house. I'm glad I'm a fakir. You've no idea – it's chaos!'

The Brig smartly delivered an outstretched hand.

'I'm the Brig, by the way; heard Enid was moving; can be an awkward time. You are?'

Ignoring the outstretched hand, Fack put his palms together and tried to look modest, pious and friendly.

'A holy man from Leicester. Are you any good at the cross-word? It's ten down that is giving me trouble.'

They solved ten down: 'fox-hunting' – alas, nearly a thing of the past – and the two men immediately weighed into more meatier matters, namely the role and efficacy of mendicant Britons roaming the country.

'The Wesleys did it,' Fack pointed out, rather peevishly; the Brig agreed. The Brig nearly always agreed; it was his job to agree.

The Brig moved on to the trickier business of Enid and her late husband, Gerry.

'He sounds a good chap, prised open part of the Establishment and let some fresh air in.'

Before Fack could elaborate further on Gerry's life and, frankly, he wasn't nearly as well informed as the Brig, Enid's car could be heard and the next thing Enid was walking in with the groceries.

'Hello, Brig! What the hell brings you here?'

'Your well-being, my girl. We can't have you galloping off into the blue with just anyone.'

'Why not – just because my late husband bought badger bristles from China? Or spent some time in Ulan Bator? Or perhaps because he had a mistress in Bombay? Or is it because all that confidentiality he practised puts me in the firing squad sights when I choose to join forces with a holy man; is that it?'

'Yes, my dear, exactly. I knew you would understand. One or two educated fakirs are quite acceptable but just think of the Social Security implications if the whole of Southall took off on some mystic walkabout.'

'With me? You must be joking! But I'm ashamed of you, Brig. It is the old, "if everyone sneezed at once" theory of life. I don't buy it and I resent you sniffing around us.'

'Not nearly as much as other people are going to resent you, my dear. One thing could lead to another and then you could be at risk.'

'What you mean is that with some rummaging around they'll find out about Gerry's confidential past and bang goes your precious confidentiality. Good! I can't offer you coffee. I forgot the bloody milk. Look Brig, Gerry would have been very amused. Anyway, it's a darned sight better than begetting some film star in Bombay. You know I've been an exemplary wife. Now it's my turn – redressing the balance, you might say. Anyway, Fack and I make a good team.'

The Brig drove away with one word on his lips, which would soon be the basis for his report: 'tiresome'. Widows were increasingly acting in a tiresome manner. Burning bras was one thing, demanding rich emotional lives at nearly seventy quite another. Chippendales, my hat! The Brig knew a great deal about Enid, but then that was his job.

'We've brought it on ourselves, I suppose,' he sighed, before turning into a mock-Tudor house at the end of a suburban drive with rhododendrons and a wife to match.

Eviscerating a house is very much like eviscerating a mouse, cat-style. It is prolonged, messy and leaves a trail of unidentifiable pieces in its wake.

Mills and Mills were perfectly capable of breaking mirrors without Fack there to help them. Indeed, a minor Mills, younger brother possibly, a man of vast proportions, had the audacity to blame Fack for the damage his men did during the move. He didn't suggest that Fack had actually done anything, but dressed 'in a sheet and padding round in bare feet' had given his reliable team the 'nerves'. He had a good mind to give Fack a piece of his mind, only…

An empty house needs a sensitive 'goodbye'. Fack sat in the car while Sophocles and Enid let their memories glide over the years and over the painful and generous occasions. There were 'those eyes' when Gerry died, Sal's childhood (they still hadn't made up their quarrel), the lonely days of early widowhood, Adam looking with little or no interest at the flowers. It had been a good house, a modest house without any pretensions. She was handing it over to ghastly people, but that was progress. She had to laugh. The couple turned up to measure for curtains and Enid was out, leaving Fack to greet them. Apparently he did it with great enthusiasm. The couple were deeply shocked to find Fack practising some obscure holy pose of deep significance, frankly a rather difficult one to maintain for a portly man not in his first flush of youth.

'Shit! It hurts!' he bellowed, as they held the measuring tape across the dining room window.

'Who is he?' the lady had murmured.

'Indian, something like that.'

'He couldn't be a friendly ghost, I suppose?'

'Don't be daft. Ghosts don't say nasty words like that.'

Enid, Fack and Sophocles squeezed into the car with just a frying pan digging into her backside. She had rung the tiny pub with rooms and booked them in for a couple of nights, feeling venomous towards her daughter as she did so.

'I put up with those pot-smoking dickheads – didn't turn a hair at rings and things – swallowed Sal's friend, who believed being a single mum was deeply significant – even had the significant two-year-old ruin a dinner party by sitting throughout on her mother's knee and finally hurling one of the best glasses to the floor. I did it all and now it's my turn. Why shouldn't mothers find their emotional selves? Everyone else does.'

Ironically, the delay in kiss and make up was complicated by Douglas, who thought Fack was good news and a better addition to the family than a lot of others he could think of. Douglas might be conventional but he was good with animals.

'But he's *Indian*,' hissed Sal.

'So what? So is Veruca or whatever her name is, and she is your half-sister.'

'Douglas, you don't think they...you know... I mean, she doesn't know where he's been.'

'Grow up! You really can't judge a man by where he puts his prick. As far as I know, your mum isn't out of bounds, even if she is a little rusty.'

'But all the same...'

'Sal, your mum has met a man she likes: end of story.'

Sal turned to leave the room, muttering, 'You're no help.'

The ghoulish twins were brilliant at polishing Sal's anxiety.

'I suppose he pees through the side but unwinds that cloth thing when he does his poos. Is it the same colour as ours?'

'Don't be so disgusting. I don't want to hear another nasty thought, young lady.' That was ripe, coming from Sal.

The house moaned and groaned with unhappy thoughts, dirty thoughts and, in Douglas's case, anger at his wife's bigotry. The meals were eaten in a cacophony of cutlery, doors were slammed, sighs were heavy and even the dogs looked glum. Another slam, and Douglas was off down the pub.

Douglas heard the rumour over a pub lunch. Cross with his wife, he slammed the door and drove down to his local, where he sought the company of other farmers and working men, whose wisdom was gleaned from the soil, not the broadsheets of the chattering classes. So it was a rude awakening he found.

The pub was modernity squeezed into a nineteenth-century shell. The beams were there, recently made in Coventry with phoney notches and an attempt at woodworm. The prints had been bought at an auction along with several barrels and stools and a great many phoney horse brasses. There was a couple of blackboards announcing sun-dried tomatoes with everything and coriander with everything else. A group of regulars were hunched at the bar. Douglas asked for a pint of Guinness and leant comfortably against the counter. Len was in full spate. Douglas started with half an ear but soon found himself listening intently, both ears on full alert.

'No, listen, it's true, I'm telling you. This lady came in with this funny little man, see. He was wearing just a cloth, see, the kind Indians wear when they shin up ropes, lie on beds of nails and that. Well, Bert, he's been there donkey's years, see – old-fashioned publican – he's not very educated, like, wasn't having any, was 'e? "Proper dress 'ere, if you don't mind." That's Bert for you. Well, this Paki bloke says, "I'm a faki-sommat and this is our proper dress." Honest, that's what he says. Well, apparently Bert knew his rights, the Indian knew his, and the lady started shrieking her head off. The other customers had an opinion or two and the police were called in. They couldn't do much, as his this and thats were covered; there was no notice about what you could and could not wear. Bloody ridiculous, if you ask me.'

'You know what they say: the posher the place, the more you can get away with.' Douglas noted it was a bloke from London who made this comment – a weekender trying to fit in. No one could remember his name – he supported Fulham; it made a change from Sunderland.

'So which was he, Indian or Paki?' grumbled Greg. There is a difference, you know.'

'Come off it, they are all the same to me.' Reg resented his story being ruined by nitpicking. It was a bloody good story. He'd picked it up the previous evening in the Goose and Feathers.

'Smell, that's wot gets me; they smell.' Dick gazed at his pint.

'Come off it! Ever met one?'

'Wot if I haven't? They still smell.'

The men were uneasy. Dick had gone too far. They turned to John; after all, he was the manager.

'Decent chaps, I say. Another round, did I see? Thanks Bert, that's £7.48.' He continued blandly, 'Remember when we were kids, we'd zap the bloody Huns, Bosch, Eyties, Ruskies and all those other intergalactic aliens.'

'We never zapped the Pakis in them days though, did we?' muttered one of the regulars. 'That came later.'

Apart from the interloper from London, John knew his regulars. He knew Douglas was becoming a magistrate. He knew how far he could let them vent their prejudices. All the same... He cleared his throat and pointed to Douglas. 'He could have my guts for garters, cost me my licence.'

All eyes swivelled to Douglas. He knew the types, the loud-mouths, hard workers, shifty-eyed. He knew them all – not necessarily racist, but certainly prejudiced to their dirty broken fingernails.

'Well, gentlemen, I have a surprise for you,' began Douglas. 'What about it if I brought that fakir here with my mother-in-law, for that is the lady you've been talking about. What about it, if John agrees, we have a pint with a guy who was born in Leicester and knows one hell of a lot more about government policy where farming is concerned than you lot of ignorant peasants? I've my wife climbing up the bloody wall because her mum has teamed up with this character. He's skint and wears next to nothing because his religion makes it part of the deal and he's off on a tour round his and our country to meet the likes of you and learn something. It's over to you, because he's as through and through Brit as you and I are.'

'He's with your mother-in-law! I'd have him locked up,' announced Bert.

'You mean he...you know? I wouldn't hold for that.'

Dick fidgeted with his glass. Failing to see inspiration, he back-peddled. 'Na, yer pulling our leg!'

'If John agrees, I'll have him here tomorrow, if you like.'

John swaggered a little.

There were rules and rules. The police were forever banging on about racism and the law. How was he ever to tell? Couldn't hear himself speak on darts nights. It would be interesting, though. They had poetry the other evening – it was a washout. Well, that kind of thing was for the younger fellas, not his old codgers. His manager was all for turning pubs into schools for the elderly. His nibs, boss of the group, had got a knighthood for it – waste of time, really; but this Paki lark just might do some good.

John's son was dating a lovely girl from Lebanon. To give her credit, they couldn't have wished for a nicer girl. It's always different once you get to know them.

So Douglas left the den of rural enlightenment with a purpose. He was doing this as much for Sal as for the murky characters leaning round the bar. Douglas wasn't a man of deep passion. His political persuasions floated round the occasional visit to the hustings. The Third World was far away from his heifers, but all this nonsense about colour was wrong, very wrong. That his own dear Sal could be so intolerant and stupid was deeply shocking. As for his mother-in-law, hadn't she always been tiresome? Was that such a crime? If anyone was at fault, it was that old buffer, Gerry.

He'd found out the name of the pub with rooms where Fack and Enid were staying and drove over.

'I don't care whose mother-in-law she is. It ain't Christian or right. He had no shoes and only a cloth thing. She didn't give me a moment's warning. After all, she rung to book the room and never said a thing. What would Sheena say? She does the rooms – is glad of the money – but I tell you, it's not right. These young-sters – homo-whatsits – I take them all but I draw the line at a naked Paki with an elderly lady, who, if you don't mind me saying, needs a damned good hiding. It's going too far. Think what his family must feel. They have feelings too, you know.'

Douglas received this delicate drop of enlightenment equably.

'It's all very difficult, isn't it? You don't know where they went when they left here, do you?'

'And they had a dog, poor little soul; now that's who I feel sorry for. Poor dear can't know whether it's coming or going.' The publican paused, possibly to breathe; all this drama was bad for his angina. Selfish, that's what people were, never gave a thought for people's angina. He gave Douglas a baleful look. You could never tell these days. The chap looked quite respectable.

'Go? The motel – they take anyone these days. They have a lot to be responsible for – AIDS and that.'

On this indisputable piece of bizarre truth, Douglas mollified the publican as best he could and raced off to the motel.

In its day the motel had been known as a hot spot for illicit coupling, but with every form of sexual expression 'hanging out' like the washing, the motel had fallen on really sleazy days of poor tired reps, anonymous grey-suited men haunted by failure and ladies long past their sell-by date giving themselves to anyone for illusory warmth. The gang bangers had moved on. They now appeared on television after the watershed.

Yes, they were sleeping there.

'Ever so funny sight they were too, with a dog – Highland, he looked like. What did the fella look like? Them Paki blokes, quite a merry look in his eye if you ask me, not like that, you know – more proper communication. We did it at school; you must look at people if you want to communicate. She was posh, spoke well and gave orders an' that. Nice, they were.'

Bless her heart, Cindy was spot on. She was off to Hull next year to read Geography with Religious Studies and Aerobics – so useful. Cindy had more to say.

'I wanted to ask if he could do some of the yoga positions an' that, but felt awkward. You never know, do you?'

Douglas could have kissed the girl. Her friendly warmth and total lack of prejudice was like a delicious balm after all the filth and innuendo he had heard.

'You're a darling. I'll just leave a note if I may. Thank you so much, and the best of luck.'

He was just finishing the note when who should turn up but a beaming Enid with Fack and Sophocles in tow.

Meanwhile, Sal was still faintly hysterical, slamming pots and pans with angry sniffs as the accompaniment when the phone went and an estate agent gave some details of desirable residences.

'"Mon Repos"! My mother is reduced to "Mon Repos" – "well sheltered from the neighbours"!' she protested.

The other place was described as a barn with many original features. Hadn't she just left a barn with original features?

Poor old Sal was consumed with nightmares of Fack and her mother furiously bonking their way with adolescent fervour through Mon Repos till reduced to the streets: her mother, sister-in-law to Henry and Eleanor, grandmother to the twins, reduced to a bag lady! In her desperation she considered approaching the RSPCA. Poor Sophocles, surely he deserved better. Of all the daft, questionable things she had done since Pa's death, this was the pits. Her mother! It was her mother, shacking up! She'd never have done it if she had been to India. She'd have respected their culture too much. Sal thought about Vijaya, shuddered and had the decency to ask herself, *What culture*?

It was time to collect the twins from school. It was always time to collect the twins from school. Sophie scrambled into the car first, followed by Beatrice, who paused to tickle Roger – fine, only Roger was asleep.

With Roger yelling and Beatrice loudly proclaiming it wasn't her fault, Sophie screeched over the top, 'Gran's done it this time. Run off with that Paki man and disgraced our family. Kevin wouldn't sit next to me – said it ran in the family.'

'Don't you believe in a free society, Sophie? Can't Granny do what she likes? And don't use that word "Paki"; it's vulgar, rude and offensive.'

'Like fuck?' Sophie knew when she was on to a good thing.

'Yes,' said Sal, and burst into tears.

Then Enid rang when they got home.

'If you seriously don't want to be on speaking terms with me, the sooner we find somewhere to live the better, but I need you as my address at the moment. We were kicked out of a pub yesterday – so silly, so unnecessary; it upsets Sophocles.'

'Oh Mum, we all love you so much, don't torment us like this. No one minds you having a fakir for a friend but don't drag him into the bosom of your family – not at once. We don't even know him.' There were more sobs.

'I haven't got enough time left for that kind of nonsense. Anyway, it's the way of the future. I'm preparing the way for Beatrice and Sophie to have an open mind. When I think of all the silly nonsense we put up with when you were at college, and you can't even accept that for the first time in my life I have a cause and a man! What more can a woman of my age want? Well, time I suppose. Neither Fack or I have time.'

'That is all very well. Beatrice has told her class that you've gone clearly bonkers and run off with a naked man with just a nappy on.'

'Good on her! That'll make the incontinence brigade join our cause.'

'What cause?'

'Fack and I – with Sophocles, if he likes – are going to liberate people from their isms. By the way, is Douglas about?'

'I suppose that includes rheumatism. Really Ma, do you have to make a complete ass of yourself? First it was wrecking the equilibrium of the over-sixties by taking them to see the Chippendales and now it's a fakir who is as authentic as Cornish cream in Kenya.'

The phone call ended on a raw nerve. People with causes can be very bewildering, like a constant flow of visits from the Jehovah Witnesses.

Sal was just recovering from the call when Douglas walked in.

'I tracked them down. Your mum is thrilled to pieces, showing off like hell and looks ten years younger. They've found a B and B in Ripon. The landlord is a devout Christian and wants to pick Fack's brains. When they arrived at this new place they were warmly welcomed, apparently.'

Indeed they were. Mrs Tankard had held open the door and said, 'Bless me, if it isn't a sadhu!'

'He's a fakir, actually,' said Enid pompously.

'Sadhu, fakir, they were all the same out there – holy men. Could do with a few round here, if you ask me. Tankard and I were out there most of our lives. He was a missionary. He'll be thrilled. We worked for a medical mission. Those were the days.

I'm always happy when I can get Indian students. You said just the one room, didn't you? Now I remember…travelling with a Jane Buddhist from Calcutta to Delhi…hot. It sizzled and he wore just a loincloth! That's what I like about the Indians. Where do you come from, dear?'

Fack looked a little taken back.

'Leicester.'

'Quite right too, dear, if you don't mind me saying. Not enough holiness about these days, if you ask me.'

Mrs Tankard showed them a small but pleasant room and then insisted on giving them tea in her parlour. There she introduced them to Tankard – a sick man, but argumentative. As for Benares elephants, they live in Mrs Tankard's parlour in Ripon, along with fiddly brass whatnots and antimacassars made from ethnic tapestry. Mrs Tankard was more Indian than Fack, and Mr Tankard, despite his angina, was not far behind. What Mrs Tankard – it soon became 'Call me Beryl' – thought about the double room for Fack and Enid was never evinced and certainly an explanation was never given. It was, however, the only subject about which Martin and Beryl had little to say. In their eyes, Jesus Christ was the holiest of holy men, but behind him anyone could have a bash. Martin liked the Muslims because they were orderly, the Hindus were in his eyes delightful, if tending to employ a plethora of gods.

'Untouchable, my foot!'

On that they were all agreed.

Douglas parked his car and walked cautiously up the Tankards' dear little garden. Bright, friendly flowers and a few impudent weeds lined the path. He rang the bell.

Mrs Tankard opened the door. Yes, Fack and Enid were staying with her, what a privilege it was to have them and dear little Sophocles. Mrs Tankard called up and a glowing happy Enid tumbled downstairs.

'Hello, Douglas, what can we do for you?'

'It's Fack, actually, I'd like to see.'

Fack eased himself out of some esoteric and, frankly, rather painful position and invited Douglas to sit on their bed. He listened quietly to Douglas's proposition before grinning broadly. Of course Enid and he would be there.

Frankly, Fack wasn't sure this was the road he wanted to follow. He preferred doing *The Times* crossword puzzle and picking up lovely ladies with generous bank accounts; no, that was being facetious and not fair to Enid. But in his opinion this crusade to fight racism in pubs smelled of lost causes, like Twyford Down or fox-hunting, not a genuine attempt to understand racism. Racism was too complex a subject to be mulled over in a pub. But Enid was a feisty lady, and why not? It wasn't that Fack was a fraud. He simply wasn't that motivated – not from the fearsomely uncomfortable situation he found himself in at that moment. After all, he had left his home not to proselytise but to learn. He admitted with a sigh that Enid's belief in him changed everything.

'God! How corrupting a good woman and comfort can be to the holy cause.'

Meanwhile, Douglas was torn between the weeping Sal, who just wanted her mum to be a mum, and his growing respect for Fack. Mr and Mrs Tankard, clutching pills, simply wanted a night out and to hear it all. It was a real outing for them, better than bingo and Bible classes.

They arrived at the pub at seven. The creaking sign proclaimed 'The Anchor'. It was nowhere near the sea. The pub looked every inch the botched attempt at antiquity. Fack noticed with wry amusement the very best in plastic woods and furnishings, just like he used to see in Leicester when he was making his way. It had the obligatory list of exotic bottles hanging upside down, bottle after bottle of undrunk liqueurs and six splendid handles to draw the well-loved favourites. There were cardboard mats with a jolly twinkling huntsman and a phoney gas fire to give it that friendly glow. John was also a fixture and fitting. He'd been there years presiding over his team of regulars and refereeing events like tonight's – no, not like tonight's; this was a one-off.

John was all for it now he had cleared it with head office. After all, he'd been in the merchant navy, hadn't he – seen Aden in the good old days – once brought a monkey home; poor beggar died of pneumonia. He, for one, knew which he'd prefer to have as a next door neighbour, his bloody monkey or one of these daft buggers who have never seen modern plumbing. But sssh! He'd been on courses run by the brewery about racism. Once he'd had to play some damned stupid game. They lay on the floor like black and white tiles and each person had to sniff his neighbour's armpit. Well, if the brewery could do it, so could he. This dozy old lot should be good for the till, his standing with the brewery should improve and he'd even invited his area manager to pop in; couldn't lose, could he?

Douglas, Beryl, Martin, Enid and Fack piled in the doorway to be met by the universal glare of Bert, Ron, Dick and the others hunched by the bar. There were a few people who didn't notice their arrival – two young men holding the inevitable discussion about cars, the silent drinkers who liked to air their melancholy in public and were totally self-absorbed. There were a few women too, those who love pubs – God knows why; lonely souls, probably.

Beryl and Enid must have known about those armpit games because Fack was spruced up in a clean cloth and had taken a snip or two to his hair and beard.

John shook hands with everyone but Fack, who clasped his hands and modestly announced, 'Namaste,' before explaining this peaceful benediction and suggesting everyone joined in by clasping their hands and greeting their friends. The regulars looked surly, a single lady brightened up, the car talk ceased for almost a whole minute before resuming about the cleaning of spark plugs.

'Free pint on me for the first person to clasp their hands and welcome me with a "namaste".'

The single lady won hands down. It just shows what fun going to a pub can be. She leaped to her feet, her pent-up loneliness exploded. She almost leaped into Fack's arms.

'I'm Phyllis. You're a holy man. I saw a programme on telly once about people like you.'

Dick, Ron, Bert and mates sat a little more erect, waiting for the possibility of another freebie to wing its way.

John, the crafty bugger, led Fack right up to the group and held his hands together before loudly saying, 'Namesty, gentle-men.'

Eye caught eye. They swirled, swivelled, blazed, glistened and whistled silently to heaven for inspiration. It came.

'Not even for a pint?' coaxed Fack with a chuckle.

It sounded like a herd of cows with laryngitis trying to moo, but it was a start. They greeted Fack. Now Phyllis had left her seat and been bidden to the bar, the holy of holies – her aspiration. It had taken her years to be invited to be part of the group.

Meanwhile the other holy of holies, Fack himself, was deep into a bitter lemon and telling risqué stories about encouraging people to say 'namaste'.

'What's wrong with 'ello, I'd like to know.' Bert could feel the free pint clasped in his hands.

'Yeah,' agreed Reg, emboldened by the moment.

'It's not fucking India 'ere, yer know,' observed Dick

'India, India – where's that?' asked Fack, looking round.

'Don't give me that crap,' growled Bert.

'I've never been there, unless you count Leicester.'

'More's the pity,' rumbled Bert.

Soon, racist comments whizzed and fizzed among the rafters of the old pub. Not that namby-pamby stuff about what you mustn't say but the liberating tension-relieving exercise in calling bloody shovels bloody shovels and be damned. Smelly armpits were but nothing. Yet in all the reversion to anal behaviour there grew in the raucous, embarrassed hilarity a new code of sensitivity, a sharing of the bent and battered, leaking chalice of friendship, from all that malice and ignorance. John, not to be outdone and thrilled with the takings, lobbed in his pennyworth of vulnerability, with his son about to marry a Lebanese. Fack admitted he couldn't climb ropes or levitate and was damned if he was going to lie on a bed of nails, unless the NHS counted. He did some tortuous feats of supple joints and seemed such a know-all that John asked if he would like to join the quiz team – Thursday week, against the Golden Goose. Good idea, thought the regulars, and that included Dick and Bert.

When the gemütlich atmosphere had reach its peak, Phyllis ruined it by suggesting John put on a girls' night. It was Enid who dashed the idea flat.

'Not here, love. Ring Ann Summers if you want that kind of thing.'

Why do women have to ruin everything?

But it was dear old Fack who won the day. He disarmed the porcupine quills of prejudice and had the bar stalwarts throwing back their pints, which pleased John and the area rep. He proved such a success that the area rep, a smart alec on the make, took him aside and offered him a job going round pubs and shaking people out of their prejudices and into their pints.

As Douglas pointed out to Sal, 'Look, love, Fack has a good mind. He's read a lot and thought a lot. He's a good guy and if he tickles your mother's fanny from time to time – so what?' Douglas wrapped his arms round Sal's waist as she beat some murky mess, which would never transform itself into Yorkshire pud – well, not edibly so.

'Douglas, how could you? Look what you've done. How can you condone your mother-in-law living in a B and B and wandering round the local pubs discussing racism, with a – with a barmy layabout togged up in a sheet?'

There was a very difficult moment at school that week. Tommy had just finished boring everyone stupid with an account of giving his rabbit some turnip to eat when Sophie asked ever so politely if Miss Roberts thought grannies should have their fannies tickled, cos her granny was having hers tickled by a funny man who wore a sheet. There had followed a silence which stretched like spaghetti. Sal had been summoned and sat closeted with the headmistress discussing fannies, or rather what Sophie had meant by fanny.

Then the local paper tracked down Sal. It made a lovely story. Not that they could quote Sophie, but they could hint at some of the contemporary problems modern grannies can cause.

A bouncy car braced itself against the mud while Roger and Sal were heaping a miscellaneous selection of grey, grubby clothes into the machine.

'Who the hell?'

A strangely androgynous boy with large, serious eyes introduced himself as Paul from the local paper. He looked vulnerable and sensitive, slightly out of place in his neat well-cut trousers and jacket. He tiptoed into the kitchen, sensibly avoided all contact with Roger, who had been drawing all over his clothes with a chocolate biscuit, and tentatively accepted a coffee. He had learnt that rural coffees covered a variety of flavours. Sitting rather hesitantly at the kitchen table, he coaxed Sal into talking about her mother.

What a wonderful, eccentric mother she must be, he suggested rather hesitantly. One felt his heart wasn't in this story.

'She's been looking for a cause ever since my father died. There are so many women her age – intelligent, energetic, lonely. Fack is just a catalyst.'

The journalist cocked his head to one side. He thought Fack was a fakir and he had checked it on the Internet.

'Well, it's not easy,' continued Sal, suddenly relieved of all the pent-up tension of the last few weeks.

Roger was not impressed with emoting mothers and strange men, so he tipped some sand onto the well-worn kitchen floor and breathed a deep, 'There.'

'Roger – just look what you've done! Don't do that! Oh, God! I sound just like Joyce Grenfell. Look, I have the children to bring up one end and my mother making a fool of herself the other.' Sal began to cry. The journalist looked at the floor. How he loathed the messy bits of life. He avoided his by doing a nifty act as a drag queen in a Leeds nightclub once a week. It was a change from cow shit and farmers' wives, especially those whose mothers had taken leave of their senses.

'It's hell, isn't it?' the journalist sighed. 'I want to be a woman – now, not in several years time after some rotten op which has a waiting list filled with foreigners queue-jumping. Now! I want to be a desirable, glamorous woman, now!'

After that, Paul and Sal cried, much to the disapproval of Roger, who just wanted another chocolate biscuit. Meanwhile, he heaped the sand back into the bucket, making, if anything, even more mess.

Sal looked closely at the journalist. 'But you are perfect!' She leapt to her feet. 'You see, I am going to start an art centre and we desperately need models. You would be perfect, encouraging students to draw out your femininity. You can live, breathe and feel a real woman – but no ghastly wig, please; femininity is in your bones and muscles, not in peroxide curls.'

'I'm in therapy. I'll have to discuss it,' said Paul eagerly.

The tears were now mutual tears of solidarity, Paul already thrusting his head forward as a model, letting the hot wet feel of emotion course down his rather stubbly cheeks, while Sal blubbed gulps of frustration at Douglas's duplicity in encouraging her mum. Why, oh why, had she teamed up with this fakir chap and, biggest why of all, why did Douglas encourage her?

It never crossed her mind that commandeering a transsexual journalist to be a model was in a modest way exactly the kind of thing Enid might have done. Even our Sal hadn't lost it all in the plethora of dirty washing and don't say 'fuck' – it's not nice.

Paul also wanted to unburden himself. Enid temporarily forgotten, Paul told Sal the blow-by-blow compulsion that was driving him to have the operation. It was nothing sexual; it was about gender, he explained. So Sal found herself listening to the frustrated, pent-up emotions of the young journalist and Roger got not one, but two chocolate biscuits.

That night it was her turn. She turned her bum angrily away from Douglas.

'My sweetheart, my treasure, don't cry; let me try to explain.' He had the patience of a saint.

Sal had told Douglas all about Paul. She had waited till the twins were in bed; the idea of the twins embracing transsexuality was too much.

'It is his cashmere shawl that has done it, you know, the one he wears to withstand the winter blasts. I tackled him about it,' Douglas began.

'Oh, Douglas, you didn't! You know how pompous Fack can sound.' Sal rolled over, her mood and anger already assuaged by Douglas's warm body.

'Guess what he said, seriously? "A holy man must be many things, Douglas."' Douglas spoke the Indian lilt lousily. It made Sal giggle.

'"Where did you get that cashmere shawl?" – I asked straight out. "I suppose Enid gave it to you." "No, Douglas," he replied. "I am not a cad. I repeat for your benefit, I see myself as a holy man, and Enid as…"'

At this juncture, Fack had stroked his beard, looked at the ceiling and plucked the word 'handmaiden' out of the ether.

Douglas had nearly choked – but didn't, because he realised that Enid too was taking a pilgrimage. Gerry's death had started it all, that dreadful stepdaughter and her husband had precipitated it and Fack was the natural conclusion. If only Sal could see it.

'It belonged to my late wife. I gave it to her when the rheumatic English weather made her winters purgatory. She was Indian, you know – carted across the world to marry a distant cousin. It's barbaric, isn't it? Almost as bad as filing for a divorce the first time sex isn't up to snuff. Which is worse, Douglas? All those Asian brides trapped in unhappy arranged marriages, or the loveless bastards running about because their parents have got bored. It's a sick, sick world, Douglas.'

'How do you fit into it, Fack?'

'It's a long story, Douglas. I had to do something. My sons inherited my business, mainly textiles. My dear wife was dead and there was I, not welcomed down the local and not welcomed at the temple. Neither wanted to seek the truth, both wanted to continue propping up the status quo. Sadly, my wealth – yes, Douglas, I am a wealthy man – had bought me recognition and acceptability, but what about my poorer brethren? Gandhiji had it worse; he was a truly great man, but at least I could try. But I wasn't really trying. I was playing till I met Enid. Then she believed in me – no fucking, no sex. She believed that someone dressed for the heat of India who had renounced the fleshpots of Leicester could make the dog basket of this country a little more equitable and comfortable for every breed of dog. My taxes have helped the equitable side, and now I want to help the spiritual side. For me, that is about being comfortable with each other. As for me, little children stare, women titter, men squirm with irritation…and why? I'm a bloody foreigner, playing bloody foreigner games in their eyes, yet have the temerity to be British.'

Douglas, who up to that moment had been mildly suspicious of Fack, decided he liked him, really liked him, even if he was batty. He must get Sal to understand before it was too late. That is why he slipped his arms round his wife and gently kissed her.

Meanwhile Enid had indeed found a purpose. She sat over

coffee with her friend Dolly and smirked, having told her all about it.

'I've met my Mr Shortbread, Dolly, only it isn't quite like that. There's not much sex, for starters. Fack talks too much for sex. He says sex is splendid when you're young but too much work at his age. He says so many things. He's wise. He spends hours just sitting with his arms and legs in weird positions. I don't think he really cares about me – he just sees me as his handmaiden.'

'Are you crazy? Enid, you must be out of your tiny mind! You hole up with some weirdo wrapped in a piece of cheesecloth who spends his days sitting like some damned lotus flower, while you and Sophocles stretch your legs in the usual fashion. Then, after tofu sandwiches, you head for some public house to challenge the dozy old locals by talking about racism. What about a home, putting your feet up with a good book? When do you get to a washing machine, get your hair done? Look, you nearly went off the rails with the Chippendales – sex for the over-sixties and all that. Well, now you've gone too far. It's so difficult to get back, Enid. Boring old normality becomes increasingly hard to achieve. What does Sal think?'

Enid's eyes filled with tears. She looked a tousled, frumpy mess, living out of suitcases. The Tankard's bath was hot but not luxurious. It was weeks since she had cut her toenails, done her hair or used hand cream. Dolly was right. It had to end. This frenetic love affair with the spiritual life was too much. At her age it was meant to be bridge, collecting for the Red Cross, the occasional film, good books and gardening. At the end of the day it was cocoa, and don't even think of romantic thoughts! Yet snuggled next to Fack's backside, she could think what she bloody well liked.

'Oh, Dol, I know, but it's not easy. This experience has been such fun – a real challenge. I've learnt so much. I might look like the wreck of the *Hesperus* but I've discovered so much about myself.'

'Then do an Open University degree,' sighed Dolly sourly, then adding, 'At this rate you are going to alienate all your family and few remaining friends. Is that the old age you want?'

Driving back, Enid noticed and not for the first time that the car needed servicing. Any voyage was perilous. Clasping the steering wheel, she continued her monologue after Dolly had booted her out with dire warnings in her ears.

'Can't you see, there's very little time left? All I ask for is "one short hour and sweet". I just want to achieve something with my life.'

These had been just the same sentiments she had used with Sal when – bliss, oh bliss! – there had been a rapprochement of a kind and Enid had been asked to lunch.

Dear little Roger was rapidly becoming an alarming beast. He tottered around on two rugby-playing legs, checking the electricity by plunging knitting needles into the sockets or pulling tablecloths slowly off the table set for Sunday lunch. His chances of making adulthood appeared limited. Enid looked upon him with discreet loathing. The twins weren't much better. They bought make-up at car boot sales and plastered their faces. Their pert bums just asked for naughty thoughts and, at school, they spent their time putting condoms onto carrots. When asked 'Why?' they couldn't remember whether it was health and relationships or religious education.

Neither Sal nor Enid mentioned Fack by name.

That evening, after the car graciously managed not to conk out coming back from Dolly's and Enid had just finished the tinned rice pudding, the phone rang. It was the ever loyal Dolly asking her if she'd got home safely. No – it was really to ask her to make a four at bridge ten o'clock Thursday. What a damn silly waste of a phone call! Enid said 'yes' tentatively, because bridge, let's face it, was a 'coming down in the world' indicator if ever there was one. Not bridge in itself, but making up a four in the middle of the morning. It smacked of nothing better to do, a grisly reminder of an awful gentility accompanied by Earl Grey tea and expensive biscuits. But Fack was away being Indian. A group in Hartlepool had invited him to read some obscure poetry. Fack was increasingly being Indian and that made Enid feel more and more alienated and likely to do something daft like play bridge.

'Shit, I'll have to tart up and not say "fuck". Three no trumps, partner,' she said to herself.

Apart from not noticing that she was one button out with her blouse and two safety pins' width round the waist when doing up her skirt, Enid made it to bridge.

About four different half-understood conventions floated round her head and Enid couldn't quite remember the pecking order, with spades at the top and clubs at the bottom. Dolly had pulled out a card table, loaded the coffee tray – the biscuits were there – arranged some flowers and brought an extra chair from the hall. The two other ladies swung a professional eye over Enid before being introduced.

'I prefer the kicking convention, myself,' said Enid with enthusiasm to her partner, Isobel, as they sat down.

'Please don't, you'll ladder my tights,' quipped Isobel.

Aren't we funny? Ha, bloody ha! I only hope the bomb doesn't drop now. I couldn't bear to be found playing bridge by yours upstairs. Enid was feeling mildly hysterical. No more time for those kinds of thoughts – Dolly had opened with a heart. Was that a weak heart? At their age it was about the only kind. They lengthened before strength, or rather those that could remember did. Even Enid could count her points before launching into an over-cautious opening.

'If only you had called your spades, we could have made game,' sighed Isabel.

'But I only had three and the highest was a ten,' protested Enid.

'Ah, but if you had thought about it properly...'

Enid would never think about bridge properly, her heart wasn't in it; bridge remained for her a despised game for intelligent middle-class women with not enough to do.

It wasn't the bridge that occupied her thoughts on the way home, it was Dolly. She hadn't been herself. Not just forgetting the milk, anyone can do that – no, she was absent-minded, not quite at ease in some way.

Had Enid raised her head from her two no trumps and looked out of the window, she would have noticed it was spring. It was always bloody spring. The birds were making a God-awful racket. The grass was leaping out of the ground but the weeds leaped higher and more furiously. Beryl had done her back in, so Enid did the weeding and sighed as she saw less and less of Fack, who was becoming horribly popular. Limousines purred outside the B and B. He expected Enid to keep him in clean loincloths. Apparently it was something handmaidens were expected to do. Enid realised slowly and painfully that her role in his life was awfully similar to her role in Gerry's life – dogsbody. She pulled the groundsel and chickweed out of the border and felt let down.

Then Sophocles became sick. He was very ill. Enid took him to the vet, then tenderly carried him home. Sophocles developed diarrhoea which, in the confines of their bedroom in the B and B, put a great strain on Enid's and Fack's relationship.

'Poor old Sophs, after all we've been through. Mind you, I never really wanted him. He was Gerry's idea.' Enid washed her hands and gazed at her coffee.

'Enid, I know that your dogs are the equivalent of our holy cows, but I have never heard of a holy cow expiring in someone's bedroom. Would it be too much to ask for you to take him to the vet and have him put down?'

'Just because he smells a bit! Anyway, you should be tolerant of smells, and of animals dying. Sal says India absolutely stinks of rotting corpses.'

'But Leicester doesn't.'

Sophocles, no doubt on hearing he wasn't wanted, expired soon after.

Enid felt awful. She rang Sal and wept. She drove over later that day, leaving Fack sitting on the floor, his legs crossed, looking inscrutable.

'Remember, it's a pub over Northallerton way this evening. I'll ask Beryl to get me something for lunch.'

Fack liked several handmaidens. It was becoming increasingly clear that he was used, not only to comfort, but for a degree of sophistication as well. Beryl had confided in Enid that she thought Fack might well turn out to be something rather grand; it was his humility, or rather lack of it.

Enid put Sophocles' inert and rather smelly body into a plastic bag.

The twins were delighted. They rushed up to the car as it came to a halt.

'Where are you going to bury him? Did you say a prayer? Does God let dogs into heaven?'

That was it; they would have a funeral. The first thing was to wrap the body in one of Roger's old nappies. His corpse was lovingly placed in the plastic basket more accustomed to the washing.

'There you are, you poor old thing. It's all Granny's fault. Me and Beatrice are writing a letter saying she mustn't keep dogs any more cos she doesn't have a proper home, only a B and B.'

'He's awfully stiff.'

'Yeah, it's got a funny name. Dad showed me with a cow. It'll go. Then he'll rot and make the courgettes grow.'

'There's a box in the barn, let's use that.' It had, in better days, been for latex disposable gloves.

Everyone had a role, even Roger, who was made into an altar boy and given a hanky soaked in aftershave to wave around.

Muttering imprecations against grandchildren and C of E primary schools, Enid was decked out in a witch's cloak left over from Halloween and a large sloppy sun hat and made to follow the cortège with Sal, her hands floury from the kitchen, and Douglas from the farm, who joined the brief walk to the graveside.

'Oh, girls! You've—'

'Ssh, we are being holy. Let's sing, "Away in a Manger". Roger, don't go too near the… Oops! He's fallen in.'

'Away in a Manger' was ruined by Roger's frightened screams. After that, Sophie recited a natty little poem from the playground all about worms crawling in and out. It had a chorus of 'Ooh ooh ooh ooh, aah aah aah aah'. After that, the girls shoved the box in the hole vacated by the bawling Roger, told Douglas to fill it in and asked what was for tea.

It was Beryl who wormed out the story of Fack's past from him. It would appear that Enid had done it again. They often say that people invariably marry the same person twice, if not three times. Once more she had chosen a well-heeled – no, a very rich – man, who had put it all out of his mind for something more spiritual, with just the proviso of a gold credit card in his bull's balls pouch, just in case. Fack had caused consternation in Whitehall, caused the stock exchange to waver, stiff upper lips in his club to wobble and the taxman to lament. Above all, his two sons were worried stiff.

The two sons sat in their elegant penthouse office. One sat on the edge of the desk swinging one leg, while the other lounged in a comfortable chair. They wore expensive cufflinks and silk ties with Armani suits that swallowed up four figures. The office was in achingly good taste and included a view over Leicester. Leicester, bless its heart, was old and wise enough not to be particularly impressed with such status-ridden displays.

'He's in Ripon; that's somewhere in the North, isn't it?'

'How do you know?'

'There's a piece in the local paper up there about a fakir in a pub – wait for it – with his companion, a Mrs Enid Tanner.'

'Oh Christ! Whatever has he picked up?'

Sandeep consulted the paper. '*The same Mrs Tanner recently arranged for a group of elderly ladies to visit the Chippendales in Leeds,*' he read.

'That's those hunky lads that wriggle their pelvises to music.'

'You're not telling me that Dad has doubled up as a Chippendale! That would be testing credulity too far.' Tapan started doodling on his desk. His father had caused many a doodle since his departure six months before.

Fack had begun life as Mahesh Sharma and risen like bread from the small streets of Leicester. He had sold gaudy bolts of cloth and saris by day and taken a degree in business studies by night. He went from rag trade to textile business during a slump, when he held on for dear life. He held on with the wily skills of someone used to surviving against all odds. He married – frankly, he couldn't remember when and could barely remember who. It was a heart-rending guilt trip just to please his parents.

Success brought choices. Mahesh chose to move away from an Indian way of life in Leicester, so he bought a beautiful, run-down Georgian house near Melton Mowbray. He acquired a somewhat querulous gay man with good taste to decorate it, but soon opted for his own style. He sacked the interior design expert and brought bolts of bright cloth to drape over the couches and hang at the windows. His wife created shrines with flowers and incense, prayers and fruit, adding mystery to the decor. They had two sons, Tapan and Sandeep, who added Lego and plastic cars, which they raced up and down the corridors. Their mother supervised delicious curries from the kitchen and reluctantly turned the pages of Delia Smith for those occasions when Mahesh wanted to show off his cellar – which was essentially French, thus demonstrating how British he was. Mahesh bent over backwards to straddle the two cultures. A jovial chap called Adrian, who hunted foxes, maintained his cellar. Wine's a difficult hobby for someone born a teetotaller.

'You should try hunting, Mahesh – better than polo and pig-sticking.'

It amused Mahesh that Adrian assumed that his relatives in India played polo and went pig-sticking – whatever that was. If the truth be known, Mahesh's family were lowly souls who scratched a living round a loom.

An expensive horse was bought, with a sour-faced man to look after it. Mahesh mildly regretted the expense and wondered what the sour-faced man, Ted, would do all day. Surely one horse couldn't take up all day? Ted proved to be a gem. He had graduated to hunting, having been warned off the turf for pulling a horse. He doubled up as the chauffeur. No one bothered to check his driving licence, which was a pity. Another character called Antonia entered their lives. She taught Mahesh to ride and gleaned curry recipes from his wife. She looked a mess, had a loud voice and was reputedly the daughter of an earl.

Not for his boys the dubious virtues of a comprehensive education. Mahesh shuddered at the memory of rampant racism and an overwhelming dreariness in the classroom where mediocrity ran amok. No, he could afford the best, so off they went to a public school, the only one Mahesh had heard of. While Daddy flew in Concorde, they learnt Latin; while Daddy consulted with ministers, they rubbed shoulders with minor royalty. They learnt that racism is a condition of the lower orders. They avoided the lower orders and went on to university.

At home in the Georgian mansion, the vicar shared the problem of the church roof with Mahesh. He shared it over a decent whisky, discreetly and without any reference to Jesus Christ. He didn't say 'noin' or wear white socks. He was a real gentleman and Mahesh, relieved not to be harangued, gave him the lot.

Having hunted for several seasons, Mahesh understood how many of the antis felt. He gave up the whole horse thing and gave a wodge of money to their cause. Ted was relieved, the horse was relieved and those smart-arsed gents who hunted with the Quorn were relieved.

Then his wife died – a brain haemorrhage. Her name was Veena. She died as the corn rippled in the late summer wind, the thistledown like tiny paratroopers blew across the fields and the sour apples were starting to ripen. She died with the first chrysanthemums, collapsed in a haze of cumin and turmeric, clutching some saffron. She slithered to the floor, her eyes rolled and the cook fled in panic for help. Mahesh was in London making a deal and the boys in their offices learning the ropes.

'Mother dead?'

'Veena dead?'

It was when they tried to remove the shrines that Mahesh first found himself saying 'No'. He found himself reading the autobiography of Jawaharlal Nehru, and began missing the wife he never knew. He found her in books and in the mean, poky streets of Leicester where he walked for hours in sad introspection. Meanwhile, secretaries tapped their pencils irritably, PAs looked at their watches, boards shook their heads and shares dipped. Still Mahesh walked in a trance. Savile Row suits had been replaced with cotton trousers. Sandeep and Tapan consulted each other, then they consulted the board. Mahesh gave way with alacrity. He had worked for years and risen like yeast; now it was his time to do what he must to assuage his guilt and understand his neglected soul.

'We'd better drive up, San?'

'It's a free country. He's not actually doing any harm.' Sandeep was busy.

'He'll go too far and get arrested. What if he marries this Mrs Enid Turner?'

'It would be too awful if she was one of those elderly tarts with a heart of gold, wouldn't it?' Sandeep shuddered. Actually he was imagining what it would be like introducing father and his floozy to Arabella, his intended. Her parents were sniffy enough about him, but a father in a loincloth and a stepmother, no doubt with an accent you could cut with a knife, would really be hard to live down.

'Well, you hold the fort and I'll go.' Tapan was always the most easy-going of the two.

'Go where, exactly? Ripon is quite a large town.'

'I'll ask the local rag, see if they can help; or the local police, they are bound to know.'

So it was that a dark blue Porsche was added to the equation.

Tapan drove carefully. It was one of the drawbacks of owning such a car. He had left at four, gone home to change, though God knows what you change into on such an occasion, and bundled some wash things into a bag just in case he had to stay overnight. He played operatic arias all the way, singing along mildly out of tune. It was eightish when he arrived outside the Tankards'.

'Fack and Enid? We like to use Christian names here – ever so much more friendly.' Mrs Tankard beamed at the beautiful young Indian gentleman standing in her doorway.

'Let me see. It's the Black Bull out towards Northallerton tonight. Doing wonders, if you ask me. I would ask you in, but it's *The Bill* on telly and Tankard don't like to miss it. Tell you what, they'll be home about eleven – knackered too, I shouldn't wonder.'

The door closed and Tapan was left with little option than to seek the bright lights of Ripon for the next three hours.

Parking a Porsche might be a doddle at Ascot or other such watering holes of the rich, but in Ripon it is not just a responsibility but a bloody nuisance. Tapan chose the town square, partly because he could see it from the Chinese where he ate duckling and ginger…or was it chicken and ginger, or maybe it was beef and ginger. It was hard to say.

Four squaddies, mildly pissed, looked at the car.

'Charlie, bought yerself a new car or sommat?'

'Na, me ol' man gave it to me for me twenty-first.'

'Thought yer said yer ol' man was on the dole.'

'So I did; just wishful thinking.'

Ted rubbed his hand along the smooth lines and said in an eager, puzzled voice, 'Ever felt like nicking sommat like this?'

'Yeah, often', replied his mate, adding, 'it's a mug's game.

You'd never get away with it.'

'How much do yer think it cost?'

'Ask him,' Charlie jerked his thumb towards Tapan, who had paid and left on seeing his car surrounded.

'I didn't buy it, actually; my dad gave it to me for my twenty-first.'

'I suppose he's one of these geezers what has racehorses an' that.' Ted was being polite.

'We're from Leicester.'

A Paki from Leicester – that was an outrage! Jealousy begat by ale surfaced. They turned stony-faced on Tapan.

'You're a Paki?'

'No, I'm not. I'm British, like you. My dad was born here, in Leicester. Now I must be off, I'm meeting someone.'

Tapan slid into the car and started it with a roar that might well have come from a lion at Longleat before gliding through the square and off to find his dad.

The squaddies stood there, thunderstruck. How dare a Paki, talking posh an' all, call himself a Brit? And drive a Porsche! An evening of moderation turned ugly. They went back to the pub and vented their spleen. There were others ready to listen and agree – agree with what exactly was hard to determine, as each person used the bait to fuel their own anger. Housing, they got better housing; their children were chosen for them posh schools; they grabbed the best jobs; yer couldn't visit a hospital without some damn blackie prodding you. It wasn't fair. Bleating this mantra like sheep, they spilled into the main square. There were ten of them by now – angry, inarticulate young men. They made their way to a nightclub which was filled with teenage girls – whose only crime was gormless stupidity – and young men a little jerky on ecstasy. The fight was nasty. Some 'blackie' doctors were called upon to sew up wounds. The squaddies were confined to their barracks and no one really knew what started it all.

Tapan drove cautiously back to the B and B. He didn't relish seeing his father looking like some bloody fool in a loincloth with some dotty old lady in tow. He walked reluctantly up the small path to the front door and rang the bell before turning round, as if avoiding the sight that might meet his eyes. He needn't have worried. It was Mrs Tankard who opened the door.

'There you are. I said you had called – spitting image, that's what I told him you were.' Mrs Tankard then called up the stairs, 'Fack, it's your lad.'

A door opened and Fack bustled downstairs, dressed, as every nightmare of Tapan's suggested, in his loincloth, with an old cardy of Enid's to keep the Yorkshire chill at bay.

'Tapan, my boy, what joy, what joy! Mrs T, I'm sorry, it's so late. Any chance of the settee for the night?'

Hearing his father say 'settee' was a shock too many. Tapan replied that he had no intention of sleeping on the sofa. He wanted to get back home as he had a business to run. He just wanted Mahesh to know that he was greatly missed and both he and Sandeep wanted him home. It was at this moment that a bedraggled Enid arrived on the scene.

'Hello, you're just like my daughter. She is forever trying to tie me down – a nice little house. Who the hell wants a nice little house?'

Mrs Tankard did, and her sleep. She made a speech about locking the front door, another about the virtue of being a holy man and the filial duties of a son and then mentioned that she must read the Bible before she went to sleep. Mr T and she had done so ever since they got married. And she left them to it, straddled on the staircase.

Fack was inviting Tapan into their room.

Tapan didn't remember much. As he told Sandeep, it was knee-deep in copies of *The Times*, had enthusiastic floral wallpaper and a double bed.

'So you are saying she is an elderly lady?' Sandeep sounded alarmed.

A floozy was one thing, if a trifle embarrassing, but an elderly lady bedded down with one's father was unmentionable. Sandeep wracked his brains and decided that it was the kind of thing the Romans went in for. Their textbooks at Eton were filled with asterisks for expurgated paragraphs where juicy parts were banned from little boys' eyes.

'They both sounded so bloody happy, slumming in Ripon –

they think they are doing good with all this racism lark, visiting pubs and provoking the natives. You know, Sandeep, did you ever see Dad lean across the counter sipping lemon juice with the lower orders?'

'Not unless there was money in it; he wouldn't have anything to say.'

'And this Enid is just the same. She might be old and very wrinkled, but she isn't what we imagined. She's very eccentric.'

'How ghastly!' An elderly eccentric lady shacked up with one's father is hardly appropriate. Sandeep, who thought nothing of sniffing coke with his decadent Etonian chums, was inclined to be censorious about his father's rather naive failings.

'Actually, she wasn't too bad in a wrinkly, crinkly way. She has Indian relatives – whatever that means.'

Tapan had driven home, his head full of contradictions. His father looked so merry and so hopelessly committed to all this daft proselytising in pubs, hobnobbing with the working man. And that Enid woman: she somehow suited the whole daft business. Tapan wondered what her family thought.

If he'd heard the twins, it was not a lot.

Beatrice, after careful consideration, thought her gran should be banned till she signed a pledge to wear granny-style clothes, bake cakes and buy bigger Christmas presents. Sophie went further and added that funny, undressed men were absolutely forbidden; indeed, any man of any age and sex, including Prince Charles, was not allowed near her. They anguished after lights out whether Enid did it with Fack. They spoke knowledgeably about seeds and sex, but on reflection decided that Fack and Gran possessed neither since they were well over thirty. They had heard their parents' unhappy quarrels about Fack's colour, but at their age it posed no threat. It wasn't such an issue as his lack of appropriate dress was.

'It's his skin, it's all like leather. I mean, they wouldn't let him in McDonald's like that.'

'I wouldn't be seen dead shopping with him.' Beatrice shuddered under her duvet.

'I think old women should be old. I don't think they should be friends with different men. They should help Mummy and buy big presents.' But Beatrice wasn't listening. She was fast asleep.

Of the two boys, Tapan was the most reflective. Ashamed and embarrassed by his father, nevertheless he vaguely understood Mahesh's need for a pilgrimage. He knew, because he ingested it with his mother's milk, the rags to riches story of his father's life. He used to be shown the shabby little shop, still selling bright saris and garish fabrics. The new owner, who swore he was a distant cousin, would fawn and insist they drank revolting tea. He'd pinch the boys' cheeks and murmur Indian phrases, which Mahesh never bothered to interpret.

'Damn it, we're in England now, thank God!'

'It was Mother, wasn't it?' Tapan spoke aloud as his gleaming car headed towards Leicester.

Veena had been a quiet, loyal wife, quite unsuited to the dizzy heights climbed by Mahesh. She avoided London entirely, never went to a meet during the whole of Mahesh's hunting career, rarely sat in the hotchpotch grandeur of their sitting room and was deeply uneasy eating Western food sloshed down with expensive wine. Veena remained faithful to her culture rather than to her husband. She watched with sadness her sons being systematically brought up as English gentlemen, particularly since the type of gentleman Mahesh wished them to be was decadent, sad flotsam from another age. She watched them clutching Pimms by the tennis court or popping over to Paris for a party and she hated it. They filled the house for the hunt ball with arrogant, loud young people, some of whom mistook her for a servant. Veena never complained. She was proud of being Indian and quietly practised being Indian on her own.

Her death had shaken Tapan. Not just that the loving bit had gone but the Indian bit as well. Her body had been cremated and the ashes were to be flown back to Benares. It all sounded so ridiculous. No one said anything, but there was a distinct feeling of condemnation in the air when family cousins, dressed in their Indian clothes, met Mahesh and his sons dressed in elegant handmade suits. Mahesh had to leave the cremation early; he had a meeting in Geneva.

That had been the start. He came back from Geneva, furious to find that the flowers on the shrine were dead and no incense had been lit for days.

'Dad, do you have any idea which gods our mother worshipped? And do you honestly believe an elderly Cox's orange pippin is the way to salvation?'

'Do you have a better way with all your goddamn education?'

He had been right. Tapan, driving back from Ripon, couldn't think of a better way. It certainly wasn't his dad bailing out of a lifetime's success, going back to his roots, finding himself and all that baloney. It wasn't the revolting cotton cloth worn Gandhi-style. Even the racial awareness crap in pubs was questionable but nearly acceptable. A new bride would have been understandable but an elderly lady, probably on her uppers and – who knows – randy as hell! That really stuck in Tapan's craw. And yet...

Sandeep and Tapan still lived at home. The house was big enough and it never crossed their mind to leave. They shared the flat in London too. If this cultural behaviour had been explained as typically Indian, they would have probably left like a shot. Sandeep was particularly sensitive about being Indian, probably because of being in love with an English girl.

Sandeep heard the purr of the car arriving in the small hours. He wrapped his cashmere dressing gown round his sleek, beautiful body and met Tapan in the hall.

'How did it go?'

'You haven't stayed up, San?'

'No – your bloody car! It sounds like a tiger – reminds me of India and all that crap!' They laughed.

The boys took a couple of beers from the fridge and wandered into the study. Once it was the holy of holies but, with their father away, it had become a useful, comfortable room to sit in with legs hanging over the sofas and loud music blaring away.

'Well, I found him, or rather them. They are staying in a B and B. Have you ever stayed in a B and B, San?'

'Bed and Breakfast! I can just imagine it – a retired couple making ends meet – their children's room turned over to the guests – notices asking you not to smoke in the bedrooms and underdone fried eggs with that jelly-type marmalade; aching good taste and lower middle-class values. Thank God we were born rich! No, Tapan, I prefer Claridges, if only for the marmalade.'

'It wasn't too bad, actually. The landlady had lived in India and knew far more than Dad about his background. As for Mrs Tanner – well I don't know what to say, quite. She's not what we thought. She's rather like Dad, but with her clothes on. You know, good family and all that. She's very old though – about the same age as Dad.'

Sandeep sat up clasping his can of beer.

'You don't think…I mean, he won't marry her?'

'I wondered that too.'

'Bloody hell! What shall we do, Tapan?'

Tapan stared into space; he didn't see much. Space is awfully empty. But he thought. He thought of his dad clambering up the greasy pole of success with *The Times* crossword under his arm. He thought of the revolting food served in his house at Eton. He thought of snorting coke, sharp, ecstatic, surreal bliss, beautiful girls collected round the roulette wheel, all ephemera but gorgeously tempting. He and Sandeep had soon grown out of it. They left and obediently made their way back to Leicester, where it all began.

'Play it by ear; it's his choice.'

'Well, Arabella's mine,' said the defiant Sandeep.

'San, are you Indian?'

'Not really. Are you?'

'Not really.'

Their father would have been horrified, their mother deeply sad. The louts who lurk in the alleyways of Leicester's red-light district would have disagreed. At Eton no one cared. Only the hoi polloi were persecuted for having a Ford Fiesta and winning a scholarship.

Perhaps – who really knows? – these were the reasons Mahesh left his home for a wanderer's life, with a gold credit card just in case.

Ten

Enid was back in her daughter's kitchen, without Fack. Sal was making macaroni cheese for lunch but, as there was some peas and kedgeree left over from the day before, they were popped in too. Enid nearly retched. Beatrice was trying to help Roger walk backwards four paces and they both fell over.

'For God's sake, leave the child alone.'

Sophie was tending her worm farm. They were dying at an alarming rate so she was giving them some vitamin drops.

This happy family picture, one of many, was not quite what Enid had fantasised about when Gerry had died. However, she had cried when Sal's olive branch had arrived in the form of another lunch, just her.

She had left Fack reading some obscure Hindu text, legs not crossed – nobody was looking. Mrs Tankard had met her on the stairs.

'Going somewhere nice, dear?'

'I'm off to see my daughter and the grandchildren.'

'Lovely, you can't beat family, that's what I say.'

It wasn't an argument Enid wanted to discuss. However, it repeated itself over and over again as she drove over to the farm.

They'll find a nasty bungalow in the village and encourage me to help in the garden. Christ, is this all life has to offer? First the loyal marital years of brushing shit off the loo; then confined to a bungalow and valued as a bloody garden fork. Where are the cruises? I'd hate going on a cruise. I'd probably find it dreadfully infra dig. Where's the romance, the payback for a life of loyalty? Where are the men, the sensual pleasure of nestling into a strange bed with a strange man? Where's the food for thought, the poetry, the music and plays? How long is it since I went to the theatre – not that Alan Ayckbourn stuff, but real nitty-gritty theatre? I want to be bloody somebody, experience something, help make the world a better place before I die. Fuck it! Surely that isn't asking for too much!'

Yes, far too much. Put away your body. It's probably past it anyway. Put away any notions of choice. You are a nasty, ridiculous old woman. You married a seedy, clapped-out spy and now you've shacked up with some barmy black – well, brown then – and you are doomed to spend the rest of your life living a vicarious existence through your frightful grandchildren. Tough bloody luck, mate!

I could stay with Fack, weld myself to his dream, I suppose. Better still, guide him home to his luxurious Georgian house in the Quorn country and invite Eleanor to stay and make her green with envy.

If the truth be known, Enid wasn't that keen, night after night, on haranguing locals about race. Nor was Fack, but sssh!

Indeed, poor Fack, despite his wealth, was wrestling with many of the same demons as Enid, only he could afford to wear a loincloth. His tits and wrinkles weren't a problem. Not for him any of the problems of an aging woman; and, after all, he had that credit card.

'Are you going to marry this Indian?' Sal looked at her aging mother.

'What is marriage?' said Enid, rather pretentiously.

'Oh, Ma, do grow up! Are you going to settle down with Fack?' The twins had been booted out to watch a video and Roger persuaded to have a sleep. He was still protesting in his cot but Sal was taking no notice.

'Sal, it's not about marrying Fack, don't you see? It's so complicated. You want me to do good works, play bridge and be a merry widow like Dolly. I'm not like that. I'm a bad-tempered, confused old woman. I miss Gerry, even now I miss him, the private him that nobody knew but me. He's dead, and now…well, I love you and the children, but there's something in me that wants to live before it's too late.' Enid leant forward. She might have been a teenager pleading for her freedom if it wasn't for the tired, wrinkled face, the dumpy figure and the worn sensible shoes.

'Fack is fun. He's an arrogant bastard but I can handle bastards. I lived with one for years. I can't say night after night chatting up racist bores is quite my thing. I don't think it's Fack's;

I know it's not. We're both a little long in the tooth.' Enid added in a high, slightly out of control register, 'But we're in the same boat. Don't you see?'

Sal loved her. She looked with frustration and compassion at the silly old woman. Yet women of Enid's age can't afford to have dreams. If they do, they pay a high price. Yes, Dolly was exactly what Sal wanted her mother to be. All this emoting about finding herself was tedious, pathetic and frankly a bit late. But asking a woman of Enid's age to grow up was pretty useless.

'Ma, why don't you buy somewhere close and help me with the gallery? I've got planning permission. I want to teach. There will be more than enough work for two.'

'What a happy ending!' Enid shook her head. 'I want a man and I want to make something of my life'

'Oh, Ma!'

They sat in silence, a horrible, incompatible silence. Upstairs the baby protested; somewhere the video squawked; outside Sal's dreams ate up money – a double mortgage at least, just so that mediocre paintings could be flogged to the uneducated tourists who knew what they liked. Then there would be a gift shop and a tea room and Enid would be making scones till all hours. What a future! Enid began to cry for her Gerry. He would have understood. He'd been a failure too. They had clung to each other, understood each other and now that he was gone there was nothing. All these attempts to find a new life, a new person – it was just bullshit. Fack was bullshit really.

'Scones, bloody scones, here I come,' murmured Enid.

It took a bloody age, what with planning, architects, being strapped for cash, bank managers and grants. Grants were almost the worst; they held beguiling promises if you could jump through the hoop of idiosyncrasy – just take the Pennine Arts Association.

'Question forty-two. How does your project reflect the artistic ethos of your local community? Please give details.'

'What's an artistic ethos when it's at home?' wailed Sal.

'Hunting prints,' suggested Douglas.

Then Enid was asked.

'Artistic ethos! They must be mad. I suppose it means the annual church art festival. You know, the frightful display of paintings they pin to that grotty old screen – "Sunrise Over My Garden", by Phyllis Bugner, or "My Cat", by Kathy Green. I try to look at them with my eyes closed.'

'Mum, it's people like Phyllis and Kathy who are going to be my *clients*. They are both thrilled with the idea of life classes.'

'I bet they are. Fumbling under the bedclothes is as near life classes as they are ever likely to get.'

'Mum, do grow up!'

Then there were the rows. The contractor and the architect went at it hammer and tongs over the loos – something about the doors and how they were to hang – and, of course, Sal and Enid had a barny too over the choice of china for the 'shoppe' – don't start, they'd already had words about it – a primrose design.

'It's *ghastly*, Sal. Can't you find anything better?'

'It's all very well for you to talk. I have a very tight budget and this is all I can afford. I don't suppose the old dears will mind anyway.'

'For Christ's sake, less of this "old dear" business. We are sentient beings and deserve better than an insipid primrose in that ghastly shoppe nonsense.'

'Well, if you're going to be like that about it, I don't know why you bothered to come. God knows, it wasn't to be a help.'

'Well, I like that! I've backed you every inch of the way, which is more than you did when I lived with Fack.'

'You can hardly equate an art complex with having a disgusting relationship with some itinerant Indian.'

The fur didn't half fly – and the sobs, the scenes, the sulks and recriminations. Meanwhile, over several painful years, the barn shook and shuffled into its new guise as an art complex. And true to her word, Sal won hands down and shackled Enid to making scones.

Stale scones, lumpy scones, dry scones, scones with raisins, cheese and saffron. Then there was the jam, sometimes rather runny when the pectin didn't do whatever pectin is meant to do. At other times it was a triumphant success, when vast cauldrons, or rather a battered old preserving pan, hubble-bubbled away at whatever fruit was available. No one could deny that Enid tried her hardest with this scone and jam lark. She made batches of the bloody things, mixing baking powder, bicarbonate, sifting flour. She usually didn't bother about measuring that, adding one and a half ounces of marg and flour galore and – hey presto! – the burnt offerings emerged. This was her contribution to art, being a brick. Who the hell wants to be a brick, for God's sake? She made herself indispensable and did it provide the rich, fulfilled emotional life she longed for? Did it hell!

On one particular morning a phone call and the time the scones were due out of the oven coincided.

'It gives them the authentic home-made look,' she told Sal.

The scones were served in the tea shoppe – another bone of contention, but it sounded 'oldy worldy' apparently and just what the – wait for it – 'old dears' liked, with Enid's blackberry jam, marrow and ginger jam nobody wanted, and various other 'Let's get Granny to turn them into jams' – more ageist crap. They never said, 'Let's get Granny to pose for the life class.' Actually, the jam making was more like sorcery. Pots were a problem. There were never enough of the wretched things. Many a time Enid had stirred vigorously at some fearsome concoction, only to have half the stuff left congealing in the preserving pan while she rushed round looking for something to put it in. Once she used an old potty that had lived under Gerry's bed. That gave her great satisfaction. Maybe she was destined to be a witch after all. The grandchildren certainly thought so. They were really very nasty to her most of the time.

As Beatrice pointed out to her, 'You have only yourself to blame. No other grans that we know appear in the *Sun* with a fakir.'

'Well, yes, I have appeared in the *Sun*, but not as a witch, I'll have you know.'

Enid was secretly rather proud of herself. She had been living with Fack in almost chaste indignity at the time. Enid gave a giggle at the memory.

Fack had been lovely but expensive to keep. He was clever,

sophisticated, dirty and exasperating. He was attractive and very funny. As for his background, he was definitely Indian but apparently thoroughly anglicised. Hadn't he even drunk champagne with the Prime Minister? He had that yeast quality which turns the son of a carpet seller into a magnate. Enid paused, her floury hands poised in the air as she remembered how he had, according to him, married a gentle, quiet soul and locked her into a Georgian house with two rowdy boys while he went hunting – just to show what wasn't exactly clear – and soon he had gratefully slid from the saddle and handed the horse back to the groom. After his wife's death, Fack felt sad. Introspection crept into his life and what had he done about it? According to Fack, he had left his sons to run his business and aspire to the Royal Enclosure at Ascot, while he read the holy scriptures, shed his pinstripe suits and started wandering the country with only his gold credit card as a compromise. Crafty bloke that he was, he didn't tell Enid about that card. She found out one day when laundering his dhoti. Floury hands fell to her sides – bastard, like all the rest, but a lovable one. They never fell out exactly. It was more the case of scones coming between them. Fack wanted to hole up with the mystic men of Gateshead – yes, there are some – while Enid felt obliged to help Sal with her art complex and in due course make bloody scones. How scones were meant to provide the rich emotional life she craved was hard to understand, which was why the results were occasionally burnt. Seriously, do men have to bake scones in order to be wanted? The worst that happens to them is a session among the brassicas.

'Cooee!'

The front door slammed. Enid's lodger had finished work. Paul, the lodger, was none other than the reporter who had interviewed Sal and become the model at her art complex.

'Oo, they smell yummy, but my figure…one lives in permanent warfare with one's appetite.'

'Well, my lad, I keep telling you, being a woman isn't all bras and roses. Out of my way while I pack these up for the dreaded shoppe.'

'Edes, could I borrow your…' Paul turned to go to his bedroom; he paused, turning back with winsome coquetry... 'pearls?'

'What's wrong with your own bloody pearls?'

'They aren't the real thing. I must feel completely authentic when I'm out on the tiles.'

Enid agreed with maximum feigned irritation and Paul skittishly nipped off towards the bathroom. He spent more time there than in his bedroom – so much so that, in the summer, Enid found herself more than once having to take an emergency pee by the courgettes. But the courgettes had turned to dank slush by the frost and Enid was increasingly reluctant to bare her bum without the dignity of surrounding foliage.

Paul had been given to Enid rather like a puppy. She hated being on her own, a fate of most widows, and even more hated the prospect of sharing her life with another woman, but a transsexual was just her thing. Paul was a bright young reporter, having difficulties with his own family. Paul was having difficulties, full stop. His remit was covering the Yorkshire Dales, with their emphasis on cow shit and dagging sheep, solid Methodist virtues and absolutely no time for hanky-panky. As a lovely old farmer put it, observing the weekend indulgence of eye make-up and foundation only partly removed, Paul, having run out of make-up remover, 'Eee, lad, you're all muck and muddle, if you don't mind me saying.'

Yet Paul was an excellent young reporter who did his local paper proud. However, he was convinced that he was – or rather she should be – a woman. The local farmers eyed him suspiciously and their wives let their imaginations wander. He was the subject of ribaldry. He even appeared in a local pantomime, or rather 'she' did – the best Widow Twanky they had found in years. It was *Cinderella* written by the rugby team. Paul was mortified by the jokes; endless jokes that finally got to him. He sought professional help so that he didn't have to spend the rest of his life being the butt of disgusting jokes. The pantomime was a turning point. After that, Paul found a hospital in Leeds with a lovely doctor who put him on hormones.

'It takes a long time. You can't just put on a dress and walk away.'

What riled Paul was the number of foreigners waiting to see the doctor.

'Just because I'm NHS I'm being treated as a poor relation,' he moaned to Enid, who put it down to paranoia. Apparently there was a group of Romanian transsexuals in the waiting-room with Paul. They spoke little English and simply rolled their lustre-brown eyes. Poor Paul! He felt really angry seeing them looking utterly foreign yet terribly familiar. Any impartial reasoning flew out of the window.

'You just wait, young man, till you are a genuine poor relation, a woman like us. I personally think it's wonderful that we have a special agreement with Romania or wherever to do their operations for them. It's why I would vote Labour, if only they didn't encourage people to speak with awful accents and only semi-educate them. You don't know the half of it,' Enid had snorted.

In those days, Paul, as Sal's part-time model, didn't half confuse some of the ladies who were daringly tackling nudity.

'Concentrate on Paul's shoulder muscles and his neck. I want to see the strength and power of his body,' enthused Sal who taught the class, while all Paul wanted was to show the vulnerability and soft contours of his slight figure.

All Miss Tatham wanted to do was to gloat over his penis – fifty-something years, and this was the first one she had ever seen. If that was what all the fuss was over she didn't think she had missed much. Stories about penises were greatly exaggerated, she decided. Several other women found their concentration waning over muscled shoulders and waxing elsewhere. Miss Tatham was not alone.

'Edes,' – Paul liked to call her 'Edes' – 'do you really think women have a raw deal? I mean, look at you. Doesn't making scones provide the warm glow of a matriarch, the authentic touch of family continuity? Surely you are the most fulfilled woman in Sal's art complex. I do wish she would change the name: "Art Complex" is simply frightful. As for "Shoppe"!' Paul and Enid agreed about many things. However, the role of a widow was not one of them.

Enid glared at the beautiful young man who had become her lodger. He was right, of course. 'Art Complex' was a dreadful name for a barn trying to provide life classes, including Paul's, a permanent gallery selling safe rubbish and a shoppe for the bus-loads of old people who didn't care much for art anyway. Why, just the other day Enid had overheard a couple discussing the art on offer.

'What's it say, Maud?'

'"Pen Hill in the rain."'

'Pity 'e didn't wait till the sun came out.'

'Why's the hill all purple, like, Maud?'

'The rain, I've just told yer.'

'But rain's not purple.'

'It's them artists. They see things. Let's 'ave a cup of tea.'

They and the rest of the coach-load would sit down and moan about the jam – too many pips for their dentures, the scones not like their mothers used to bake. As Enid never tired of pointing out, her mother never baked a scone in her life – but then they had servants – well, a cook, at any rate. And there was Paul standing in her kitchen, fantasising about some beautiful enriched teacake lifestyle based on bloody scones.

'The difference between you and me, Paul, is that a few hormones and some snipping away of your private parts and – hey presto! You've got what you want. They can snip away till kingdom come, inject monkey glands into me for as long as they like, but that won't bring back my youth or give me any of the aspirations I have had all my life – and still have. I'm reduced to fucking scones and you are reduced to a waiting list. I would give anything to be on a waiting list.'

Enid started to cry. The scones mopped up a few tears. Paul felt awful. He gently removed the tray with the scones, sat Enid down and let her bemoan her fate as a lonely old woman.

'But you don't still miss it, do you? I mean, old people have their own way of life.'

'I'd like to know what it is, then,' mumbled Enid into Paul's elegant hanky.

He was a perfect lodger. All he wanted was what Enid didn't want. It brought about a curious reconciliation. In the evenings, when he was occasionally in, Enid would show Paul the art of being a desirable woman – how to hold a handbag, a glass, how to move gracefully and above all how to sit – before saying, 'Come off it, Paul! It's crap. Nobody does that kind of thing any more. I learnt all that rubbish at finishing school – just look where it got me.'

One magical night Enid put on a tape of a waltz. They closed the curtains, put out all but one light, pulled back the furniture and carpet and then slowly and clumsily waltzed together. Enid knew how to lead. They had done it at her finishing school. Now, nearly fifty years later, she found herself nurturing a young woman in the gentle pleasure of dancing. Their bodies moved and their cheeks all but met. It was bliss. The years crumpled away. Even Paul's scent was a shared smell, a whiff of nostalgia. The tape ran out.

'This calls for a drink. I'll open a bottle of wine, you get some glasses, the nice ones.'

Then the phone rang and Paul was invited to a drag club in Leeds. Enid drank the bottle on her own. The carpet was still rolled up and the furniture pushed against the walls. His scent still lingered and Enid, a little pissed, put on the tape again, found a large soft cushion and danced the night away. The soft cushion gave a feeling of a compliant partner, one that wouldn't bugger off to Leeds at a moment's notice. After a while Enid began to cry, not so much for something she had lost as for something she had never had – a real romance in her life. Gerry had been a gruff, rough, awkward kind of character and there had been little or no romance about him; not for her, anyway. He had reserved that for his mistress.

Was it too late? Could she ever experience the kind of delicious emotional anarchy that his affair with his Indian mistress, Savita, and their beautiful daughter, Vijaya, were surrounded with? Enid desired to throw away respectability and just for once dabble her toes in the role of being a beautiful woman. Enid wasn't even sure what such beauty would mean. Just to feel desirable would be a start.

Then she thought of her lovely friend Dolly. Dolly was chirrupy, pretty and always optimistic. Her clothes looked nice, they fitted well – soft colours and expensive scarves. Her hair was just right for her face and she regularly visited the beauty clinic to keep the whiskers under control. Not far off seventy, Dolly was popular round the bridge tables and charity dos and always had a cruise lined up for the inclement months. Recently, Dolly hadn't been well, poor love. Enid would bleat that all this comfortable life Dolly led was not for her. She hated well-fitting clothes, hated bridge, hated cruises – even if she had never been on one. No, her idea of fulfilment was completely different, so different that she could never, even to herself, work out what exactly it would be. While all these self-indulgent thoughts were churning round her head she failed to noticed that Dolly was rapidly becoming seriously confused.

She thought that her few dizzy months living with Fack was what life was all about – Fack, that rich bastard who had decided to become a holy man. Then Fack took to mysticism and was last heard of thinking about doing Thought for the Day and Enid found herself making scones. It was so unfair.

Fack wasn't any different to my Gerry, Enid mused. Just wanted his clothes washed and his shoes cleaned... While all she had wanted was excitement, to be taken seriously and a whiff of sex. Men are so bad at whiffs of sex. They either want to settle down to beavering away like some piston in the Science Museum, or hand the whole business over to their partner. It was another of Enid's grievances.

After the waltz, Paul came back a day later in a foul mood. He didn't feel part of that scene any longer. He wanted to meet real men and real women. Mind you, he had picked up some useful tips, particularly about his hairline, apparently quite a problem among ageing transsexuals with receding temples. 'But I'm young. That makes all the difference. The hormones should take care of that.'

Later that day he insisted on Enid looking at his nipples. They were positively 'Keatsian', he told her. Paul had studied English at Oxford.

'Well, your true love's ripening breasts are doing nicely, Paul. Are you in to supper?'

Whatever the reply, the sexual innuendo would be there. It was as near to sex as Enid got these days. 'I should think so, too, at nearly seventy,' you can hear them say.

It wasn't so many days later that Enid tucked her garden away for the winter, snipping here, pulling there and digging everywhere. Digging does wonders for frustration. Anyway, it was a break from scones and a good excuse to puzzle about her lodger and his compulsion to change sex.

'Why?' she kept asking.

'Oh, Edes! Haven't you ever felt something so strongly that you'd give your right arm for it? Seriously, I'm prepared to be operated on, have my privates whipped off, reorganised, just so I can feel I'm female. It's about feelings at the end of the day, isn't it? What about your feelings, Edes? Of course, you come from a generation that didn't have them.'

Spot on! Not only that – what feelings she had were mown by convention so they never grew to fruition. That was the theory, but Enid refused to conform. Her feelings weren't Paul's, thank God! But they were about sex. The arbitrary way it arrived and disappeared, only to become an object of humour. It was so damned unfair. Life is damned unfair, my girl!

The last time Paul had banged on about feelings she had hit him over the head with the trowel – then added an extra pinch of salt before slamming the bloody scones in the oven.

'Feelings, feelings! Who's going to make the scones if everyone is having feelings?' she sniffed angrily.

'Ever felt like learning how to cook, Paul? It's required knowledge for earth mothers.'

'I'm not that kind of woman, Edes; you should know that.'

'What makes you so certain that *I* am?'

'Well, love, you are a bit long in the tooth for much else.'

'Paul, there are two basic types of feeling, yours and everyone else's. You have mastered, or should I say become mistress of, the one. What about tackling the other?'

She wouldn't have parted with him for a moment. It would be Paula who would leave her, for something better. She knew that well in advance.

But that is as it should be, she told herself – not that she wanted to believe a word.

She had left her parents to marry Gerry. He was going to change the world. Now that was something she could believe in. Only it didn't turn out like that. Gerry became a cog in something he wasn't 'at liberty to divulge'. However, as the widow of a cog who shacks up with an Indian holy man – now that was better! At last that gave her just a hint of recognition. Didn't the Brig come over to check all was well?

Enid found that the post, in those days with Fack, contained a number of 'Do you remember me?' letters, some going right back to her wedding and even one from a girl with whom she had been at finishing school. Fiona, she remembered, was rather plump and inclined to spots. She had been very good at holding a wine glass, handbag and pair of gloves while eating stale biscuits covered with fish paste. It was called 'poise at parties' and deemed very important. Enid seemed to remember that Fiona loved dogs and wanted to breed Labradors. Her letter revealed that Fiona had married a farmer and sunk very slowly into the mud, sans Labradors, sans children but clinging to the local WI lifeline. She had clung with such tenacity that now she was something very grand and had to appear at the National AGM. But that was not the gist. It was simply an extension of her address: 'I am someone who goes to the National AGM.' The gist was pitiful. Fiona had lost her way, or rather headed down a dead end track. Her life, her values, her aspirations had stopped and finding a hat for the AGM was now the high point of her existence.

Enid had read the letter sitting on her double bed in the bedsit she shared with Fack, her holy man, who was doing *The Times* crossword beside her. In those days her life was rich, even if her bank balance was appalling and materially she and Fack had nothing.

'Poor bloody woman!' exclaimed Enid.

'Too many letters,' murmured Fack, clearly not listening.

'I wonder why she reads the *Sun*. I mean, I would have thought the *Mail*, if anything, was more her scene. What do you think, Fack?'

'For the crossword, of course. I expect the *Sun* has a faintly naughty one, or maybe she's very bored and wants to find out how real people live.'

'You and your real people! I'm going to try and get in touch.'

Fack looked up. He didn't say anything at first but then he spoke slowly and thoughtfully, usually a style of speech he reserved for talking about himself. 'Just be careful; don't hurt her.'

'What do you mean?'

'Just that. Now what do you make of "A sailor, more or less" – six letters?'

Fiona was thrilled to hear from Enid. The years rolled away as the two women squealed down the phone. It was Fiona who did most of the squealing while Enid, mindful of what Fack had said, found herself playing the lady of unusual rectitude. Why? She wasn't sure. Had they done that at finishing school too?

'Now, girls, when you meet someone whom you suspect has fallen on hard times, generosity never comes amiss; it is the hallmark of a lady. However, any largesse must be tempered by rectitude.'

'Fiona, I'd love to meet you. Why don't I come over – it's not that far.'

'Well, we could meet, I suppose. I mean, are you sure? I mean, with your busy life in the limelight. Oh yes, let's! Why don't we meet in Worcester. There's a lovely coffee house. It's easier than coming here. I don't want you getting lost in the lanes.'

Fiona spoke with hearty insincerity. Fack was right; there was something wrong.

Enid had driven over, hopping from one motorway to the next. The arteries, as she considered them, were clogged with what Enid thought of as cholesterol. Huge lorries belching diesel trundled – utterly, revoltingly, butterly, with tonnes of either expensive or ruined goods: exhausted tomatoes with thousands of miles under their belt and not very new potatoes in between the ceramic bathroom fittings from Cumbernauld and 'Reed Maid' garden furniture from Hull, both blown far off course, apparently. There were the busy cars with no discernible purpose other than to delay progress with their pestilential whizzings, just like insects. Enid stuck in the middle lane, her favourite place, and remembered nostalgically a hitchhiker for whom she once went over a hundred miles out of her way, because…oh well, in those days one still had some hormones left.

The Olde Sheepe Coffee Shop boasted all the modernity of a haphazard planning policy that required the exterior to remain stubbornly set in some fantasy century while the interior subscribed to the latest tourist trends. It was nearly empty when Enid entered and the light was faintly dimmed. It took her a while to make out that Fiona was sitting there quietly, almost unobtrusively.

'Fiona?'

'Oh, it's you, my goodness! Oh Enid! How rude of me. It's simply lovely to see you again. Gosh, you are wearing jeans. If I'd known, I would have put on mine.'

Can you imagine two men meeting after all these years and mouthing such platitudes? Of course not! They haven't been conditioned to such fatuity.

The two women were both uncomfortable and ill at ease. They nearly kissed but shied away into an uneasy handshake and clumsy embrace. Fiona had made painful sartorial efforts. She wore a cream blouse with a hideous brooch and had a jacket hanging over the back of the chair. They settled for coffee and some carrot cake. The chit of a girl taking their order had all the hallmarks of someone destined for better things. Her chin alone smacked of class.

'This your gap year?' asked Enid, after hearing the bored 'Yeah' to some query about the cakes available.

'Yeah.' This time it was spoken with more enthusiasm. 'I'm off to Brazil next week.' All her vowels were intact, even in the middle of Worcester.

'That will be a real adventure,' enthused Enid.

'Not really. My mum lives there.' The girl was bored – two old biddies twittering away; what did they know anyway? Why, only last night she had snorted two lines of coke and her head had left her body for another planet. As for sex, these old pussies wouldn't know the meaning of the word. God, she hated working in this soulless, crappy old bar. Typical of her mean old pa – absolutely loaded and wanted her to meet real people. Real people didn't snort, hadn't a clue – and anyway she felt knackered. Shit, if only they knew the half of it…

Fiona smiled a bright little brave smile far removed from the world of the spoilt waitress. Fiona had her own fantasies – minious, like meeting important people. She waited till the girl had gone.

'Gosh! You are good, Enid. I never know what to say. It's not having children, I suppose. She's just like Fergie – her mother lived somewhere like that. Mind you, I don't think it makes them any happier – just look at that poor Lady Di.'

Have I driven all this way to twitter about the fringes of the royal family? Enid asked herself. She looked keenly at Fiona. Yes, the pleasant features were familiar but overlaid with an anxiety. There was something fraught and definitely wrong.

'I just loved the Queen Mother. She really kept that family together. Whenever I feel I can't cope, I just think of her. Oh Enid! It's so lovely seeing you after all these years. Golly! You must have had an exciting life. You married a Tanner, didn't you? Very grand! Did you inherit a stately pile?'

Enid laughed, as much as to herself as to Fiona.

'Not exactly. He gave his inheritance away.'

There was an awkward pause. Fiona started to finger her engagement ring. Then she found something deeply absorbing on the floor.

'Little did we know,' she murmured. 'Susie Parker's done well. She's Lady Bingham now. And Felicity – guess what! She married a football manager. Goodness knows what her people thought.' Fiona lifted her head from the floor and began rubbing her hands together as if she was washing them. 'All those years ago. Do you remember learning to iron a hanky?'

The two women cautiously began to reminisce about the dotty time they were thrown together to be taught the skills judged necessary for their future lives.

They remembered not only ironing a hanky but how to introduce bishops to dukes, choose wines and write 'thank you' letters. Soon they were both laughing at the absurdity of doilies, stopping a run in one's stockings with soap and how to make a short speech of welcome and thanks.

'Why weren't we taught how to make longer speeches, proclaim great wisdoms, argue politically? Why weren't we taught how to save the world?' Enid threw her arms in the air and, with a voice raised more in ostentation than the sincerity of the moment, exclaimed, 'Castration! That is what we suffer from; we need balls.'

'Yeah' looked round and thought, Silly old bats – they wouldn't know what to do with a stiff prick if you gave them one; haven't a clue, never had anything stronger than aspirin, anyway. If I don't get finished here soon, it's something naughty in the toilets for me.

Fiona cringed. It was so embarrassing. No wonder Enid ended up in the *Sun*.

'Ssh! People are looking, Enid.'

Hardly! There were two stout ladies, their sticky cakes about to topple into their coffees. Nothing other than an air raid siren would have shattered their conversation on the merits of missionary versus several other positions for overweight sexual adventurers. Castration wasn't something they or their partners worried about. There was a young man in a roll-collared shirt reading a script – probably *Puss in Boots* for the Christmas pantomime. A couple of uncertain age munched silently through several cream cakes. They heard – but then they had heard many things. Only the table next door forgivably felt mildly uncomfortable. They had a dentist appointment in half an hour.

'Don't worry, Fiona, no one cares a monkey's. It's true, though, we were destined to be the handmaidens of life, to live in reflected glory. Only we didn't marry men with reflectors. Come on, you haven't told me your story.'

'Oh, I so dislike being unfair, yet I can't help feeling Clive has made a bit of a hash of things.' The diamond ring was desperately fondled as Fiona mastered the images of failure that had marred her adult life. She couldn't look Enid in the eye as she described a marriage where home and happiness were jettisoned over the years to cover debt, bankruptcy, social disgrace and finally a breakdown, leaving Clive and her just a piece of embarrassment.

'We're not even invited to the Bingham's annual wine tasting at Christmas, and they invite the Porters, even though neither of them drink. Oh Enid! It's ghastly. We live in a bungalow – that says it all really.' A silence spread across the table as the two women contemplated their demeaning circumstances.

'Many people prefer them as they get older or if there are problems with health.' Enid spoke with the desperate enthusiasm of someone who didn't believe a word she was saying.

'I mean, just think of me. I live in just a bedsit, even though I married a Tanner.'

That did it! The idea of her long-lost friend living in a bedsit, even though she married a Tanner, energised Fiona sufficiently for her to reach out her hand and touch Enid's arm.

'I think it must have been in my stars, meeting you like this. I'm a Capricorn. I'm very sensitive about how other women feel. That's why I got in contact with you, don't you see?'

The balance of power was shifting.

It's my Tanner legacy, thought Enid, who wished Fiona would remove her understanding arm off hers.

'I knew I must get in touch. Just a bedsit? Is this because your friend has rejected worldly things? Is it a devout union?'

It would be so easy to answer her with utter rubbish. But Enid remembered what Fack had said. This unhappy creature, emoting over the carrot cake about dropping several notches in the social pecking order, would cling limpet-like if Enid let her.

'Fack is a holy man. He sponges off me because I let him. He's worth it, he amuses me. Most entertainment costs money, and being a widow is not entertaining. Living in a bedsit makes you envy a cosy bungalow – just remember that.' It was a lie.

'But you're a *Tanner*,' Fiona mumbled enviously.

'I know I bear the illustrious name, Fiona, but Gerry had already got rid of his fortune by the time we married. He was a radical, see. He didn't approve of all the nonsense of, well, you know… Only, after he was dead I found he had left his fortune to a beautiful Indian actress by whom he had a daughter – not exactly the generous good works I had assumed.'

'How simply ghastly. All the same, you had the Tanners.'

Grow up you simpering, silly owl! Who the hell cares tuppence about the Tanners except the bloody Tanners? She just restrained herself in time and left the retort unsaid. Instead, she beamed at Fiona, who had suddenly taken on the appearance of a spaniel.

'Old age is the best age, that's my motto. We must branch out and enjoy our lives, not moan over yesterday,' said Enid, adding to herself, *May I be forgiven, the liar that I am…*

'I know, but Clive still likes a proper dinner with a pud. The

WI is marvellous; you get simply snowed under with ideas. Actually, you mustn't be snooty. I used to be, but they are wonderful. I even went on a course on public speaking. Mind you, we did do a bit at finishing school, but that was different. Do you know, I think they've saved my bacon.'

Haunches of bacon were being hastily carried by several ladies and dumped out of sight. Enid's imagination was working overtime. She very sensibly said nothing but mentally noted that it was a long way to drive in order to meet a very silly woman with whom she had nothing in common. But silly women have a propensity for nattering on.

'Actually, I was wondering whether I could persuade you to give a talk about life with the Tanners. You know – stately homes and hunt balls. It's rapidly dying out now the beastly Labour Party is in power, and I know several ladies would be very interested. We're all dead keen on the royal family.' The spaniel looked eager, almost pleading.

'More coffee?' Their bored waitress chewed gum insolently as she waited for their response. *Coffee, my arse; what I want is something real cool*, you could just see her thinking.

'Yes, please,' nodded the spaniel with hangdog enthusiasm, her face muscles suddenly sagging with the enormity of it all.

'Nobody changes for dinner any more. We did till we moved into the bungalow but the Scouts came round for bob-a-job or whatever they call it – probably screw-you-for-a-fiver – and we felt so silly. One kid asked if Clive was some sort of comedian.'

'I hope you said yes.'

'There's an insatiable appetite for stories about grandeur, not about the cocaine-sniffing decadence that is the hallmark of success these days – football players, second-hand car dealers and politicians with accents you can cut with a knife. No, my ladies want to know about the green baize door, the real gentry who ran the country and the families who married each other to create the continuity that we all looked up to. I remember being green with envy when you married a Tanner. Mind you, I thought I was safe enough with Clive. He went to St David's, you know. Then things started to go wrong...blocked Fallopian tubes.'

Enid didn't think blocked Fallopian tubes were a sign of social incompetence, but the public speaking course had a lot to answer for. Fiona was in full spate and unlikely to shut up for quite a while. It intrigued Enid that life with the dreary old Tanners was regarded as the apogee of wish-fulfilment for the ladies of Lower Berkstead. It also perplexed her that appearing in the *Sun* with an Indian holy man hardly got a look in edgeways. It was being a Tanner that mattered.

'By the way, where did you read about Fack and me?'

Fiona stopped, looked round furtively to make sure the 'Yeah' girl wasn't listening and hissed, 'I know it's awful but Clive likes fish and chips. We have them on Thursdays now that we don't change. I put them on some decent china and put the ketchup in a nice piece of Royal Worcester. I saw your face, instantly recognisable. There's the girl who married a Tanner, I said to myself.'

She wouldn't have bothered if I had married a Smith.

Any sensible person would have taken the hint and firmly forgotten about extending their hand to someone in need. They would have bolted for the door before the bill or Fiona could further compromise them. But not our Enid. She too knew what it was to be lonely and socially isolated. After all, she was only a Tanner by marriage. So, despite the values that Fiona draped over the table, or perhaps because of them, Enid found herself saying, 'Yes, I'll come over. Have you got room in the bungalow? I'd love to meet Clive. I'll give a talk about the Tanners and their ilk, but I can't guarantee it's the talk you imagine.'

'Goodee! Oh, that will be wonderful.' Fiona's face crumpled again and she wore a look of utter spaniel perplexity as she said, 'You don't mind – we only have one loo.'

As anyone coming down in the world knows, you are judged by your loos. It's not enough that the lavatory bowl sparkles with demonic cleanliness, it's not enough that you made a toilet roll holder last winter which looks just a little like Carmen with a sore throat, or buy the softest bum tissue on the market. No, none of these things count if you only have *one loo*. Even modern council houses boast two. Enid was only too aware of this social disadvantage. Her best friend, Dolly, had reminded her on their house-hunting tours.

'But you can't and it only has one loo. What if your posh Tanner relatives come to stay?' Dolly had remonstrated outside 'Sunny Moments' – a repulsive pebble-dash bungalow.

'That will be the day!' But sour grapes were not Enid's thing, nor were the slights and deprivations bubbling like boils all over poor Fiona's psyche.

'I'll bring a potty. It might even have the Tanner crest on it.'

'Oh do! I'd love my ladies to see it.' Bless her, she had entirely missed the point.

The staff loo was a dingy place to hit it cool, but that is what 'Yeah' did and it wasn't even the end of her shift. Meanwhile Enid had kissed Fiona, who had dissolved into bubbles of excitement at the prospect of hearing about the Tanners. Enid steered back onto the motorway and exasperated a white van by sitting in front in the middle lane, deciding to take the speed limit into her own hands. After all, she couldn't afford to speed with such weighty matters as Henry's hunt buttons and the family crest to consider. She was considering a little too much and overshot the junction, adding an extra twenty miles to her journey. That, she reasoned, was grounds for banning the Tanners of this world. She was very tired by then.

Enid bought a small notebook and wrote *Fuck the Tanners* on it. In it she jotted down any reference to the upper classes. Many of these she knew were mercifully now out of date – from passing the port to plain girls dolled up as debutantes and skinny little boys shipped off at eight to Latin verbs and buggery. Above all, she wrote most passionately about the servants' hall and the teeming number of adenoidal maids skivvying at all hours. It was symptomatic that Henry's family were so prominent in her booklet. The Tanners were a dull but worthy lot, frankly not worth a talk. Even Eleanor, a Tanner who had married Henry, would agree to that. Actually, the week before the talk something happened so mind-bogglingly frightful that the ladies were all agog when Enid rose to speak – and it wasn't because of some cracked old potty, either.

Henry, her brother-in-law, had tried to kill a rambler the week before.

Her brother-in-law wasn't a Tanner. He was an Ashington Stanley Smythe, or ASS for short. He lived in a splendid pile of masonry which Elizabeth I graced on her grand tour. After that, an ASS decided to give it the Georgian touch. Not content with that, Henry's great-grandfather added some Victorian modern touches such as plumbing, a chapel and new kitchens. Sadly, Henry still thought of these innovations as modern and it took his wife (a Tanner, with money) quite a while to convince him that the huge spit in the kitchen was just a little awkward. Anyway, it was difficult to find a lad to turn it; they were too busy sniffing glue. His father had converted the chapel into a game trophy room, where a large lugubrious bison, a cheetah and innumerable deer gazed down from a gilt frieze with holly leaves intertwined with berries. A life-size elk peered out of the pulpit and the lectern carried a litany of the chase. Where the altar had stood rested the pièce de résistance – Henry's great-grandfather's elephant gun. Other guns rested in mahogany cases. There were several stuffed animals nestling in other cases, including a couple of ferrets that had been to Eton and back with Henry, and a goose deemed too tough to eat. Next door to the goose was a huge fish and next to the fish were rods galore. There was every bit as much devotion in the room, or so Henry insisted, pointing a finger, as there was 'up there'.

'I had a word with God, and he agrees with me.'

God, not having been to Eton and not being in *Debrett's*, wasn't required to give an opinion – only to acquiesce with doffed cap in hand.

Henry lived for shooting and fishing – hunting too – but he had had a disastrous fall. As his doctor pointed out, had he had a brain it most certainly would have suffered. All the same he missed the salmon fishing that season and only just made it in time for the Twelfth. Henry was benign most of the time. However, he continued in his particular loathing for ramblers who innocently, and most of the time legally, roamed his acres and admired his woodlands. He detested their woolly hats, the maps swinging round their necks and the dreadful accents they used. He was convinced that their accents frightened the pheasants, their bobbly hats terrified the partridges and, if they were allowed to wander as they liked, even the grass shrivelled. They were anathema to him and anathema was a mighty long word for Henry.

According to his elegant wife, Eleanor, who rang Enid the night of the big bang, Henry had been reading *The Field* after a light luncheon of cold grouse with a glass of port.

'The old boy dropped the magazine and was just having a couple of winks – well, it's our age, isn't it? He's had some nasty dreams recently. They say it's the war; though how, after all this time, a war spent cataloguing regimental silver can lead to nightmares, I really don't know! Anyway, Henry suddenly leaps to his feet, shrieking his head off and heads for the holy of holies. I saw it all. You know what Henry is like. Well, he wrenches open the gun case and staggers to the window. Only then did I notice the ramblers.

'"Henry," I said, "do put that thing down at once."'

'Well, "at once" works beautifully with the Labrador, but not apparently with Henry. He turns round looking quite deranged and shouts something about the Stalin-Hitler pact. I blame all this television! He really should stick to sheep trials with his weak disposition.'

There was a pause. Enid looked at the mouthpiece of her phone accusingly. To have her grand sister-in-law on the edge of hysteria was absolute bliss. What had happened next? she wanted to know. Bloody phone! She shook it.

'Are you still there, Enid? I'm in a state of advanced agitation – just catching my breath. Well, the thing went orf, Henry fell over and I ran to his side.'

That's why we have the NHS – just in case a deranged gent looses off – I mean *orf* – his great-grandfather's elephant gun. Enid was enjoying her imagined contribution to this tale. She could see Henry dressed impeccably in elderly tweeds, the gun the size of a log too big for the log basket and Eleanor, of committee fame, twisting her hands anxiously and calling her husband to order.

'Anyone hurt, Eleanor?'

'Of course he's hurt! Poor Henry is quite demented. If only those ramblers had thought about that before they came tramping over our property.'

'I mean, what about the ramblers; were any of them hurt?'

'The sights weren't working properly; a tree caught the blast. It really is too tiresome. I've got Henry in hospital. I'm chairing the Red Cross tomorrow and a horrible little man wants to interview me for one of those nasty papers they used to read in the kitchen when we still had staff.

'Look out, Eleanor. He'll want to know all about your sex life.'

'My sex life? Don't be so frivolous, Enid. You of all people should know about these things. What do you think I should wear?'

'Jeans and a T-shirt.'

'You know very well I don't have jeans or a T-shirt. Some of us still have standards.'

'Then for God's sake don't show them, unless you want to be ripped apart. Seriously, Eleanor, you are going to look a real ass unless you're careful.'

They didn't part on particularly amicable terms. They never did. However, the WI lapped up every word Enid told them, true and false – Tanner and non-Tanner alike. But, before all that, Enid had to drive down to Worcester and she wasn't her cheerful self as she drove down to see Fiona. She blamed Fiona's fawning, ingratiating manner. How could she be so silly as to let herself in for a dreary night with the pretensions of a failed couple, followed by massaging the fantasies of some lower middle-class ladies with clean knickers? Then there was Henry. He was clearly round the twist, with poor old Eleanor playing King Canute with the press. There weren't many times when Enid felt real relief at being out of it all but, as she drove down, the anonymity of her modest car and the well-washed neutrality of the clothes she had chosen seemed like a welcome guard against elephant guns.

Fiona had remembered everything she had been taught at that finishing school, but still made it all seem inappropriate and clumsy. There was nothing wrong with the bungalow – if you like that kind of thing. The guest bedroom didn't really need some biscuits, a jug of water with a lacy thingamajig over the jug as well as a face towel and a rough bath towel. The flowers had a suspicion of 'arrangement' about them but, all in all, it was no worse than some of the B and Bs she and Fack had visited.

Clive was a dear. A little bewildered and obviously embarrassed by his wife's notions of grandeur, he'd been made to wear a suit for supper – oops, dinner! He had a perfectly decent job as bursar in a language school and he spoke amusingly about the rich children of African potentates no doubt being taught the same rubbish she and Fiona had learnt, only in their case it was already pathetically out of date, while for these kids it would be for real. They were the future. Over something with a grand French name but essentially stew in substance, Enid suggested such heresy.

'You can't! Honestly, Enid – you don't really believe it. I mean, those children – you've no idea; they arrive with worms and tribal marks.'

'All children have worms, it's like puppies.' Enid then touched on the one institution that Fiona believed in implicitly. 'I bet Prince Harry and the other one had worms.' Enid found naming contemporary princes about as tedious as naming dim and distant ones.

'I don't think so for a minute; the Queen Mother would have seen to that.' Fiona was rattled and her voice a touch quivery.

'Come off it, Fi, any kid who has a chance to play on a farm is bound to catch them. I did.' Old Clive was enjoying himself.

'Don't, Clive, not when I've gone to the effort of making a bombe surprise.'

So they returned dutifully to the 'Do you remember when?' days, when they learnt the differently shaped glasses for different wines and how much to tip at the end of a perfect weekend of tennis and privileged inanities. Enid let it be known that neither she nor Gerry ever went to such a weekend. Indeed it would have been the epitome of decadence in their eyes.

'Well done, Enid, if I may say so. The world moves on, and if we can't keep up, we move over.'

'For a lot of rich Africans with worms,' said Fiona and then she burst into tears.

'Now, Fi, don't cry. That's silly. Enid here has left it all behind and I like to think I've found a cosy nest for us, my love. I'm delighted to leave the rat race to the rats.'

Enid watched the modest figure peer into his bombe surprise and decided she couldn't go ahead with the rubbish she was expected to dole out to the WI. Indeed, and not for the first time, she wondered why she had agreed to speak in the first place.

The WI met in a bright, cheerful village hall. There were

gingham curtains, photographs of the village in bygone days, and a notice to turn the lights off. Two ladies were already putting the chairs out – pleasant ladies dressed in discreet comfortable dresses just below the knee, but wearing scuffed shoes bought for comfort rather than elegance. Behind the chairs there was a table with cups and saucers ready for afterwards. Other members began arriving and soon the hall was awash in floral prints. Enid need not have worried. Her faded Indian dress was so out of date as to have done a complete fashion circle and mixed favourably with the rest. Henry's attempt at shooting a rambler caused a sympathetic ripple among those plagued with car theft and the mindless damage of young hooligans. Indeed, listening to these women, one felt he had done a valiant act. As Enid had anticipated, Fiona, overdressed in a silk suit, was a mine of useful information for those still concerned with colliding bishop and dukes. But the most animated discussion was about how to hold a knife. Enid had added holding a knife as extra padding if she ran out of other equally useless snippets. After she had dismissed a large proportion of the population for holding their knives incorrectly, there was a stony silence – the kind that precedes thunder. A lady in the third row rose to her feet.

'Excuse me,' she said, in the way Boudicca might have spoken, 'are you telling me that holding a knife elegantly, the way we were taught at grammar school, is sneered at by the gentry?'

'I don't suppose anyone cares these days. Anyway, aren't we all gents – and ladies, of course?' replied Enid.

'The royal family would never hold their knife any way but the proper way.' The silly Fiona didn't know when to stop.

Another lady, enraged by the term 'proper way', leapt to her feet.

Ding-dong the battle raged, hands shot up, ladies became heated (ladies don't perspire), many had found biros and were practising how they held their knives. It appeared that a few favoured the 'assegai' approach. The majority must have had a grammar school education or its equivalent and only a few could really call themselves 'ladies'.

'That's the problem,' said Enid genially. 'It's a bit like sex. We've all been doing it for years – then along comes someone and tells us we're doing it the wrong way. Even you, Fiona, can't tell us how the royal family do that.'

'Is being offensive to our beloved Queen also an attribute of the gentry?' asked a lady, who must have lived somewhere like Iceland, judging by her tone of voice.

'Yes, it is, actually.' On that note Enid came to what almost amounted to a sticky end.

'You asked about life with the gentry and I've told you. Had you asked about life with the super-rich, life with Splosh and Bec – apart from not knowing – nevertheless, I would bet my bottom dollar they hold their knives totally incorrectly.'

'Don't you mean the Beckhams?' hissed the ever-helpful Fiona.

'Probably.'

A Mrs Cawdle had been asked to give a vote of thanks. She rose quaking from head to foot and, producing a piece of paper, in a quavering voice spoke about her mother's days in service and how she had taught all her children to 'talk proper', ending that she was glad Enid spoke with a pinch of salt.

Finally Enid found herself eating a slice of sponge while holding the notes from her talk and advising on what should be said in a speech by the best man at a wedding. Keep it cheerful, keep it clean and above all keep it short. Enid never went to weddings.

There were still some glares from ladies who had spent a lifetime doing it the wrong way; whether 'it' was sex or holding knives was hard to tell.

'I don't think we need leave poor Clive on his own much longer, do you?' asked Fiona anxiously. They went back to the car. Fiona was petulant.

'It's as if everything we were taught is now out of date. It's so unfair! Shall we watch the television when we get back? There may be some more news about your brother-in-law.'

There was.

Henry had been arrested and was being held in custody. Bail had been refused. It was all stiff upper lip stuff, with a fabulously crusty old lawyer eyeing the camera as if it was an insect that needed swatting. The ramblers had wobblier lips. They laid into the landlords who refused access and banged on about their rights. The television then went into the ASS family history and dug up illustrious ASS members who had fought and died for their country – and one Tarquin, the ASS who had fought and died in a debtors' prison.

Enid was bored, frankly – bored with Henry and bored with nice ladies in floral prints. She had done her stuff and now wanted to go back to her holy man. Fack was the kind of arrogant sod who knew exactly what to do with his knife, even if he did wander the country as a holy man. Enid had long decided that the reason the police and other authorities didn't touch him was because he used his metaphorical knife the right way. Or, to put it crudely, he had class on his side. Indians tend to be Maharajahs at heart.

Before leaving, a sad little scene took place while Fiona went to communicate with Delia Smith in the kitchen. Clive looked furtively at the door before asking Enid's advice.

'The old girl can't accept it. She wants to lead what she considers a proper way of life. I know things haven't gone that well for us. I had to sell the farm and I'm afraid her money and mine went up the spout along with the furniture – Lloyd's and all that. Frankly, Enid, a lot of out of date pretensions went with it. But we've got this place. I have a job. Between you and me, all those African youngsters are what the future's about, worms or no worms. Poor old Fi doesn't see it. All part of not having babies, I'm afraid – Fallopian tubes, poor old thing.'

Enid liked Clive more and more. They had eaten another stewy thing and finished with lemon meringue pie.

When she got back she found Fack massaging his calves, having sat too long in some sophisticated position.

Eleven

'Edes, I'm worried about my labia.'

'Prune it in the autumn and give it a good mulch once a year.'

'Edes!'

'Sorry, love, it's these bloody scones. I must get them in the oven by seven.' She clattered the mixing bowl and scales irritably. Labia, my foot! Anyway, it does sound like some exuberant plant – with pink flowers and all that. When had she ever given hers a second thought? Paul took being a woman far too seriously.

'Well?' she asked, resignedly.

'It's just that I want to have really juicy lips; they can dry out, you know, especially as you get older.'

'I hadn't noticed.' She slid the scones in the oven. 'What labia secret are you about to impart – special jelly at £50 a go?' It was the kind of silly nonsense that Paul was taken in by and one reason for living with her. When she wasn't making scones, it made Enid giggle.

'No, it's a question of whether to have a special operation to get them absolutely right or take pot luck when they are snipping away everything else.'

'As a taxpayer, I think your labia can take pot luck.'

'Do you think it really matters? I mean, do you worry about yours?'

'I think I can say with all honesty that I was well into adulthood before I knew what they were and, since knowing, I've not given them a single thought till now. You know, part of a woman's charm is her modesty. Modesty and labia don't go hand in hand.'

'God, you are a stuffy old wrinkly, Gran!' Enid whipped round to see her granddaughter Beatrice standing in the doorway, waving the key to the house kept by Sal in case.

'How dare you speak to your grandmother like that! Anyway, what are you doing here?' It would have been nice if Paula could have said it, but she didn't. Why was it always left to her to be the heavy?

'I'm just chilling out till Ma arrives. D'you know, we've been studying the boundaries of decency and acceptability this afternoon – it's called "Personal Health and Social Education". If you hang on long enough, it turns into full-blown sex – better than maths any day. Labia are old hat. We did those yonks ago. It's the clitoris we're going to do next – gateway to the orgasm. Gran, sorry about the stuffy old wrinkly bit. Honest, I didn't really mean it. It's my age. Perhaps I should have just murmured something about being out of date. Any choccy biscuits?'

The half-grown woman clumped into the room and flung a bag bulging with books onto the sofa. Her hair was a mess of several plaits – very fashionable if done properly. Her face was flushed with health and her hands were unimaginably filthy.

Enid had endured her grandchildren with a mixture of pride and deep misgiving. From the word go they had mouthed precocity with a wispy-haired, grubby-faced innocence. They had sworn and used sexual terms almost from birth, or so it seemed. Yet Sal and Douglas were intelligent, warm, loving parents who 'drew the line'. Enid wondered what line. Now the twins were nearly fourteen and at secondary school, where the school playground topics were about drink, drugs and sex, and where the curriculum was about drink, drugs and sex – commonly known as 'Relationships'. Enid had picked up a copy of a magazine Beatrice had left behind once. It, too, was about drink, drugs and sex.

Nobody writes a magazine like that for us, she had thought sourly. It's all knitting patterns, recipes and dowdy clothes.

'Ma says she'll pick up the scones and me when she's finished at the dentist with Sophie.'

'Oh my God! I was meant to tell you that. It's worrying about my labia that has done it.' Paul did an elaborate clutch of his soon-to-be-removed genitalia.

'You'll never be a real woman, you can't have the curse.' Beatrice, with her matter-of-fact attitude, might just as well have been talking about making a chocolate cake. 'It's yukky and hurts. Did it hurt in your day, Gran?'

Enid was holding the latest batch of scones. She looked at her androgynous lodger and her Lolita-style granddaughter before replying. 'Can either of you conceive of a way of life when nobody spoke about these things?'

'Queen Victoria smoked dope for her period pains,' announced Beatrice.

Enid was irritated with these winsome shock tactics. She was bored with teenage sexual banter. She was irritated by Paul's obsession with his fantasy female self. They never included her in these non-stop revelations about their bodies, never discussed tactfully the possibility of new teeth, fewer whiskers, the libido of older people. So she asked harshly, 'Why don't you two just get screwed and belt up?'

'Don't be so uptight. Honestly, Gran, you just don't know when to draw the line. Anyway, you've always had a filthy mind. Mum says so. Mum thinks you're a pain. You should stick to what you are good at – making scones.'

Enid was by now enraged.

'Have either of you ever heard of *private* parts – private labia, private vulva (they were somewhere down there, weren't they?), private clitorises, penises, scrotums? Have I left anything out?'

'Foreskins,' announced Beatrice.

'I thought they were just the name of a pop group.'

'Vaginas,' trilled Paul, as if the very word itself held some ritual power.

'I've had enough of you two. When you get to my age these things have a delicacy quite wasted on you. Enough is enough. Sex is banned, bits of the body are banned, I am too old to share these…these intimate terms. I had a perfectly satisfactory sex life for nearly forty years without referring to anything as crude as my private parts.'

'Poor old Gran, she's really past it.' Beatrice spoke behind her hand to Paul.

The scones flew through the air, thudding with a faint pop against a table and on the carpet. Several hit Beatrice, which was most satisfactory. One hit an already burgeoning bosom, while another caught her in the eye.

'Ouch!' shrieked a startled Beatrice, as the bell went. Enid opened the door and Sal walked in with Sophie. Several more scones scored direct hits.

'What the hell!'

'It's Gran, you mustn't ask her about her… Ow, that hurt! She's probably lost them, that's why. *Ouch!*'

'Her what?' asked a clearly perplexed Sal.

It is always interesting how priorities reassert themselves. There was no doubt in Sal's mind.

'But the scones! I need them for tomorrow – a mystery tour is coming from Darlington.'

'I'll make some more and bring them over fresh in the morning. But I do wish you wouldn't take me for granted. Honestly, I'm a sentient being and wish to be treated as such. As for your bloody daughter, what does she think I am – cream cheese?'

'Gran's so uptight about the facts of life. They all are at her age. It shrivels up.'

'What does?' But no one bothered to answer.

Beatrice was dragged to the car and continued her soliloquy in the back, while her mum and Sophie tried to shut her up. Beatrice's account of what had happened earlier before they arrived was hilarious, cruel and not repeatable.

Enid and Paul cleared up the scones and Paul was sensitive enough to realise that Enid had been hurt by the goings-on.

'Edes, I think you're wonderful. Forget those monsters. It's their age.'

'No, Paul, it's mine. We are pushed away as an embarrassment.' Her lip wobbled and Enid started crying.

'I've got fucking years ahead of me, years when I'm of no interest to anyone.'

It was several days later when Enid arranged to go over to Dolly's for a soothing chinwag. If Enid thought she had good reasons to cry, so had Dolly. Pert, pretty Dolly was sliding down some obscure greasy pole into a maudlin muddled state. She welcomed Enid with a petulant moan about the fishmonger. She sat, huddled and unhappy, failing to answer Enid's questions and occasionally bleating some irrelevant observation. Poor, poor Dolly! Something was seriously wrong. Enid looked at her friend and shuddered. It might well be her turn next.

'Dolly, I mean, it's so bloody lonely. No one is going to team up with us. It's those patronising clubs for the half-dead or nothing.' Dolly wasn't really listening. She sat with an air of blank misery spread across her face.

'Just look at the time. I must get back. It's bloody scones for some mystery tour or other. How long is it, do you think, before we're on that mystery tour?' She bit her tongue. She wished she hadn't said it. Dolly was well away already.

Enid left soon after. She drove back carefully, thinking of her poor friend. That night, when Enid started to get undressed, she undid the rather tight fastener of the skirt, unbuttoned a blouse that pulled a wee bit over her bosom. She removed a vest with holes under the arms and then slipped off a rather grey, ill-fitting bra. The tights had a hole developing and her pants were pitiably over-washed. Standing naked she looked sheepishly at the droopy bits and pieces.

'I would be dead by now if this was a Jane Austen novel. I suppose I would be dead or nearly dead if I was in an Indian village or deep in Africa somewhere.' Every time Enid heard or spoke of India, she was reminded of Mumsi. Teaming up with an Indian fakir and airing tiresome views might be seen as an indication that all was not entirely resolved. At least Fack was entirely her business. It was then she had a flash of pure genius.

Why not? She twirled round in front of the mirror. Enid was a great one for great ideas but this 'out-greated' even them. It was terrific!

'After all, Mumsi is the same age. We can presumably find plenty to talk about. It's an excuse to buy some long flowing dresses that flatter the figure. I don't have the money, but ingenuity will find it. What is more, I'm going to prove I'm… Oh my God! The bloody scones!' Grabbing her dressing gown, she rushed into the kitchen and slopped and pinched the mixture for the oven next morning.

She drove over, mulling her famous idea in her mind as she went.

'Here they are, straight from the oven.'

'Oh Ma, I meant to tell you; they've cancelled. The old dears have caught a bug or something. Actually, I'm not that put out. I need to hang some new prints that have arrived – studies of the Dales.'

Enid looked at her daughter. Was there a ghost of that blonde art student who wouldn't settle for anything less than Jackson Pollock, who announced vociferously that the Impressionists were old hat and Symbolism was the name of the game? Was this – frankly very plain, prematurely middle-aged – woman about to hang some God-awful prints of Hawes and Askrigg, Aysgarth Falls and Bolton Castle, really the same woman?

'No, you're not. You're going to sock your old mum a large cup of coffee.'

'The cafeteria isn't open yet. Janet doesn't get here till ten.'

'You still have a kitchen, I believe.'

The kitchen was a loveless pit. Enid could see that they had eaten supermarket lasagne the previous night. The night before appeared to have been spaghetti. The washing-up was done on a rota basis, apparently – but the girls had quarrelled and refused to do their share.

'Can you remember doing the washing-up as a kid, Sal?'

'That was different. You didn't have a job.'

'When did you and Douglas last have sex?'

'Ma! How dare you! You're rapidly becoming a disgusting old woman, for Christ's sake.'

'Well, these things are neglected at their peril.'

'No, they are not. It's just your immature, puerile mind. It's about time you snapped out of it. Dad's been dead ages now. You've had your unsuitable romp with God knows who and now you really must settle down.'

Apart from the washing-up, the kitchen had a half-dead look of something that needs feeding, grooming and a little care. Roger, the youngest child, had piled a number of paintings and weird devices made from cereal packets on every available surface. There were notices pinned to the wall, many out of date, and a broken jug waiting to be mended which had been there as long as Enid could remember.

'Sal, I don't mean to pry, but success is more than an accolade from the regional tourist board. As for me, I'm sorry if you reject my odyssey. Frankly, it's a pity more women of my age don't break out.'

'I've worked my bloody guts out to get that award.'

'And sold yourself to mediocrity in the process. Sal, think back, think back to all that vitality, that wackiness, all those wonderful, larger than life pronouncements you would make. I can see you now over toad-in-the-hole: "I think that art is so important. We should utilise it as a form of weaponry. We are the soldiers of the mind." I can see Gerry looking at you with that quizzical expression of his and deciding that his own daughter was practising bullshit as an art form.'

Sal had flared up and shrieked, not for the first time, 'Why doesn't anyone take me seriously?'

'Why indeed, Sal! Because we know you don't mean this. You don't really want studies from the Dales and scones.' Enid watched her daughter's face.

'You know nothing about art. You don't know what you're talking about. Half the time I don't think you know much about baking scones, either. Sometimes they look as if you've cooked them under a sunray lamp, brown and shrivelled. I need support for this place. It's bloody hard work. I still owe the bank a fortune, so of course I play safe. Do you think I like showing half the rubbish in the exhibition centre? Do you think providing shrivelled scones and tea to the elderly is what art is all about? I'd love to go totally abstract – so would about four other people I can think of. Four people don't pay the bank. I'd love to encourage young painters who are off the wall. I can't afford to. Your generation just doesn't understand. Well, that's not fair – I know you lived with a fakir for several months, but frankly that cost you quite a few friends, a great deal of money and even you must see it was a pretty silly thing to do. Oh my God! Just look at the time; I must open up.'

Enid put out her arm to prevent Sal leaping off into the engrossing world of being busy.

'I accomplished a great deal with Fack. We've parted completely amicably. Sal, I implore you to think hard about Douglas, the children and how much this place is costing you. You know the old maxim, "Is the fucking you're getting worth the fucking you're getting?"

'I must go, Ma. You know, if I fined you every time you swore, the bank would be paid off by now.'

Enid looked with frustration at her daughter's broadened backside poured into shapeless trousers, her once-smart shirt and dreadful old cardigan completing the unbecoming outfit. Sal's teeth, always a bone of contention since she refused to have them fixed at thirteen, made her look like a huge ferret. She wasn't yet forty, God help her! Enid drove back to her bungalow. That wasn't entirely accurate; she drove back to Paul. Enid loathed living alone and she wasn't too enamoured with the bungy, as she called it, either.

She had been enticed into buying the bungy when she eased herself out of the B and B. God knows, there was no lack of choice. Heaps of particulars flopped onto her mat. They all had one thing in common. They were ugly. Finally, with Sal's patience at snapping point, Enid agreed on the one at the end of a cul-de-sac with a sizeable kitchen and garden. It had two double rooms, one bathroom and a large L-shaped room for everything else. It was grim, frankly.

When she got back, having had those words with Sal, Paul was out – no doubt up to his dainty knees in cow shit while dreaming of joining the editorial team of *Vogue*. He had sent off his entry for a scholarship and had set his heart on entering the world of fashion and design. Enid would tartly edit that as meaning 'fashionable'. Even if Paul was out, the bathroom harboured the smell and the false eyelashes, lipsticked tissue and unwashed nylons from the previous night. It was enough to give Enid the comfortable sense that she was not alone. All the same, she didn't really go for the pale blue fluffy mat round the lavatory bowl, with matching bath mat. Paul had won them somewhere.

What was Mumsi's real name...Savita? That was it. Enid was sitting in her front room, hands loosely crossed on her lap and mulling over the idea she'd had earlier. But first she had to repeat the whole story, as if by doing so she verified it. Having just left a tired out plain Jane of a daughter, it was more imperative than ever for Enid to feel she hadn't played second fiddle to this siren across the waters with her ravishing film star daughter. That was it! The idea was very much there. She sat bolt upright. It was brilliant. Yes, she would invite herself over with the beautiful Paul as her other daughter. Ferrets needn't apply. No, no, that was horrid! She loved her Sal, loved the grandchildren – well, kind of – but she loathed their busy, busy lives, their frozen lasagne values. No way was she going to India with that lot. She didn't mean it like that – it's just that Sal was frightening her; she was heading for a ghastly world of mediocrity and Enid couldn't bear to watch.

Suddenly Enid found herself feeling happy – a very rare condition. She felt that tightening of the stomach, a surge of energy quite unnatural for a failed woman of her age. She felt her mind free from the fetters of making bloody scones. She'd sell her pearls and her engagement ring; everyone would squeak...so what? She never had an occasion to wear them. If she did, inevitably she forgot to put them on. Only Paul used them and he would understand, surely.

Paul listened patiently. The story was a breech delivery. In her excitement Enid couldn't remember the beginning, middle and end, the point at which Paul came into the story and what part her pearls played. He understood the gist, however.

'Edes, wouldn't that be too divine? I must contribute something. Let me think. By the way, how were the old pussies at the art complex?'

'Didn't turn up. They were dicing with death and diarrhoea, so I moaned at Sal for becoming middle-aged and dreary. Honestly, just looking at her exhausted face, neglected figure, shapeless clothes...'

'Like mother, like daughter,' chirruped Paul.

'I'm over twenty years older, I'll have you know! What's more, I like to think that I haven't sunk quite so far into the mire of mediocrity.'

'Sal's a dear. Don't be nasty about her. It belittles you. Shall I look up the price of fares so that we have some idea about costs? You did mean after the op, didn't you? Just think, I can wander round the... Edes, what is it we'll be seeing?'

'I've no idea till I've written. I suppose it's palm trees by the sea, abject poverty and opulence all intertwined. Can't you see it? Emaciated children shoving their hands out for change.'

'And servants padding round in bare feet with platters of sumptuous curries. My figure! – I mustn't give in to temptation. Edes, where exactly is Bombay?'

'Sorry, Paula, it's my Oxbridge, I suppose.'

'Don't worry, we can suss it on the Internet.'

Enid, despite a course for older people in Ripon just as the scones were getting underway, was no dab hand at the Internet. Her granddaughters could find porn in thirty seconds flat, or where their favourite record was in the charts. Not so poor old gran! The course was confusingly difficult and Enid simply couldn't devise a system for memorising what she had been taught from one week to the next, indeed from one moment to the next. Part of the problem was motivation. The other grey-haired ladies and gentlemen eagerly made lists of friends to send Christmas cards to, or designed the card itself. 'Sentimental rot' was not for our Enid, who ended designing menus with her bloody scones in pride of place. She even tried drawing a scone or two but they ended looking like dinosaur dung – 'the mouse it was that ran away'.

So, what with an uncooperative mouse running in circles and an inability to draw scones or spell lapsang suchong, Enid's efforts were not among the ones held up for praise and by the next week Enid was still unable to draw lapsang whatsit and unable to spell scones. No, the computer skills got no further than turning the machine off and on – well, a little further; she could write a letter, change the format so the letters went all wiggly and vaguely save it – although she could never see why it was worth it. The great day came when the grandchildren had been banned from surfing the Net for undesirable material in their mother's office, so very sensibly came hotfoot over to their gran's for some action.

'They want to bike – such a good idea – all that fresh air. They must be growing up at last,' babbled Sal, who was trying to do at least six things at once – and supervising her children wasn't one of them.

Enid wasn't so sure that fresh air and a bike ride was all that was on her grandchildren's minds. This was made abundantly clear when they arrived and, with heaving air still imbedded in their diaphragms, explained that they had arrived as angels of mercy to teach their old gran about the Net. Sophie sat down first and, suffused with giggles, showed Enid how to log on.

'See, it's easy; just follow these simple instructions. Now you're using your telephone line.'

'That costs money, my girl. Anyway, what the hell do I want to know about?'

Girlish giggles began and rippled round the room.

'Gran, say you were about our age and wanted to know about – well, you know – you would just press this, fill in the little box, and hey presto!'

It didn't seem very 'hey presto!' to Enid, who now found herself engrossed in some very dreary and frankly embarrassing film about a couple groaning their way to as phoney an orgasm as filming can show. She watched with curiosity tinged with awkwardness at the proximity of the giggling girls.

'So this is the reason you bicycled over? Honestly, I thought you did this stuff all in school these days.'

'Pulling a contraceptive over a carrot is hardly the same thing,' began Beatrice, only to be interrupted by Sophie.

'At St Antony's they were given real plastic whatsits. You know what they are, don't you, Granny?'

'Didn't a politician say something about "On your bike"? It wasn't to search out sex films, either. You two are the pits. Now, off you go. I won't say a word – a senile promise is worth it's weight in gold teeth fillings. What's more, I'll give you some money for the baker's shop.'

That had all happened just before Paul became Paula. Paul/Paula was a dab hand on the Net. Where Enid had found herself languishing among the Bombay restaurants of the UK, Paula made a beeline for some smudgy photos of the real thing.

'Look, I was right. There's some palm trees. It's on the west coast.'

Not a lot to go on, but Enid was determined to put Gerry to rest. It's one thing to darn socks and quite another to find your rival owns a sock shop. That, frankly, was how she saw the situation.

'It's a big port. I think I knew that. Lots of hills running down to the ocean and Bollywood. Gerry's daughter is an actress – so was her mother. You'll be in your element, Paula. I'll feel lumpy and English, while deep inside I'll feel contorted into knots of jealousy.'

'Why the hell are you going? You've got nothing to prove, Enid.'

'Yes, Paula, I've got everything to prove. Before I get too old I want to know…be absolutely sure…that I was top dog, if you see what I mean. I don't mind the mistress bit, the fortune bit, but I must know that Gerry wanted to live with me, grow old with me. Growing old is difficult enough, but to grow old with a lie like that would be terrible. It's like you rather. Life would be far easier if you remained Paul but you can't, you simply can't. I can't grow old comfortably if I suspect Savita meant more to Gerry than I do. It's strange, but the things that most women define as important to them and their man have never interested me. I've been rather earnest and watched women liberate themselves from the sidelines. Gerry and I had a contented marriage. I made it so. I was bloody good at it, too. But there's this niggle. I must know that she was about sex and I was about contentment. Don't get me wrong; I was pretty good in my day.' Enid had said far too much. She had lifted the lid off a burden she carried silently and, in doing so, a little tear escaped.

'Edes, I'll support you, after all you've done for me.'

It was a lovely thing to say, but Enid didn't hold him – or her – to it, which was just as well. Paula had wrapped a strapping arm round Enid and looked at her with a curious mixture of simpering emotion and a protective calm. Her eyes were smudged with green and framed with long lashes. Caked foundation covered the still leathery skin and Paula's lips were a delicate pink. Poor love, she looked quite awful. Still, it was a lovely thing to say.

For a week Enid smudged her nose against the travel agent's window. She had to drive to Harrogate. Ripon's travel agents were into skiing and showed whizzy teenagers skateboarding over the entire resort – a feat of photography and of hope, thought Enid as she passed the usual group of underachievers mooching round the town's marketplace. Harrogate was quite different. One agent had posters of Hindu dancers, all fingers, toes and huge eyes. Enid must have looked at them for over half an hour before finally entering the shop.

'But what about my scones?' Sal's voice rose hysterically above the roast beef. Enid had been invited to lunch. The amount of ceremony performed for her benefit was minimal.

'Hi Gran! How are the wrinklies of Ripon making out?'

'We are an economic force to be reckoned with, Beatrice. Only last week the health clinic announced yet another programme for the over-eighties, while the Derby and Joan Club are off to Paris and the *Folies Bergère* for a knees-up champagne evening.'

'Yuk!' announced Sophie, who had sidled up in a pair of stretch trousers cutting her crotch in two and a glittery top that pulled her adolescent breasts into taut peaks.

'Yuk to you, too,' retorted Enid before she put her head round the kitchen door.

The kitchen had last been decorated about ten years earlier. Since then the twins and their younger brother, Roger, had daubed paint, jam and various indefinable murky messes over the walls. A proliferation of nails held a notice board with out of date dentist appointments and school dates, a great many telephone numbers and a cartoon about untidy kids. Another nail held a small dustpan and brush which was for cleaning the table but was rarely used. Several others held saucepans and a wok. Working space had shrunk in the wake of a microwave which had never worked properly, a chip fryer, a worm farm which had gone bankrupt and a huge radio permanently tuned to some wretched raucous noise without which the children pined and threatened to ring ChildLine and complain about bullying tactics. Enid saw it as all part of the state school conspiracy to give every child a philistine, impoverished education just to make sure no one ever achieved enough to threaten the status quo. Certainly, her grandchildren were unlikely to threaten anyone. Only the other day Beatrice had revealed that she thought the Mona Lisa was a boring old mountain somewhere. But back to the kitchen. The paint, once a sparkling white and tan colour, had mellowed into a dirty mud, with the floor tiles a mixture of torn holes to trip the unwary and a circular stain from a burning pan, a pancake having embedded itself in the lampshade and all that had been ancient history.

'Be a love and make the gravy, Ma. I just want to check the price list in the gallery.' A dishevelled Sal galloped across the yard to her baby – her art complex – already the recipient of that regional award.

Douglas entered the kitchen and took for granted Enid stirring the gravy.

'Where's Sal?'

'Your bloody wife is suckling her baby.'

'Don't I know! How are you, Enid?'

'Douglas, what's gone wrong? One of your daughters thinks Mona Lisa's a mountain, your other one is incapable of differentiating between vowels and consonants – and sounds, frankly, exactly like a cat, while your son has already demanded for Christmas a toy so astronomically expensive that I'll have to find a full-time job just to afford it. Anyhow, what is a Space Dream Center, spelt the American way?'

'You don't want to know, Enid. At least my kids are no more dreadful than everyone else's. No one can complain that with me as a magistrate they are at some mysterious advantage. I have to patrol the greenhouse for cannabis. God knows what they nick after school. Beatrice tells me it's an initiation rite and not to worry. As for drink, I've tried easy-going talks while driving the car but I'm told to mind my own business. Don't I know anything? Meanwhile the price of beef is a joke, cereals are another and I had a field of maize trashed by some dimwits. Where's it all going to end? As for Sal's "baby", as you call it, it's bloody ridiculous if you ask me. What makes it worse is that it is the only thing around here that makes money. Subdivide that further and it is the coffee shop that brings in the money. All this edifice to farming and it's the wife's bloody coffee shoppe, spelt some ridiculous way, that makes the money.'

Poor old Douglas. He was in a bad way. Who could blame him? He had been another 'brick' over the years – so kind when Gerry died and far more understanding than Sal when she had roared round the neighbourhood with Fack, shaking the locals out of their racist sloth. Those were the times. Why did she ever jump off that bandwagon? Because she was pushed? Enid looked at Douglas shuffling round the kitchen – because? It was because of the family – her family, Gerry's family. The once proud Tanners hurtling into the oblivion of bungaloid values. That's what it was. She and Gerry had wanted a new, more equitable society. They turned their backs on – well, hunt balls, grouse and

Ascot, all that rubbish. So this was it. The new world they had longed for. A son-in-law shuffling round a totally disgusting kitchen, preoccupied, depressed and at odds with his wife, her daughter. Sal was looking more like a harassed ferret than ever. Hell! The gravy was bubbling away, just like her thoughts.

It took a while to persuade Sophie not to wear her Walkman. Roger had to be bribed to sit next to his grandmother, whom he declared was boring and knew nothing about Man U.

Beatrice had decided to be a vegan for lunch but, on peering at the dispirited vegetables, changed her mind and became a fruitarian. It was into this happy Sunday lunch that Enid dropped her bombshell about India, to which Sal had squealed with dismay, 'But what about my scones?'

There followed a silence – but more than that. The girl's eyes narrowed, Roger looked up at his boring granny's face and Douglas held his roast beef suspended between plate and mouth. Enid studied her daughter's face. It had puckered into a spoilt, panicky reminder of when she was seven.

'Anyhow, you can't possibly afford it.' Triumph spoke.

'I can if I sell some jewellery. Anyway, that's my business. It's not as if I'm paid by you. OK, you pay for the ingredients, but I make the bloody things voluntarily.'

'You've always hated going abroad. Why this sudden interest in India?'

This was no friendly questioning. Sal's voice had a tone which bore a hint of venom.

'I want to meet Mumsi before she dies. There are questions I want to ask her.' Enid swung round to Beatrice, who was sitting nearest.

'You know that your grandfather had a beautiful Indian mistress?'

'Dead exciting, Gran, and she was the mother of that gorgeous sour-as-hell lady that came over. Mum, you were jealous, weren't you?'

'Oh, shut up! You don't know what you're talking about. Anyhow, this really isn't suitable for Sunday lunch. We can discuss it over coffee.'

'Goodee! I think I'll have coffee. This is a bit like a soap in a way.'

Sophie removed the Walkman and looked at her grandmother expectantly. 'Did you mind about the mistress?'

'Sophie, not here! Little pitchers have long ears.' Sal's concern was rising like a soufflé. Meanwhile Douglas had finished his beef and was scooping the last of the trifle, which had all the hallmarks of the supermarket. Long gone were the days when he and Sal swore to give their children good wholesome food. Then long gone too were the promises of care and love tempered with treats. He couldn't remember when he and Sal had last dined together over a bottle of wine in a good restaurant. He looked at the frumpy mess of a wife and could no longer see the lovely, earnest art student with her long blonde hair. Sal had thrown it all away on studies of the Dales. He looked out of the window straight onto the car park with the barn already lit up for today's visitors. Only a few days ago he heard a couple muttering as they made their way back to their car.

'Don't know why we bothered, Arthur. I prefer the telly any day. Who wants to sit with Pen Hill in the rain staring at them?'

'At least there weren't any sheep dipped in formaldehyde! Come to think of it, might have been more fun if there had been some.'

It summed up the art complex.

Roger, who up till now had behaved like a perfect grandson, waved his spoon and whispered conspiratorially, 'How's great-uncle Henry doing?'

'Badly, Roger. You'd better disown him. Your great aunt Eleanor tells me he's coming out of prison soon.'

'Will they tag him, like they do real criminals?'

'I don't suppose so. They've confiscated all his guns, poor love. It is a bit like lopping off his balls…'

'Mother, that's enough of that. You know very well I don't like you using language like that in front of the children.'

'Well, I am in the doghouse! First I want to go to India. Then I'm rude about some old codger who was stupid enough to try shooting a rambler. Where's your sense of humour, Sal?'

Later, sitting in a once comfortable armchair, now shabby and torn with age and misuse, Enid held her coffee and noticed with pleasure that her hand wasn't shaking. She wasn't that old, at least. The two girls draped themselves over another armchair expectantly. Douglas had done a runner, while Roger was seeing if it was only cats that have nine lives by taking his bicycle over a particularly perilous assault course.

'Well, what's all this about India?'

'It's just that I've got so much unfinished business out there. I really need to meet Mumsi. I want to know if it was just beauty or something more…'

'Spare us the details,' said Sal, as she did some very inept Morse code, implying 'not in front of the children'.

'Mum, don't patronise us. We want to know about Granny and her past. It sounds really cool.'

'It's your grandfather's past, not mine.'

'But you had that funny Indian man. He didn't like kids much, I could tell.'

It was obvious that the twins were going to act like a Greek chorus throughout this conversation.

'Err, he was grotty. You didn't have sex with him, did you?' Sophie asked, pulling a horrified face.

'Sophie!' remonstrated Sal.

'Our relationship wasn't about sex. We lived cheek by jowl in perfect harmony.'

'How boring! Grandpa had that actress. She was his daughter. She was very smelly, but then they are if they act and that – it's called allure. Where in India are you going? I wish I could go.'

'Well, you can't. I've asked Paula.'

Enid really didn't expect the wrath that her reply elicited. She said they would go just after her operation. Sal exploded with fatigue, jealousy and a host of unresolved emotional knots that were tying her into misery.

Paul had come into her life when he interviewed her before the art complex was open and when Enid was dashing round the countryside with Fack, making a right fool of herself. Paul had become a model when the art complex opened and soon teamed up with Enid – never one to live by herself if she didn't have to. Sal had thought it an excellent idea – at first. But lying exhausted in bed that night, the seeds of jealousy began to grow. She thought back to her student days and the seeds grew larger. They began to sprout. She thought of her mother's behaviour as a widow, how she had revelled in finding out about her late husband's mistress, had gone completely off the rails with Fack and was now teaming up with a transsexual while she, Sal, sank into debt, married to a farmer with three insolent children and an art complex selling crap. Why couldn't Paul have turned to her? Just because Enid had decided to behave like a superannuated teenager and renege on the scones, it didn't mean that it was fair, because it damned well wasn't. As the tears prickled her eyes, Sal was overwhelmed with guilt as well as jealousy. Guilt at something that had happened earlier – several weeks before.

She had been exhausted, compromising all that she had loved and learnt about art with the realities of the bank and the advice from the tourist board. One night she wept in the bath and crept into bed an angry, tired, frightened woman. She lashed out in anger at her frivolous mother for doing her own thing. She, Sal, wasn't free to do half the things she would like to do. Put on a really abstract show and get screwed by... Sal let her imagination wander over the men she knew and plumped for a stranger. She would wear crotchless tights and a bra that barely fitted her ample breasts. Such sexual thoughts made her sigh and move restlessly over the bed. Douglas lay exhausted; he had been up half the night with a cow calving. No way would he want to make violent love to his wife. Sal slid a hand down to her alert, throbbing clitoris. Why shouldn't she? She started gently rubbing herself – no slow build-up, either. Almost immediately she felt violently aroused and found herself groaning beside her sleeping husband.

'What's that?' he cried groggily.

'Nothing, I just... I think I was just asleep, a nightmare!'

She lay, then, beset by guilt. She saw what she had done as a betrayal, so revolting that it shocked her more than an adulterous encounter would have done. So much so that she felt compelled to get up and wash her hands for violating her.

For all Sal's liberal attitudes, masturbation was a dark and revolting sin.

It happened again and again. Now, weeks later, faced with her mother flying off to India with Paula, Sal felt as if they were doing it to spite her. They knew what she did and they were going to retaliate – taunt her with tales of her successful half-sister who never needed to masturbate. What if Ma got on with Savita? The prospect made Sal shudder.

'Paul can't just go like that. He's got his career. Anyway, what are you using for money?'

'The usual – I'll sell various things. The marvellous thing about being a widow is that I have only myself to worry about.'

'But I rely on you for the scones, you know I do.'

'Get Beatrice and Sophie to do them. Buy them from the bakery. Honestly, Sal, the scones aren't really that important. Forget them. Isn't that the easiest thing?'

The unseen, binding emotions were twisting and turning themselves into more and more knots, so that by the time Enid went home, the twins, Roger, Sal and Douglas all felt curiously dismayed by the trip to India.

'Paul'll be a girl by then,' said Douglas reassuringly, as he dried a saucepan, noticing the wodge of mashed potato sticking firmly to the side of the pan. Somehow, for Enid to travel with another woman gave the trip a vague notion of respectability.

'I wouldn't trust my mother with an orang-utan,' muttered Sal angrily, as she banged down another saucepan with a suspicion of cabbage leaf still clinging to it.

'That makes Granny a lesbian,' suggested Sophie, who was meant to be wiping the place mats – hunting prints – but who was hanging on every word her parents were exchanging.

'Not the orang-utan, stupid. Paul, or rather Paula…' continued Sophie. But, changing the conversation midstream, she added, 'Hey, Ma, why don't you commission a range of decent place mats? These are so naff.'

How can the young switch from lesbian grandmothers to place mats? thought Sal with incredulity, as images of her mother passionately embracing Paula swam round her imagination. It stopped there, before further masturbatory scenes started to penetrate her easily-roused sense of guilt.

'That's a good idea: scenes from the Dales, that kind of thing?'

'No!' exploded Douglas, Sophie and Roger, who knew little about art but a great deal about contemporary culture.

'Get some really cool ones, y'know, the type that we'd like. I'd buy them for Christmas and whatnot, for you and Gran.'

'We'll make our fortune yet,' teased Sal, but she was chuffed that he'd made the effort. It is always thrilling when the young start to join in.

'What about cow placentas?' suggested Douglas. 'Beatrice has a camera. They should go down brilliantly in a rural area; never know, we might be spotted as some cultural icon.'

'Shut up, Dad! Anyway, you haven't a clue. Has he, Mum?'

'No, thank God. He's only teasing!' But Sal was thinking of something else.

In the end, 'Scenes from the Dales' sold steadily on mats, as they did on the mugs. The aching good taste crept over many aspects of the gallery and shop like a paralysis and the whole enterprise became a beacon of mediocrity that flourishes in the name of success and was the epitome of bank manager art. The Yuk Complex would continue to win provincial awards for excellence.

'I mean', said Sal much later after Enid had left, when she and Douglas were watching *Antiques Roadshow*, 'she's so frivolous. I'm sure it's not working. That woman has never worked in her life. Look, that's worth about two thousand. What do you think?'

'Less – I'd say about a thousand. But you went to India. You loved it, and you had a fair amount of hanky-panky by all accounts.'

More than I have now, she thought, but didn't say it. 'I was young and beautiful; well, more beautiful.'

Only a few years ago, Douglas would have taken her hand – it was in easy reach – and reassured her how beautiful she was still, but now he simply looked at her.

'Your Mum has done nothing but wait. Her life has been a waiting game. Now she's wanting a bit of fun…'

'But at her age!'

'What the hell has her age got to do with it? She's a sentient being, a lovely person, even if she does dress badly, use coarse language and at times have us screaming up the wall. No, on reflection, I defend your mother's right to go to India and if Paul – I mean Paula – gives her a buzz, let her go too.'

Just as Sal was tidying up before she went to bed and when she felt that she could relax from the relentless shock tactics of her children, she found Beatrice in the kitchen. The child turned round and in an entirely matter-of-fact voice said, 'Did you know that Indian penises are smaller than African ones?'

'Beatrice! Must you? I thought you were making cocoa. Can't you just stick to that?'

'Just thought you would like to know.' She spilt the hot milk and rubbed it with her slipper before slip-slopping off to bed. Why do fourteen-year-olds have to slip-slop everywhere?

Sal looked at her daughter with adoration and envy. Where did she find out all this nonsense?

Henry the ASS, despite expensive lawyers, had left hospital and found himself on remand. As he pointed out, the ramblers, the Labour Party and state-educated judges had no sense of humour. He shared a cell with Mick, an awfully nice chap and professional burglar. When a harassed Eleanor next visited him, he insisted on telling her about Mick's state-of-the-art burglary protection plans.

'He's going straight and needs just a few bob to set himself up as a security adviser. Damn good idea if you ask me. He's going to ring you when he gets out.'

'Are you completely off your head?' remonstrated an alarmed Eleanor.

'Move with the times, that is the name of the game. I say, old girl, you couldn't get a copy of *The Field*, could you? Do you know, they have decent lavatory paper here, the kind we always had in the Gents. The fellas are all right – can't understand a word they say, particularly the black ones. Keep asking if we ever owned land in the southern states of America. I think it's a political question.'

'Now listen, Henry, you're in a spot of trouble. You know that. I've spoken to Jarvis, the family lawyer, but this isn't his thing. Criminal work isn't done by, well, the kind of people we know. It's handled by Jewish firms and bright young men with accents.'

'Don't I know it,' sighed Henry.

So it was that Henry's barrister made an impassioned speech

314

in a Birmingham accent about the right of English gentlemen to fire off their elephant guns after lunch. Much play was made by the press of Henry's lunch – just half a grouse. His lawyer was uncertain where grouse actually came from, apart from Harrods.

'Where did you get the grouse, and where is the other half?'

'You'll have to ask the memsahib. All questions concerning food are handled by her. I ate another half in prison, or rather shared it with several friends. They supplied some frightful hooch and I supplied the grouse. Luckily, nobody liked the grouse and the hooch was desperate. Afterwards, we all shared a kind of cigarette – very relaxing it was too.'

The seven injured parties gave evidence of a thundering roar and raining lead shot, a piece of which installed itself in a rambler's shoulder. A woolly hat was holed but the wearer was unscathed apart from bruising. Several branches were splintered, and a rucksack clearly peppered. Then the ramblers were asked about their relationship with Henry the ASS and they shook their heads. He shouted scurrilous suggestions that they used trees as toilets, left litter, opened gates and spoke loudly, frightening the pheasants. Above all he was offensive about their backgrounds, yelling gratuitous insults if he came across them. For their court appearance, the ramblers wore dull suits with white shirts. They probably weren't all insurance salesmen – one or two might have been accountants. Not so the jury. They were a motley collection of big-bosomed matrons who would never willingly walk over mud, a couple of small shopkeepers resenting every minute wasted over this nonsense and a delightful black man who kept winking at Henry. The remainder sank into boredom, made up their mind and didn't allow their prejudices to be dented by fact. After a while the giggle factor became bogged down with windy rhetoric and Henry was sentenced to eighteen months.

'Chin up, old girl,' he said in the cells, before giving some instructions for his keeper. Henry then disappeared into the prison system.

No one could fault Eleanor's chin. She treated her husband's fall from grace in much the same way that she had treated her son's tenure at public school. She asked an incredulous prison officer if she could send him hampers from Fortnum's.

Eleanor could sniff a committee at a hundred paces and that is what it took for her to breeze into the visitors' centre quiet room, where the local branch of the prisoners' wives were holding a meeting. The quiet room was a new innovation. No children allowed, but snogging permitted. Heavy petting surreptitiously entered the agenda and one or two keener spirits proudly boasted that the latest nipper was conceived there. When Eleanor entered the quiet room she was met by eight tired women carrying the burden for hundreds of others. They wore thin summer dresses and cheap, badly cut jackets over plunging necklines to keep the old man's pecker up, and not a decent warm bit of clothing between them, even though the Christmas decorations were already in the high street. Suspicious looks swivelled round and even Eleanor, not the most tactful of souls, wished she wasn't wearing such impeccable tweeds. That cameo brooch was a mistake, too.

'Nice to see a new face – what's yer name, love?' snapped a lady with eyes like X-rays.

'Eleanor Ashington Stanley Smythe.'

'What, them husbands all at once! Which one is in the nick?' demanded the same lady. Then it dawned.

'You're married to that funny old man who tried to shoot some ramblers.' It was an accusation. Stoically, she continued, 'You're posh, not one of us. What do you know about travelling by train for over three hours with young kids and no toilet facilities when you get here?'

The prisoners' wives closed ranks. Their eyes bored into Eleanor. But chin to the fore and settling for Smythe, she picked up an agenda and then breathed the magic word: *fund-raising*.

'Fund-raising! Do you have a separate committee for that?' They looked at her with incredulity and thought about the meagre grants occasionally handed out – or a sale raising £40 when they needed £10,000. 'Illegit' money was hard enough to come by; 'legit' just impossible. What had their kiddies ever done to be treated like shit? These were bitter women.

'Why don't you be a sodding fund-raising committee if you are so keen about it?' It wasn't said in a friendly tone. It was loaded with sarcasm, anger and class hatred.

'Brilliant, I'll see what I can do.' Our Eleanor had the hide of a rhino.

'Poor dears, you've no idea,' repeated Eleanor to her friends who looked furtive and asked how Eleanor knew it wasn't going on drugs.

'It's not the wives who take drugs, it's the prisoners. Henry is spaced out most of the time.' Eleanor even gave a chuckle.

'What's new?' they muttered.

By the time Henry was transferred to a cushy open prison, the prisoners' wives' fund was £3,000 richer. And a pair of the Home Secretary's underpants were auctioned in a stately home, along with a motley collection of 'yesteryear novelties'. A local youth training scheme helped with the evening and nothing was taken apart from the virginity of Brenda, who was not as others. Brenda was in seventh heaven. She'd only been helping with the washing-up.

Dear little Brenda had been doing sex education at college. No carrots and condoms for her. She did it standing up in the boiler room with four different lads – or was it the same lad four times? It was hard to tell. Suffused with excitement, she ran from the boiler room straight into the arms of Enid, who was looking for a broom to clear up some broken glass. Enid very firmly handed the overexcited child gabbling something about sex to the severe Methodist disposition of Annie, who was organising the ladies. Never had little Brenda – well, not so little; she had a metabolic weight problem and was over sixteen stone – been so animated. She was ecstatic as she grabbed the startled Enid.

'Do you know what, miss? I've been intercoursed four times standing up!'

Everyone agreed that the college had at least extended Brenda's vocabulary.

Eleanor had exhausted her address book, stormed the elegant houses of Oxfordshire and twisted arms with Chinese burns to fill Warton Hall for this evening on behalf of prisoners' wives. She agonised over inviting the prisoners' wives themselves, but the thought of those cheap clothes and worn-out faces contorted with bitterness said it all – she had to. And she had invited Enid in her pretty blue dress. What a buy that had been!

'I now know what you went through with Gerry away. After all, you don't know – he may have been in prison.' Eleanor frequently rang Enid. She felt Enid understood more than her other friends.

'I don't think he was ever in prison, Eleanor, unless it was in some far-flung place like Ulan Bator.'

There was no place in Oxfordshire of that name, so Eleanor didn't enquire further.

The sour ladies invited Eleanor to their next meeting in the visitors' centre. This was just before the ASS came to the end of his sentence. The quiet room was in use, whatever that meant – so they met in the kiddies' room. The women sat on diminutive chairs clutching polystyrene coffee mugs. Friezes of rabbits and toadstools surrounded the walls, garish teddies and decapitated dolls languished in large plastic drums, while torn books filled the shelves.

Eleanor had agonised for hours about what to wear. She even rang Enid.

'Don't you have anything simple, like you'd wear to do the garden?'

So Eleanor wore a full tweed skirt, much pulled at by roses, and a jersey starting to go at the elbows. She arrived early, hoping to avoid too much attention, but because she walked straight into the quiet room, not realising the change of venue, she was flustered by the time she came face to face with Sheryl, who coordinated the prisoners' wives.

'Excuse me for having to smile. You look exactly like those ladies do on telly in the gardening programmes. Friend of Titch, are you?'

'I didn't have time to change,' said Eleanor, feeling on the defensive.

Sheryl thought it unlikely that the likes of 'er would be doing the garden in February first thing on a frosty morning and deeply resented this dressing-down.

'Yeah, it's all very well for you. Come by the Roller, did yer?'

'I've brought the cheque – pump-priming finance, I imagine. What's the next plan?' Eleanor sounded cheerful and authoritative. She wasn't going to be intimidated by this Roller nonsense.

'We all 'ave indoor plumbing, ta very much,' declared a lady who was a little confused by Eleanor's terminology.

'Sheryl, any news from the Lottery people?'

'Yeah, Babs, guess what!'

Yes, without so much as raising a finger to help themselves, the prisoners' wives had got the lot. Poor old Eleanor's efforts were surplus to requirements. It had taken several months but, with a little help with filling in the form, a whacking grant had landed on their laps.

The women were thrilled, the cheque substantial and, for a while, they reminisced about the lottery draws they had, to a woman, lost. Then, with an ingratiating air, Sheryl thanked Eleanor.

'Yer a bit out of date, really. We don't need the likes of you, see. It's not as if you're suffering from yer ole man being here, not like us an' all. Why don't you fund-raise for all those poor buggers like...oh, I don't know...'

It hurt. It was humiliating. That sea of bitterness, those malevolent eyes sparkling with derision. Even the bunny rabbits, the headless dolls and one-eyed teddies conspired to oust poor Eleanor in her gardening skirt and jersey worn at the elbows. As for the Roller, Henry hadn't had one for years. She started the Volvo and, with tears at their ingratitude, drove home with Tory sentiments beating in her breast.

That evening she rang Enid.

'I blame the Lottery. These women thought it was their right to get a grant. They never did a hand's turn. Meanwhile I did all that work, including the Home Secretary's underpants – and did I get an ounce of gratitude or even recognition? I tell you, they don't even speak the Queen's English. Half the time you can't understand what they are saying and the other half they don't understand ordinary English. I did what you suggested, wore just my gardening skirt and jersey; one of them asked if I was a friend of Titch's – whatever that means. You know something? It's not having servants any more. One gave a damn good education to those girls. Nowadays the same girls go straight into the House of Commons and breastfeed everywhere. I tell you, Enid, we are making a rod for our own back. Everything Daddy stood for is ridiculed. Gerry and you, for instance: look how you both embraced socialism. You and Gerry have a lot to answer for.'

'Eleanor, calm yourself. Why should these marginalised women kow-tow? Anyway, they've paid out for their lottery grant. You know, Gerry and I at least moved with the times. Here in my boring bungalow I'm anonymous, but you! Just look at the fuss at the trial. You stick out like a sore thumb.' The phone went dead.

Enid sat down heavily. Dear Gerry, what a close shave! What a pathetic dinosaur Eleanor was. No wonder Gerry had blown the lot. It was just a pity he had blown it on Mumsi. All the same, bless his old heart, it was a brave stand to turn his back and then choose to do something confidential – whatever that meant. There had always been the enigmatic figure of the Brig, who knew whatever there was to know, but he had died just the other day and with his death had gone the secret of Gerry's career. Enid imagined her gruff, rather ordinary husband sitting on his hunkers fermenting revolution among the diehards in dispossessed countries. It seemed far-fetched. She tried again, this time providing table tennis bats to the more obscure provinces of the Third World with secret instructions for making bombs sealed in the handles. No, that was Boy's Own rubbish. Gerry wasn't like that. He simply thought that the values and rubbish that had kept his family in power from generation to generation were fundamentally wrong.

Well, who doesn't? added Enid for her own benefit.

Why didn't I mind? Kick over the traces, get a decent job, a lover?

She was irritated at how passive she had been. Growing up at sixty-plus is a little late in the day, she considered wryly, before thinking of poor old Eleanor: efficient, good-looking in her day, hard-working and steeped in all that class bullshit. It often made Enid wince. What really amused her were the illustrious jobs the latter-day Tanners held. Glorified gardeners! Their son had married the heiress to some remote stately home, open at weekends, and James spent his time cleaning the guttering – over a mile's worth – and clipping the edges of the lawn. Henry, when he wasn't blasting ramblers, was forever cutting logs for the winter like any peasant, which, of course, was exactly what he was. Their daughter, Cynthia, had married a medieval castle in the Borders and turned it into a B and B. It was pathetic, really: they had the family coat of arms on boxes of tissues in every bedroom. After that, Enid wanted to start on the art complex, but good sense prevailed. She gave that one a miss. After all, it wasn't really Sal's fault she didn't have regular exhibitions of Jackson Pollock lookalikes.

'Harry, look at this!' A stout lady stands in front of whirls of angst.

'Eh, luv, know what tha' is?'

'Nowt on our farm,' dismisses the house-proud farmer's wife.

'Ah, but what about old Jethro's?' They double up with laughter.

This private joke was not enough to sustain an exhibition.

Paul/Paula was a dear and Enid relied on her companionship more than she realised. Nevertheless, there was an area of friction between them. Paula would seek Enid's advice on a whole series of female actions, from blowing one's nose to laughing appropriately. Enid knew she was the wrong person to ask. Marriage to Gerry, who never noticed and didn't care, at least with his English family, rather put a stop to titivating. What residual desire to capture her man which Enid had felt was soon replaced with a sense of the absurd for trying to look like some desirable fashion statement. Enid would listen to Gerry's tirades, like the time they were invited to a fund-raising dance for a local bird sanctuary.

'The bloody establishment is behind this. Thieves and turds – that's what they are, feathering their own nests.'

'I think "turds" is a bit strong, darling. It's only a charity trying to raise money for a bird sanctuary. Feathering dear little robins' nests, I would have thought. Do we go or not?'

'Not! They'll turf out all the locals who have shot there for years – then organise a posh shoot or two on an annual basis with the excuse they're just culling geese or whatever. Local kids who have learnt their poaching there for generations will suddenly be banned. Typical – one bloody law for the birds and no attempt to provide decent rural activities for ordinary kids. Just look at the fuss bloody Henry makes. You don't want to go, do you?'

'You're right – no, of course not.'

But she did, deep inside. She longed to float round in a beautiful ball gown, her face glowing with just enough make up to set off her natural good looks, and her hair softly cut and arranged to enhance her looks. She could feel the excitement rise, the feeling of another man's arms round her. But Gerry didn't want to go; that was that, multiplied by over thirty years.

No wonder Enid's confidence as a woman wasn't always good enough for Paula. However, what was really galling was the way Paula would consult her gay friends, who were queens to a man. That really hurt. Those camp, strapping big lads impersonating femininity were nothing more than a grotesque distortion of the subtle mannerisms learnt from a tender age. Paula had wanted to learn to cross her legs while sitting on a chair. After Enid had snorted that only shop girls sat like that, Paula had consulted the lads and now flaunted her new talent in front of Enid.

'Just look at that bulging calf muscle; it's a dead giveaway.'

'Edes, I've come to the sad conclusion that if I follow all your ideas on femininity I'll end up as dowdy as you.'

As a barb it was entirely accurate. Enid felt completely humiliated; more than that, she felt betrayed. It was true, but what Paula would never understand was that once Enid had wanted to be a desirable woman. Hadn't her parents been overjoyed when a Tanner invited her to be his wife? Hadn't they overlooked Gerry's chip on his shoulder and failed to notice that his values and interests lay outside the smug, privileged world he was born in? Rose, Enid's mother, for years would fantasise about her daughter's lifestyle. It was only when it became palpably obvious that Enid was left alone for months on end, with a small baby and little else, while Gerry did something 'confidential', that she realised her daughter's bed was not of roses but of cabbages just like everyone else's. You can't gossip about a son-in-law whose job is 'confidential'.

One evening, while Paula did her ironing – she was at that stage when she ironed everything – Enid watched her while sitting and staring, an activity that becomes increasingly popular with age.

'You know, Paula, your fag friends will never be able to help you discover the essence of femininity. That is what makes drag such a joke. It is the art of the impostor. No, the real thing is very different. It's not lipstick, high heels, elaborate curls or smooth hands. It's not a firm bust, trim waistline or soft skin. It's none of these things. I suppose it is an attitude of mind. Real women might look like that character in *Coronation Street* – what was her name? – Ena Marples…'

'You mean Ena Sharples. I had an aunt who looked just like her.' Paula had turned off the iron and was standing looking at Enid, hesitant, clumsy, gauche, with spread legs and awkward arms. Her face was a leathery mess of powder and make-up and a raw, ugly yearning to be something he wasn't and she wasn't.

'What does, deep down inside, being a woman mean to you, Paula?'

Paula gave a strangled noise and waved her arms around while muttering words like 'clean, deep down inside', followed by a coquettish flourish of the hands before adding 'glamorous'. As a wannabe, she had a long way to go. So Enid answered her own question instead.

'It's an instinct to succour, to cradle the dying man's head as he lies in the gutter. It's the instinct to give unstintingly. It's whiskers, varicose veins, arthritic joints and incontinence. It's to be ridiculed, pushed aside and forgotten at the same age as a man is at the peak of his success. That is being a woman. Now it's possible for clever, pushy women to be honorary men. They ride roughshod over – well, the rest of us. If you really want to join us, Paula, forget ironing your bloody smalls, forget putting on your lipstick every time the doorbell goes. Just practise what it means to succour. We give birth to more than just damp bundles. We are the barometers by which society measures compassion, patience, understanding. Only no one cares any more.'

Enid began to sob, hiding her head in her hands and mumbling, 'It's about being a fucking failure and no one thinks that is anything unusual.'

I was loyal, she told herself. Yes, that too is a female virtue. I stood by my second-rate, seedy civil servant or whatever he was officially. I told everybody that Gerry was right, privilege was wrong. 'Oh, no,' I'd say, 'Gerry thinks it's all wrong.'

A brave little face would look questioningly at whoever was listening and a brave little smile would radiate that face while Enid remembered Gerry hadn't left enough to pay the heating bill.

Reverie over, Enid burst out, 'Fuck it, look what you've done, Paul – I mean Paula, sorry. I was going to write to Vijaya about our trip. Vijaya, I might say hastily, is not a good role model, Paula. She's a bloody awful one.'

Enid snorted in very unladylike fashion on a piece of kitchen paper before shuffling off to the bathroom, where she locked herself in and let herself howl. Paula put it down to the menopause. She was years out, but then Paula herself had a long way to go. With luck, she would never get that far, never reach the deep waters of womanhood, where loyalty twisted and tortured every aspiration, till, like a limp rag, there was nothing left. Poor, poor Enid.

Howling over, Enid wiped her face. It looked no more blotchy than Paula's. Then, avoiding all further conversation, she made for the computer.

Dear Vijaya

At last! I would love to visit Bombay for about two weeks towards the end of March. I am coming with a young friend and would love to meet you all – Mumsi, Aunt Jamila, Rani and, of course, you and Ran.

The letter tried to steer a course between staying in a cheap hotel and being invited to stay in Vijaya's apartment. Enid couldn't visualise either, which made it even more difficult. Nor did she reveal anything about Paula – she felt that was all part of Paula's personal odyssey – but simply said she would be bringing a friend. There was a sinking feeling as she wrote. She had really hated Vijaya. This was pure exploitation, asking herself to stay, but then she did want to meet Mumsi.

Would Vijaya have her to stay, would Mumsi want to meet her?

The bonds were sold, the press was squared but the middle classes were still grumbling about the scones. It had been agreed that the twins would, for a tidy sum, bake the bloody things themselves. They came one Saturday to go over the finer points with their gran. No sooner had Sal's car disappeared from view than they turned on Enid.

'Gran, no hard feelings, like, but we never get a chance to shop like our friends who live in town do on Saturdays. You've been showing us how to make scones, like, for years. Could we? I mean just for a couple of hours, honest, we won't buy drugs or booze or have sex behind the supermarket. I mean, just for you we won't. But please, it would be really cool.'

'Not so much cool as bloody cold cheek if you ask me. Go on then, I'll seek retribution another time. Have you got enough money?'

Clutching an additional fiver each, the twins, giggling fit to burst, shot out of the door and weren't seen for another five hours. Enid looked at the recipe book, scales and flour. How she wished she was fourteen again.

Sophie and Beatrice, giggling harder than ever, returned just over five hours later clutching rather revolting and totally unsuitable little pieces of sequinned material which they insisted were all the rage.

'When on earth do you wear them?' asked an incredulous Enid.

'Clubbing; let your boobs hang out.' Beatrice wriggled provocatively.

'Have you ever popped yours out in public, Gran?'

'Sure,' lied Enid.

'You *what*?' Beatrice stopped wriggling.

'Of course not! The only time I ever saw naked breasts at your age was in the *National Geographic Magazine*. Apart from buying bits of unsuitable flimsy, what else have you been doing?'

This question brought a further bout of hysterical laughter. Sophie looked like a lobster while Beatrice had her mouth shut but seemed to be blowing like a whale.

'Drink, sex or booze?' asked Enid, getting a little irritated by this display of adolescent behaviour.

There is a curious notion that time, if not a healer, at least dulls the deed. It was weeks later, just before Enid left for India and all the scone paraphernalia had been taken over to Sal's and deposited on the tumble dryer, which was the only surface available, that Beatrice sidled up.

'Gran, you know the other week – we did topless dancing...' there was a pause '...in Maggie's bedroom.'

'Did you? Good on you, Beatrice! I just wish I had done the same thing at your age.'

'You are funny, Gran.'

'Why, Bea?'

'You seem to have got old without doing anything you wanted to do, apart from Fack and all that.'

'Well, I didn't do topless dancing. You're right, Bea. Would you like to do proper topless dancing with tassels, if I can organise it?'

'Could you? Oh Gran, you're really cool. Most people at school have well-dressed grans who buy them expensive presents, have their hair done every week and go to Cyprus on holiday. You are so unpredictable. Shacking up with some Indian guru one moment, then making bad-tempered scones – y'know what I mean. No one at school has a posh great-uncle in prison for trying to murder a rambler, either. We're all oiks. That's why topless dancing is such fun. It's really oiky.' Beatrice paused. 'Gran, how do the tassels work?'

'You stick them over your nipples, then wriggle so that they swing together.'

'Cor! You think you can arrange it?'

'That's what grannies are for, my love.'

The enormity left Beatrice speechless.

But before topless dancing became an issue, Paula went home to make an uneasy peace with her family. As the exceptionally clever, talented, member of her family and the first to get a scholarship to Oxford, her parents regarded his compulsion to become a girl as all part of this nonsense of going to university and 'getting ideas'. Their dream boy had turned his back on chapel and everything decent. What were they going to tell the neighbours? Paul had bought them books which they hid. He even borrowed a video which they watched in silence. His father's only comment was, 'Let's have a cup o' tea, Mother.' Next day, when his father was at work – council refuse, and proud of it – Paul's mother turned on him.

'How can you do this to him? It's worse than having you in prison. Can't you see it's dirty, disgusting? Can't you just be a homosexual, quietly, when you're not here? Everyone is these days. That Simpson boy is, and your cousin Ben…mind you, I blame his parents, far too easy-going. But we brought you up decent to believe in the Lord, the royal family and your marriage vows. What kind of vows are those going to be? I suppose you are going to be injected with… oh, I don't know! But don't expect your father and me to welcome Dolly the sheep as our grandchild.'

Paula had told her parents about India. They listened with the same resignation and probably the same sad prejudice as they did everything else to do with their son. He would always be their son. Their sour disparagement reduced India to elephants and curry.

'Why, when he had a good job, did he go haring off to India?' There was no answer, not one they could share. As always, after a visit, Paula felt absolutely wretched.

Paula arrived home with Enid much in need of TLC and a stiff whisky.

She sat astride the edge of the sofa, quite elegantly, and ran her hand through her well-groomed hairdo.

'Why is it thought of as disgusting, Edes? I can see it might be embarrassing with the neighbours. God knows, I've had my moments as a journalist, but I've always been able to explain. My parents just don't want to know. They see the whole wilful desire of a transsexual as some kind of perversion. It's not about fucking, bonking, screwing or any other sexual practice; it's about body image. I want to be a woman. What's more, I'm prepared to kill myself if I can't be a woman.'

'None of that, Paula. I expect your parents might come round – give them a while. Meanwhile, I've got some news for you.'

Paula was so involved in her chrysalis stage that 'news' meant news about herself. Enid sarcastically brought her to heel by waving a letter from India – only the reply hadn't come from India. It had come from California.

'I warned you, Paula. We could be letting ourselves in for anything. Listen to this:

Dear Enid

Where have you been? Surely you must have read that I'm in Hollywood. It was in all the papers. I have signed a very prestigious contract to play the part of a beggar girl who becomes president and marries her psychiatrist, who is Michael Douglas. I shan't tell you the plot but it is very beautiful.

Ran and Rani are here and we have a house on Malibu Beach. I have spoken to Mumsi and she will give you an audience if you are in Bombay.

'*An audience*! My dead husband's mistress will give me an audience! Who the fuck does she think she is?'

'Edes, it sounds rather exciting, I think. Does the letter mention anywhere to stay?'

'Not exactly, but she's given me Aunt Jamila's address. I'm going to write to her next. Paula, come on, girl – let's make this a cat among the pigeons holiday.' So saying, Enid grasped Paula by the arm and swung her round.

The reply from Aunt Jamila arrived while Paula was having her plumbing altered. Enid marched excitedly up to Paula's bed – in a side ward, since she was a statistical freak in prurient terms and the NHS are squeamish about such matters. When Enid arrived, there were a couple of queens sitting on her bed painting their fingernails. Posy was the owner of a club in Leeds and another in Newcastle. He wore expensive suits to see his bank manager and was as shrewd as they come. Amber was a dancer in his club. He had trained with the Royal Ballet but bailed out after years of *Swan Lake* and *Nutcracker*. Amber had an expensive habit – coke – which made him bad-tempered and paranoid, as well as doing a power of damage to his nostrils.

Enid couldn't help just a tinge of jealousy creeping over her smile when she remembered that it was these clowns Paula turned to when her skills as a woman were found wanting. But now was not the time to make it an issue.

'Hi girls, how's the patient?'

'Silent! It's bliss. No querulous moans.' Posy waved her fingernails.

'Edes, darling, you don't want another lodger, do you? Paula is so ridiculously understood by you and you're taking her to India – no more room in the bag?'

'Amber, I have a favour, since you're here.' Enid explained how her granddaughters and some school friends wanted to learn topless dancing with tassels. Could Amber find anyone who could teach them?

'Well, I sure as hell can't, honey, but let me think.' The seed had been planted.

The queens tiptupped away into the twilight, leaving Enid alone to read her letter from Aunt Jamila. It was by far the most sensible letter she had received from that family.

Dear Enid

How lovely! I would be honoured if you and your friend stayed with me during your visit in Mumbai. I know every charity in town and run most of them myself. My sister, Savita, leads a very quiet life but I know she will want to see you. Your late husband was quite a character. Let me know when you will arrive.

'Isn't that wonderful news? I can now book our flight.' There was a whispered affirmative.

Paula's confidence soared with her new guise. It was as if her penis alone had been the impediment. She walked with an elegant confidence, bag slipped over her arm and not waved around like some ammunition carrier. They were busy weeks and the only undercurrent of unhappiness was that her parents didn't want to know. It added pathos to the frenetic round of parties and farewells and 'hellos' to Paul and Paula. Her boss, recognising a damn good journalist, had done everything possible to welcome her back, knowing full well that someone as good as Paula was bound to break into the big time. What was most touching was the quiet kindness showed by some of the farmers Paula had worked with. Not just cakes, flowers and get-well cards, but phone calls and visits while she was in hospital from rough-handed, big-booted farmers, at home in the lambing pens but not in a hospital ward. Paula's parents didn't visit her or send a card.

The first thing Paula did was have her hair done.

'Y'know,' Beryl confided, tucking a towel round Paula's neck, 'some of them, the older ones that is, have it done just before... y'know.'

'They die?'

'Spooky, isn't it?' Beryl massaged Paula's scalp.

'I think it's rather beautiful.'

'Mind you, it cheers up the patients – makes them feel human again. I'm not allowed to ask, of course, but you hear such funny things.'

'I've just had my penis chopped off. I want to be a girl.'

'Yer what?' So Paula repeated herself.

'What posters will you now pin on your wall?' It was a good question.

Paula thought she had covered everything in her obsession to become a girl, but Beryl's question totally flummoxed her.

'Who do you suggest?'

'Well, at your age you can't beat Cliff Richard.' Beryl started blow-drying.

My first snub! How gorgeous! thought Paula.

Paula was no sooner in her own bed than she wanted Enid to have a tiny peep. She pulled back her bedclothes and revealed a very bruised, red, scarred undercarriage.

'Are the labia going to be all right?'

'What's "all right" when it's at home? For God's sake, pull down your nightie and start behaving like the woman you are and not the freak you are in danger of becoming.'

That did it. All the tears of rejection, particularly from her parents, coursed down Paula's face. She had to reapply her make-up before the boys arrived. They, too, were given a peep and were less censorious than Enid. Indeed, an hour later they were still in full spate about the merits of different private parts. The only other people to see the results – but ssh! Enid mustn't know – were the twins, who were enthralled and asked really down-to-earth questions like:

'What happens if you wobble your clitoris?'

'If they injected a baby into your false womb, would it grow?'

Sophie tried the same question on her civics teacher, Mrs Hemmings. Civics was on the national curriculum, so a heady dose of sexual morality was added to make the boring pill of the Lord Chancellor's Woolsack more appealing.

Mrs Hemmings paused for barely a moment.

'What an interesting question. I think Professor Winston is the man to consult. Find his website, Sophie, and see if you can get an answer. Now, back to the House of Lords; can anyone say what function it has?'

'There's some old goat that didn't want the age of gay sex reduced to sixteen,' said a pupil called Eric, rolling his eyes at this petty discrimination.

'And they are a cruel lot of bastards, supporting fox-hunting.'

'Someone called Black Rod walks backwards once a year. Sums up the bloody place, doesn't it, miss?'

A bell shrilled loudly, waking most of the class, who didn't know what the House of Lords was and certainly didn't care. 'Miss' was a decent sort who let one sleep, draw, dream, eat sweets – so long as they didn't have paper wrappers.

'For homework, I want you to write the moral arguments for and against transsexual women having babies.'

When that reached the local paper, the shit didn't half hit the fan.

'You see, Gran, the trouble is, miserable mediocrity.'

'Like your mother's bloody art complex.'

'That's not fair. You know Mum would love to have really wacky exhibitions. It's the locals, Gran, you don't know the 'alf of it. I really tried for civics homework, so did several others. Then along come all these wankers and complain Mrs Hemmings had overstepped the mark. Same with Shakespeare; our books have all the juicy bits removed, but you only have to look it up on the Net and there it is. Do you think adults have double standards, Gran?'

'Yes, my love, but not just double. They have multiple standards and we each have to choose our own. But Sophie, don't let that miserable mediocrity catch you; that is a really shitty standard.'

Sophie gave her gran a rare hug. Grans might be wrinkly and slightly batty – no, very batty – but on the whole they were easier than mums and a darn sight more interesting than teachers. Her gran was, anyway. Sophie couldn't think of another gran who lived with a transsexual and was about to hop it to India to meet her husband's mistress.

Enid had neglected her old friend, Dolly, during Paula's perpetual ongoing drama of becoming a woman. Now she wanted this old friend to herself for what would probably be their last evening together. For Dolly was getting worse. Dolly was to be driven over for supper. Paula was starting to gallivant again and Enid could plan a lovely evening just for herself and Dolly.

'I think of you as my "through thick and thin" friend, Dolly. How are you?'

Dolly looked a mess. Her hair, always so beautifully coiffured, was straggling round her face, which was a powdery mess with some lipstick badly drawn across her lips. The trousers no longer fitted and were covered with stains, as was her jersey.

The two friends embraced warmly – that is what friendship is all about, embracing an unlovely mess when the magic has gone – and walked with their arms round each other to the warmth of the bungalow.

'They are hiding under my bed. I know they are.'

'I wish I could help, Dolly. I really do.'

They drank a glass of wine ('Please don't let her drink any wine, it's not good for her'), and Enid listened to Dolly's querulous laments.

'Those names, they are impossible to remember. But I met some charming Americans. What were they called, Enid? It's terrible, I can't remember a thing. Anyway, they were charming. Enid, what's happened to me? I don't even know these people.'

Suddenly, as if scooping something out of the ether, Dolly snapped her fingers.

'Mavis and Dwight Dewhurst! I met them on that Greek cruise, but I couldn't go again. They might get at me for not remembering.' Dolly paused. They sat quietly and a moment of grace blessed them both.

'Another glass?'

'Better not, they'll get cross. I get so tired and muddled.'

'Come on, you are my guinea pig! One of those telly chefs – he assured me it was foolproof.'

The chef had bunged his mess into a hot oven for forty minutes. But when is hot actually *hot*? And not too hot, or not hot enough? Enid removed something resembling Mount Etna in a tetchy mood. She unearthed enough unburnt dish to serve Dolly and gave herself part of the lava flow with a large wodge of vegetables.

Dolly rambled on. She was concerned. Her son wanted her to come out to Canada and live with him and his wife. She loved him dearly, but the idea of uprooting herself, leaving her friends... She was too old to start a new life. Anyway, they wouldn't let her. Enid listened with great concern and sympathy. Dolly had been her brick ever since Gerry died. She had been her confidante. When bricks are removed, buildings fall down. Dolly was suffering from dementia.

'Please don't go. I would miss you horribly. Old age is pretty good hell, isn't it? I mean, it's not the aches and pains – it's the being shoved aside.'

They widened the brief. It wasn't just the dilemma of whether to move or not but the whole bloody business of growing old and being hounded by unknown people. Talking to Dolly was a three steps forward, one step back performance.

'I've got the whiskers under control; my teeth don't protrude as black Dracula fangs; bladder and bowels, fingers crossed, do roughly what they are told. My figure is an unlovely rectangle which needs about ten minutes in the morning to get going. Where are we going, Dolly?'

'It's not a question of where we are going. Other people are taking over, that's the problem. I've become a problem – me, his mother, has become a problem.' Dolly was not the crying type. She sat in fierce, angry silence.

'Rubbish! You of all people. Dolly, you're one of my icons. Don't let them do anything, not until I've come back from India.' The words were banal; Enid was frightened. They said their farewells with tenderness, as if their ways were about to part.

Enid cried while clearing the table and doing the washing-up. What was going to happen to them all? Not a ghastly home – no, not that. It had taken her years to reconcile the shrivelling of mind and body as it was. All that business with Fack was denial of a kind. For a while Enid was by his side, in his bed and washing his loincloth – till the truth dawned and she realised that everything she did he could find in Yellow Pages. And now Dolly, as fierce and loyal a friend as any widow could find, was being bullied to up sticks, cross the Atlantic like some pitiable immigrant and, at seventy, put down roots.

'Not Dolly, please. She's needed here.'

Enid wondered if there were nice counsellors who listened to the confused unhappiness of aging people who don't want to be uprooted. Were there utopian communities for the elderly, driven by their children's insensitivity?

'We can put you in Heidi's room. You can have your own furniture and it might be possible to add another bathroom. I'm sure we can work out the finances somehow.'

Heidi's room is slightly smaller than the average prison cell. The furniture will all be sold to pay for the bathroom and the grandchildren will have formed a pop group called 'The Devil's Own', the only place to practise being the new bathroom.

'As I see it,' said Enid banging several saucepans, 'we want to live until we feel, by dint of poor health or old age, that we want to die. But there's this dreadful no-man's-land where we are kept clean and comfortable while neither alive nor dead. If it happened to chickens it would cause an outcry.'

Enid thought back to when she did that stint for a charity working with old people, and replaced the customary mystery tour with a visit to a ritzy night club to see the Chippendales. Their faces were a picture and several died quite cheerfully soon afterwards.

Twelve

It wasn't speculation about death, apart from the flight and the usual 'would anyone miss me if I died?' but speculation about India. Enid suggested she used the rent money for the flight and Paula fluttered her newly fluttering arms and muttered appreciation.

They both went on separate shopping sprees. Enid got as far as dear old Harrogate, while Paula went all the way to Leeds. Paula returned looking quite magnificent and very theatrical while Enid looked slightly – all right, *very* – different. She had shopped on her own, clutching a modest amount of money and, having searched round Marks and Spencers, decided on charity shops. Somehow it fitted with Aunt Jamila and her charities. If well-washed but not very well-fitting clothes are what you want, charity shops are for you. Enid bought several flowing skirts and cotton blouses – then, having counted the change, she sidled into M and S again for a breather and cup of coffee. Never has a cup of coffee stirred such dilemmas. It had Enid wondering, Should I or shouldn't I? all the way to a beautiful trouser suit in russet reds. She felt a million dollars in it and immediately wished she hadn't bought all those dreary skirts and blouses.

There was one incident before they left which convinced Enid that considerable distance needs to be put between grandmothers and their grandsons.

Roger, growing fast, was large with a penetrating voice. He had the good grace to keep out of his grandmother's way but just occasionally he did something. As Enid carried her final batch of scones into the art complex, her mind being among the torrid slums of Bombay, Roger yelled with peremptory vigour, 'Hands up!'

Up, up and up went the scones. It was a race between hands and scones – and another race between Roger, running for his life, and his grandmother shrieking un-grandmotherly abuse after him while hurling the scone tray like a Frisbee at his departing backside.

Roger was at that age when he would justify everything.

'She shouldn't be so stupid. Everyone knows "Hands up" is just a joke.' Roger stared at his trainers which he kept scuffing on the carpet.

'Anyway, I was just saying goodbye, like...and good riddance,' he muttered.

'What's that?' asked his father, in those tones reserved for recalcitrant children.

'The scones are bloody revolting, anyway.'

'That's because you only get the stale ones.' Enid was trying to be helpful.

'Then why make bloody stale scones?'

'You mustn't talk to your grandmother like that.'

'Like what?'

'You know perfectly well.' Douglas was tired and exasperated with his son.

'Sorry, Gran, maybe you should find a sense of humour.'

Before Douglas and Enid could stop him, the coltish figure was off. He took with him the aura of wilful childish behaviour. That was one thing Enid would ban in her Utopia – children.

With Roger, no doubt planning his next evil deed, out of sight; with Sal teaching a group how to paint flowers – hyacinths; and the girls busy doing homework, Douglas was relieved and inclined to give his mother-in-law a drink.

'Give the fire a kick while I get us both a whisky.'

'At least I don't have to go to any nativity play, Douglas. The last one had dear little Roger as a wise man. I don't think any of your children are cut out to be biblical characters.'

'That's the point, Enid.' Douglas swirled the drink round his glass and stared into its amber depths.

'One starts with such hopes and high ideals,' he said. He still didn't look at Enid.

She looked at him. She liked Douglas and worried when he was like this.

'Something wrong?'

'I just wish I was going to India with you, that's all.'

Later, Enid helped Sal with the washing-up. That at least delighted the children.

'Are you ready for India? You'll need plenty of pills for gippy tums. I'm green with envy. Why can't I go to India?'

'Sal, if I had the money, so you would. But I need to go. The more I think about Mumsi and that money, the more I need to know that I was important too. I know it's silly at my age, but it is because I'm this age that I want to get everything in perspective. What if I was just a glorified washing machine?'

'And me, just plain Jane,' added Sal sourly.

'Darling, you're not yet forty and you look exhausted. It's that damn art complex.'

'Not exactly, Ma. It's now at the time when aspirations and reality meet head-on; they don't have very much to say to each other. I look at the twins, who are terrifyingly worldly-wise, waggling their pert little bums and talking about sex – what do they know?'

'What about Douglas?'

'What about him?' repeated Sal savagely.

Not a very happy departure.

The great day arrived. Paula took a reasonably sized suitcase and a vast amount of hand luggage, which she assured Enid was just for her face. Enid had borrowed a case and bought a cheap bag to sling over her shoulder.

'Edes, I just can't wait.' Paula squeezed her hand.

Nor did they have to. Even Air India took off on time. The two women tucked their legs at awkward angles. Paula wailed that she was sure she was getting an embolism but cheered up when a delicious curry arrived. She read one of Martin Amis's books and chortled accordingly. Enid spent the flight wondering about the enormity of what she had done and mouthed conversations with an imaginary Mumsi. Already she wished she had bought something more glamorous than the Mind charity shop second-hand skirts.

All the same, she told herself, it's not clothes that matter. It's what's inside them, adding, that is just the kind of tripe I used to say to Gerry when we were first married.

Arriving anywhere after an economy flight requires a fist fight to find one's limbs again.

'Excuse me, I think that is my leg. I have an extra arm here if you'd like that.' Enid said this jokingly. Even so, several heads turned. They walked down the steps to the warm embrace of an early Bombay morning. Only it wasn't Bombay – only the English and their hangers-on use that word; the locals reckoned they lived in Mumbai. Already there was a foreignness about the air, a faint smell of spice and damp nappies; even the airport buildings had an aura of mystery after hours cooped up with arms and legs bent and twisted out of recognition.

Like all good women the world over, the first thing Paula and Enid did on landing was visit the Ladies. They opened the door to find a young woman lying fast asleep on the floor. She wore a shabby green sari fringed in red, several bangles rested on her arm and her bare feet were calloused from lack of shoes. She didn't stir. They stepped over her, used the lavatories and washed their hands, but as they were about to leave she sleepily rose to her feet and cupped a hand out – perhaps for payment. How were they to know?

'I don't know how much, do you?' hissed Enid.

'Do you think she has a home somewhere else, or is this it?' whispered Paula.

Enid found a handful of Indian money; the sleepy-eyed girl darted a greedy look before continuing a more demure gaze.

'Give her a couple of rupees. She looks as if she could do with another sari.'

'You did *what*?' said Aunt Jamila later on, shaking with laughter. 'That girl will soon get her dowry if she meets many people like you two!'

A driver met them bearing a card with the word 'Enid' written on it and whisked them away in an elderly but comfortable car which had the feel of the fifties about it. The whisk became a crawl, as a melancholy cow with droopy ears, staring ribs and judgmental eyes insisted on walking in front of the vehicle like an official mourner at an East End gangster's funeral. First impressions jumbled in kaleidoscopic frenzy. Emaciated men pulling rickshaws with fat slug-like men in the seat. There were vast bundles perched on people's heads, buses belching black exhaust, ancient cars abandoned all attempt to stick to the rules of the road, potholes themselves making it impossible to do so. And children...a copulation frenzy must have overcome the citizens of Mumbai.

Not if Aunt Jamila had her way. Over a delicious meal she explained the need for family planning and her role and influence in running centres for primary health care.

'It was about a film on family planning that Gerry met Savita. She was making the film for free; only the very prestigious are asked to make it for free.'

Enid couldn't think of anything to say. It was as if she had no role in this bittersweet drama. Then why had she come all this way?

'How is your sister?'

'Savita? She is still very beautiful. I don't think being beautiful is always a blessing, do you, Enid?'

'Maybe. I've come here to find out,' retorted Enid.

Aunt Jamila didn't choose to hear Enid's reply. She had turned her attention to Paula.

Having worked out that Paula was no relation of Enid's, Aunt Jamila had winkled out that she was a journalist. Any journalist was fair game for Aunt Jamila and she organised for the two women to visit the projects in Mumbai that provided primary through to tertiary care and were financed by funds raised by Aunt Jamila. Enid couldn't help feeling that Paula was taking over as honoured guest and, as usual, she was playing second fiddle.

Second fiddle Rose, that's me, she thought with humour.

Aunt Jamila lived in a large, ginger-coloured rambling villa above the sea. Tall palm trees stood guard while spiky green plants grew exuberantly. Orange, blue and yellow flowers sprouted like unruly soldiers in what had been planted as straight lines, but they had long since decided that straight lines were not for them. Enid was frightened of snakes. There probably weren't any there, but Enid felt sure that every rustle meant a snake. Sometimes Enid and Paula met silent men leaning on their forks, their huge melancholy eyes following the two women.

'Have you ever seen them do any gardening?'

'They probably do it while we're asleep,' suggested Enid, who felt a sad melancholy which suggested to her that most of life took place while she was asleep.

In the villa there were more silent men who pounded on underwear to give them the washing of a lifetime, who left nothing untouched in their bedrooms and even lined up loose change in some fanatical order – a symbol of wealth they would never achieve. What they made of Paula's pills, potions and creams was never revealed. As Paula said, very simply, 'I'm a woman. Do you realise what that means?'

It made Enid realise that no, she probably never had. She felt goaded into approaching Aunt Jamila again. After all, wasn't that the reason they were here?

'I really do want to meet Savita, Aunt Jamila. I feel it is very important that we meet.'

'Are you the physical, thumping type? Savita watches *Dallas* – too much if you ask me. She is worried you could be a violent type. Savita doesn't like violent types.'

'What a relief; nor do I. I didn't watch much *Dallas*. It was so unreal. I just want to know what kind of woman I shared my husband with. That is what I've come to India for.'

'A goddess in her day, one of the most beautiful women in India.'

Aunt Jamila's description was tinged with what might have been derision. She, too, had an agenda with the beautiful Savita.

But first the poor. What tulips are to Amsterdam, the poor are to India. The car lurched over potholes, round a dead cow which someone was hauling off – no doubt to cut up and convert into wealth of some kind or other. The street was now more or less a pedestrian thoroughfare, with a throbbing mass of people weaving intricate patterns in their desire to get from one place to another. The driver stopped, waved a stick and opened the door. At once some kids appeared, their dirty little fingers shoved under Enid and Paula's inexperienced noses. Other fingers reached out to touch their clothes. It was an eerie experience. Aunt Jamila's years of experience cut a swathe through the band of eager hands and the two women gratefully followed in her wake.

The Women's Health and Happiness Clinic was held in a

large concrete shed. In the waiting room were about fifty mothers who between them had given birth apparently to hundreds of squirming babies. Older children stood with that posture seen the world over, which is a combination of having worms and sticking out an empty stomach. The walls were covered with advertisements for basic hygiene. There were no words. They were designed for the illiterate.

'Notice, not a Nestlé bottle-feed advertisement to be seen.' Aunt Jamila swept a hand round the waiting room. 'We give those mothers who can't feed their babies special counselling and only then show them how to use a bottle-feed correctly. It's almost impossible, since they don't have access to clean water.'

'How long do they have to wait here?' asked Enid, mildly overwhelmed by the sheer number of women and children.

'Waiting is something these mothers know all about. Ignorance makes people wait a long time. India is still waiting. While these mothers wait, they learn, see; they have these mothers just like themselves, who can now teach basic baby care.'

Sure enough, amid the mass of babies, mothers and slightly older children were two women clutching relatively chubby babies which they were bathing.

'How do they get enough hot water to bath a baby?' asked Paula.

'We encourage them to come here. Our water is clean and if there are any problems our nurse can see the baby. While they wait and learn, these women will explain about birth control. Not a popular subject. No one can afford more food just because they have fewer children. It doesn't add up.'

They left the waiting area and walked straight into a small room containing a woman lying with her legs in stirrups and about another six women peering up her vulva. Taking not the slightest notice of the woman in question, Aunt Jamila continued, 'Here we can take swabs and check on women's internal health. We have students helping us.' Paula had sidled near the prostrate lady and was having a long look at the part Enid was trying to avoid looking at.

Later, Paula was to observe, 'I suppose I can't expect everything, but quite honestly there were several discrepancies. Her labia were considerably smaller.'

'Don't worry,' said Enid, 'I expect I'll say the same thing when I see the ravishing Savita. Only the discrepancies will be easier to see.'

Paula started to get quite excited by her visit to the health clinics. Her pencil and pad came out, she sidled up to Aunt Jamila and soon, with the hard to refute comment, 'You wouldn't be interested,' would leave Enid gazing out to sea while she dived into the crowded slums of Mumbai to visit schools, clinics and – don't tell Enid – even brothels. Of course, 'Don't tell Enid' didn't last long and Enid heard all about Paula's escapades. She heard it with a heavy heart. It was – once again – the slight she could expect from being a widow with no profession. As much as she rationalised the fate of women of her age and standing, she still found herself as enraged as she had been on the day she found her not very exciting husband had cultivated a mistress and child. Paula's excursions in the bowels of Mumbai just rubbed it in.

Aunt Jamila finally pinned down Savita by yelling at great length down the telephone. Savita had found it necessary to consult her astrologer, who dictated that the meeting could last no longer than an hour and must take place at ten thirty at night.

This time it was Enid who could explain to Paula that she wasn't needed. The snub was wasted, as Paula immediately arranged to go to a 'club' – whatever that meant. It transpired that Paul had run to ground some transsexual Indians who played a significant part in several religious rites. Armed with her journalist's notebook, Paula wanted to know all.

'Those boy-girls are spoilt rotten. They do too much film work. It isn't good,' was Aunt Jamila's opinion. Aunt Jamila had an opinion about everything.

Enid changed into her one glamorous outfit. She dabbed some lipstick and noticed that her heart was bumping impertinently hard. She practised walking in the mirror. How had she allowed herself to develop a waddle? It was too late, but she rather wished she had bought a gift, just something.

The astrologer had requested that Enid came on her own. She sat in the back of Aunt Jamila's car and, heart still thumping with nerves, was driven through the night to Savita's villa. The villa was in an enclave surrounded by a high wall and an intimidating entrance, rather like a military command post in some out of the way part of the bush. A white pole was across the road and three men in gleaming uniforms rushed out at the sound of the car. One guard rather spoilt the professionalism of the trio by having his walkman still fixed in his ears. Enid's driver mentioned the magic name, the pole shot up and they drove into a sanitised world of the very rich – not a piece of paper, no dog shit, not a sign of a cow, sacred, holy or otherwise, just sumptuous villas mostly hidden by dense green foliage.

'And all paid for by that dimwit of a lover.' Aunt Jamila had thrown away that morsel by explaining that Savita had sunk the inheritance into developing a prestigious community protected from the filth and poverty of the poorer parts of Mumbai.

'But my sister can't escape my clutches. I make her pay for her privilege. My God, I do!'

The car turned into dense foliage and stopped at another military outpost. Only the driver must have known the guard. They met like old friends. At last Enid was free to leave the car. She thought of those photos of Mrs Whatsit inelegantly bent double with a tiara slipping over one ear and was thankful there was no one to see her shoving and pushing her bum to the edge of her seat before cautiously setting foot on the gravel.

Did Savita open the doors and warmly welcome Enid? No, she did not. She kept her waiting for twenty minutes in a small room designed just for that. It was a jewel of a room with exquisite paintings and an erotic piece of sculpture. There was nothing to read. Enid just sweated it out. The manservant reappeared and indicated for Enid to follow him. Enid by this time was on the edge of laughter. It was just too ludicrous. He flung open some doors and mumbled something Enid didn't catch.

She was standing at the far end of the room – ah, what a room! It was like some seedy Bollywood attempt at a Raja's anteroom, with a soft light falling – no, shimmering – softly behind her. The light had one of those nasty devices that Indian restaurants use to give the illusion of water falling over rocks. In this case it fell over a tiny woman with a face hacked out of the hardest stone you could find. It reminded Enid of those erotic drawings the Indians were always trying to get tourists to visit. She was beautiful, undoubtedly, with striking bones, huge eyes and magnificent lips. The lips spread into a smile. They knew how to smile with every nuance of a smile and for Enid they gave the smile of the victor. It played about her lips, but her eyes were dancing with jealousy. Not being a theatrical creature, Enid didn't know her role, which was to shut up and stay in awe till the end of this scene. Instead, Enid interrupted Savita with, 'After all this time! Isn't this fun?' It was many things but fun it was not.

'Ah, Enid, I feel I have known you all my life.' Two hands gathered in greeting. Savita bowed slightly.

'I suppose you do in a way.' Enid knew it was wrong, playing her trump card far too soon, but she was bursting to know – had been for several years, ever since that letter Vijaya had written soon after Gerry had died. 'Did you know Gerry was married?'

Silly, silly girl, or rather middle-aged woman. It caused the atmosphere to change at once. Savita's face broke into a snarl.

'I have consulted my lawyer. You have no grounds…' Savita was flustered by Enid's uncouth approach.

'Oh, Savita! I never imagined you would be so vulgar. I gather you own this development. Isn't that wonderful! No, I just wanted to meet you, out of friendship, really.' (Not true). 'We have a lot in common.' (Actually, nothing, if the truth be known.) 'You loved my Gerry all those years and raised your beautiful daughter, while I loved him too and raised my daughter.'

'Vijaya tells me she is married to a farmer. How terrible for you both. What a shame on Gerry's family name.' Savita was stalking up and down like Lady Macbeth. Obviously gentlemen farmers were quite outside her experience and were not two a rupee in India.

Savita threw open the doors to another Bollywood reception room. All that was missing was some elephants. It was then that Enid saw another figure reclined on sumptuous cushions, his podgy little eyes darting with merriment.

'Fack, you bastard! How the hell?' Enid was looking straight into the eyes of her Fack. The bastard! He would, he just jolly well would! He hadn't changed a bit – slightly cleaner, perhaps, but that was all.

'Hey, Enid!'

Now was the time for Enid to get really jealous and flash her eyes and lash her tongue. But she couldn't; she was just so thrilled to see the old rascal.

'Fack, you old devil! How are you?'

'Do you know, Enid, so much happier for seeing you.'

To think she had played his handmaiden while longing for sexual recognition! She had got as far as his bed, mended his worn shorts, washed the sheet wound round his waist, bought his toothbrush, appeared in the local press…but all she really wanted was a damned good fuck. And here he was lolling in Savita's villa. He would be, wouldn't he? It was humiliating, though. Even Enid could see that. It was typical too. Of course he knew about Savita. Enid had told him, just as one tells children fairy tales. How does a penniless fakir transmigrate like a soul from Leicester to Mumbai? Of course, she might have guessed it! He probably whipped the address out of her address book and the rest was history. Probably been fucking this Indian whore like holy shit ever since, though that wasn't his style – or rather, hadn't been with Enid, much to her chagrin.

'How the hell did you end up here?'

'With ease, Enid. It is the feast of Kumbh Mela, I couldn't miss it. Such fun, such stories and so much to be learnt. Once part of a family, always part of a family – that is what I say.'

Savita's smile added contempt as she watched what she thought of as the helpless worn-out woman struggle to find a dignity that simply wasn't there. Enid was just some white maggot, one of the British. They were all white maggots; hadn't her Gerry poured contempt and ridicule on the British?

'I can do things you can't, Enid, because I have money. My Gerry knew that I would make all that money work, but you? Buy more cows for that farmer son-in-law? We Indians are more sophisticated. Maybe Fack will start an ashram chain of hotels after the Kumbh Mela. Meanwhile, he looks good, huh?'

'Gerry's inheritance went to you, because I imagine he thought you would spend it on helping the poor. He was a great idealist, as you know.' It was a knee-jerk reaction. Enid could almost see how ridiculous she must seem to them both, standing there, dumpy and old in front of this beautiful, frightful, elegant woman while in the background lolled the man she liked to think of as her lover – even though…not very often…not enough.

'Helping the poor! Where's the money in helping the poor?' This was said with head held high and eyes flashing malice.

By now it looked like a set for an opera, complete with heaving bosoms and flared nostrils. Savita, a little plump it must be said, stood centre left waving her arms like a downtown policeman during the rush hour. Enid's eyes never left Fack, much to the irritation of Savita, while the roly-poly fakir, his face wreathed in smiles, lay back on his cushions enjoying every minute.

'All the same, I'm glad I was able to give Vijaya her dowry holiday. It meant a lot to me. How is she, by the way?' There was a tragic simplicity in Enid's voice. Perhaps she was becoming an actress after all.

'Making lots of money in Hollywood. She is very successful and not married to a farmer.'

'You know, Savita, I realise that you are a stunningly beautiful actress and I fully appreciate my husband falling head over heels…'

'He never fell head over heels, never, that is a lie!'

'May I sit down? This room is very elegant but there don't seem to be any chairs. I'm not very good at sinking into cushions.'

'You were, Enid, very good. Goodness me, do you remember how we used to laugh when I tried to Indianise you?' The bastard spoke out with a chuckle. Enid found herself falling for his charm all over again. Perhaps he was here to protect her. He would tell her at some point when they were alone how ghastly Savita was. Fack was a tremendous social snob, as only a rich Indian who had hunted with the Quorn and sent his sons to Eton could be.

'Come and sit beside me, Enid, just like you did in that B and B in Ripon.'

'I can't, Fack – not in front of this famous actress.' Here Enid flung her arm round the room. 'Don't you see, it's all wrong! I'm just out of my depth.' Enid began sobbing quietly, but still with dignity.

'This is where I give audiences. Some people cry at my beauty. I don't think you are crying for that. Perhaps you would be more comfortable in my private boudoir.' Even Savita looked mildly put out by the way things had turned out.

As Savita led them through yet another door, Fack put out a hand and touched Enid, who flinched like a virgin. 'It's all rubbish, really, she just wants to impress you,' he said.

Savita did some deep breathing and her eyes turned blacker than ever. Obviously the astrologer hadn't anticipated this turn of events. She opened a further door leading into yet another room. There were couches covered in sumptuous rich colours and huge cushions and chairs that looked like thrones – the lavatorial variety. Enid at once recovered her sense of humour, thanks to Fack's touch, and she found a throne and cautiously sat down, mentally noting she must keep her pants on. For long afterwards she wished she had lowered her trousers and presented a bare bum. It would have been the ultimate snub. She was sure Fack wouldn't have turned a hair. Indeed, he might even have giggled.

'Figuratively speaking, of course, Gerry had no doubt found himself head over heels.' Somehow Enid felt the need to make a mental dent in this surreal social nightmare she found herself experiencing.

Savita flashed a smile, still bright, still beautiful, but essentially the smile of an old woman fighting her last battle. She lay seductively opposite Fack on a couch covered in zebra skin. Weren't they illegal?

'My Gerry was my love, my hero. Ours was a real romance. I came from a modest family. He encouraged me with my acting. I was brilliant. I made a fortune. What have you ever done, Enid?'

'I've always kept our modest home spotlessly clean.' (Not true). 'Of course, now that Gerry is dead I help Sal. I make scones, a little like naan bread, really.'

Savita's reptilian features searched Enid's with complete disdain. Enid, well aware of the tack she was taking, smiled back blandly.

'We have servants to do all that.' Savita waved her arm to cover all the maintenance roles that Enid apparently did.

'You see, Savita, Gerry and I were modest people. We were idealists.'

'Ah, like my unmarried sister! Gerry and I were lovers, he lavished me with gifts, money.'

'Well, they always say you have to pay for a fancy lady. I have no quarrel with you, Savita. How could I? You are magnificent – but tell me, what did you talk about when you were just together?'

'Me, we talked about me. Did he ever talk about you?'

'No, there is nothing to say, as you can see. We talked about saving the world, especially India. We talked about the best policies to provide family planning, clean water, decent housing and health. He flew round the world concerning himself with these issues.'

'Yes, I see. How boring! But then, with my talent, he could forget all those dreary things, you know. When you are at the top, Enid, you see things differently.'

Savita had sunk down into the zebra's skin as if she was a parasite, while Enid sat upright on the loo, quite imposing. Savita was busy replaying her role as the siren in Gerry's life. She lay back languorously and sighed. But the astronomer had been adamant and time was running out. Savita rose to her feet and made a farewell speech about her heartfelt love for Gerry and how beautiful it was that his humble old bag of a wife had made the pilgrimage to meet her. Enid retaliated, erect and remembering all the nonsense from finishing school about where to put one's feet, clear annunciation and projecting the voice. Her theme was slightly different. She was so delighted that Gerry had just some common, self-centred trollop for a mistress, interested in money and more money. If building a prison for the very rich, in order to become even more rich, was what Savita regarded as a successful relationship... and here poor old Enid got rather muddled; however, she ploughed on to the end and felt so relieved she even pecked Savita's cheek as she took her leave. To her astonishment, Fack followed her out. He stood by the car and took both her hands in his. Bloody Indians – it's such a beguiling act!

'This is India. We are both foreigners in a way. That is why I listened and understand what you said.'

Bastard! she thought.

Enid didn't turn into a pumpkin, white mouse or any other apparition as the clock turned, nor did Savita, but the stars were shocked into quite interesting predictions. Enid could lie still that night and feel that her breasts were as good as Savita's, her nose, mouth and private parts were every bit as desirable as that blowsy, venomous cow's. What's more, if care and concern count for anything, she'd rather have cleaned lavatories all her life than build that spooky enclave determined to keep out the poor.

'How did it go?' asked Paula, dying to find out.

'You've got far too much make-up on for just the morning.'

'Oh God, I forgot to remove it last night. I was very late home.'

'Paula, don't! It's one thing to prance around with the "girls" back home but quite another to do the same thing here.'

'They wanted to see what the operation does.'

'You didn't!' Enid looked aghast.

'I want to set up a trust so, funds permitting, at least one of those kids every year can become a woman.'

'But you've heard Aunt Jamila. Being a single woman without family is disaster here.'

'Look Enid, those kids would prefer to be women, disaster and all, than rub their cocks against tourists the rest of their lives. But, to change the subject, what happened?'

'She was repellent. She was everything Gerry despised, so I thought. What men will do for their cocks… I can't believe he loved her, I really can't. Guess who was there. Go on, guess.'

'I don't know – her latest lover?'

'I don't think so. It was Fack – well, he was there. He obviously got Savita to finance him – just to goad me, I suspect. I gather he's persuaded her to fund him for the Kumbh Mela. That's typical of Fack.'

'The what?'

'You know, the festival that comes round once in twelve years. Why is life all turned into a monstrous festival periodically? I don't know, or rather I do. Forget the heart and all that soppy business. It's the nitty-gritty that counts. Talking of nitty-gritty, Aunt Jamila wants us to see her home for the dying – when the nitty-gritty comes to a juddering halt.'

That afternoon Paula and Enid, in sprightly cotton dresses, one elegant and the other decidedly frumpy, with Aunt Jamila very much in command, arrived at a building that looked like a seedy bingo hall but had been a cinema till Aunt Jamila acquired it for her mission. At least it wasn't Christian, so there were no crosses, gentle Jesuses or other impedimenta to confuse the dying with mortal sin, guilt and that waiting room in the sky called purgatory. Instead the dying lay or sat on their rattan mats, while girls padded round them with water and simple medical care. There were swollen limbs, emaciated figures and eyes swivelling furiously in bodies that had long since disowned them.

'Do you provide painkillers?' Paula was still a journalist.

'Very expensive, painkillers are. They give false hope, so why give painkillers and extend all that business of dying? No, we give comfort.' Aunt Jamila waved her hands as if to verify the obvious.

'People want to die, dying is a great comfort for these people. It's living that is the hard part. Look at them, they know how to die.'

Enid tried to stop looking at all the bodies and concentrate on one, a shrivelled woman way off the top of any age scale, but about fifty according to Aunt Jamila. The woman looked like an Egyptian mummy unwrapped after thousands of years. Her eyes were sunk in a strikingly handsome skull, the skin stretched taut over a head with strands of wiry grey hair. Her lips were dry and sore and mucus was starting to dribble out of her nostril. A breast hung like a brown paper envelope, barely covered by the filthy shabby cotton sari, and her legs were drawn up as if to protect the emaciated stomach.

'This was a baby, blessed with hope once,' said Enid aloud.

'Now, my dear,' said Aunt Jamila in a placid voice, placing a plump hand on Enid's arm, 'she's one of the lucky ones. Last week we scooped her out of the market. She sold vegetables. Next week she'll be dead. Or do you prefer your system where old people are kept in dying homes for years and years, just because your religion gives you horrible hang-ups about death?'

'What about AIDS?' asked Paula, always frighteningly professional.

Aunt Jamila waved her hands, shrugged her shoulders and said it was the orphans that were the problem.

'We train the girls most thoroughly and find husbands for them.'

Just like my parents did, thought Enid bitterly, as she recalled that bloody silly finishing school with its emphasis on female skills.

'The boys too; we make sure they can survive.'

'It is the prostitutes that are the real problem. Girls of about twelve sold by their parents. They know nothing and, even if they did know about AIDS, what could they do about it?'

Aunt Jamila was full of self-satisfied success. She smiled at the dying, the newly born, and used both to extort more funds from the rich, who lived in their own prison for their own protection.

'By the way, Aunt Jamila's sussed you, Paula. She asked me if you were a girl-boy?'

'What did you reply?'

'That you had had an operation and were now strictly kosher.'

'Did you have to? I don't think that's very sensitive.'

'You're going to be the butt of jokes for the rest of your life, so just get used to it.'

'But…'

'Don't "but" me, my girl. We all have an Achilles heel. How would you like to be some useless widow with slender means, and no future apart from making scones?'

'I don't think of you like that, Edes. You've helped me over some pretty rough times. This trip to India, it's been fantastic. Do you know the best thing about it? I know you complain that I think of nothing but myself. Here I haven't time to think about myself. Do you know, I went out without spraying on any perfume this afternoon.'

Probably noticed what a cheap and nasty smell it has, thought Enid. That's the trouble with education – it takes an age to sink in.

Jamila was running round like a headless chicken. Servants scuttled with armfuls of linens – and why? Sitting cross-legged in the morning-room in deep concentration with his eyes shut most of the time was Fack. He had been kicked out unceremoniously by his benefactor, who was speechless with fury that he had winked at Enid and taken her hands in his.

'That rotten old she goat. How dare you! What an insult to the beautiful Savita. I, I plucked you from oblivion.'

'Jarrow, I was living in Jarrow and contemplating the internal workings of a Hoover and the deeds of that noble mystic, the Venerable Bede.' Fack loved a good row.

The viper hissed. Jarrow, Hoover – these names meant nothing to her. No, all she could think about was the duplicity – that this miserable, phoney son of a bitch – same thing in Indian – could reject her beauty; and failing that – even Savita was a realist – not recognise that he was a bought man, bought with the sole purpose of crushing any confidence that fat white cow might cherish about herself. Hadn't he written to her, pleading to be allowed to walk in her shadow? Hadn't he discarded his fat white handmaiden with her whiskery chin and prongy-toothed daughter, just to bask in the rays of Gerry's true love? What Savita would never know was that Fack sat in Jarrow public library with a copy of Catherine Cookson to write this rubbish.

He had become deeply mystical since his departure from the B and B in Ripon. It brought him into contact with an intellectually superior type of Indian. In Middlesbrough he enjoyed the company of a delightful old man who had taught himself Sanskrit, having handed over the grocery business to his son. They sat in the room above the shop with incense burning and Indian fabrics pinned over the damp patches. There was a woven picture of the Taj Mahal. It was simply dreadful and Fack insisted they took it down and shoved it behind the cushions. The old man didn't seem to mind but his son kicked up a fuss. Fusses with Narin were short-lived, as there was always someone waiting to be served baked beans and naan bread mix.

It was in Middlesbrough that the idea of authenticating his spirituality first occurred to Fack. He had been given short shrift by a surly policeman when the librarian got cold feet about this weirdo reading *The Financial Times* while wearing next to nothing.

'Can you tell me where you come from, sir? This library is for the folks in Middlesbrough.'

'How can you tell, officer? I mean, are they stamped at birth? I am a holy man. I wander. Would you ask the Pope where he came from if you found him in Dublin public library?'

'Nutcase,' Plod whispered discreetly into his phone.

'Can you keep him talking?' A bored sergeant flipped to the appropriate numbers.

Keep him talking? The bloody officer couldn't shut him up. The librarian waved her arms menacingly and declared that it was important to maintain quiet in a library. Fack declared that as he and the officer were the only people there and since he, Fack, didn't care a toss about the quietness nonsense, it didn't apply. The librarian tried another tack.

'So sad; it all comes from educating people like that too fast.' By 'like that' she meant all people who wore very little and came from hot, dirty countries with no plumbing. No one was going to accuse her of being a racist. The policeman had been briefed to move on the riff-raff. They were causing a rash of burglaries. He was rather pleased with himself. This was no riff-raff. This was a plain barmy Indian with philosophical pretensions, probably schizophrenic. He had been on a course, he had been on a course for every bloody subject including politically correct arse-wiping or was it arse-licking?

As luck would have it, the community psychiatric nurse was a lovely Indian lady from Uttar Pradesh. Talk about talking in a public library! Fack and this Indian lady clocked up overtime for everyone else. Does that make talking 'a good thing' after all?

'But you must, every sadhu must. It is the most profound experience to dip in Mother Ganges, feel those holy waters. My Dad took me as a youngster, along with my three brothers and baby sister. We would watch the fire-eaters, the magicians, holy men covered with ashes and nothing else. Then the music – discordant melody, but catching. I love it. And the holy men talking about the holy scriptures, rapturous; their voices are still with me. Their eyes! I shudder. What are you doing here? Blown by your prayers?'

'You are a lovely girl, intelligent too. Yes, I've been blown by my prayers. Not very far, mind you. Fabrics, wonderful colours – we made them in India till our bellies grew large on emptiness. My father heard about Leicester, a sweet dream for education, for enough food anyway. Many cousins were there already. But no sadhus, no holy men, to remind you of your prayers – just

Christian priests ready to shove Jesus Christ down your throat. He got stuck. Behind him the money piled up. My sons were so sophisticated. All they wanted was nightclubs and kicks. Ugh! I had raised two boys without a shred of spirituality. Then my wife died and with her the last act of piety in my life. Money without piety is like Divali without paint: colourless. So I handed over my home, my Purdey guns and my Gainsborough – at least, Sotheby's think so – and have been wandering here and there, letting my faith creep back. How could I be so foolish ever to have let it go? I have fought racism. I tell you it lingers in corners, in Downing Street even. Now I must move on. Middlesbrough is empty. God has left and, quite frankly, I don't blame him.'

He stayed a little longer, because the old man who taught himself Sanskrit was lonely. There were few people to share his passion for Sanskrit. But really Fack was waiting for the right moment to approach Savita. It's very difficult for a rich man to learn to be poor. It doesn't come naturally! Finally, he heard about Jarrow, a cradle of early Christianity. Surely God must linger there. The Venerable Bede had written a long letter and placed it in the bottle of time – only no one was interested, not in Jarrow. With bitterness as their only sustenance, the men of Jarrow had walked for bread and justice, and Fack walked too. But Fack was expeditious and hitched lifts off beautiful women. Fack arrived in Jarrow when it was raining. The lights shone down on burgers, bingo and cheap carpet warehouses – hardly bread and justice. The pubs were noisy and spilt into the streets, where a harsh neon glare caught glimpses of that other God which young people follow, as little plastic bags changed hands. Fack was bored with drugs. Their fatuity irritated him. They were the dead end roads on that long journey we all must make. They reminded him of his spoilt sons – perfectly nice, intelligent but arrogant, as if snorting cocaine with the rich and powerful invalidates the crime.

Fack frightened the police. He squeezed the boil of racism that lingered in the mean, rain-slashed housing estates. He was chased through the park as a paedophile and denounced from the pulpit as the Antichrist, but resurrected by a dear little old lady who invited him to stay in her bow-fronted house. All she asked was that he did one or two of those little jobs she found quite difficult these days. Fack fumbled with the dustbins, he tried putting up a shelf, mending the Hoover and digging the garden. He, who had advised the PM, wined and dined with the great and the good, hunted in the shires, and paid school fees – he, who flew regularly in Concorde, snapped his fingers for champagne – found the interior of the Hoover quite mystifying, quite Graham Greene.

Was Fack in touch with humility at last? More like reality! He decided to write off to Savita straight away, explain not so much what he was as who Savita would like him to be. He mentioned the great Hindu festivals and a great deal about searching for beauty. It was a very beautiful letter if you were a vain and stupid woman.

Which she was. Poor good, kind Enid, plain as a pikestaff and in need of a little aftershave – how could she compete with this siren? It was no contest in Fack's eyes. Savita's eyes could smoulder as much as she liked, but all it ignited was a desire to chuckle. As poor Enid had been stitched up by that grand meeting, Fack found himself feeling increasingly tender towards his old mate from the B and B days. What was it she would say? 'I believe in you.' That was it. God knows what it meant, but Fack had liked it. He liked the careless intimacy of unmade beds, broken-down cars and pompous policemen always wanting Fack to wear something appropriate. So, when the confused, plain-faced widow found him crashed out on the cushions, his heart leapt. It's good to have a mate, a real mate that laughs. It's one thing to discard all earthly relationships but it's more authentic if there are relationships to discard.

Fack's focus throughout his life had always been on himself. He had done well, been successful; people liked him, respected him, sought his opinion. His dear sweet wife had remained faithful to India. He hadn't. He had deserted India for the gin and tonic values of the huntin' rich. Worse still, he had pursued those who spend mindless lives in the corridors of power. They never enter any room; never express any view of their own. So he had deserted the memory of his wife and Mother India. Yet without a mother and a wife, what is a man?

Aunt Jamila scuttled round Fack with the cynicism he deserved. After years of playing second fiddle to her beautiful sister, years of extracting blood out of the stony-hearted rich of Mumbai, a spoilt fakir with hazy notions of Hindu mythology was, let's face it, no more than par for the Bollywood course. Even in India a plain sister knows when she's plain. She also knows where her power base lies. Fack under her veranda was like a juicy plum. He absented himself from meals but could be found sitting quietly at his devotions – if working out with the aid of a timetable how to get to where the Kumbh Mela is counts as a devotion. Savita had withheld the money she had promised him. There had been one hell of a row over the telephone. Only Enid knew about his gold card kept for emergencies.

The girls walked by the sea under the swaying palms. They watched the little crabs scuttle away from their toes and, like scavengers the world over, they picked up flotsam thrown up by the storms. Little boys ran behind them or thrust grubby hands out for money. Paula had become quieter. The enormity of what she'd done had begun to weigh. No longer was her labia the only issue she thought about. She watched her sisters washing, feeding, begging to survive; she saw the emaciated old women scooped up by Aunt Jamila. Paula bought some saris at about three times their market value and became very angry about a half-dead cow left to die painfully, until reminded by Aunt Jamila that many children suffered worse deaths. Inevitably, the beggars shocked her most of all. Their scars, gnarled, twisted limbs and their faces contorted with…

'Expressions to make you weep? But, of course, Paula, what did you expect?'

It was another observation of Aunt Jamila's that really made Paula curl up in knots, the comment that really got to her.

'I realised at once, my dear. It's your profile. Doctors can fiddle like garage mechanics but they can't change the make of the car.'

Paula was speechless. She just stared at this plump, elderly Indian lady. Aunt Jamila continued, 'I thought Enid was being shy about her companion. Savita's friends are never shy about anything like that, only about tax.'

Another time Aunt Jamila was explaining that very Indian matter of caste, when she suddenly smiled and said how the

English had an equally obscure social custom. Paula assumed that the conversation would drift towards dukes and dustmen, time-honoured stuff, but not at all.

'Vijaya tells me you eat at different times according to who you are. Sometimes it is tea, other times it is supper, and people like Ran and Vijaya eat dinner, all at the same time. How very complicated!'

'I think Vijaya has got it a little bit wrong. She's right about the dinner bit – and how! She used to turn up looking like a peacock. We use different language to show what background we come from, but it is all dissolving in our microwaves and mobile phones. I have neither.'

'Yes, and that is another thing. Vijaya tells me you are not progressive. Mind you, Vijaya is not one to say so. She is too successful to understand. As for Rani, he is doted on by my sister – a scallywag, is that the word? We came from a very modest background, you know. One sari a year and plenty of poverty. One by one they died till only the ravishing Savita and me remained. Our father was skin and bone. He sharpened. Our mother withered. I watched her wither and Savita flourish. My good works are in their honour.'

The tubby little woman with freckles round her nose had also flourished along with her sister. Was she jealous?

'Were you educated, Aunt Jamila?'

'Here and there.' She waved a hand and twisted the edge of her sari.

Paula, who had asked the question, realised she had over-stepped the mark. Was it the journalist, the man still lurking in her profile, or just plain insensitivity? Paula was ill at ease with Fack. His charm and podgy body caught her unawares. She needed time still when facing a man. Anyway, he was appallingly chauvinistic and treated Enid like a dishcloth. Enid loved it and was forever running errands.

'Why do you run after him all the time? The lazy sod's done nothing but sit and smirk all day.'

'I know. Gerry was the same. He wants me to get him some books, unreadable stuff about the Kumbh Mela. I don't feel confident walking around on my own. Let's walk to the bookshop. It's in that main street where that particularly revolting dead cow was.'

'And you pay for them?' Paula might be a woman but she wasn't that soft a touch.

'He's a fakir. He doesn't bother about worldly goods.'

'He's a con and you know it.'

'When you get cross, you look all masculine.' That shut her up.

The girls left in the early afternoon. The gardeners were resting in the shade and watched them go. One of them spat out some betel juice as though it was an observation. The road was quiet with two or three villas hidden behind high walls, but all too soon they joined a shabby thoroughfare with huge advertising boards, endless scooters and clapped-out buses interwoven with taxis, rickshaws and bicycles in swarms. Then there were the children – scruffy, wide-eyed children murmuring plaintive noises and poking skinny arms out as they collected round Enid and Paula.

'Oh, do go away.' Enid sounded like an irritable teacher. One boy tentatively lifted Paula's skirt. She yelped angrily. All the way they noticed people watching them. Women in saris, some pulled across their faces, squatting by huge piles of melons, aubergines or wonderful spices. Men used the pavement to mend their cars, sit and have a chat, or weigh unidentifiable pieces of metal on ancient scales. Then there were the stands selling saris, jewellery, watches and gaudy underwear, plastic ducks, saucepans and watches, while the shops set back from the road sold insurance, banking, travel and advice. Still the little boys chattered and whined behind them, still the curious eyes followed them.

'I think we've done very well, don't you?'

'I'm glad you came too. Look, here we are.'

They entered a velvety dark bookshop smelling of a leathery, musty fragrance. The floor was uneven and books appeared to be piled in no particular order. An elderly man wearing a grubby dhoti padded towards them in bare feet. He bowed, smiled, bowed again and walked backwards into a pile of books that immediately collapsed on the floor. He didn't or wouldn't speak English. Maybe his lack of teeth didn't help. Enid gave him the piece of paper. Suddenly, a piercing shriek came from the bowels of the shop. It was a bird in a cage. Both girls were frightened. The old man shuffled and mumbled round the shop. At last the door opened and a younger man entered. After a brief conversation he turned to Enid.

'Do you know the Bull Ring in Birmingham?'

'Not really. That's the centre, isn't it?'

'My cousin has a restaurant, the New Moon. You should visit it. What can I do for you?'

Enid, feeling a little flustered, repeated what she wanted.

'Just as well I turned up. My father doesn't read. He's blind.'

The young man padded round the shop till he produced the books, asked a fortune and Enid paid it.

'You bloody fool! Never pay the asking price. This isn't Leicester,' was Fack's response.

'Oh well, we got there and back. That was a miracle in itself.' She hated it when Fack was cross with her. She knew that Paula thought that she ought to stand up for herself but she wasn't that kind of woman.

Later, as the sun dipped and insect noises started, the girls sat out on the veranda sipping delicious soft fruit drinks.

'Even if I got the ingredients, it wouldn't taste the same,' said Paula, wistfully.

'Isn't that the point?'

'No, you don't get it. The point is that here women have a raw deal. Children don't get educated. Poor people have a wretched time. Being a sacred holy cow isn't all it's cracked up to be. And for every value we share, there are hundreds of niggly ones we don't. They don't put that on the tins and bottles of exotic drink. You could never put India in the bottle any more than you can put India into curry.'

'Do I detect buyers' remorse?'

'You mean about being a woman?'

'For God's sake, Paula! Not everything is about you being a woman. Can't you forget it and move on?'

Paula leapt to her feet and muttered, 'You don't understand,' as she disappeared into her bedroom.

Enid waited, sloshing her drink around the glass. So much had happened, yet none of it was really Indian. That business with Savita – it was all about Gerry. And Fack – well, he was pretty English in a way. As for Paula, why couldn't she let go? Charging off to find transsexuals – she could get into trouble in some places. Anyway, it was rather seedy. Aunt Jamila had sussed her straight away. She would. She was like a mother earth figure with her easy-to-live, easy-to-die charities. Tomorrow she was going to take the two girls round some of the more interesting parts of Bombay.

Tomorrow dawned with a gentle mist and a neighbourly rooster. Aunt Jamila was waving her arms and shouting. It was as near to cooking as she got. Her devoted manservant padded round the morning room adjusting – unnecessarily – chairs and cushions, while placating his mistress's stream of noisy injunctions. Fack wasn't to been seen. He had taken to serious prayer in his simple bedroom. He'd join the ladies in the afternoon. Fack was delighted for other people to sightsee and tell him all about it. He had upgraded the shabby grey dhoti he had worn in England for pristine white garments. Enid rather hoped he would be rolling in the dust before joining the Kumbh Mela. He had confided in Enid that his time with Savita had been very tiring and disquieting for his soul.

'I am not a poodle, Enid. What is more I am a man of honour. That woman! Your poor husband – you should feel only commiseration. Beautiful women are a nightmare. Be relieved, Enid, you are not beautiful.' As always with Fack, it sounded so reassuring, so heartlessly cruel.

It takes a curious leap of the imagination to find a common denominator for sightseeing. Aunt Jamila knew exactly what they ought to see. Turn-of-the-century municipal architecture is grim in Birmingham, grimmer in Brighton but grimmest of all in Mumbai under a bright blue sky, where extraneous twirls and motifs rub shoulders with street vendors sizzling beguiling delicacies. Asked about the food vendors, Jamila shrieked, 'Oh my God, no! To eat is to die! They never wash their hands – how can they? There isn't enough water to go round.'

Enid thought of the water poured onto Savita's garden every evening and said nothing.

The railway station was indeed remarkable. It grew out of a million people rushing round to tend the train – the great 'she' creature. This time the vendors were far outnumbered by Indians rushing hither and thither. But was this India? Enid wanted to stroll through markets, fingering sari material, smelling spices; she wanted to haggle over souvenir beads for the twins, buy silk for Sal. But Aunt Jamila waved all that nonsense aside and insisted they visited the Institute for Indian Affairs, where they spent a long time, a very long time, poring over Sanskrit scrolls. There were beautifully carved figures, charming paintings – nothing naughty – and a sobriety quite at odds with the teeming streets outside.

'Do you think we could… ?' But no! They couldn't. Aunt Jamila would show them the Mumbai that she regarded as worthy of her visitors. With a seraphic smile, capacious handbag and a sturdy gait, she dived from one Victorian building to another.

What about a temple, the arts – surely there were studios? Education – couldn't they visit a school for the needy? But no, only more stiff buildings formally there to impress, buildings the British couldn't take away when they left, and mildewed paintings of moguls and maharajahs, politicians – no women; huge ugly urns and courtyards where the patient sat and only the very patient ever saw whom they were looking for. But India isn't India for nothing. The pall of squalor didn't entirely leave the place. The faint smell of pee and rot, unwashed bodies and diesel – it all added a particular note.

'Those temples – you can see them on your own; and the poor – you can see them any time. I remember, Gerry would dive into the poor area as if it was a swimming pool. What is it about you English? You seem to treasure poverty.'

'I don't want to let Fack down and shrink from sights and sounds I don't feel comfortable with. I gather the Kumbh Mela is all sights and sounds. I rather wish I could go too.' Paula rolled her heavily made-up eyes.

'Fack always looks after himself. He is not a true fakir. You must have learnt that if nothing else.' Enid struck a prim note.

Already Enid was learning that nothing is true in the English sense of truth.

Fack was at least learned, witty, amusing and great fun to be with. It suddenly hit Enid, looking at a portrait of a particular stiff-collared, much-bewhiskered gentleman, who died at an early age of forty-two, to ask Jamila, 'What did Gerry wear out here?'

'Simple Indian clothes – good quality, of course. He never compromised.'

Then he wasn't being unfaithful in a sense, was he? After all, you can't run around Ripon in a dhoti, not unless you're Fack.

Paula had been quiet and bored. The journalist was having a morning off. She looked almost beautiful in a tantalising, 'neither one thing nor the other' way. India was giving her room. Later that day she had felt confident enough to go off on her own – something about the zoo and another contact about sorghum yields.

'No one knew. Do you know how much that means? He was a lovely guy – studied at Nottingham. I'm coming back to India, Enid. I'm going to roast like a chicken on the beaches of Goa – temples galore and dirt cheap. All this stuff Aunt Jamila has shown us is dead boring. We haven't seen anyone under thirty since we arrived. I want to eat out at little restaurants – just a touch of Delhi belly – you can't go to India without Delhi belly.'

The day before they both were to fly home they were taken to 'Bollywood' and walked round a set of an ancient Indian fort. A man had to jump through a burning window. The actor was far too precious and a scrawny stuntman took his place. There was all the drama of footage being filmed. Unfortunately, the man got it wrong – the footage was brilliant but the man was killed.

'That is why we use extras and stuntmen, insurance and all that.' The pragmatism shocked the girls.

'What about his family?'

'He has seven children, I believe. Someone will do something.' Jamila, who did all she could to raise money for her waifs and strays, couldn't have been less concerned about the accident they witnessed. Wherever they went, Savita's name and memory were evoked. Jamila answered with good humour.

Paula said in their bedroom afterwards, 'It must always be like playing second fiddle, I suppose. I'll never forget this holiday, Enid. I've learnt a lot – about myself, I mean...'

It would always be about herself, mused Enid. Paula had been fun when she was a chrysalis but now she was a self-absorbed bore. Am I any better, obsessed with Gerry wandering around in pristine white cotton trousers at the foot of his beloved stainless-steel bride? It sounded more romantic than mistress. Yes, I'm also a bore! Poor old India – playing host to the two of us.

One secret ritual Enid had developed during their stay was in the lavatory. For years, first as a child then as a mother and occasionally as a grandmother, Enid had read of slithery snakes emerging through the lavatory plumbing, only to coil themselves round the cistern pipe – was the writer Kipling or possibly Conan Doyle? No one ever explained exactly what happened but Enid's imagination covered all eventualities and she braced herself for a terrified search minutes before her bowels were given notice to function. This little ritual she withheld even from Fack and Fack you could say anything to.

Enid couldn't resist. She ate some delicious spicy delicacy from a vendor. A bout of gippy tummy occurred. While doubled up with a griping pain and while hovering over Paula's demise, if demise it was, Enid found herself wondering what would happen if a young royal showed a definite gender move. Would the Queen mention it in her Christmas broadcast – the royal household issue bulletins? Enid offered her services and happily made up appropriate bulletins to mark the royal process from dashing heart-throb to the nation to role model for teenage girls in ten dizzy months.

It had been Enid who left Fack that last time. She had walked out of some dim B and B in Middlesbrough and braced herself for making scones for the rest of her life. She would be making them now, only… and it is the 'onlys' that make life worth living. This time she would be leaving him with Aunt Jamila, comfortably neutral, with the pious intent to visit the Kumbh Mela. Enid had her doubts. The level of discomfort expected of gurus was way beyond Fack's capacity to do without; after all, he had a Savile Row tailor.

Then it happened – very quickly and completely out of the blue. Paula was meant to be fiddling with her packing, writing last minute postcards, or so she said, but when the time honoured 'Cooee' was met with total silence Enid found she had vamoosed – lock, stock and false eyelashes. A card was left on her pillow:

> I know you will understand. Fack has asked me to join him at the Kumbh Mela.

But she hadn't any money. She was due back to work next Thursday and was running out of pills, without which hair would sprout, her labia possibly shrivel and God knows what else…

Aunt Jamila wailed. Even bossy women can wail. It involved a deep gargling noise, much flapping of the hands and a gait somewhere between a waddle and a trot. Whatever her quarrel with Savita, this transcended all argument. She immediately rang her sister.

'That man – he's run off with the she/he. He's abused our hospitality. I thought he was holy; he's not holy – he's just sex, sex, sex!'

Fack's card on his pillow read as follows:

> The spirit of Kumbh Mela impels us to go. We are one spirit. We pray for you.

'He carried a gold bank card, just in case,' explained Enid bitterly.

'These boy-girls are all the same. How do you say? They like to have some cake and eat it. You are completely different, my dear. As for that man, Savita had a rich, serious man once – not Gerry, after Gerry. He was serious, but now she is old. It is freaks and frights that can be persuaded to flatter her. Beware flattery, Enid. Fack was not serious. He was, how do you say? – a flight of fancy.

'No, Aunt Jamila, you're wrong. Of course I'm jealous, but I believe in Fack. What my emotions tell me is one thing. Another part of me wants to believe in Fack. He's not driven by sex. He's…well, serious and if Paula pleaded that she wanted to go he'd take her. Oh, hell! Why didn't I ask? It's those bloody scones that held me back. *I* should be with Fack, not her.'

'Scones, dear?'

They dined on spices and hot dishes prepared for her last

night – actually for their last night; the cook didn't know half the guests had left.

Aunt Jamila didn't let her heaving bosom worry about the intricacies of betrayal last for long. She wanted to pick Enid's brain about her hospital for the dying. Would the worthy souls of Ripon help with the fund-raising?

'Why don't you fund a scholarship for a couple of school leavers to work out here for a year? They would love it.' Enid thought of Aunt Jamila and the twins. She shuddered. Anyway, she was absorbed in the mayhem of emotions that Paula and Fack had created. Savita had rung back just before dinner and spoke for over half an hour to discuss with her sister the best way of maximising this glorious coup de grâce.

'That frump! I need to rub her nose in it!' yelled Savita hysterically.

'She needs to rub your nose in it,' announced Aunt Jamila, not really understanding what her sister meant.

'Over my dead body,' said Enid quite firmly.

'It's over her dead body. Don't you see?' yelled Aunt Jamila who had lost the plot. This was followed by another phone call.

'You can't look your best next to a dead body. I know, I'm an actress,' announced Savita, who had in some half-baked way imagined a reconciliation with Fack where Enid's corpse was in the foreground, rather like a trophy from a big game shoot.

'I don't want her dead, but Jamila – don't you see? That silly, stout lady must know her place. Fack came to me just as Gerry had. I was their romantic vision, their goddess, their orgasm.'

'Really Savita, that is American talk, Hollywood talk – disgusting. Just remember who you are talking to.'

'Jamila, we beauties have an important role in life. It includes orgasms because we are beautiful enough to create them by our looks alone. We don't struggle like some harassed lady fumbling in her handbag – we just ooze such appeal that we are irresistible. Gerry irresisted me.'

'Irresistible,' mumbled Jamila, all flustered by this sex talk.

Our Enid might be a silly stout woman in Savita's eyes but she was damned if she was going to be walked all over by her dead husband's mistress, let alone the inscrutable Fack.

'You can tell your sister next time she rings that she can go to hell, but before going there she can realise that Paula's labia are likely to fall off or something and Fack's sex life requires more than a slap and tickle with a boy-girl or some clapped-out wreck of an elderly actress.'

Wow, that shit hit the fan! Sex talk, sex talk – most improper. Aunt Jamila wailed about the dead who would be unsettled by all this nonsense. She knew all about it, but the servants were dropping crockery – always a bad sign! Enid started slamming doors while packing her suitcase and thinking about the duplicity that had taken place before her eyes and what to tip the servants. However, by bedtime both women had calmed down and agreed poor Savita was more to be pitied than envied. Jamila suggested a fair sum for the servants and Enid mentally doubled it. The two women sat on huge cushions sipping tea and discussing death and why so few people in the West were comfortable with it.

'A good death is so desirable and it is free to everyone. You cannot buy it. Certainly my sister will not have one, but some of my poor friends – yes, they have a beautiful death. The Kumbh Mela is all very well – all that cavorting; but a good death – that, Enid, is what we should try to achieve.'

Aunt Jamila's chauffeur skirted round a cow not having a very good death and Enid saw some enraged chickens hanging by their upside-down legs and facing imminent butchery. The usual beggars clung or sat in bleak hope. Already they were no more than the cheerful background of squalor – colour and telephone wires everywhere. A cart pulled by an emaciated horse nearly collided with the elderly car outside an amazing modern building housing some multinational. Elegant people entered the building. No one so much as turned their heads. Soon the shacks and seedy concrete sheds with wires like roots in the sky sprang up and followed the vehicle all the way to the airport.

Enid's last view of India was a man on a bicycle with three huge bundles of reeds tied to its sides and a fourth worn like some exotic hairstyle. The man could neither pedal nor walk. He simply wobbled indeterminately with such fierce intent that somehow the traffic avoided impact. Enid wished she could use this absurd sight as some kind of metaphor for India, but soon the more irritating experience of a delayed flight and a week-old magazine had to suffice. While waiting a dreary hour, after a brief glimpse at an article on classic gun designs, Enid smiled shyly at the crumpled figure sitting beside her.

'Typical!' she ventured.

'Heathrow's much worse,' he snarled. 'It's the bloody same the world over. It's no good blaming the bloody Indians. The bloody Brits, the bloody everybodies – they are all the same.'

'Then who is to blame?'

'We are getting too big for our boots. That is what is behind all this.'

He'll be blaming family values next. Really, people are weird, she thought idly.

They sat, sweating gently, and didn't say another word till their flight was called, when he turned and said, 'Let's hope we make it.'

It had rather the same effect as someone shouting 'Fire!' in a cinema – to Enid, anyway. She flew home consumed with terror. Every adjustment the plane made, every jerk, whirr and buzz, created new terror in her heart. By Heathrow she was a dishrag and queued in the wrong line with her passport.

Where exactly was her car? What exactly was her car? Dirty, yes – but what colour? As for the make, that was completely beyond her. She knew when she found the right one. Apart from the key fitting, it smelled of that duplicitous cow. Slowly, Enid drove north, with memories of that other time with Ran – and what was her name? Try as she could, the name escaped her. So much for beautiful women! Everything looked so lush, so ordered, as the trundling lorries clocked their busy journeys up and down the motorways. At first Enid noticed all the obvious differences but all too soon fatigue took over and she fought a bitter battle with sleep. It did not occur to her that she was a danger to others but, believe me, she was. Finally she was parked outside the bungalow as if nothing had happened and she hadn't even gone away. There were letters, some gone-off milk and definitely suspicious bacon. But Enid had remembered, for there stood a carton of long-life milk. Bliss! A hot cup of coffee – and an invitation to lunch.

'You don't look at all brown, more green if you ask me. Douglas is dealing with an aborted calf. The joint didn't get in the oven till eleven thirty, so we're running a bit late. Ooh, how glamorous – a sari.' Sal wiped her floury hands on her hips before unwrapping what looked like recycled paper and holding up a beautiful marriage sari in the deepest red.

'There's enough for a simple straight skirt and—'

'Perfect for the hunt ball,' murmured Sal, without conviction, 'and a bodice gathered over one shoulder.'

'I've bought the twins tops. They are very glittery. I wasn't sure about their boobs. They are always a problem, aren't they? India doesn't cater for boys. Do you think Roger will find incense very naff?'

'Hell, I've forgotten the potatoes; we'll deep-fat fry them instead.'

Enid then knew she would miss delicious Indian food, if nothing else. How could the English cook so badly?

'You will be able to start the scones tomorrow, won't you? The twins did their best but we had a few complaints, I'm afraid – mostly about bits and pieces that made an unwanted appearance, like pencil shavings.'

'Oh dear! No suing – nothing like that, I hope.' At that moment Beatrice arrived and made a point of not kissing her Gran.

'No,' explained Beatrice. 'The worst that happened was a batch of the bloody things falling out of the boot of the car onto a muddy patch. It was awesome. But Gran, I tell you one thing. I'd rather die penniless than make scones for a living. It was so demeaning.'

'The whole point, my arrogant beautiful granddaughter, is that the vast majority of people who spend their lives doing exactly that – loading scones, making scones, selling scones and eating scones – feel exactly like you do. Only they have no choice. I went to India and watched the loo cleaner lying fast asleep on the floor of the ladies' loo because it was the only possible place for her – not because she liked it. The beggars…'

'Not the bloody beggars!' Beatrice raised her arms in a dramatic pose.

'We knew it would be beggars, didn't we?' said Sal, as she rendered some cabbage inedible. 'Why you couldn't have visited the seamier side of Leeds with all the druggies, I don't know; at least there the beggars speak English. Hey, talking of Leeds – where is Paula and how are her private parts coming on?'

'You mean her labia,' giggled Beatrice.

'Beatrice! Please, not in front of the roast potatoes. I know your gran couldn't care less but there are things best left private and Paula's private parts are one of them.'

'*Private*! You must be joking!' It was hard to tell whether Enid or Beatrice made the retort.

Just then Sophie burst into the room. She eyed her garish Indian top and, with the skill of her coltish age, announced that it would look marvellous under a T-shirt.

'She's done a bunk, Paula has. Guess who with…' Enid's voice trembled just a little.

They guessed and guessed. Paula's labia gave a great variety of possibilities but not in a thousand years did anyone guess Fack.

'Why, what was *he* doing there? That fat fraud – I should have guessed.' Sal had never really come to terms with her mum's idea of a companion.

Enid told them all about Savita the witch with Fack by her side, about the weird prison camp atmosphere surrounding the villas for the rich, the nothingness of their lives and the money – Gerry's money – keeping it all going. Well, she didn't know for certain, but having met Savita she could well believe it. Then she spoke of Aunt Jamila, stout, plain and purposeful, with teeming millions of the poor and the dying lying on the floor, her floor of her hospice; of how Paula found her way to the freaks and frights of Bombay – only it wasn't Bombay at all, but Mumbai; of how she left a note to say that she and Fack were off to the Kumbh Mela to find the inner depths of their souls or some such rot. She added that she didn't think there was any hanky-panky, not if her experience was anything to go by.

'You mean you never…' began Sophie, before getting a savage kick from Beatrice, followed by not very surreptitious giggles.

So much for being back in the bosom of her family. It was back to the traces straight away, with bicarb, flour and marg once more cluttering the kitchen. It was back to less comfortable emotions as well. Already Enid was lonely and the whiff of scent in the bathroom was there as a reminder. She couldn't bring herself to go into Paula's bedroom and tears trickled down her cheek as she realised she would rather have her back than face being alone. If there can be tears for one, there can be tears for two. She rang Dolly. Some woman answered and was non-committal about Dolly speaking.

'I'm her carer, you know. Only if she's up to it.'

'Dolly! Hello, it's Enid.' But Dolly was having none of this 'hello' nonsense.

'I asked for chops, lamb chops,' a sad, querulous voice, pretending to be Dolly answered.

'Dolly, it's me, Enid! I'm back from India. I've got a little something for you.'

Tears, confusion, paranoia – they were trying to put her away. 'Please come, Enid. They refuse to let me eat what I want and say I've got – you know, what do they call it? Oh Enid, I want to die. It's quite horrible like this.'

Enid was over in next to no time. She thought of Aunt Jamila's hospice and shuddered for her dear friend. The dashing Dolly looked awful. Her neat body was stuffed carelessly into some elderly trousers and a shirt which hung out at the back in a colour combination that Dolly would never wear. Her face was haggard – not a trace of make-up – and worst of all she was wearing her bedroom slippers just like some old codger. Enid had jumped out of her car, trepidation, care and curiosity all wobbling inside her. She clutched her parcel and gave Dolly a big hug.

'Look, Dolly, something pretty to cheer you up.'

Dolly flinched and then took the parcel.

'You never can tell,' she murmured darkly. 'But it isn't my birthday!' she exclaimed, while admiring the beautiful stole.

'Oh come on! Every day should be a birthday at our age. Guess who was staying with the arch-witch Savita.'

'Who?' Dolly had connected once more.

'That scoundrel Fack. You have to admire him. He has balls if nothing else. He's run off with Paula and, before you ask, I don't mind – well, not much.'

Over coffee made by Enid the two women discussed 'well, not much' – so much so that even Enid began to believe it herself, just as she believed there wasn't really anything wrong with her dear friend. However, a phone call from Canada put paid to that illusion. It was Dolly's son.

'She'll have to go into a home. It's costing a fortune in carers and I've no way of knowing if they are ripping her off or anything. I know you've been a good friend but it's no good. She can't manage and I can't look after her from here.'

'Buts' were useless; he'd made up his mind. Enid couldn't believe her ears, the insensitivity of it all. She left poor Dolly and her carer and drove back, sick with worry.

Well, you have to think of something while making scones – so Enid thought about Dolly. Ten ounces of flour flipped into the mixing bowl where it covered several rock-like lumps of marg. Soon the machine lumped and bumped its way to the crumbled look while Enid tried desperately to think of ways to bring just one more glimmer of happiness to her old friend's life. That's it, she decided – the freaks and frights album. She would use it as an excuse to show her the photos from India. God – the milk! She poured in the appropriate amount and whizzed it once more before rolling out the nasty, lumpy mess and cutting it into scone shapes. Would Dolly like to make scones? Yes – for five minutes and she made even more mess than the twins had done. But having her for the day was rewarding and Enid hoped she could repeat it, giving back just a little of what Dolly had done for her.

But it wasn't poor Dolly that was uppermost in Enid's mind; it was her old bugbear – boredom. The only reason why she got married that she could think of, frankly, was to stave off boredom. Life had been for Enid, apart from that brief interlude with Fack, pure undiluted boredom, with Gerry producing a slow intravenous drip of something different. No, that wasn't true; Gerry did better than that – he wasn't at all dull. It was she who was dull. But he had made her angry at times, as well as the familiar irritation from the way he snored to his inability to earn pots of dough based on some esoteric class hang-up. Gerry resolutely wanted to go down in the world and, by God, he did. All Enid wanted to do was be a faithful, loyal wife and, by God, she was.

So the combination left her an impecunious widow with vast tracts of time on her hands. And for a really dull visitor, try Time; it invites itself to stay and rarely leaves. Enid had made a pact with Dull to piss off while she was in India. Anyway, she had Paula to keep her company; but through that doorway her old partner, Boredom, welcomed her home. However, for the first time since Gerry's death, she was able to mourn their silly, bloody life together. She hadn't felt confident to tell Sal to her face all about Paula, but a cheery postcard with 'Wish you were here' sentiments so enraged her that she telephoned Sal.

'I didn't want to draw attention to it in front of the children. You know what they are like.'

'But Mum, aren't you furious?'

It comes to something when your only shoulder is your daughter.

'Not really – well, yes I am. If anything, I'm rather pleased in a way. After all, he's ditched Savita and – call me bitchy if you like – that gives me a great deal of pleasure. She was a real femme fatale – no, right bitch. Her house was designed to intimidate people, all cushions and huge goblets, gold this and gold that, nothing comfortable and the skins of dead beasts to prove her prowess at the chase and her command over men. Yukky, yukky – she's unreal! Sometimes I think she, Fack and now Paula are all just my imagination. I mean, they are at least a reprieve from scones.'

'You always say you'll do anything to help and then you complain.' Sal was plaintive. She had better things to do than listen to her mother wail.

'I know – I shouldn't have solicited your shoulder. It's just I'm an incurable optimist. First I used to think being adult would open up vistas of – well, you know. Then that being married would do the trick. I could put the world to rights while your dad moved continents or whatever. By the time he died, I really thought I could begin again. Now, surely, there is more to life than scones…and don't suggest bridge.'

'Well, I think you are utterly spoilt. You had a life of Riley out in India – even a transsexual to appeal to your prurient ego – and all you can do is moan about being bored. Grow up, Mum.'

Enid put the phone down with an ill-tempered commitment

to scones. As usual Enid was searching for something better. As usual her family were unimpressed and wished she would settle down like her friends.

'I love her dearly but...' prefaced many a conversation with Sal's friends. Actually, not so many; Sal did her best to put Enid out of her mind. All the same, the batty old bag needed care and attention.

India improved in Enid's imagination. In Mumbai itself there were half-living cows, not half-dead ones, and Aunt Jamila's clients were grateful and resigned rather than endowed with unreliable bowels and a silent rage that their miserable time was up. Even Savita retained her lovely looks and her words slithered over Enid without effect. She didn't think about Paula or Fack. Somehow that was unfinished business. India grew more lovely by the day, curries were given to unsuspecting guests and the smell of incense kept everyone guessing if Enid was making cannabis an issue.

Living on imagination is not enough. Scones came and went. They whirled round unconvincingly in one wet, gloomy muddle. Enid's body joined in the excitement, with a plethora of whiskers covering her chin and her knees locking themselves in some obscure arthritic contortion. Paula was still away, her finances presumably non-existent, as far as Enid could make out. As for Fack, he wrote. His letter was very beautiful and melted all the misunderstood sadness lurking in her breast.

Every week Enid went over to see Dolly. There were no lovely ladies coaxing memories or providing pets. No, for Dolly it was an Australian lady, brisk, proficient and hard as nails, who referred to Dolly as 'we'. Dolly was past caring and was convinced she was about to play tennis a lot of the time – quite dangerous when she took a swipe, which she did when irritation overcame her.

'Have you brought the balls? We're down to three. That silly woman doesn't understand.'

'I can't play, Dolly. It's my arthritis; my knees are killing me!'

'At your age!' retorted Dolly, slipping visibly into a sulk.

'I played bridge last week. I revoked and we lost. Do you remember how cross you used to get with me?' It wasn't true, but did that matter?

'It's silly to play bridge before tennis. Don't be so tiresome.'

'There, Dolly! Don't we have some pretty flowers.' The brisk lady plonked the vase where Dolly couldn't see them.

'Must they go there?' remonstrated Enid.

'You don't have to deal with a vase of flowers being thrown at you. She can be a little monkey, you know.'

No, Enid didn't know. 'She's not a little monkey. She's been a marvellous friend and is a feisty, lovely woman...' Even if, during her last visit to Enid's, an offering of scones had been thrown in her face. The one certainty was Dolly's decline. It was horrible. As her brain turned to mush and everyone talked about her dignity, Dolly slithered into a tiny, shrivelled wreck and all Enid could do was wish her to India where death is alive and the dead everywhere.

Of course, Enid was convinced she had it too. Every item forgotten, date missed, muddled thought bubbling to the surface – all was a clear indication that she was next. She failed to see what she had was her old enemy, boredom, her personal widow's blight – years lived out bravely if a little noisily without an escort. Enid was still yearning for that other half whom she had dumped into the crematorium several years ago and, if it wasn't him, it sure as hell was for something or someone else. She decided that he had died in the earthly sense while she was dying in the spiritual sense. But, Lord knows, she had tried – kicked over the traces, done everything she could to live life to the full, bar Ecstasy; she drew the line at Ecstasy. The twins had offered it to cheer her up but it would be too humiliating if she shuffled off this mortal coil on some teenage drug. So back to scones it was.

Thirteen

Another postcard announced that Paula was coming home. Home – the cheek of it! But Enid dusted her room and even put some flowers in the sitting room. She wanted her back. Paula arrived with too many parcels and not enough money to pay the taxi driver. She flung her arms round Enid and enveloped her in some powerful perfume.

'Edes, darling, I'm back. You've no idea the adventures I had. I've left Fack there. He didn't really know what hit him, taking me along. Now look, I must just see to my face. Travel is so destructive. It takes years off my face every time. I've bought some duty-free plonk. Let's have it with supper and I'll tell you all about it.'

All those cross remarks disintegrated, all the hurt vanished. Edith couldn't wait to snuggle up on the sofa and listen to Paula's account of the Kumbh Mela.

Apparently Paula had shared a tent with six other women and none of them guessed. Now Fack stayed a little more upmarket. He decided that his health and well-being required a proper bed and a room to himself. He explained that Leicester fakirs were not used to the climate or levels of deprivation and he claimed he would rather run a mile than expose his penis to the common man.

'Well, that's something new,' chuckled Enid.

The day would evidently start on a fractious note. Hours after they agreed to meet, he would emerge smiling broadly and meet Paula with, 'So you're here. I hate women who are late.'

Only, being a newly-fledged woman, Paula would snap, 'Bloody hell! I've been waiting here nearly three hours. I'm about to faint from thirst.'

'Dear girl, this is what the Kumbh Mela is all about. Now, first a glass of water – here.'

Fack was always generous with anything free.

They wandered for hours among the fire-eaters, magicians, boys on stilts, charlatans and knaves. They sat at the feet of gurus, gazed at the hordes bathing. They ate, they drank, they peed. They might even have made love, only Paula was worried about her hymen.

As it was, Paula was beginning to regret allowing Fack special dispensation in his sleeping quarters. No other fakir had it. They slummed with the best of them.

'He's taking advantage because I'm a woman.' She sniffed, a newly acquired skill. (Men don't sniff, do they?) So, what with clutching her not so private parts and learning to undress – almost – in public, learning to listen to the wisdoms of the fakirs and to give, give, give and how to her beaming ebullient companion, Paula learnt a great deal about being a female and Fack learnt that he missed Enid, oysters and a good claret.

Paula the journalist had a ball. She almost forgot her identity among the fascinations of the teeming characters all around. They squatted round fires, children mimicking their parents as they stared at the thousands of people milling round. The acrobats and jugglers moved effortlessly through the crowds, leaping and throwing their sticks, wearing wonderful gaudy gear. Gurus sat, toes and fingers disciplined to represent all that inner peace their fierce voices mocked. Nor were the crowds and their leaders Hindu – far from it. A large American preached Coca-Cola values in a raucous upper New York State twang. Paula listened to the familiar mishmash of organic beans, values and horoscopic well-being, while all around stared uncomprehending peasants hanging on every word. After all, it was free. The more prophetic demanded money and required the audience to sit in rapture for hours on end, their hands in supplication. Only Fack exuded his indomitable ego, but excused himself from a dip in the holy waters on account of his arthritis. He bubbled at Paula's side, looking at the mass of people and secretly feeling just a little foreign.

The Kumbh Mela is a time for reaffirmation and Fack reaffirmed, much to his chagrin, that he did miss so many aspects of his former life. He missed his own roses. The municipal parks he remembered from Gateshead did wonders, but fakirs sniffing their blooms could be a startling sight. Then, apropos of nothing, he thought of Meissen. He had learnt to appreciate Meissen over several years of wandering through the Bowes Museum on a Sunday with Enid. He had been amazed at the treasures harboured for the local populace – but that was all yesterday. So many things were yesterday. And tomorrow? Fack was not so much in two minds as a multiplicity of minds, with one in particular nagging more than the others. And it wasn't Meissen. He missed Enid. Lolling among Savita's cushions he felt a surge of affection for the carthorse figure of Enid clomping into the room. If Enid was a carthorse, Paula was a mule, a hotchpotch muddle of a woman. Fack was mildly intrigued. He must take the girl-boy in hand, which is why they were now having a blazing row in the middle of 10 million people all searching for peace.

'But it says "men only".'

'So what? I used to be a man. Anyway, I'm a journalist. Perhaps I've an assignment with *Health and Beauty* to study hygiene and here I am studying – or would be, if you weren't kicking up such a fuss. For God's sake, they are only toilets.'

Boy-girls were impossible, squeaking about their eye make-up one moment and hitching up their skirts to leap over a perimeter fence the next. Paula's calves were a dead giveaway. She used to play rugby. Of their ten days, the first three were fine. Like two thirsty drinkers, they lapped it all up; but on the fourth day Fack began to think about Meissen and Paula was running out of pills. The gurus no longer offered infinite wisdom. Indeed, infinity seemed a very long time and life would be precious enough, if only…

Suddenly the Yorkshire Dales rose up and imprinted their raw loveliness on Paula. They were her home. They nurtured the new-form woman. Here she would always be the boy-woman – accepted, tolerated – but a boy-woman, while the farmers 'up t'dale' understood and knew nature had many quirky ways; just look at aborted calves with heads like a hydra. And for Fack, too, the questions were being answered. He no longer needed the spirit of the common man to teach him humility. Fack would never learn humility. But he had learnt something else.

Paula had sucked up to the Fack with shameless intent. Fack

liked a handmaiden or two and, having been dumped by Enid, he would make do with the coltish boy-girl and maybe teach her a thing or two. The mists rising off the river knew none of this. The millions pressing down the banks to wash away their sins cared little. Their own sins were weight enough. The jugglers were making a mint; the little food stalls were making a mint. The gurus smiled with knowing charm. They also were earning a buck or two. The teaching of the wicked and the forgiveness of sin was a marvellous money-spinner and, in the laid-back atmosphere of those millions, who cares?

Paula packed her belongings, apart from a red scarf which she gave to a Canadian nurse, and an Indian skirt which had been stolen by a German girl who felt totally liberated by all this spirituality and started nicking anything not tacked down in the name of a shared experience. It was Paula who left first. But there was still the tricky business of the fare. Her original ticket back home had gone up the spout. Stuck in India without her pills was pretty scary. Anyway, Paula had a hospital visit shortly. Fack was no help. Bleating boy-girls were not his thing. He relented with the fare back to Mumbai, but refused further responsibility. He sat outside his sleeping quarters, back upright and toes neatly hidden, his dhoti spotless and, in no time, was surrounded by a throng of teenage boys interested in football. A football guru can earn a packet. Fack didn't know the name of a single Indian football player.

'Really, Paula, you must be responsible for your financial affairs. Letting go and liberating your tortured soul, that's one thing. But coming to me for money is quite another.'

'I only came here because you encouraged me.'

'The same could be said of someone standing on the top of a high diving board. Of course, I led you here. Look at all the enlightenment, the wonderful entertainment, the food – oh yes, the spiritual guidance. Leave it if you must. Your trouble is lack of understanding of yourself.'

He was right. Fack so often was. Paula, the journalist, packed her bag save those items destined to remain and, wonder of all wonders, was picked up by a Swede, also travelling to Mumbai. Or was he a Swede? Perhaps he was Norwegian or a Finn. No –

they are totally different. One thing he was, though; he was single-minded, a dentist with the sensitivity of a rhinoceros. Who would wax lovingly over the molars of hundreds of Indians? Who indeed? Only a dentist taking sabbatical leave. Later, Paula would doubt the authenticity of his name – Olaf, or was it Gustav? But the more she doubted it, the more it stuck – Olaf, or was it Gustav? Nothing happened – thousands of miles of flat teeming countryside and only molars for light relief. He was a companion, though. Someone to begin a sentence with 'Let's stare at the spicy food and take a deep sigh, moan about the lavatories and the price of taxis.' If he had genitals they were on sabbatical leave too, or, God forbid! Paula's plethora of body signals weren't up to snuff. The gentle touch of her leg and his hairy hoof beat a hasty retreat. Her eyebrows shot up and down trying to catch his eye but he only had eyes for molars. She shot her breasts forward and flipped her hair back, but it was molars all the way. The taxi dropped her outside Aunt Jamila's gates. They were shut, very shut and Aunt Jamila's factotum, Hamid, didn't improve the situation. He looked sternly at Paula. His moustache drooped a little, his eyes drooped a lot. Madam was out.

'I expect she's down at the hospice. She is marvellous. I've just come back from the Kumbh Mela. It was marvellous too – in a different way, of course.'

'My flight isn't for a day or two, I was wondering…'

'No wonderings – Madam doesn't like wonderings.'

'No, I see. Well, I need a wash after that train journey; then I'll ask her when she gets back.'

The conversation took on a pantomime flavour.

'Oh no, you don't.'

'Oh yes, I do.'

This might have continued indefinitely had Aunt Jamila's ancient car not crawled to a halt. Hamid's moustache flew to its distinguished best, his eye sparkled and now he could sit back and enjoy the row – a jolly good row, just what he liked.

'Ah, Paula! On your own, or do you have that fat little man from Leicester with you?'

'I'm on my own. I must go home but I need time to arrange my ticket.'

'I'm glad you mentioned ticket. You say you haven't got a ticket? Not very English manners, is this? Enid was a lady. She would never have lost her ticket and run out of money.'

They agreed. This argument was pretty dull. Hamid went to pick up Paula's suitcase. Aunt Jamila put out her hand and said something to Hamid. Paula was no linguist, unless you count bad French. Certainly Hindi was well beyond her. The suitcase stayed put; a bright red climbing plant framed it rather prettily. The gardeners had stealthily padded not so much into view as out of sight but in hearing. What they lacked in linguistic skills they made up for as a rapt audience.

'How do you say?' puzzled Aunt Jamila. As she spoke, an army of little boys crept silently into a semicircle. Hamid was having none of this. He barked as only a man with a moustache can bark and they scurried away, creeping back afterwards one by one. Meanwhile Paula felt tired and tearful. Her bladder, mercifully unisex and working well, was patient, but not for long.

'At least let me have a pee.'

Now, discretion is imbibed with mother's milk in India. All that Delhi belly nonsense was highly regrettable for European bowels. As for having a pee, one simply doesn't have a pee in India. One might say 'Excuse me', but no further utterance is required as to what is to be excused.

Paula was losing her cool. She was frightened, wanted to pee and was furious with the group of onlookers swirling round her and Aunt Jamila. Suddenly there was a lithe body touching her too many times. Paula lost her femininity and threw a powerful punch. The crowd murmured menacingly, the bloodied child shouted imprecations and Hamid (at a hasty signal) quickly let Aunt Jamila and Paula, with the suitcase in tow, through the gate. A lavatory later, Paula was lounging back in minor discomfort. Her eye make-up was all awry.

'I am not against boy-girls – don't get me wrong – but I hate scroungers. Why did you go if you hadn't got enough money? You didn't think that man was going to pay, did you? Really, you should have gone home with Enid and no troubles. But I am open-hearted. You work for a month in my hospice and I send you home – now no nonsense.'

The deal was brilliant. Paula's boss understood and Paula was commissioned to write about her work in the hospice. Only the dying were put out. Many regarded it as bad luck to be nursed by a boy-girl in their final hours. To do her justice, Paula quietly retreated to the sluice paid for by the women's group from Pennsylvania and there she wallowed in filth and felt better and more feminine. Paula longed to be feminine more than anything else in the world but, as any woman will tell you, it's a tough task and doesn't come naturally. Snip, bob and tuck all you like, remove this and that and the other will pop up, especially if it's hair. If it isn't hair, it's temper. Females can land a hefty blow, a spirited bite, and choose a mighty weapon to wield. And tears – few men can cry at a drop of a hat, but many women can dab their eyes apropos of nothing. Poor Paula longed to cry but her tears refused to well up except in self-pity. It took a month of washing sheets, a month of alarmed dumb expressions, a month of snide glances and a month of writing up the experience for the worthy folk of the Dales, so that hints for curries were juxtaposed with dying breaths. Her editor loved it. Didn't it just show that all she needed was a good holiday? Frankly, having her whatsits rejigged was, in his opinion, a pretty frantic way of being overtired. Mind you, he thought the world of Paul – oops, Paula.

So, while Paula hogged the frame in India, Enid might not have bothered to go there in the first place, for all the change it made to her life. It was scones and being disparaged all over again. Indian gifts were for the best part already pushed to the back of thoughts, if not bedroom cupboards. Sal as always was preoccupied with bus-loads of people not the faintest bit interested in art. The twins were totally preoccupied with themselves, while her grandson and son-in-law had formed an unholy alliance with the steers mooing for their silage. Even a postcard from Paula failed to lift Enid above the scones, although she did rather grin at Aunt Jamila making her work for her ticket. Good old Aunt Jamila! But then it's always the rich that are tough.

Poor old Paula, that will teach her to run off with someone like Fack, thought Enid. She felt the mild pleasure of realising that she had done better in keeping his attention than Paula the harpy or Savita the man-eater.

Back in India, Aunt Jamila ate with Paula but the meals to start with were somewhat terse in atmosphere. It's one thing to accept a guest's friend but quite another thing to have the same person wished on one by expediency. Middle-aged ladies are choosy about expediency. What do you say to a he-she who owes you money night after night? Aunt Jamila prattled about her hospice, the problems of fund-raising and the difficulty of finding people in public life whom one could trust. Occasionally she clicked with Paula the journalist and, bit by bit, a tender affection grew and Aunt Jamila's prejudice was soothed away. Then Paula, the she, would moan about her hairy shin, or worse, and Aunt Jamila would shut tight like a clam and pitied the British and their future in a society run by the Paulas of this world. Class she could understand. After all, it wasn't much different to caste. But transsexuality was not nice and not necessary.

Savita heard that Paula had returned and, assuming some demonic row with Fack, she ingratiatingly invited Paula to dinner. To do Paula justice, she said 'No' on three occasions. Savita flew into a rage and sent the car down to collect Paula. Paula cowered in her bathroom with the door locked, wishing she was tough and confident when confronted by the Savitas of this world. There was much padding of feet and voices rose, Savita's more than Aunt Jamila's. When Paula crept out, Aunt Jamila was apparently lying in bed with a migraine, so she dined alone, with the servant silently plying her with dishes.

Working her way back to England was playing havoc with her pills. Paula needed a great many pills, including those suppressing hair growth. Many women are frightened of spiders. For Paula it was body hair. She scuttled to an expensive doctor. Her medical insurance had gone the way of her ticket and she had to pay a fortune to remedy this deeply personal problem. Aunt Jamila reckoned it cost her an extra week, but paid up. Paula nipped off to see her new friends in the red-light district of Mumbai, but they weren't interested in her problems or her adventures at the Kumbh Mela. They were freaks, daily honing their freakishness; she was foreign and dreadfully normal. Poor Paula, despised for being normal! Aunt Jamila was a hard taskmistress. She despised any deviation she noted in Paula. Paula's lot was a sharp learning curve. She learnt to take a rickshaw and haggle for tissues and other minor toiletries. She learnt to walk like a shadow and behave as unobtrusively as possible. India was tough, but it gave Paula as good an initiation as she could expect.

So it was that Paula packed her flimsy shirts and swirling skirts, her dainty sandals and countless scarves, her pills and notebook and pen. What she didn't pack but took by hand took almost as much room again. Pills for the journey, tissues for her hands and face, something to read, another scarf just in case and a jersey for a cold reception – there were bound to be several. Paula wished her new friends well and hoped they would keep in touch. What a lie! The desire to help the girls be real girls had already receded. It wasn't mentioned any more. After all, these girls were Indian. India absorbs her problems in her own way. There was one farewell Paula was glad to make – to the profoundly handicapped boy who lay in his mother's arms attracting alms by the bus stop. Already the boy was larger than his mother, or rather the woman who had bought him at birth as a lucrative investment. Paula would miss the large comfortable bungalow glowing russet in the sunset – its shady veranda, the slow gardeners and contemptuous house staff, their eyes revealing their prejudice, and Aunt Jamila, who had kept her like some bargaining chip before jettisoning her back to the myriad problems awaiting her back home. All the same she would miss the heaving squalor – the standpipes providing bathing and sundry other activities, as well as the glittery shops she was too nervous to enter. That bitch Savita she wouldn't miss.

Nobody met her. Why should they? There was a Pakistani in the toilets wielding a wide broom. Paula smiled in recognition. The woman looked surly. The tube was filthy. No one looked at her. Paula was cold. The grey day started to rain. King's Cross was filled with cross people peering at the board for trains. She bought *House and Garden* to read on the journey and tried ringing Enid. It entered her head that she might get a surly reception. After all, her clothes were there. She left ringing her boss till she reached home. It might be another difficult call. The express train trundled. It was doomed to trundle; cuts and political expediency had forced the trundle as the only gait the poor train had. But it suited Paula.

The re-entry into the Yorkshire atmosphere had a sobering effect on her. She crossed her legs and settled down to read about beehives. A more demure posture would be hard to find. She flinched a little as if the odd sting had pierced her composure. Out of the window she watched as cows munched their way along a line of water meadows but, in a flash, huge fields of grain swapped places with black tilled soil and Peterborough Cathedral. In between the flashbacks to the operation and the self-doubts, she delicately probed her holiday – still too raw, too close. She shivered at the dank weather. India was hot, unequivocally hot, but not the nights. At the Kumbh Mela they had been surprisingly 'nippy' – a word her gran had used. What would her gran have thought about her now?

'Must be comfortable, pet. People who do silly things aren't always comfortable. That is what I say.'

She had been right, but she died before Paula could thank her. Beehives passed into vinyl tabletops followed by Georgian facades – the odd smug couple and Labrador dog standing on the steps to accentuate the desirability. Paula put the magazine aside and looked at the woods sprouting like pubic hair. Then the train slowed down and Northallerton hove into view.

Tits out and chin up, Enid had to be confronted some time. Anyway, Paula was skint. She needed just something to tide her over. But confrontation is never like that. Paula warned the taxi driver of a financial disadvantage but he drove her just the same. That meant Paula and Enid spent the first fifteen minutes looking for cash and supplementing it with a dodgy cheque. The driver was plied with coffee and invited back any time if the cheque didn't live up to its promise. It was only when he drove off that the two women embraced warmly and wept a little.

'Oh Paula, I could kill you. I hate being on my own.'

'I know, but I had to do it.'

'Your "had to do its" are getting out of control.'

Enid had to smile at the next imperative foisted on Paula. Her boss, not particularly pleased with his idealised reporter, had sent her to cover a story of Byzantine complexity. A herd of cows had to cross the road to a farm adjacent to the church. It was milking time. It was also the time when a wedding emerged after a romantic, bucolic service. None of the participants was Christian. The cows took exception and the bride's father took exception but the solicitor rubbed his hands in glee. Back in harness, even Paula could find the funny side and, more importantly, she forgot her gender for a while.

'Honest, Edes, I had to laugh. The poor bride's dress was ruined and some hungry cow tried munching Harrogate's hired hat creations. But it was the bloody bowels that ruined the day – just like India all over again.' There was a comfortable pause. 'It was fun. I'll always remember your kindness, Edes.'

Which meant she wouldn't.

Enid became a lady with a mission. Her daughter must have a holiday – not just camping in Shetland or Brittany, but a real holiday without those bloody children. She would look after them. Surely she could prevent pregnancy, drunkenness, Ecstasy, spots and the other pitfalls of adolescents. But first pinion your victim. Sal wasn't easy to corner, but armed with a left-behind umbrella – they had dozens – Enid caught her round the neck.

'What the hell! Oh, do grow up. Honest, Ma – you are worse than Roger.'

'I want to talk.'

'Dangerous. Anyway, I don't and you can remove that bloody thing from round my neck.'

'Well, when, then?'

'A cup of coffee after I've tidied up.'

Watching her middle-aged daughter swing her arm with a damp cloth made Enid's heart break. The coach-loads of philistines didn't deserve it, or rather her. It strengthened Enid's resolve.

'You'll end in the divorce courts, or a breakdown. Then what would happen?'

'Stop exaggerating, Ma. We can't all push off to India on a whim!'

'Just look at you, Sal. You give charity shops a bad name. Just think of the children! Do they want to bring their friends home to a mother like you?'

'Now you just listen to me. Just because you are a spoilt elderly lady with nothing to do, you can jolly well belt up about what I do. What were you doing at my age? Munching mints with that silly dog of yours and waiting for my pretty dubious Pa to put in an appearance. If I choose to work my tits off, that's my business. Anyway, we have planned a holiday – to New Zealand – once Roger is old enough.'

'New Zealand? What's there for you? Maori art, bungee jumping and dagging sheep! It's Douglas, isn't it? He wants to go there and you are just like a faithful dog, like my bloody dog, and you go wherever he wants. Where are your balls, for fuck's sake?'

'If this is going to degenerate into bad language I'm leaving now. Really, you are impossible! Holiday, my foot!'

Clutching the offending umbrella and flushed with agitation, Sal clattered to the back of the shoppe, this spelling being another bone of contention.

Later she spoke to Douglas while lying for those few delicious moments before sleep.

'She wants us to take a holiday.'

'Did you tell her about New Zealand?'

'Yeah. Doesn't count – not sexy enough and lacks artistic merit.'

'Poor old Enid. Will she never learn that some people are deeply attached to their place, their time, their rhythms of life and loving. Do you pine for India, Sal, or long to fly up to London to visit the latest exhibition? Am I an ogre, keeping you trapped?'

'Move over, you're hogging the bed.'

It was a mating call and had been since their honeymoon. Douglas and Sal had many problems and conflicts, but deep down New Zealand was all right. They might arrange a flight so they could just spend a few days in California – probably not really Douglas's scene, but Sal could get the Getty Museum under her belt.

Enid had got it so wrong. It seemed inconceivable to her that people could live and love without longing. God, how she longed to right the rights of yesterday and to ease the pain of longing into the future! For the pain at sixty-something is pretty frightful, every bit as bad as that at sixteen. Enid blinked in a dull ache with every dawn, shuffling to the lavatory full of foreboding. She'd look at the small improvised bathroom with the seal round the bath flaking and Paula's rubbish covering every surface, the bowl itself usually pathetically clean, as if success in life depended on a clean lavatory bowl. Back in her bedroom conflict reared its ugly head – whether to be comfortable and able to nip out into the tangled garden at a spare moment, or give herself a momentary thrill of looking glamorous in clothes that lifted her spirits but restricted what she could do. Already Paula had amassed a great many stunning casual outfits at expense of the rent. She must remind Paula about the rent.

'Edes, don't! Rent is such a bore for you and for me. I don't know why you bother. After all, you're miserable without me. You said so yourself. Honestly, Edes – you look so dowdy like that. Seriously, if I didn't know you had had an affair with a fakir, I certainly wouldn't think so looking at you now.'

'I know,' came the reply in a dull voice. It was, after all, well before nine. 'But I really want to grapple with those low branches, as well as weed the border and the supermarket really doesn't care a damn how I look. Nor do I, quite frankly.'

'Really, really?' Paula snorted. 'Well, at least speak properly if you're going to look such a drab mess. You are a real moaning Minnie this morning. Don't you have any self-image, any drive inside you that tells you that you're a mess, a frump?'

'I do try when I go out. What about my little blue dress? The twins are always giving me hell. Sal's worse than me. I often wonder about their sex life.'

'You mean *her* sex life! I don't believe sex is just that momentary. It's all the tiny signals leading up to it. I'm keeping my hymen for Mr Special. You can only be a virgin once in you, life.'

'That's rich coming from you. But what about all that rubbish about a journey of passion with Fack?'

'You don't think we…? Yuk! I did think about it but Fack is inscrutable, isn't he? No, our journey was essentially about tiny signals, only the signalling system broke down.

Enid felt immeasurably better on hearing that. Apart from anything it showed Paula was on the move. Despite Enid's generosity – or was it dependency? – at Paula's lapse of taste in doing a bunk with Fack, something had snapped. The intimacy had left their relationship. Enid bowed to the obvious. She had given too much and Paula couldn't handle it. Anyway, Paula was keen to meet a Mr Right and get that bloody strip of skin torn. Enid shuddered faintly at the thought and you can't live shuddering at the thought of your lodger's love life. Of course they would keep in touch, write even, phone regularly and share a bottle of wine in Harrogate. And Enid would send on all mail and give Paula's new telephone number. Oh, and there might be some bills – you know, niggly things bought from magazines. It went on and on. Paula borrowed an extra suitcase and both women parted in tears.

'Oh my God – the scones!' Enid snapped out of tears and into rage, which was her personal fuel for those damned scones.

New Zealand hit the agenda with £1,000 from Ernie. Bugger the overdraft – they were off! Sal was a chip off the old block and whizzed round the charity shops and gave way in M and S, arguing that one nice trouser suit would be worth its weight in gold. It certainly cost enough. Ironically, Sal's clothes might be worn, but she chose good quality and left without her mother or daughters wincing in embarrassment. Roger would have been quite agreeable for his mother to have left starkers: 'starkers' was his 'in' word, along with 'bonkers', which applied to his gran. Bonkers or not, Gran was left in charge of the domestic side while Cyril was hired to look after the farm. Enid met him in the farm kitchen. She had delivered a batch of wobbly scones. Cyril caught her amid perfection, down to a streak of flour across her brow.

'Here's my mother-in-law, Enid Tanner. She will be in charge of everything here.'

'Hello, Cyril. Excuse me being all floured. I'm the scone lady, among other things. Please don't take the "in charge" bit too seriously. I won't say I'm useless – let's say I'm vague.'

'There's nothing to it,' Sal had insisted.

'Then why are you completely knackered all the time. I don't mind mucking in with the children but I draw a line at running the complex. For a start I'm lousy at keeping the books and all that. I don't guarantee not to be rude to the frightful people who come round and make those banal remarks and I'm not making scones, supervising homework and worrying myself sick about the girls whooping it up at the school disco – sex behind the cloakrooms or popping pills in the back of boyfriends' cars. I'm in charge!'

'Ma, don't exaggerate. The discos are supervised and they are too young to do it – they just talk about it all the time. So do you, come to think of it, and how often do you get laid?'

'Really! How dare you talk to me like that.' Enid descended into a sulk and the more she sulked the more she refused to run the silly pretentious art complex.

'Get someone else. It's a pity Paula's not about – she would have been perfect. But Sal, I'm adamant – no complex and no scones.'

So, with much indignation at her silly mother's refusal to take responsibility, Sal flapped her way off to the airport with Douglas shouting calf-feeding instructions as they departed.

Friends – yes, she still had some! Chirruping down the phone about goldfish and grandchildren was her point of contact while stranded.

'Honestly, Letty, do you know anything about goldfish? Frankly, I say bugger the goldfish – excuse my French.' (It had been, for a nanosecond, Roger's favourite beast.) 'I've mastered almost everything in this place but the goldfish still leaves me cold. I can't stand its large bulging eyes – they spook me. Oh! I must tell you. I made cottage pie last night – it was a disaster. Roger told me I'd made it out of dead cat. I could wallop that young man. Apparently they go for pizzas with sun-dried tomato. I don't know about your lot, but Sal ate what she was given – lots of fish fingers and sausages. Well, this lot won't touch them. There's Sophie, who is a vegan. She's pretty vague about what that means and still likes ice cream and Beatrice won't eat birds that have had their beaks cut. Roger is a splendid trencherman but refuses rice which he is convinced is "poofy". I ask you! Then there's telly... You what? Oh well, Sal told me to use my discretion about TV. I did query a documentary about Siamese twins being separated, but Roger told me to grow up. He watched it and complained that it lacked sex. So I told him that there was a famous couple of brothers who married sisters and sired something like nineteen children between them. Roger felt better then. I'm a little worried about an adult film called *Orgy* which is on tonight. I can't guarantee that Roger will be in bed. They never get to sleep much before midnight and fail to understand the correlation with lousy, sleepy behaviour in the morning. Oh, and another thing – the washing! How twins can generate fifteen pairs of knickers in five days – I just don't know what they do with them. I found a pair – why is it pair, I wonder? Anyway, they were in the dog basket. Several others were lurking under furniture. My arthritis is strained to the limit peering under chests of drawers. It is the weekends that are particularly dreadful... Hell! There's the doorbell. You'll have to hear about them another time. Bye, Let.'

Had she bored her friend? Quite possibly – they all had grandchildren, and helped out without making a fuss about goldfish. That was the trouble – loneliness did that. It made an issue about goldfish. All the same, at least she hadn't banged on about those bloody scones. The highlight during her tour of duty had to be the difficult calving, with the hired help getting her out of bed, dressed and pulling on the end of a rope while the silly old moo moaned like any lady in labour. Three hours later Geoff was warming his hands round a mug while he regaled Enid with tales of difficult calvings he'd helped happen. When she suggested he should have been a midwife, he gave her a stare.

Parents' evening was pretty dreadful. Being in loco parentis is at its most daunting when faced with a moustached lady complaining about Sophie's religious studies.

'But she doesn't believe in God,' bleated Enid.

'That has nothing to do with it. She doesn't believe in the religion of Ancient Greece when she does classical studies.'

'Yes, but...'

'There are no yeses or buts; Sophie is a clever girl and I expect a high standard of work.' There are some things that never change, formidable teachers among them.

'It's fish pie,' announced Enid, carrying a hubbly-bubbly mess to the table.

'But that's not vegan,' pleaded Sophie.

'There are no dairy products in it,' retorted Enid.

'Yes, there are. You made the white sauce with milk.'

'How did that fish die? Horribly, I bet. I won't eat cruelly killed fish.' Somehow Beatrice's contribution to the argument seemed flimsy.

'Fuck the lot of you.'

'Ooh, language! You promised Mum you wouldn't swear,' said Sophie in that sanctimonious way kids have.

'And you promised to eat everything put before you.'

'So long as it was vegan.'

'Killed humanely.'

'Didn't have germs.'

This wasn't just once but every meal, with just a few variations to keep Enid on her toes. As for the washing-up – another routine sworn in front of Sal. Their words were worthless and they sloped off mumbling excuses as thin as tissue paper. Enid couldn't help seeing her role in military terms with her bloody grandchildren as recalcitrant squaddies.

Her exhausting role was punctuated with 'Hi folks' postcards and the occasional phone call to find out if the cow had calved and was Roger practising his trumpet. A blast from the latter answered that one. What Enid found completely annihilating was the lack of time to be herself. 'What is this life if full of care?' was spot on, but not because she wanted to stand under a tree and stare but just to have a split second to be herself, think impious thoughts, feel free to wonder what the rest of the world was doing and how soon could she rejoin it again – or horror to end all horrors – what happened if there was a plane crash and she was doomed for ever? Were other grandmothers lying when they cooed over their smelly grandchildren? Did they really enjoy looking after their dear little ones every year so their children could revitalise their marriages? Were they really fascinated by the minutiae of growing children? Because she, Enid Tanner, was not. Then she thought of the dreadful Savita. Was she rapidly becoming a nasty old shrew like her? That would be too humiliating. She must try harder.

Enid should have known better. Thinking about that Indian mob was to court disaster – and it did. No sooner was a bronzed and cheerful Sal berating her over the scones once more and Douglas hot on the phone to 'A1 guys', than Enid received a letter from Vijaya. The letter made Enid's stomach turn.

Hello Enid

Mumsi has told me all about your trip. What a hullabaloo! Now you can help me. Rani is spoilt rich – or is it rotten? I thought his poor relations would show him how to respect his parents. We work but he is just dead lazy. Can he stay for the summer, work on the farm and learn proper English? He will be company for the twins. You will soon be able to see my next blockbuster film.

Vijaya

The letter left little room for 'no'. Enid moaned and groaned and rang Sal, who had hysterics and rang back half an hour later to say the twins were spending the summer as far away from home as possible. Douglas categorically refused to have anything to do with the boy. Enid sighed, cajoled, pleaded and cried. Sal subsided into rage, the twins scoured the Internet for holidays abroad and Douglas mentally searched out revolting tasks on the farm that no one liked doing. Enid collapsed into pathetic acquiescence and Sal started sighing at the inevitable. The twins considered fortifying their rooms and Douglas planned some serious talks in the county on the status of the British farmer, leaving only Roger to wonder what all the fuss was about. After all, he was simply going to zap their guest.

Yes, Sal would have him. Rani could work on the farm and live the same life as the twins. They would be at school till July, and during the summer there would be the occasional treat. Rani must understand they led very simple lives and she would be responsible for him during the visit.

Is this what widows on slender means are meant to do with cuckoo kids plonked in their nests? Gerry had a lot to answer for. Anyway, poor Sal was going to bear the brunt.

At one level Enid was aghast at the implications of this visit. A spoilt Indian boy, used to the absurd luxury of Californian life, was about to be dumped on her – well, Sal actually – to ruin her – well, Sal's actually – summer. Yet, in a sneaky part of her psyche, there was just a hint, a glimmer of adventure, and even more, retaliation. The bloody boy could learn to make the scones! The very thought gave Enid a smile and produced a tuneless hum as she fried a lemon sole for her supper.

It took more than a letter to organise Rani's visit. Among the more alarming matters to settle was the query about whether Rani would be going to a hunt ball, to grouse shooting or to Ascot. Having assured his mother that absolutely no way would he be doing any of these very British things, Enid had to explain that if Vijaya insisted that she wanted the boy to do such things then she better organise a different holiday. There was a sulk in the correspondence before Vijaya came to heel with the revelation that her son was a little too big for his boots and, if he enjoyed his visit, he could always return to – and here she added the joke – 'Oxbridge'.

Abject ignominy – Rani had to travel as a minor! At least he flew first class and managed to bribe the cabin crew with pairs of pants belonging to, and signed in biro by, a minor member of the pop fraternity. In return he required champagne and smoked salmon. By the time he reached Heathrow he was a revolting shade of seedy yellow with a tinge of green. A whey-faced lady handed him over to Enid. He stood, rocking slightly with a seraphic smile; then he threw up. He threw up in the car park and finally in the car, all over the passenger's seat. Enid insisted he mopped the lumpy bits up with his designer T-shirt which she promptly chucked in a corner. It was about then that he spoke.

'Mama says you gotta show me Buck House, Harrods and that cathedral place where Lady Di was married.'

However, Rani was sound asleep before Enid swung onto the motorway and headed north with the whiff of puke in her nostrils and a puppy-fat adolescent snoring beside her. And that is how it remained all the way to Ripon.

'I'll give you some hot soapy water in a bucket and a scrubbing brush.'

She had popped him into a bath and peeled his clothes off him and into her elderly washing machine – 'that thing', as he described it.

It was then that the shit hit the fan. Rani refused to clean the remaining vomit which had congealed on the floor and down the edges of the car seat.

'Get your servant to do it; it's disgusting. Anyway, who the hell do you think I am?'

Enid was adamant, Rani was wilful. While her back was turned he picked up the phone and rang his mum. It was the middle of the night. Her beauty pads covered her eyes. Vijaya was fast asleep. She woke enough to scream abuse at her son and more abuse at Enid. Why couldn't the maid do it? Poor love, he was missing his mother – and in the same breath she gaily pointed out what a little bastard he was.

They were invited over to Sal's for supper.

'You'll smell of sick, you know that.'

'How was I to know? I only drank one bottle. I'm still a kid. It's cruel to make me clear it up. I'm too grand,' he added.

'Grand, forsooth! You grubby little boy! You clear up the mess you made in my car because you were drunk. As for *grand*, let's get something straight. So long as you play straight with me you'll have a good time. Phoning your mother is out unless you ask me – it's too expensive. Drinking is out, smoked salmon is unlikely, and as for "Ma says you gotta do" or whatever preface you constantly make, that is banned.'

He did it reluctantly and using expletives even Enid hadn't heard before. The car seat was reduced to a disinfectanty watery mess and a great deal of kitchen paper was then used then to clear up the mess. It took months to get rid of the smell. It acted rather like a curb chain. Whenever Rani stepped out of line he would be reminded of the smell. It also meant that the scones must have had just a touch of aroma about them – not that anyone complained.

'Honestly, Sal, I'm sure they must. It just goes to show how hopelessly lacking in judgement, smell and taste the great British public are.'

Rani was a strapping lad, pale yellow with a greenish tinge even when he wasn't about to be sick. He had no concept of the word 'no', ate for comfort and was more than a trifle overweight. He peered at the twins and seemed a little frightened of them. He preferred Roger and would pad off ferreting in the evenings, always a little nervous of finding rabbits. His knowledge of farming came from Westerns and Douglas would find him scaring the milkers by waving large sticks and making cowboy noises.

To do him justice, there was one incident that turned Enid's head and melted the stone which up to then had been her heart. Douglas invited him to watch a cow calve. He watched the calf slip messily onto the straw, clamber to its wobbly legs and finally find the teat of life. Rani grew a thousand years that morning. So much so that Enid felt she could start him on scones. He baulked like any young colt, but the curb was pulled and the lack of servants evoked and away Rani went, sifting flour, rubbing in fat, adding sultanas or cheese – and soon a splendid variety of scones were on sale. But a sad, bad incident also occurred. He was seen by a group of elderly pensioners carrying the scones into the complex and a small group announced loudly they wouldn't eat scones made by a darkie.

'But I'm not a darkie! My dad is Norwegian and my mum is a very beautiful, famous actress.' He said it wistfully, as if discussing people he barely knew – poor love.

So from the alarming beginnings of being a quite revolting boy who threw his not inconsiderable weight around, boasting of Madonna's knickers being in his luggage and startling the twins with descriptions of snorting coke, he metamorphosed into a pathetic loveless child fed a diet of dreadful values. He was so proud of his mother and so bewildered by her rejection.

Furious at having her dormant mothering instincts roused, Enid found herself eating shepherd's pie and listening to the basics of American football – just so the bloody child didn't feel rejected. The inevitable occurred. Rani doted on her and followed her round like a dog. She did one good thing. Despite the shepherd's pie, she helped him lose weight. He preferred her company to that of the twins, who alarmed him by their indifference to all the totems he tried to win their favour with, not just Madonna's pants but Michael Jackson's hairpiece – a terrible mangled mess, rather like a dead cat, quite frankly.

Rani received a letter from his grandmother. He guarded it carefully but not carefully enough. Enid had no scruples about finding it and read it with glee. Savita wanted to know what pitiful little hovel Enid lived in and exhorted Rani to remind her how important he was. It was a matter of honour she insisted. Enid folded the letter and replaced it, muttering, 'Poor little sod.'

The reconstructed Rani made scones and lost weight and whiled away his childish summer sans coke, smack, dope and booze. The poor little rich boy had come home – well, to a home of a kind – which meant one in the eye for Savita. There was one memorable day when the whole family decamped to the sea – that murky grey choppy sea that borders North Yorkshire. But on that day the magic had made it piercing blue with ripples of silver, a minimum of mess and enough sun to burn everyone's noses. The party staggered over the rocks with squishy bags full of sandwiches, cushions to sit on, and towels – just in case the briny proved too tempting. Enid presided over the clutter while the children – everyone was reduced to childhood that day – cavorted and spun nearer and nearer the sea. At last Roger tumbled in and, fully clothed, one by one they flopped and splashed in the shallows. Poor Rani had never experienced cold like that sea, never cavorted with quoits and buckets, chucking water and being chucked at. He frolicked like a young dolphin – much less puppy fat wobbling and brown eyes ecstatic with an unexpected glimpse of childhood. That night he rang his mum. She was not amused and castigated her son for such tomfoolery.

'People who live in Buck House don't do this nonsense. How will you go to Oxbridge chucking water? As for cooking, let me speak to Enid.'

'What are you doing to my son? He is not a cook, he is rich and sophisticated. Just remember who you are, Enid. I am Gerry's beautiful daughter.'

'Come, come, Vijaya! You know your history. Queen Victoria taught all her children to cook and these days there is hardly a cook on television that doesn't have a triple-barrelled name.'

'A triple-barrelled name – is that better than mine, for instance?'

'Your beauty is worth many names,' said Enid with her tongue in her cheek, 'but a few more are always useful – think of them like confetti…'

That lost Vijaya, who couldn't for the life of her think of any correlation between her name on all the billboards and cooks with triple-barrelled names.

'You are pulling my legs. Now, listen – no more silliness. Rani needs proper family life. I am too successful for motherhood.'

Vijaya sometimes spoke the truth.

The roly-poly Rani grinned his way through the challenging climate of a British summer. He chummed up with Roger, held the twins in awe and made scones with a passion that would get him on any TV show, whatever his name. Only the faint smell in the car reminded everyone of his disastrous debut. It was with genuine tears in his eyes that he thumped Roger on the back and just a hint of bemusement that his present to the twins – more Madonna knickers – was met with crude ribaldry. He shook hands solemnly and even pecked Enid on the cheek.

'He really is a dear and has shades of his grandfather.' Silly old woman – what sentimental rubbish! Still, the moment he departed Enid was aware there was a new gap, a slice out of the apple of life. Enid drove back North once more, overwhelmed with the emptiness which Rani had held at bay and which no amount of scones could fill.

But what a surprise! She was tired, tetchy and longing for a bath. However, there was an out-of-tune song bellowing from the tub and every indication that someone had moved in. She had to admit her spare key was no secret, under the geranium pot.

'Who the hell!' she shouted, just a little alarmed.

'Me,' came the reply from some superego.

'Paula, is that you?'

'No,' squeaked a falsetto voice.

Well, at least he knows who Paula is. Suddenly it dawned.

'Fack!' And the bathroom door opened to reveal a clean, beaming Fack, dressed in casual, scruffy Western attire.

They didn't kiss, they hugged for a lovely time – a standing-still hug.

'Enid, we are getting too old to challenge the system. My days as a fakir are over. You and I are going to live comfortably together and I promise, no more scones.'

The boredom and loneliness just melted away.

Typical! He never asked, he just assumed. Equally typically, Enid wrapped herself in his arms and felt utterly happy for the first time in years.

Printed in the United Kingdom
by Lightning Source UK Ltd.
134142UK00001B/1-36/A